Praise for the Novels of Tim Lebbon

"Tim Lebbon displays the sort of cool irony and uncanny mood-making that drive the best *Twilight Zone* stories."
—*New York Times Book Review*

"Tim Lebbon is a master of fantasy and horror, and his visions make for disturbing and compelling reading."
—Douglas Clegg

"Tim Lebbon is an immense talent and he's become a new favourite. He has a style and approach unique to the genre."
—Joe R. Lansdale

"A firm and confident style, with elements of early Clive Barker." —Phil Rickman

"Tim Lebbon is an apocalyptic visionary—
a prophet of blood and fear." —Mark Chadbourn

"One of the most powerful new voices to come along in the genre . . . Lebbon's work is infused with the contemporary realism of Stephen King and the lyricism of Ray Bradbury."
—*Fangoria*

"Beautifully written and mysterious . . . a real winner!"
—Richard Laymon

"Lebbon will reward the careful reader with insights as well as gooseflesh." —*Publishers Weekly*

"Lebbon is among the most inventive and original contemporary writers of the dark fantastic."
—Ramsey Campbell

"Lebbon is quite simply the most exciting new name in horror for years." —*SFX*

"A riveting adult fantasy." —*Rocky Mountain News*

"The exhilarating story line paints a dark, gloomy Poe-like atmosphere throughout, especially when the adversaries take center stage. The key characters, in particular the teen and his champions, are unique individuals that make their realm seem even more nightmarishly real. Tim Lebbon paints the darkest *Dusk* that will have readers keeping the lights on until dawn breaks." —*Midwest Book Review*

"I've come to admire Lebbon's masterful blend of beauty with the horrific.... This stunningly visualized fantasy is beautiful, gripping, and delivers an unexpected emotional blow at the end ... [a] wondrous and frightening tale of magic's demise and the impenetrable human spirit." —*Talebones*

DAWN

"A terrific horror fantasy ... The story line is action-packed and filled with the usual creative war gadgetry that keeps Tim Lebbon tales fresh.... A superior tale." —SFRevu.com

"This sequel to *Dusk* again demonstrates Bram Stoker Award winner Lebbon's consummate talent for viscerally visual fantasy [with] strong and unusual characters and a plot of epic proportions." —*Library Journal*

"The relentless imagination and evocative prose that made *Dusk* such a thrilling read are still in evidence.... Lebbon has shaken up high fantasy with his duology, and it was a pleasure to read." —SFSite.com

FALLEN

"Stoker winner Lebbon successfully combines quest adventure and horror in this gripping and disturbing tale.... Lebbon creates vivid and convincing major and minor characters, places and creatures, blending wonder and nightmare in this dark and memorable novel."
— *Publishers Weekly* (starred review)

"The joy of reading one of Tim Lebbon's Noreela tales is discovering what new surprises the author has conjured up....The ending is just mind-blowing...shocking, tragic, and haunting.... *Fallen* is just another outstanding addition to the Noreela mythos, and every time I visit this terrifying yet fascinating world, the harder it becomes to tear myself away."
— FantasyBookCritic.blogspot

ALSO BY TIM LEBBON

NOVELS

Bar None
Fallen
Dawn
Dusk
Hellboy: Unnatural Selection
Mesmer
The Nature of Balance
Hush *(with Gavin Williams)*
Face
Until She Sleeps
Desolation
Berserk
30 Days of Night
Mind the Gap *(with Christopher Golden)*
The Map of Moments *(with Christopher Golden)*
The Everlasting

NOVELLAS

White
Naming of Parts
Changing of Faces
Exorcising Angels *(with Simon Clark)*
Dead Man's Hand
Pieces of Hate
A Whisper of Southern Lights
The Reach of Children

COLLECTIONS

Faith in the Flesh
As the Sun Goes Down
White and Other Tales of Ruin
Fears Unnamed
Last Exit for the Lost
After the War

THE ISLAND

a novel of Noreela

TIM LEBBON

BALLANTINE BOOKS/NEW YORK

A Spectra Trade Paperback Original

Published in the United States by Spectra, an imprint of The Random
House Publishing Group, a division of Random House, Inc., New York

SPECTRA and the portrayal of a boxed "s" are trademarks
of Random House, Inc.

Library of Congress Cataloging-in-Publication Data
Lebbon, Tim.
The island : a novel of Noreela / Tim Lebbon.
p.   cm.
ISBN 978–0-553–38468–0 (pbk. : alk. paper)
978–0-553–90657–8 (e-book)
I. Title

PS3612.E245I85   2009
813'.6—dc22
2008042600

Cover design: Jamie S. Warren
Cover art: © Cliff Nielsen

Printed in the United States of America

www.ballantinebooks.com

BVG 2 4 6 8 9 7 5 3 1

For Tracey, with love.
Now you've got to read it.

Acknowledgments

Thanks once again to Anne Groell and the whole Bantam team, and to Howard Morhaim for continuing wisdom.

THE ISLAND

Chapter One

drink out the storm

KEL BOON DID not like magic. He knew all the arguments—
*it's natural as breathing; Noreela gifted it to us; it's the
language of the land*—but it was something he did not understand. And in his time serving the Core, things he did not understand had usually ended up terrifying him, at the very
least. At the other extreme, they had tried to kill him. So he
used magic, as much as anyone in Noreela used it, happily
leaving its manipulation to the Practitioners. But he did not
like it.

Strange, then, that his best friend and lover was a witch.

Kel looked at his latest carving, sitting back and stretching
the ache from his muscles. He'd been working on the piece
for two moons, picking a moment here and there between

commissions, or spending more time working on it when paid
projects were sparse. He made a scant living selling his carvings; he could afford to eat, drink and keep a roof over his
head. His craft would never make him rich, but he was fine
with that. Rich meant visible.

Lately, he'd had plenty of time to work on this, his own
very private sculpture. When it was ready, he'd give it to his
love, Namior Feeron. It would be his gift to her on the day he
proposed marriage.

It was good. Namior's love of the cliff hawks that lived and
hunted along the coast had meant that Kel's choice of what to
carve for her was easy, and the hawks' own particular grace,
charm and mystery made the task a pleasing one. He had
completed the basic form and was now working on the detail,
trying to capture the bird's light elegance in the weight of
wood. He'd chosen a hunk of wood from a young wellburr
tree's higher branches; light and solid, beautifully grained,
still rich in natural oils. His climb to cut the branch had been
an adventure in itself, and Namior had asked how he'd gained
such bruises and grazes on his legs and stomach. He told her
he'd been involved in a drunken scuffle at the Blue Ray
Tavern. *You fool*, she'd said, already starting to kiss the bruises
better.

Kel brushed wood dust from the hawk's eyes, grunting in
satisfaction. A good afternoon's work. He stood and began
tidying his worktable. A blanket went over the carving, just in
case Namior called on him unexpectedly, and he oiled and
sharpened each of the chisels, blades and files he'd been using. Then he wrapped them in greasecloth, rolled them together into their leather pouch and tucked them beneath the
table. The wood shards he swept by hand into a bucket and
threw onto the unlit fire. When burned, the wellburr wood
would freshen his rooms and fill the air with an exotic, spicy
smell.

He looked once again at the unfinished carving, given
ghostly shape by the blanket. He imagined the blanket mov-

ing, the sculpture screaming like an attacking hawk, venting violence through every pore. Closing his eyes, he breathed deeply and listened to the first gust of wind outside.

Something whistled behind him, and for a moment he thought it was the breeze finding its way beneath the door. But the thick curtains over his windows and door were still, the candles around the walls flickering only slightly, and he knew what was making the noise.

Namior called it a voice carrier. It was a machine. She'd insisted on him taking it, rebuffing his objections, because he lived at the top of Drakeman's Hill, and she was sometimes too busy to climb all the way up there to see him.

Another breath of wind rattled the front door in its frame, and candlelight shivered in sympathy.

The machine whistled again.

"I'm coming," Kel muttered, but he smiled. It would be good to hear Namior's voice, and he hoped they could arrange to meet that evening.

Kel crossed the room to a curtained alcove in the corner, and behind the curtain sat the voice carrier. It glowed softly, emitting the whistle from tiny holes in its chalky shell, and it had risen a hand's width from the shelf, floating in the air as though Namior's intention made it lighter.

He reached out and touched the small machine, cringing at the slight warmth that bled through its exterior. It almost felt alive. As his fingertips made contact the whistling stopped, and he heard the expectant silence he was used to.

"Namior," he said. She was cruel; she always waited for him to speak first.

"Kel the woodchopper." Her voice came clear and sharp, almost as if she were in the room with him. From instinct he glanced around, just to make sure. And as usual, he was alone.

"How are those mad old witches you insist on living with?" he asked.

"Listening."

Kel was silent for a moment, eyes half-closing as he considered exactly what he'd said.

"I'm fooling," Namior said.

"Wait until I see you," he whispered.

Namior laughed. "You and which army, exactly? But Kel, my mother and great-grandmother sense a storm coming, and they think—"

"It's uncanny, how they can sense a storm just by listening to the wind and seeing storm clouds boiling overhead." He stepped sideways and pulled a curtain to one side, looking out over the rooftops of the village below. "And observing the white-crests out to sea."

"A *real* storm, Kel!" Namior said. "A surger. High tide, big waves, heavy rain, like nothing you've ever seen since you've been here. Trakis and Mell want to go to the Dog's Eyes, drink out the storm and defy nature. Will you come?"

"I'm a sculptor and a tortured artist. Do you really think I want to use bad weather as an excuse to drink?" He always felt it strange talking to a glowing, floating machine, so as usual he had his eyes closed as he spoke to Namior this way. And that helped him picture what she said next.

"Of course. Followed by my taking you to my rooms and examining your greatest sculpture."

Kel smiled. "It needs oiling."

"I'm up to the task, I think."

Kel opened his eyes and looked around his rooms. The curtains at the door and windows were shifting now, candles dancing in excitement, and the wind and rain beat at the walls. "Sounds like the world's ending out there," he said.

"Well, you *will* live at the top of Drakeman's Hill."

Kel glanced back at the hawk he was carving for Namior, and once again tried to imagine her face when he revealed it to her at last. "You're welcome to live with me up here."

Namior was silent for long enough for it to become uncomfortable. *Training,* Kel thought. *Mother, great-grandmother . . . a whole family of witches.*

"See you at the Dog's?" he said at last.

"I look forward to it," Namior said, and the machine stopped glowing and settled back down.

Kel closed the curtain on the voice carrier and stepped back, smiling. She might be good at avoiding certain questions, but Namior was also adept at saying exactly what she meant. *I look forward to it,* she had said. Five words that drove away the cold and made Kel feel warm all over.

He shrugged on a heavy coat, a scarf, and a hat made from furbat skin, and strapped a knife to his belt. Storms reminded him of that terrible night in Noreela City. With every blink he'd hear the screams and see the children dying, and if there was lightning, it would imprint those memories on his mind even more harshly. He'd once told Namior that he hated storms, though he could never tell her why, and she had laughed as she asked why he chose to live next to the sea.

Same reason I fell in love with a witch when I don't trust magic, he'd responded. *I'm a man of contradictions.* She had smiled as though he'd made a joke, but he often spent deep moments considering this, and thinking that he'd been hiding for so long that he no longer knew himself.

PAVMOUTH BREAKS WAS a fishing village on the western shores of Noreela. It was built on either side of the River Pav where it merged with the sea, extending up the slopes of the valley on both sides: a gentle rise to the north, with a slow fall to the sea; and a steeper rise to the south known as Drakeman's Hill, ending with a sheer cliff into the sea on that side. The harbor was natural, enclosed and expanded centuries before with a long, curving stone mole projecting out into the sea. The river was spanned by bridges in two places. The first, oldest stone bridge stood closest to the sea at the harbor throat, while a mile upriver was the newest crossing known as Helio Bridge—a hundred steps high and half a mile across, spanning between the sides of the steepening valley inland.

Namior Feeron lived in the northern part of the village, her family home perched on the shallow hillside and built so that it had views both out to sea and across the narrow river mouth to the south. From Namior's room on the roof she could see far up Drakeman's Hill, though Kel Boon's rooms were hidden from view by other buildings. Still, she liked to sit at her window sometimes and imagine him descending the steep paths and steps to reach her.

She'd climb, but that sometimes seemed too eager. *Eager sends them away*, her mother told her, and she should know; Namior's father had sailed west with nine others two moons after her birth, never to be seen again. *Give them a chase*, her mother would say. *And sometimes, give them a catch*.

Namior stared out at the darkening, rainswept village, feeling violence in the air of the storm yet to come, and she knew that tonight she would be happy giving Kel several catches.

Her mother and great-grandmother were in the main downstairs room, gathered about the groundstone, still scrying to see whether they could assess the coming storm more accurately. They'd excused Namior when her nose started to bleed—she still had much to learn about magic and its gentle, deep manipulations—and her mother knew that soon she would be going out. *I'll take care*, she had told her, and her great-grandmother, blind in one eye and deaf in one ear, had said in one of her less troubled, saner moments, *Find a secret each day, and in a few years you may know him*. Namior knew that her great-grandmother did not approve of Kel Boon. *Eyes the color of blood*, she had once complained. But like all witches in the Feeron family, past and present, Namior was blessed with freedom and gifted with choice.

A machine drifted up the narrow path below her window, reaching out jointed metallic arms to relight oil lanterns that had gone out and turn up their flames. She saw rain patter down in a hundred spots across its gray-stone hood, and it sped up as though to escape the downpour.

She should dress. Kel would not be down for a while, but she'd like to be at the Dog's Eyes before him. Trakis and Mell would be there already, downing Neak's stormy brews and debating whether to spend some of their hard-earned on the Ventgorian wines he kept in his cellar. A storm like this one seemed to raise the village's blood; partly excitement and partly, she suspected, the idea that they were defying nature. The sea would rise, the rain would fall and the wind would blow, but Pavmouth Breaks clung to the coast, boldly facing the tempest and waiting for morning to arrive.

She frowned, remembering her great-grandmother's sickness that afternoon. Her mother had administered ceyrat root, but it had perturbed them, and set a chill in the air that Namior had still not shaken. The old woman was subject to periods of madness—she called them her crazes—brought on by age and the stew that time made of the brain, and such a sickness was usually the beginning. *She's just old and ill*, she thought. *Bad meat for supper yesterday. Too much scrying.*

A blast of wind gusted in from the west, and Pavmouth Breaks seemed to shudder beneath its force. Namior stood and moved back from the window. The glass flexed slightly, distorting the village and warping her own reflection so that she looked to be in pain. She turned away and went to wash and dress.

NAMIOR DESCENDED THE twisting staircase at the heart of the house. She'd changed from her loose witch's robe to a pair of tight canvas trousers, soft sheebok-wool shirt and a long leather coat, and she felt ready for the night. She could still hear her mother's voice chanting softly as she sat by the groundstone, and she slowed to listen to the words. There was something not quite right, and it took Namior a dozen heartbeats to figure out what that was: her great-grandmother was silent.

"Namior," her mother whispered. "Come down; come in."

Namior descended the last few stairs, not surprised that her mother had been aware of her presence. The two women had sat around the groundstone for most of the day, her mother touching surfaces smoothed by hands for decades, gathering strength from the land's magic and using that strength to try to discern things yet to happen. Namior's senses still felt heightened from the time she had spent with them. Noises rang inside her head, and she could smell the anger of the sea.

Her great-grandmother sat across the room from her, huddled down in a mass of blankets. She twitched and mumbled in her sleep.

"Sit," her mother said, patting the floor cushions beside her. Namior sat cross-legged and lowered her head, paying respect to the groundstone.

"Storm's getting harsher," Namior said.

"Yes. There's something…" Her mother shook her head, setting her many earrings jangling.

"Wrong?"

Her mother nodded. "A blank spot in the storm. There are waves and rain, breakers smashing the shore, and a waterspout farther along the coast that may touch land."

"I saw most of that, too," Namior said, and she felt a brief flush of pride in her expanding abilities. They exhausted her—if it were not for the lure of Kel, she would be happy staying in and sleeping for the evening and night—but they also excited her. Her mother and great-grandmother knew that, and they encouraged it, though the older woman was always the one to urge caution. *Life's too short to rush*, was one of her favorite sayings, and it had taken Namior a long time to see the sense in that. Life was short, so she needed to do things right.

"And we should have seen more," her mother said. "There's something missing. A weight. Something out to sea."

"A weight of what?"

Her mother frowned, staring at the groundstone. "I'm not sure." Then she smiled. "Probably just the storm stirring the magic. It happens sometimes, especially when there's lightning."

Namior looked at the groundstone—as high as her chest, planted deep in the family home generations before, polished and smoothed by centuries of her ancestors' contact—and she almost reached out again. But there was still a gentle throb behind her face, and her nose prickled at the thought of communing with the land's magic again that evening. A dribble of blood ran down to her top lip.

Her great-grandmother shuddered awake and looked up. "No more for you tonight, Namior," she said, her voice weak and tremulous.

Namior nodded, dabbing the blood away.

"Don't go too far," her mother said, leaning in close enough to kiss her daughter's cheek.

"Only the Dog's Eyes," Namior said. "Kel is coming down."

"There'll be damage to clear up in the morning. Stay in the heights, away from the harbor."

"I will." Namior was becoming unsettled by her mother's concern. "You know I can look after myself."

The woman nodded and smiled, but her eyes were still clouded by whatever was missing. Namior could hear it in her voice, and she was unused to the sound of fear. "You're a good girl," her mother said. "And you're growing to be a great witch."

"I'll be away," Namior said, smiling, then glancing pointedly at her great-grandmother. "Don't forget you both need sleep!"

She felt them watching her as she left the main room and

stood in the hallway behind the front door. Closing the hall
door was almost a relief. Alone again, listening to the wind
batter the door in its frame, hearing the whistle of a machine
rumbling by, she cast her mind back to her own visions from
that afternoon. She had sensed a storm coming, as had they
all. She had seen the waves and rain, boats swaying and bobbing in the upset harbor, and cloaked shapes pushing against
the wind as they navigated the dark streets, steps and winding
paths of Pavmouth Breaks. She had not been aware of any absence; no void where there should be something; nothing to
disturb.

She sighed, hoping that her great-grandmother would not
descend into one of her crazes.

"I'm still young," she whispered. She touched the stone
charm that hung around her neck—a shard from the same
rock that had gone to make her family's groundstone—and
breathed in the energy it gave her. "Still young, and I trust
their word."

Vowing to be careful, she pulled the door open and went
out into the storm.

STAY IN THE *heights, away from the harbor,* her mother had
said. But upon leaving their house and taking the short, cobbled path down to the wider street, Namior looked right, down
the small slope toward the harbor, and in the dusky light she
saw the sparkling glare of spray as the sea struck the mole.

Storm's not anywhere near its height, she thought. So she
turned right and walked along the hillside, heading toward a
lower path from which she knew she would be able to view
the whole harbor. It wasn't every day a storm like that came
in, and Namior reveled in the power of nature.

The path curved slowly around the hip of the hill, exposing itself to the sea winds, and with every step Namior felt the
power of the gale increasing. She hugged the jacket close

across her chest and lowered her head. It was raining so much that the water was not draining away fast enough, and her feet sloshed, leaving wakes like those of small boats. She winced as a gust of wind threatened to unbalance her, driving rain horizontally against her face, stinging her exposed skin, soaking her trousers. Still the storm felt young, and she sensed that it had yet to find its rhythm.

She walked on, passing a couple of people going in the opposite direction. They offered her a brief nod, and she nodded back, unable to identify them in their storm gear. Their faces were covered. They could have been anyone.

The path sloped down toward the harbor, and once it was free of the buildings crowding it, Namior could hear the roar of the sea as it broke against the land. It was immense, shuddering through the ground and into her feet as well as shaking the air. She paused in the lee of a tall retaining wall to watch, sheltered from the worst of the rain but still with a good field of vision. Waves broke against the mole and pushed their spray right over, and the water of the harbor itself was in turmoil, tossing boats against each other. The front was awash, the swell lifting against the harbor wall and occasionally surging across the ground. She could see a few hardy people struggling here and there, dashing from one building to the next, but mostly the streets were sensibly deserted.

Worse to come, she thought, and for the first time she felt the twinge of concern she had seen in her mother's eyes. There would be broken boats to fix when the storm had spent itself, and perhaps more.

She turned and hurried back up the hillside, and when she drew level with the narrow path to her house, a transport machine rolled down the street toward her. It stopped before her and lowered itself on wooden wheels, and she climbed onto its back, touching the control stone beside the metal seat and casting her thoughts. The machine turned, trailing limbs stroking the ground as it drew power from the land, and started along the hillside toward the Dog's Eyes Tavern.

WHEN KEL BOON entered his favorite tavern, a score of faces turned his way. He smiled and received a dozen smiles in return, but some of the older men and women barely nodded. He'd only been there for five years, and it would take a lot longer than that for him to become one of them.

Such was the atmosphere in a small fishing village. Even on a day like that, when the skies were opening, the sea was battering them and the rest of the world felt very far away, Pavmouth Breaks' residents feared the stranger.

His attention was grabbed immediately by the small tone-bone band playing in the large window bay. There were two men and a woman, the same three who regularly supplied music in the tavern in return for drink and food. And though he'd heard much of the music before, it never failed to stir his soul. The woman had caught a fresh whistle fish that day, and she had it draped across her lap, stroking its scales and passing her fingers across the many bony protuberances on its back and sides. A whistle fish took days to die out of water, and its death sounds could be manipulated into hoots, clicks and whines. The two men played a variety of instruments, ranging from a whalebone harp to a large hollow bone around which much legend had been built. No one knew where it came from, but these were fisherfolk; there were a thousand tales of its origin, and all of them true.

"Kel!" Trakis called from a smoky corner. The big man stood and waved his arms and Mell, sitting beside him smoking a pipe, nudged him in the ribs.

Kel looked around quickly but saw no sight of Namior. Maybe the witches had held her back, after all.

"You look like a drowned furbat!" Trakis said. As Kel drew closer, his friend's face grew stern. "You need ale." He strode toward the bar.

"Hello, gorgeous," Mell said. "You're dripping on the table."

Kel stepped back and shed his coat and hat, hanging them

on a hook set into one of the tavern's many rough timber columns. It was one of the oldest buildings in Pavmouth Breaks, so the landlord Neak said, and he also claimed it was home to the most wraiths. Kel always smiled when he heard Neak telling that to a visiting fisherman or a newcomer to the village: *Most haunted place in Noreela!* Kel had visited a dozen places in Noreela City itself that also laid claim to that dubious title.

"No Namior?" Mell asked.

"She's coming. I spoke to her earlier."

"Storm from the deepest Black," Mell said, taking another draw on her pipe. She gasped, then exhaled a stream of pure green smoke. "You can almost hear the wraiths screaming in the wind."

"No wraiths out there," Kel said, perhaps a little too harshly. "It's just weather."

Mell nodded and stared at him a little too long. Of everyone in Pavmouth Breaks, she seemed most suspicious of his past. Sometimes he thought she could see deeper than he knew.

Trakis returned and lowered a tray of drinks carefully to the table. Four jugs of Neak's Wanderlust ale, and a tall, dark bottle. "I'm splashing out," Trakis said. "Tonight it's us against the world."

"A militiaman who can afford Ventgorian wine," Mell said admiringly. "You must be corrupt."

"Eat sheebok shit, fisherwoman."

Kel raised his jug and offered his squabbling friends a toast. "Us against the world." He drank, closing his eyes as the initial bitter taste changed into something sweet and wonderful. Neak swore that he brewed naturally, without the help of magic or machines, and Kel believed him. Nothing that tasted so good could be so false.

The tavern door opened, conversation stopped and Kel joined with everyone else in looking at the newcomer. Namior Feeron entered, slamming the door behind her and shaking water from her long hair. She spied Kel immediately and smiled. As she came across to them she swapped greetings with most of the tavern's patrons, and Kel looked away. Seeing how well she knew this place sometimes stung him, because he also knew how much she wanted to get away. She was desperate for travel, exploration and adventure. She craved to see Noreela City, Pengulfin Heights, the islands of The Spine, which curved out from the north of Noreela, and she even dreamed of a journey far enough south to see the dangerous mountain ranges of Kang Kang. But every time she mentioned this, Kel Boon told her no. He was staying there. *I've had my adventure*, he would say, and however much she pressed, he could tell her no more. That was the dark space between them—a gap that seemed, at present, unfordable.

"The harbor's mad," Namior said even before taking a seat. "Boats are crashing about, and some of those waves are breaking over the mole."

"There's been worse," Mell said. She had been a fisherwoman for almost eighteen years. She'd been involved in three wrecks, seen two friends drowned and one taken by sea creatures, and nothing seemed to disturb her anymore. At almost forty—just younger than Kel, and two decades older than Namior—Mell had lived enough to fill many lives. *We'd have such tales to tell each other*, Kel sometimes thought. But if he wanted to stay in Pavmouth Breaks, he could never speak of his past.

Not if he wanted to stay alive.

"And what do you say, young witch?" Trakis asked Namior.

Namior's eyes darkened for a beat, then she smiled. It lit up her face. "My mother says there's to be a waterspout just along the coast." She glanced at Kel, the smile slipping so slightly that he thought he was the only one who noticed.

"I'll drink to that!" Trakis said. He raised his mug, and the rest of them joined him in toasting the storm.

Namior sat on a bench close to Kel, and it only took one

mug of ale before she pressed herself against him. He slung his right arm loosely around her shoulders and drank with his left. She looked at him frequently, her ale-tainted laughter a welcome addition to the tavern's underlying noise. Kel drank slowly; he had never enjoyed the sensation of being drunk and the loss of control it brought on. But he had always enjoyed watching Trakis and Mell drink together, and that night both of them were truly in form. Conversations turned to bickering, bickering to full-blown arguments, then they would hug each other, laughing and swearing undying friendship. Kel supposed this was just one of many taverns filled with such people, but these were special because they were his friends.

The door opened occasionally, letting a sample of the storm inside to blow out candles and spatter the wooden floor with rain. Whoever stumbled in was subject of the tavern's appraisal, and more often than not they would have stories of how the storm was progressing. Waves fifteen steps high, they said, battering the mole and smashing boats against the harbor wall. Rain so heavy that some of the paths up to Drakeman's Hill had turned into impassable torrents. "Looks like I'm definitely staying with you tonight," Kel said at this, and Namior's hand squeezed his thigh, remaining there afterwards.

The evening turned to night, though daylight had been stolen long ago by the thundering clouds. Lightning flashed at the tavern's windows, followed soon after by the rumbles of thunder. The heart of the tempest was almost upon them.

Kel knew that Namior saw this as an adventure. Whatever had troubled her earlier had been melted away by the Wanderlust ale and fine Ventgorian wine, and her smile was a pleasure, her laughter a welcome song.

But with each flash of lightning, as though the space between blinks was another world, Kel was taken back to that night in Noreela City.

ONE DAY YOU'LL learn to pack your fucking weapons properly," O'Peeria says, grabbing Kel Boon's belt and tugging him to her. The Shantasi woman runs her hands across his body, beneath his cloak, around his belt, loosening and tightening straps and webbing, shifting knife sheaths a finger's width, lengthening the string on throwing stars. Kel raises his arms from his sides and watches her, enjoying the opportunity to examine her face while her attention is elsewhere. She's beautiful, in a harsh way, her pale skin set off against her long dark hair like day against night. He looks down at her own weapon-clad body, lithe and strong.

She passes one hand between his thighs and adjusts the straps of his sword scabbard. Pausing, she glances up, her eyes darker than the Black. "If I feel your cock growing hard, I'll cut it off."

Kel goes to say something, but he's not entirely sure she's joking.

O'Peeria stands, grabs his shoulder and shakes. Kel stumbles and leans to the left to avoid falling over. None of his weapons makes a sound.

"Good," the Shantasi says. "A Core agent should know how to wear his weapons, at least." She turns and heads for the door, sweeping her hair over her right shoulder and tying it in place. That way, it won't interfere when the time comes to fight.

"O'Peeria," Kel says. She turns and stares at him. She's been his lover, and she swears that she's his friend, but she's a hard woman. And with all they've been through he's never found a way to get close.

Kel shakes his head. "Doesn't matter."

"You ready?" O'Peeria says, raising her eyebrows.

"Yes." Kel's voice is quiet, and he cannot meet her gaze.

"Sure, Kel? Are you fucking sure? This is killing stuff, tonight. No more fun and games. We've been watching him long enough, and the Core wants him dead. So are you *ready*?"

"Yes," Kel says, more firmly this time. He looks over

O'Peeria's shoulder at the door. Beyond lie the nighttime streets, alleys, parks, squares and secretive buildings of Noreela City. "I'm ready."

O'Peeria smiles, and not for the first time Kel thinks that he might love her.

By midnight, she will be dead.

THE THUD SHATTERED one of the Dog's Eyes' windows, cracked floorboards and shook the door in its frame. It knocked several wine bottles from the shelf behind the bar to smash at Neak's feet, struck at Kel's ears, and sent a heavy shock wave up through his feet and spine.

The rain and wind did not lessen — with the smashed window, the noise from outside increased — but for a few beats after the thud, the interior of the tavern was almost silent. It felt as though the ground itself had moved.

"What in the Black was that?" a soft voice said. The thought spoken, a ripple of surprise ran around the tavern, and a beat later most people were on their feet and heading for the door.

"That wasn't wind," Namior said.

"And no wave, either," Mell added.

Trakis raised a mug and drained it of ale, then stood and nodded at the door. "Shall we?"

Kel felt a sudden chill of fear — a realization that nothing was safe. His world — *anyone's* world — could be opened up and taken apart at any time. He had liked Pavmouth Breaks when he first arrived, and over the years he had grown to love it, but he always knew that safety and contentment were merely thin veneers camouflaging the random cruelties of the world.

"Kel?" Namior said. She had remained close to him, and now he saw that strange look again, the one the others had not noticed before.

"What is it, Namior?" Mell said.

Namior looked at her two friends, then across at the broken window. Raindrops spat in. A dozen people had gone outside, but none of their voices were audible above the storm. "My mother and great-grandmother...they were worried, that's all."

"And you?" Kel asked.

She shrugged. "I'm still young. Felt nothing. But if they're worried..."

"Then so are you," Mell finished for her. Namior nodded.

Trakis placed his mug gently on the table. None of them drank.

Someone burst back into the tavern, her hair made mad by the wind and rain. She wiped water from her face and Kel saw her eyes, the mixture of excitement and fear driving them wide. He'd seen such a look many times, and he knew exactly what it meant: she had seen something she had never seen before.

"Something's coming!" the woman said. "Out to sea, something out there, dark and big and fast!"

"What is it?" Mell asked.

"Don't know. Something."

"Come on," Kel said. He grabbed Namior's hand as the four of them headed for the door, skirting around the woman, who evidently no longer wished to see.

"The ground's still moving," Trakis said as he pulled the door open and stepped outside.

And it was. Kel paused for a beat and felt the vibration enter his feet and transfer up through his bones, and when he pressed his teeth together it felt as if they could shatter. From behind came the musical rattle of wine bottles clanking together. From ahead, the sounds of the storm, and whatever else it had brought.

Namior squeezed his hand. She was outside by then, arm outstretched, and he was suddenly desperate not to let go of her.

"Come on!" she shouted. "They've gone up the hill behind the tavern to see better!"

Kel realized that, other than Neak and the windswept woman, he was the only one still inside the Dog's Eyes. He stepped out into the storm.

NAMIOR WAS AWARE of the wildlife that existed in and around the village, and she was also used to seeing most of it only rarely. So when something ran over her foot she squealed, unheard in the gale. And when she looked down, pools of light cast from the Dog's Eyes' windows were speckled with dashing shadows. Rats ran uphill; swarm lizards dashed so quickly that they looked like smudges of shadows; a dog growled past. And around her head, what she had thought at first were leaves blown by the wind, were bats, soundless and terrified.

Namior suddenly wanted to be back at home. Her mother was there, and her great-grandmother, and they had seen something more than the storm—something *absent*. Climbing the steps beside the Dog's Eyes, and then the steep banking at the rear of the tavern, and finally mounting the flattened observation area where patrons sometimes drank on hot days and Neak occasionally held flat-ball tournaments, it was the absentness that disconcerted Namior the most. If they'd sensed something more, perhaps she would not have been so afraid. More could be dealt with, seen, challenged. But nothing could be done with nothing.

Mell and Trakis were already up there, leaning on the wall and staring over the harbor and out to sea. Namior held on tight to Kel's hand, desperate not to let go, and he ran up the steps behind her, drawing close.

"What is it?" she shouted before they had even reached the wall. She shouldered in between Trakis and Mell, while the watchers shouted words that the wind stole away. Rain was driven at them across the rooftops of buildings farther down the hill, and the water had a slightly smoky taste when it hit Namior's tongue, as though it had picked up chimney smoke.

Kel stood behind her, held her arms and looked over her shoulder.

"Nothing," Namior said, because when she looked out to sea, that was what she saw.

Down in the harbor, waves crashed against the mole and the harbor wall. At the base of the cliffs to the south, the sea smashed, boiled and foamed like a diseased creature, striving to gnaw into the land. Beyond the mole were violent white-crests, waves breaking and rolling and building again, surging in toward the village and promising chaos. And past the waves, out to sea, where clouds flashed but no lightning danced at the horizon, a wall of nothing seemed to be grow-ing in the darkness.

"What *is* that?" Kel shouted.

Namior shrugged, comforted by the feel of his hands on her arms.

"End of the storm," Trakis shouted. "Sea growing calm."

"No," Mell shouted, and Namior listened because the fisherwoman was wise to things of the sea. "Everything's about to get worse!" Mell looked up at Trakis, then across at Namior and Kel. When she next spoke it was no longer a shout, but still they all heard. "We should be safe up here."

"A wave," Namior said, dreadful understanding dawning at last. The thud, and now the wave. She'd heard of places far to the south, near Kang Kang, where the ground sometimes shrugged, cracked and turned over. Groundshakes, they were called, though many people thought they were the result of fledge demons deep underground collapsing another seam of that strange drug.

Mother, she thought.

"They'll be fine," Kel spoke into her ear, saying exactly what she wanted to hear. But how could he be sure? Namior glanced along and down the hillside at the chaos of rooftops, paths and courtyards, trying to place her house. It was slightly lower than the Dog's Eyes, and closer to the harbor. Lower and closer... to *that*!

She could not look away from the wave for long. It was a blankness on the horizon, a tall dark space above the foam-capped waves and below the boiling sky. And it was coming closer, making itself known at last.

The ground shook. The air was filled with the taste of the sea. And a roar was rising, building quickly as the sound of the incoming disaster found the land and announced itself.

They could only stand there and watch. Namior thought of all the people she knew who would likely be down in the harbor area; friends who lived there, others who worked through the night dealing with the day's catch. They'd have felt the thud and now they would hear and see the wave. But for them, it was already far too late.

She closed her eyes, but she had to look again.

There was a flash of red lightning across the horizon, as though the flesh of the sky had been slashed.

With a roar greater even than the wave's, the water in the harbor surged out to sea, leaving fishing boats resting on their hulls and the pale shapes of sea creatures thrashing in their exposure to the night.

And then the wave came in.

KEL STAYED WITH her. His fingers sank into her arms, hurting, but the pain pinned her to the land. She was glad for it. It was nothing compared to what her village faced.

As the wave came closer it slowed, growing higher—an impossible thing that should not be there. The rain and wind seemed to stop for a beat, as though cowed by this monster from the sea, then its base struck the mole. The heavy concrete structure disappeared beneath the foot of the wave, and the water thundered down, broke, swallowing boats and tossing them before it, smashing into the harborside and roaring onward. Buildings disappeared in its white-foamed fury.

The noise was staggering, the roar of water expending so much power, then beneath that the sound of Pavmouth Breaks suffering a fatal wound. Buildings collapsed, adding their parts to the wall of water surging inland. It scoured the landscape before and beneath it, ripping away structures that had stood for longer than anyone knew. Timber buildings seemed to disintegrate almost before the wave touched them, submitting to the inevitable. The water's texture changed, made sharp and heavy by the detritus it had picked up, and it boiled up the hillsides.

The first stone bridge, spanning the River Pav across the throat of the harbor, collapsed beneath the onslaught.

Across the narrow valley, on the much steeper slopes of Drakeman's Hill, the water seemed to rise and rise. Forced into the narrow alleys and paths, it spurted upward and outward—sprays that carried parts of the land with them. Shattered buildings tumbled into the waters.

"By all the Black!" Namior shouted in despair, shocked by what she was seeing and filled with a deep, dark sense of hopelessness.

Kel pressed his face beside hers and said nothing, because there was really nothing to say.

Namior looked along the hillside to where her house stood. It was still safe. The waters roiled farther down the slope, smashing and breaking and pouring their awful energy into the destruction of the village.

The wave was broken at last, and before a huge cloud of spray and mist rose high enough to block the view, Namior could look down at the harbor and see what was left. There was not much. The mole had crumbled in several places. She could not make out any sign of the dozens of boats that had been moored there, and the harbor wall itself was vague, shattered and collapsed so that its true form was no longer visible. The buildings were mostly gone, only a few walls left standing, and their insides were home to surging, filthy water. It was as if Pavmouth Breaks had only ever been a painting, and a giant hand had come to smudge the image away.

The ground continued to shake, and for a beat Namior thought the hillsides would slide down into the ruined valley, taking all those surviving structures with them. Pavmouth Breaks would be gone. She closed her eyes and rested her hands on the wall before her, trying to commune with the land, but she could not concentrate. Magic *observed*, she could feel that; it watched what was happening. But it could offer no easy explanation. If this wave was a part of the language of the land, then it was a roar of outrage.

The front of destruction had passed them and was traveling up the valley. The wave had dropped into a surging mass of water that pushed up, colliding with the River Pav and combining with it to wreak more chaos and devastation.

Namior could see roughly where her home was, and everything there seemed as it was. "Mother," she said.

"We'll go down," Kel said.

"No, we can't. What if—?"

"It's your family," he said into her ear, just loud enough to defeat the continuing roar. "That's reason enough."

She turned her head so that they were face-to-face, and she kissed him. She did not need to say anything else.

The others were stirring, galvanized from the shock into which they had been frozen. Trakis and Mell looked at Namior and Kel, their faces grave. Namior knew that Mell's parents lived down close to the harbor, her father a scarred old fisherman with one leg and countless tales, her mother a net maker, who cooked the best fishtail bakkett she'd ever tasted. Mell nodded without speaking, then turned to leave.

Namior grabbed her arm. "I need to check on mine, quickly, but then I'll be there," she said.

Mell's lips pressed together, and as she and Trakis left Namior saw tears in the fisherwoman's eyes.

"Come on," Kel said.

They headed back down beside the Dog's Eyes—Neak was standing before his tavern, looking down into the valley in a daze from which they could not rouse him—and then along the path toward Namior's house. A machine stopped for them, lowering itself and offering a ride as if nothing had happened.

Namior thought Kel said something as they passed by the machine, but she could not be sure. Either way, right then she agreed with him. It was a time when it felt better to trust their own two feet.

Buildings blocked their view of the valley for a while, the path they followed winding between old stone walls and newer timber structures. They passed a few people coming the other way, up from the valley, and all of them had a haunted look in their eyes. One woman was bleeding from a terrible head wound, but when Kel reached out to stop her she lashed out, knocking his hand aside, determined to walk on.

"Wait!" Namior said. With time and a chant she could stem the bleeding and heal the wound. But when Kel tried to stop the woman again, she panicked and pushed him away.

Namior went to go after her. "Wait, I can—"

"At least she's walking," Kel said. "There'll be many more who can't."

"Yes," said Namior, watching the woman's back as she staggered away. And the impact of what had happened really struck her then. She could hear the steady roar of the receding waters, the grind of the village's ruins scouring the land as the surge carried it away, and she thought of all the people who would not be with them anymore. There would be wraiths to chant down, if the village Mourner was even still alive, and bodies to collect, and . . .

"Namior?" Kel said.

She looked at him, eyes blurring with tears.

"We should go. Your mother."

"My mother." *She saw this*, Namior thought. "She knew something was wrong."

"Nothing could have been done," Kel said. "It's just nature."

"Just nature." Namior nodded.

Kel came to her and folded his arms around her, holding her tight. She thought that if he hugged her hard enough, maybe she would not be able to hear the flowing water, smell the scent of sea mist in the air or taste salt on her tongue like spilled blood. But she was wrong.

THE AIR WAS heavy with mist and tasted of the sea. It was a taste that Kel had never become used to—exotic, distant, alien. He had been born and bred in Noreela City, and he had almost died there. Though he had been in Pavmouth Breaks for over five years, still it felt like a retreat, not a home. He was a visitor. He'd started to believe he always would be.

The buildings on their left opened up, only a short wall bounding the street, and Kel looked over, down at the harbor and the surrounding area. He realized with a shock that there should have been a house blocking his view, but it had gone. The ground it had been built on was washed away, leaving a sheer drop beyond the wall of at least twenty steps. If he fell, the mud would suck him down and drown him.

Namior gasped behind him, pressing back against the building across the street.

Kel backed away from the wall. Its footing had been exposed, and the slightest touch could send it tumbling. He looked across the ruined village at Drakeman's Hill; a section of its lower slope had also been washed away, a dark wound in the land. As he watched, a two-story stone house slid gracefully down into the swollen river, maintaining its integrity until the rushing waters took it apart. He hoped no one had remained inside.

Namior nudged him, nodding along the street. A machine

stood there, stubby legs shaking slightly as though balancing against a tremor. There was a wide, deep dent in its side. The metal shell was scored, part of its stone interior crumbled, and a spread of flesh that connected the two was hanging loose, dripping blood and gore to the wet cobbles. It keened—a high, pained sound.

Namior rushed to the machine and placed her hands against its metallic carapace.

"Your family!" Kel said. He was not surprised at her concern for the machine. It was in magic's control, after all, and he sometimes thought of Namior as a slave to magic.

"It's damaged," Namior said.

"It can stay damaged. Practitioners will fix it. We should check on your mother and great-grandmother, then..."

"And then down there?" Namior stepped away from the machine, approached the wall and looked down into the valley. "They're dead. All of them."

"We have to help," Kel said. "There'll be survivors, and wraiths for someone to chant down."

"And when's the last time you tried to chant down a wraith?" she asked.

"I didn't mean me," he said, blinking slowly to try to shake the memory of O'Peeria's death. He saw the familiar look on Namior's face, the one that said, *I really know so little about him.*

Namior dashed past him, entering the short, winding path up to her own home. Kel followed. By the time he caught up with her, she had opened the front door and entered, and he followed her inside. Until a while ago, he'd planned on coming there with love on his mind, but when he shut the door it was to close out the stink of sea, and death.

I know the smell of death so well, he thought. *I can handle it again.*

For the first time since arriving, he began to think he could give the people of Pavmouth Breaks more than just wood carvings. He could help.

———

NAMIOR'S MOTHER AND great-grandmother were fine, if a little shaken. The older woman was sitting close to the groundstone, stirring shapes in dried seaweed on the ground and chanting a low, painful song.

"There are many wraiths," her mother said. She was dressing, shrugging on her coat, pulling on heavy boots. "I'm going to find Mourner Kanthia."

"If she's still alive. She lives up the valley, where the river's even narrower."

"She's alive," Namior's mother said, and Kel saw the certainty in her eyes. "But she'll need help." She paused and stared at her daughter, sparing only a quick glance for Kel. "What of you?" she asked.

"Down to the harbor," Kel said. "To help."

"Is this it?" Namior said. "Nothing more?"

Her mother frowned and nodded at her own grandmother chanting beside the groundstone. "It's difficult to see. Things are . . . in chaos. It's like the wave swept through magic as well, and our paths inside are corrupted."

"There could be more waves," Kel said.

Namior spun around to face him, her eyes suddenly stern. "Trakis and Mell will be down there already."

Kel smiled. "I wasn't suggesting we turn and run. Just that we need to take care. Listen. Watch."

Namior's mother hugged her daughter close, smiling over her shoulder at Kel. He was pleased to be included at last. "Grandmother will keep looking," she said. "And if she senses anything else, she'll let us know."

"But she's . . ." *Mad? Was he really going to say that?*

"She *will* let us know."

"How?" Kel asked.

"She's been doing this for a long time. She has her ways."

Kel nodded. He'd heard of old, old witches who could touch the minds of their families at a distance, but it was a talent that took a lifetime to perfect.

"Take care of our girl, wood-carver," Namior's great-grandmother said. And she looked up at Kel, her one good eye glittering with whatever her damaged mind cast into it.

THEY WAITED WHERE the street had vanished. Kel knew the route down to the harbor. He'd walked it a hundred times with Namior, holding hands and laughing. Now it was changed. Several buildings on their left—houses, a shop and a storage shed for some of the fishermen—had vanished. The street was gone too, cut off in a ragged line. Beyond, the water had undermined the land and washed it away. To their right stood a low row of stone houses, a couple lit from within by candles and oil lights, several of them dark. Whether the inhabitants were hidden away within, afraid to emerge and terrified of what would come next, Kel did not know. It could be that the fisherfolk who lived there had been down at the harbor, or perhaps even out to sea. Some of them liked working at night, though the risks from inimical sea life were far greater then. They said it gave them a better catch.

The water's route had reversed, and now it was rushing back out to sea. It carried with it the evidence of the violence it had wrought on the village: smashed timbers, a couple of machines rolling along, uprooted plants and trees, and a body, facedown but obviously broken and twisted.

Namior gasped, and Kel held her close. "Listen to me," he said. "We'll see lots of death down here. The entire seafront and harbor have been washed away. All the boats are smashed or gone. Are you sure you want to go on?"

She pulled away from him slightly, and in the weak light he could see her eyes flash with anger. "This is my village," she said. Kel nodded. He admired such unflinching loyalty. And envied it.

The rain had lessened, as though the wave had been the culmination of the storm. The wind was weaker too, still lifting spray from the violent waters, but no longer strong enough to have to lean into.

Ahead of them, the hill curved around until it faced out to sea, and this was where Kel had thought they could be of most help. Those living right down on the coast would be dead and washed away, but farther up the hillside, where the force of the water's impact had been less, there would be people trapped in collapsed buildings and perhaps wounded in the streets. The bleeding woman they had seen was evidence of that; he only hoped that others were less shocked and more open to aid.

"We'll need machines here, and Practitioners," he said.

Namior raised an eyebrow. "With all your love of magic?"

"It has its uses. This is one of them."

Namior was looking across the expanse of flowing water and debris.

"Namior, we can't get over there yet. The bridge is out, and—"

"The central span's gone, that's all. The rest of it held. And Trakis and Mell will be trying to get over there, looking for Mell's parents."

A hundred steps downriver, the remains of the old stone bridge held on valiantly against the backwash of water. Even in the darkness, Kel could see the shadow of debris piled up against its upriver side. It was crazy, but perhaps those uprooted trees and tumbled rocks could provide a way to cross.

He looked back down the slope at the ruins of the lower parts of Pavmouth Breaks.

"Kel?" Namior said. "We've seen how bad it is here. Wherever we go tonight, there'll be people to rescue. And they're our friends."

Kel nodded. "Okay. Back past your house, then we can cut down through the Moon Temple grounds to get to the bridge."

"Maybe we'll find some Practitioners on the way."

"Can't you do it?" With all her witch training, communing

with the land, drawing of magic and using it to cure and mend, he was sure she'd be able to control some lifting machines. But she seemed doubtful.

"I could try. I use them, just like anyone. Ride them. But I've never *instructed* a machine, not like that."

"Always a first time for everything." He hugged Namior and she smiled back, warming him through. "So come on," he said. "Or by the time we get there everyone will be rescued." *Or dead*, he thought. In which case Mourner Kanthia, if she was still alive, would have a busy night ahead of her.

They hurried back the way they had come, and Kel could not help thinking that they were just another part of the confusion. They passed the path to Namior's home and soon drew level with the entrance to the Moon Temple gardens. The heavy metal gate was open, and there were several people gathered around the ornate, half-moon entrance to the Temple. Kel knew that the moon priest lived around the hillside where they had just been, close down to the small beach, so it was doubtful that he had survived. He'd locked up his temple before returning home that evening.

Kel looked up at the open viewing area on the Temple's roof, and there was a naked woman up there. He paused in surprise and sensed Namior standing beside him, looking up as well.

"Who *is* that?" Kel asked.

"I'm not sure," Namior said. "Someone seeking help." The clouds were still heavy and thick, promising more rain, and neither life- nor death-moonlight touched the woman's body.

"We should go," Kel said. "Things will get worse."

"How in the Black could they be worse?" Namior sounded almost desperate, and Kel wondered just how close she was to panic. He would have to look after her.

"Things fall," Kel said. "Buildings have been undermined. Foundations weakened. The wave has done all the damage, but it's time that will keep destroying."

Namior said nothing. Perhaps she hated the defeat in his voice, but he could not help it. It was the way he had been trained.

And as they worked their way downhill, past the Moon Temple and toward the lower streets, Kel could not help thinking about his time in the Core, and how it had prepared him for an occurrence such as this. He had learned a lot about survival in the harshest of times and living off the land. They had instructed him on basic medical requirements and demonstrated how wounds could be closed using twisted sheebok gut, a needle and a sprinkling of shredded hedge-hock. He had learned about languages and cultures, the subjects and objects of worship and how death was dealt with by the different races and peoples of Noreela. But the lesson that had been most valuable had undoubtedly saved his life, many times: always expect the worst.

He was expecting that now.

They skirted around the Temple, heading down the steep slope toward the road that used to run alongside the river. The lower boundary wall to the Temple grounds had fallen away, and the ground there had been undermined as well, slipping down to add to the chaos left behind by the wave. It was only so close that Kel saw just how much damage had been done.

Ten steps below them was a sea of mud, rocks, protruding walls, smashed roofs, bodies, cattle and trees. Farther out, the flooded river still poured back toward the sea; but closer to the bank several struggling shapes splashed weakly at the muck, doing their utmost to remain afloat.

"What's that?" Namior said, but her voice trailed off. She already knew.

"Stay here!" Kel said.

"What? You can't just leave—"

Kel ignored her. Slipping to the place where the ground fell away, he tried to glance over, down into the mess now lit by an emerging death moon. There was a slick spread of muck beneath him, but to his right a horse's body had washed against the mud cliff, lying on its side. Kel jumped.

The horse coughed when he landed on its stomach. He steadied himself, ready for it to struggle, but the creature was dead, the air forced from it when he landed.

"Help!" someone shouted, voice distorted by a mouthful of mud.

"Kel!" Namior shouted from ten steps above.

"Rope!" he yelled. "Blankets! Smashed wood, *anything*, Namior. Find it and throw it down." He knelt on the horse and felt down into the mud for its saddle, but his hands touched the distinctive ridges along its back. A wild horse from the plains above the valley, likely come down for a drink. Just his luck.

He looked across the sea of mud at the feebly struggling shapes. He was sure there had been at least four when he jumped down, but now he could only see movement from two. *Shit, shit, shit,* he thought, looking around desperately for something to throw out to them, wanting to offer hope but unable to find either.

Kel probed at the mud with one foot and immediately sank up to just below his knee. He pulled back, grabbing hold of the dead horse's mane to avoid being sucked in deeper.

"Namior!"

There was nothing he could do.

He watched another shape going under, crying out a muddy name that he could not identify as they went from night to black.

"*Namior!*"

"Kel!"

He turned and looked up, and Namior was edging a length of splintered timber down to him. He grabbed it, cursing as splinters bit into his hand, but by the time he'd turned again, ready to throw it across the surface of the mud, the last shape had disappeared. A huge bubble rose where it had gone, and even above the roar of the swollen river he heard that bubble burst. Another person's final breath added itself to the dead atmosphere of Pavmouth Breaks.

Kel stood slowly and propped the wood back against the bank. Carefully, slowly, he climbed, grabbing Namior's hands and letting her help him up.

"You did your best," she said.

"Let's go along to the bridge, see if we can—"

"Kel, you did everything you could."

They stood, and Kel held her close, seeing the yellow death moon reflected in her eyes. "It doesn't matter," he said. He could see that his words shocked her. But he'd witnessed many people die, and just then he could not pretend otherwise.

O'PEERIA GOES FIRST. She's always the one to take the lead.

They skirt by the city's bustling South Gate, passing a huge encampment of traders congregating for the annual Festival of Spice and Season. The darkness is driven away by a hundred campfires, and the air carries heady scents of warm spiced meats, vegetables and the unmistakable tang of fresh fledge. Kel has never tried the drug, but he has always felt its allure. O'Peeria sometimes calls him weak.

The air is also filled with the chants, songs and pained moans of various sects, many of whom use certain powerful spices as their chief means of communing with their particular deities. Kel has no deities. He's seen too much to believe in such influences, and even his trust in magic is all but shattered.

There's a cursory check by the gate militia, and as usual it's Kel they pull to one side. O'Peeria is striking enough for them to leave her alone. He sighs, responds to their clumsy questions with answers he's used a hundred times before— why is he armed, where is he going, on whose authority does he travel—then follows O'Peeria onto the main street that leads into the heart of the city.

Sometimes, he wishes people knew of the Core. It would avoid having to deal with bored militia.

"We need to make sure we all get there at the same time," O'Peeria says. She does not have to explain why. Kel has been present at the extermination of three Strangers, and he has seen what they can do. They're not all exactly alike, but they do share one characteristic: brutality.

And he's also seen what happens to them when they die.

"So slow down," Kel says. "You're walking like you have a Violet Dog on your tail."

"No one and nothing gets on my tail unless I say so." She glances back over her shoulder without breaking pace, and Kel is pleased with himself when he does not smile. He won't play her games so easily.

He follows O'Peeria into the first of Noreela City's squares.

There's a real bustle there, even though it's almost dark, with stalls being erected, machines drifting just above the ground carrying building parts, several light balls floating here and there where required, and people hurrying about, all in preparation for the forthcoming Festival. Kel is glad. It means that he and O'Peeria won't be so conspicuous, even though a Shantasi like her always warrants a second glance. It is not often that these mystical, strange people venture out from New Shanti, and when they do, observers generally assume they have a purpose. O'Peeria is good at staring down curiosity.

Past the square, she steers them left into a darkened alley. There are no light balls here, and Kel is not disappointed; he has always felt uncertain around magic. He does not understand it. Does not like it. They say it comes from the land, but he can't help believing there's much more to it than that. He supposes it's a result of his being in the Core, and that tracking, hunting and assassinating mysterious Strangers from beyond Noreela makes him more suspicious of what people generally accept as true. It's a side effect that he welcomes.

"Here," O'Peeria says. She's standing by a grating in the ground, three heavy locks holding it in place.

"Down?"

The Shantasi smiles, and the life-moonlight catches her face. It's dazzling. "What, Kel Boon? Afraid to go into the dark with me?"

"Just concerned that you'll be scared."

O'Peeria raises an eyebrow, kneels and runs her hands over the locks. They're heavy, and Kel knows that it'll take a lot of effort and noise to break them. She knows it, too.

"Sorry," she says, and pulls a thin iron spike from her boot. Placing it between the random paving in the alley, she sets her foot against the flattened head and shoves down, hard.

O'Peeria touches the spike with one hand and uses a few whispered chants to break the locks. Kel looks the other way. He hears the broken metal clank to the ground, and he only looks again when he hears the spike being withdrawn from between the stones.

"You should try it one day," O'Peeria says.

"We have Practitioners for that."

"Fuck that. One day we might meet a Stranger who knows how to use it better than us. What then?"

Kel heaves up the grating and prepares to drop down into the darkness. "Then," he says, "we fight for ourselves."

He could not know that today would be that day.

KEL HEARD IT before Namior. Even when he paused, raised his hand and tilted his head, all she could hear was the still-raging river. He turned to her, his face suddenly pale in the yellow moonlight and his eyes going wide, then he grabbed her hand and started to pull. He scrambled up the remains of a house's collapsed sidewall, as though suddenly eager to return to the Dog's Eyes.

She tugged back. He was going the wrong way! But then he pulled her close, their noses touching, and she could actually smell fear on his breath.

"There's another wave," he said. "Save your breath and run." And still holding her hand, he turned and started uphill again.

She was supposed to warn us, she thought about her great-grandmother, and she feared that the old woman's current craze was deeper than ever before.

They'd made their way along the uncertain ground above the shattered lower areas of the village until they were level with the fallen stone bridge. It crossed the river from one side of the harbor to the other, and they could see the terrible destruction that had been wrought on the place. The bridge's remaining surface and walls were just visible above the flooded river level, but either side of it, there were no easily identifiable areas left. Buildings had toppled, smashed and been carried away by the power of the wave, and few walls protruded above the thick layers of sticky, stinking mud left in its wake. The water was piling massive amounts of debris against the upriver side of the bridge: trees, shattered timbers, dead horses, furniture, half of a roof with some tiles still attached, and close to the uncertain shore where they stood, a knot of bodies. Namior had tried desperately not to look, but the arms, legs, heads and torsos cried out to be seen. She had wondered where their wraiths were, and she hoped that Mourner Kanthia was still alive.

Kel let go of her hand so that they could both climb faster. The broken rubble beneath her hands was sharp, and several times she slipped and cut her knees and shins. The pain drove her on. Her breathing was rapid and heavy, but by the time they'd cleared the fallen wall and were making their way up a steeply sloping vegetable garden, she could hear the second wave.

She did not look.

Across the other side of the bridge, on the harbor side, she had seen the vague shapes of people already searching the ruin for survivors. She hoped they were making their way up Drakeman's Hill.

The wave was louder by then, and the ground was starting to shake.

"Faster!" Kel shouted. Namior glanced up and he was sitting astride a garden wall, hands held out, glancing down at her, up at the wave and back again.

Still she did not look. She remembered watching the first wave roar in, and she wondered how long it would take for her to die. She would feel the water pluck her up, sweep her along, and she would be battered by the broken parts of the village it had already consumed. One beat? Five? She doubted she would drown. The wave promised a more violent death.

She was almost crawling up the steep slope, pushing with her feet and digging her hands into the soil, pulling toward safety.

First wave didn't reach this high! But she had seen the massive amounts of water still flowing back toward the sea from that first deluge. And the new wave could be even more powerful than the last.

Kel pulled her roughly over the wall and they were on a path, and he grabbed her hand and ran, dragging her after him, unforgiving when she stumbled, ignoring her cry of pain as she twisted her ankle, his fingers digging into the back of her hand. He kicked down a gate and they ran up the slope of a garden planted with salt-herbs and spice. Other people ran with them—people she had lived with forever—but they were all alone in their panicked race for survival.

They dropped over another wall and Kel kicked at a gate between two tall, thin houses until timber cracked and the gate bowed inward. He pressed through and Namior went after him, and soon they were climbing a terraced fruit garden, tearing through fine nets protecting the fruits from birds. Bizarrely, incredibly, someone opened a window and cursed at them. She wanted to scream at them to flee, but she remembered Kel's words—*Save your breath and run*—and by the time her conscience pricked her, they were already over another wall and running up a winding, cobbled path.

"Kel..." she said, gasping, her shins and knees burning, ankle aflame from where she'd twisted it. But though she called his name again, the monster the sea had birthed roared too loudly for him to hear.

She fell to her knees and Kel fell beside her. They held each other as the second giant wave blotted out the moon and cast its shadow over the remains of Pavmouth Breaks.

AFTER THE SECOND wave, they returned to Namior's home. Her mother and great-grandmother were still there, surrounded by survivors who had fled uphill from the ruined and damaged areas below. Her great-grandmother sat close to the groundstone, shivering and crying as she held her hand a finger's width from its surface. Her mother brewed tea, and between pouring large mugs she pressed a herby paste into an ugly wound on a man's leg. The groundstone hummed very slightly, and the man groaned as his bleeding ceased.

"Will there be more?" Kel asked, not aiming the question at anyone in particular.

Namior's mother looked at him, frowning. "Can't see," she said. "We tried scrying again before the survivors arrived, but there's still a blankness there."

Kel went close to her, talking quieter. "Have you ever seen anything like this before?"

"Yes," she said. "Many times. Our eyes are our true sight; anything further is afforded to us by magic. But there's plenty that can confuse what we see."

"Anything *exactly* like this?"

She poured bondleaf tea into several more mugs, not looking up at Kel.

"I assume that's a no."

"You don't like what we do," she said, not scolding, simply stating a fact. "How can I expect you to understand?"

There's plenty about me you don't know, he thought, but sometimes when Namior's mother looked at him, he saw suspicion in her eyes. "Understand what?" he asked.

"No, Kel. I've never seen or sensed anything quite like this. And I can't tell you why."

Kel nodded, grabbed two of the mugs and returned to Namior. She was kneeling with several children, trying to calm them with a gentle song. One of them was sobbing quietly, and he wondered whom the child had lost.

"We can help here as well as anywhere," he said hesitantly, but he was pleased when Namior glared up at him.

"I'm going back out," she said. Kel smiled and nodded, then offered her the mug.

They drank the tea quickly. It coursed through their bodies, tingled in their muscles, giving strength where tiredness had set in and lessening the pain of cuts and sprains. Namior conversed with her mother, then nodded at Kel and opened the front door.

Outside, the air smelled of the bottom of the sea.

"What did she say?" Kel asked.

"She told me to look after you." Namior chuckled as she led the way back down the narrow path. To Kel, her laugh sounded almost hysterical.

On the main path along the hillside, people were hurrying in both directions. Kel could see no real sign of organization; everyone was on their own mercy mission. A woman hobbled past holding a child beneath each arm, her face grim behind the mask of blood she wore. At first he feared the children were dead, but then a little girl looked up at him and grinned, as though this was the greatest adventure ever. Despite himself, Kel smiled back.

Namior started heading back downhill. Kel grabbed her arm.

"Namior, there may be more waves," he said. He could see that she understood that, but there was a defiance born of desperation in her eyes. Their friends had been down there. Kel had seen the vague outlines of people struggling through the ruined harbor across the bridge from where they had stood. Trakis and Mell had probably made it across, searching for Mell's parents in the ruins, and the second wave...

"They're dead, aren't they?" she said, tears blurring her eyes for the first time. Shock could do that, Kel knew, protect you against the truth. By the Black, he was as aware of that as anyone.

"We can't know that," he said. "We don't even know they got that far. But we can't just rush down there, not yet. Not when there might be more."

Kel could hear the roar of the waters receding once again, and combined with that sound were the impacts of rocks, the grinding of parts of Pavmouth Breaks being sucked out to sea.

Namior wiped angrily at her face. "But there are plenty of people who need help up here."

"There are." Kel pulled her close and kissed her cheek, and he was surprised at the comfort he took from the contact. *What's coming?* he thought. During his time in the Core, he'd developed something of a reputation for only seeing the bad in things, only anticipating the worst. Often, he'd been right. *What in the Black could have done this?* He turned slightly, looking over Namior's shoulder and out to sea. It seemed calmer now, and though a storm boiled on the horizon, closer in to shore the sky was clear enough still to allow moonlight through. That would help the rescuers, at least. But the sea itself was dark, forbidding, and no one really knew what lay over the horizon. Over the years many, such as Namior's father, had gone to find out. None had returned.

Of all people he, a Core member, knew that there was more beyond the horizon than sea.

The long night stretched out before them, and at its end Kel had the feeling that many things would be different. Not just the ruin brought down upon the village, the deaths and destruction that everyone would have to start coming to terms with. But *changed*.

A man shouted behind them, a woman screamed and somebody called, "My dada!"

"Come on," Namior said. She led the way and Kel followed, and for a brief flash she could have been O'Peeria, leading the way to her death with Kel following blindly behind.

THEY SPENT THE rest of that night trying to help the wounded, the lost, the bereft. The Moon Temple doors had been forced open and it became their temporary hospital, the old one having been down behind the harborfront. Kel and Namior spent a while finding wounded people and helping them to the Temple, but then her position as a witch-in-training dictated that she should remain there, using her fledgling skills to heal wounds and soothe pain. The Temple had no groundstone, but Namior drew what she could from its deep-set walls, chanting softly over people with broken legs, water-filled lungs, rent flesh. Healers arrived at last from Drakeman's Hill—they had made their way across the swollen river and plain of mud in a small boat that had been deposited high up by the waves—and while they used their herbs and drugs, Namior supplemented that with her young touch of magic.

Kel remained close by. He had no wish to leave her, so he helped where he could, moving people around and finding them somewhere to sit or lie down while waiting for treatment. The village militia brought many people in; even the trained soldiers were shocked by what had happened, eyes wide and frightened. They had left their weapons behind and filled their belts with skins of fresh water, and they almost made Kel believe that someone was in control. But their commander had been killed in the harbor, drowned by the second wave as he tried to rescue the victims of the first. Perhaps the shock felt by the militia was more down to that than anyone else; their captain had been sixty years old, a veteran, and a father figure for many. Now, they were as lost as anyone.

He carried three dead people out of the Temple and laid them down in the moon-bathed yard. The death moon cast a yellow light over their flesh. Their wraiths needed chanting down, he knew, but that was a Mourner's job. He had tried it before, but that had been a friend, and he could not face such memories right then.

Halfway through the night, just as a third and final wave came in, he was relieved when Mourner Kanthia arrived at the Temple, guided by Namior's mother. Kanthia had struck her head and been made blind, but she willingly let Kel direct her across the yard to the bodies. The Mourner began her work.

The third wave was much smaller, but still it caused upset and fear, and its roar was somehow more painful than the sound of the first two. Perhaps it was because he knew it was merely stirring the remains of a destroyed village, now, rather than doing any more damage. It felt like an unnecessary insult from the sea upon Pavmouth Breaks, and Kel was surprised at the strength of emotion he felt. It was ironic that he could think of this place as home only after half of it was gone.

He watched from the Temple doorway. Kanthia—hooded, cloaked, flowing rather than walking—moved from one corpse to the next, chanting, making vague sigils in the air above their heads and chests. Soon she was finished, and when she returned to the Temple she stood far from Kel.

Perhaps she had sensed what he had done.

———

LATER, A LINE of four machines appeared from down the slope. They rolled on chipped wheels, crawled on clumsy legs, and they were all coated in a thick layer of muck. A Practitioner sat on the back of each construct, steering with chain harnesses, whispering their knowledge of the land's magic and urging the machines onward.

They brought the dead and injured with them. Kel and a couple of militia took them down, carried the wounded into the Temple, laid the dead side by side in the yard. Mourner Kanthia emerged from the shadows behind the Temple, converging on the corpses like the carrion foxes Kel had seen in the Widow's Peaks. He stood back again and let the Mourner do her work.

She spooked him, but he was glad that she was there. He was not sure he could have remained had the air been full of wraiths.

DAWN BROKE, CRAWLING across Noreela and reaching them last of all. Its vibrant colors piled down the valley of the River Pav and touched the pitiful ruins of Pavmouth Breaks' lower areas, glittering from the still-churning waters and reflecting a thousand disturbing images from the seas of mud. There were bodies trapped there, broken homes, and machines that still struggled feebly against inevitable rot and rust. People hauled themselves across the muck in small boats and on sheets of heavy timber, pausing here and there when they reached the remains of a building, investigating, then moving on. If they did pull someone out of the mud or water, they were usually dead.

The water was back down to normal sea level, and the dawn revealed the fate of the harbor in full. The mole was broken in two places, the rest of it battered and missing huge blocks of stone. Most buildings across the harborfront had been demolished, their debris adding to the destructive wave as it had surged inland. Farther away from the sea the destruction lessened, though even far up the valley, close to the tall Helio Bridge, buildings low to the river had lost roofs, windows and doors, and many walls had crumbled and fallen.

Drakeman's Hill finished in a sheer drop thirty steps high where the wave had undermined the ground, carrying away the hillside and a score of buildings. Survivors had rigged a rope ladder, and Practitioners were using machines to pile rubble against the new cliff to provide an unsteady staircase.

Kel and Namior stood in the Moon Temple's garden, looking down at the village and trying to appreciate the full extent of the damage. Namior shook, though not from the cold. Kel hugged her.

And then he heard a panicked, terrified voice. And he already knew something of its meaning, because Kel always expected the worst.

"What in the Black is *that*?"

The shout came from someone farther down the slope, but it was taken up by others, and soon Kel saw a man amidst the shattered roof of a house pointing out to sea.

"Another wave?" Namior asked, eyes wide.

"No," Kel said. He climbed the wall surrounding the Temple yard so that he could see over the neighboring houses. "Not of water."

"What do you mean?"

Kel looked. He could not speak. For a beat he forgot to breathe, but then shock punched his chest and he gasped.

"Kel, what do you see?" Namior was scrabbling at the wall, but all her strength had gone.

For a moment, he thought the sea had grown spikes.

"Kel?"

"Masts," he said, "and sails." They were still far out, but he could see from their movement that they were sailing in toward Noreela. He guessed there were thirty of them, maybe more.

"Whose sails?"

Whose indeed? Kel thought of the Core, and how he had fled it, and how its fears and aims were still so deeply embedded within him that, somehow, he had always known that this moment would come.

He just never expected it would happen to him.

Beyond the sails, on a horizon that had forever been long, straight and unhindered by anything other than clouds and the dreams of what lay beyond, there sat an island.

Chapter Two

on stranger shores

NAMIOR INSISTED THAT Kel lift her onto the wall so she could see for herself. Her heart was fluttering with excitement and unease, and childhood myths harried at her memory. As yet, the shock of what had happened did not allow them to manifest fully.

The masts looked like trees growing out of the sea, swaying to different breezes. Their branches were dark, their colors as yet uncertain, and from their peaks flickered small shapes that could only be flags.

Behind them, several miles out to sea, was an island.

She remembered one of those myths, then. Before she died, her grandmother used to whisper the story to her before putting her to bed, drawing vague violet shapes in the air with sparks and shadows. *The Violet Dogs came ashore like a wave of disease, more than willing to spill their noxious living-dead blood because they knew it would do them no harm. They fought through the first lines of defenses thrown up by the tribes that lived on Noreela way back then...strange, small, weak people who did not yet know the land and had no inkling of the magic it could give them. The Violet Dogs ate the dead and living alike, strengthening their bridgehead, though in truth none was required, because they were already the masters of that place. The Sleeping Gods did not stir, the Nax were not yet known in their underground fledge seams, and other creatures of Noreela were not even whispers in a sleeping child's ear. So the people were alone in their vain defense of the land.*

But though she had often gone to sleep with such stories in her mind, Namior was a young witch, with a kindly heart and a soul filled with hope and confidence for the future. Even as a child she had known those tales for what they were—stories, passed from grandparent and parent to child and remembered down through the years. If the Violet Dogs had been so powerful, brutal and unbeatable, she reasoned, where were they now?

So she watched the masts bobbing closer to Noreela, as the strange island behind them was touched by dawn and painted green and lush with vegetation. And though she was fearful of something new, she could not help but feel a child-like optimism as well.

"I should get home!" she said. "Commune with the land, see what's there."

"We have to go," Kel said.

"Go where?"

"Away from here." He sounded different, and his face was drawn, eyes wide and fearful.

"Kel, just because we don't know—"

"I *do* know, Namior." He looked out to sea again and

grabbed her arms, pulling her down as he jumped from the wall. "Just look what they've done already!" He pointed down toward the harbor, then closer at the bodies lined carefully across the Temple yard.

"Maybe they didn't mean—"

"How can you even think otherwise?" He stepped back from her slightly, raising his voice, scaring her. This was a Kel she had never seen before. She was confused, but she thought herself better than this. *Can we instantly fear them?* Every bone in her body, every fiber of her that had ever communed with the land and shared a touch of its magic, said no.

"So let's march down there and kill them as they come ashore," she said.

"It'll never be that easy." Kel's eyes narrowed, hands fisting at his sides. He looked across the river of devastation at Drakeman's Hill, as though seeking his own home.

"Caution, yes," Namior said. "I'll agree to that. But this is something new, Kel. This could be a new tale in Noreela's history, a whole new beginning!"

"Or an ending." He looked at her so intently for a few beats that she thought he was going to strike out, and she flinched back against the wall. His eyes softened, and he took her in his embrace. "I'm not all you think I am."

"I was just starting to realize that."

He guided her away from the other people still atop the wall. He was looking around, guilty, suspicious, and she did not like this new Kel. Not one bit. He had always been a man with history, and that had excited her. Now, it suddenly scared her as well.

He spoke softly. "I used to be part of an organization called the Core. A secret group, only hundreds of us." He sighed and looked away. "They'd kill me even for telling you. They'd kill you for knowing."

"Kel?" She did not understand a word of this. Each utterance made him stranger to her.

"We tracked and killed Strangers from beyond Noreela.

Spies. Intruders. We think they were planning an invasion, and it has been our duty for generations to—"

Namior pushed him away. "You're a wood-carver."

"Here, yes. But not beyond here. Even the duke doesn't know about us. Before I came to Pavmouth Breaks, I'd been on a job in—"

"Kel!" she shouted, drawing the attention of several people hurrying from the Temple. News of the amazing new turn of events was spreading fast.

Kel held up his hands, but every effort he made to subdue her angered Namior more.

"I'm going home to the groundstone," she said, softly. "If there's any threat, magic will let us know."

"Like it let your mother and great-grandmother know about the waves?"

She pressed her lips together and stared at him, never relinquishing eye contact for a beat. "I'd like you to come with me." She saw her Kel, the man she loved—the gentle man who had come to Pavmouth Breaks and settled into a quiet, humble trade selling his extraordinary carvings. And she saw Kel Boon, that stranger who had come into her village, now a stranger once more. There was something in his eyes she had never seen before. Namior blinked once, slowly, reaching back and touching the wall rooted in the land, and felt the tingle of wider perception.

Kel's eyes held fear, but the fear was mostly of himself.

"What have you done?" she asked softly.

"What?" He spoke sharply, glancing down at her hand where it still touched the wall. "You do *that*, to *me*?"

Namior moved forward and reached for him, but Kel stepped back, fear turning to anger. "Come with me, please," she said.

"I'll take you," he said. "You come with me. I'll get you out. We have to *leave*! We have no idea what's happening, and I have to get away."

"Why?"

"To tell the Core." Kel glanced down at his feet as if that was a painful idea. He spoke again, a whisper this time, as though speaking only to himself. "They have to know."

"You know where I'll be," Namior said. And she turned away from Kel Boon, left the Moon Temple grounds and ran along the streets toward her home. With every step she hoped to hear him coming after her, but she suspected that he was already going in the opposite direction, and probably hoping the same.

From the mouth of the path leading up to her home she could look out over the sea and watch the boats sailing ever closer. The mysterious island behind them was like an itch in her eye, so out of place and yet so obvious. Around her, other people stood and stared, some of them fearful, others fascinated.

She hoped she had made the right choice.

FROM THE MOMENT he had left the Core five years before, Kel had been trying to shake it from his bones, his guts, his heart. He had never succeeded. Even after what had happened with O'Peeria, he was Core through and through. Fleeing from the Core had been fleeing from himself, and it was not until he hit the western shores of Noreela that geography had forced him to stop. Inside, he had kept running, changing himself totally in the hope of erasing his old life and creating something new. The wood carving took a very particular and concentrated talent, and sometimes he went a whole afternoon without remembering the best ribs between which to slip a knife when stabbing a Stranger from behind, the feel of breath on his hand as he broke someone's neck, or how to sleep at night knowing all the things he had done.

Sometimes, that was the hardest. Sleeping. As night fell and only the sea broke the silence, so the voices grew louder.

To begin with, he thought Namior would come after him.

She was proud and strong and dedicated to her family, and she would persuade them to come along and flee with him. So he went slowly, passing the bodies in the Moon Temple gardens as he headed down toward the expanded river. Few people spared him a glance; whether they went down to the river, or back up into the village's heights, most only had eyes for the sea and what it had brought in that morning.

But the more he remembered Namior's eyes, the more he realized she had already silently vowed to stay. *If only I could persuade her*, he thought. *If only I'd been more honest with her.* But the more time that had passed without his telling her about his history, the more difficult that prospect had become.

Perhaps there was still time. Up to his place on Drakeman's Hill, get the stuff he needed, back down to Namior's home…

Perhaps.

He jumped a wall and skidded down a steep garden of flowering fruits, releasing a wonderfully sweet aroma to the air. It was soon swept away by the breeze, replaced once again by the stink of mud and sea. He burst through a gate onto a path that had been chopped in half.

He skidded to a halt just in time. Another step and he would have tumbled headlong into the wet mud, probably sinking there, and slowly drowning.

Fucking idiot! O'Peeria's voice said, and Kel grinned. He was hardly surprised that she chose now to come to the forefront of his memory.

To his right lay the stone bridge, middle span washed out and detritus piled high against its upstream side. In the dawn's light, he saw the dark shapes of uprooted trees, and in their branches the pale fruit of dead, naked bodies. Past the bridge, beyond the ruined harbor, he could see the masts of the visitors' boats bobbing closer. On the horizon, the island cast an unnatural shadow against the sky.

Kel looked across the river of water and mud at the slopes of Drakeman's Hill. He had to get up there. He needed his weapon roll, hidden for so long beneath the floorboards in his rooms, and the other things he had hidden there as well. The magic things. He needed them most of all.

I could just go, he thought. If he ran fast enough, and far enough, maybe he could get beyond the Strangers' reach before they landed. That's what the Core had always called them: Strangers. No one had ever discovered their true name, and none of the Strangers, when interrogated, gave up such information. So "Stranger" was all-encompassing, and it also conveyed everything about them that needed to be said. They were not of Noreela.

Kel felt the press and pressure of responsibility. Noreela was alone, and almost everyone living there considered their vast island to be the whole world. He and a few others knew differently. And that shattering knowledge was the reason that one in four Core agents killed themselves before the age of forty.

Instead of suicide, he could run.

But if he ran now, giving no thought to direction or intention, then he would be doing Noreela a greater disservice than ever before. He was sure that if the Core *had* managed to track him down, they would have killed him without thought. Yet this event was far greater than just him.

Invasion, he thought, and it was terrifying. Strangers had only ever come in ones and twos, tracked and caught for interrogation by the Core, or killed if they could not be caught. And the majority of Core members considered such covert visits as reconnaissance for a full invasion.

A man ran past him along the path, heading away from the harbor. "They're coming!" he shouted. "Ships! *Things!*"

Kel watched him go. And as he glanced back upriver, he saw three small boats crossing the fast-moving waters, their occupants pulling on a long rope that had been strung somehow from one side to the other.

He ran, careful to keep away from the ragged edge where the path had been undermined and scoured away by the flood. Clumps of seaweed and a few dead fish were scattered here and there, and piled on top of a tall garden wall he saw a mass of clawed things, snatching at the air as though they could see things he could not.

Namior pulled at him. He slowed, then ran on again.

When he drew level with the boats he waited, reaching down for the man and two women in the first boat, helping them climb from the soaking mud up onto the solid bank. They thanked him, distracted, and one of the women ran back toward the harbor. The man and other woman sank down onto the cobbles, the man crying and calling a name over and over again.

Kel jumped down into the boat and snatched up the thick punt clamped along its side. He could wait for the other two to finish pulling themselves across, but one was still only halfway, and the man seemed to be flagging. Or he could cast off from the rope, push his boat across the mud level with the punt, then paddle as hard as he could across the river. He'd be swept down toward the harbor, but if he paddled hard enough, he thought he could strike the opposite mud bank almost level with where he needed to climb.

The old Kel Boon—the Kel Boon of the Core—would have started hauling on the rope. And when he reached those coming the other way, he'd have battered them aside with the punt, leaving them to the mercy of the terrible currents.

"By all the Black!" he shouted, venting his rage where the river could carry it to the sea. He looked in that direction, and from that level he saw the masts just above the broken bridge, coming closer and closer with every beat he stood hesitating.

Kel pushed off, angling upriver as he shoved the small boat across the mud levels. It was hard work, his muscles immediately began to ache, and with every shove he felt Namior calling him back. He wished he'd tried harder to persuade her . . . but she was stronger than he'd ever given her credit for. Perhaps he could have knocked her out and carried her. But there was her family. Save her, let them die, and he would gain nothing.

And is this all gain? he thought, those familiar suspicions and fears of his own motives crashing in once more. He cursed again, swore that it was not. He loved Namior, and that was the reason he so wanted her to come with him. It was about her, not him.

"I'll go back for her," he said. But speaking those words aloud made it no more likely. He'd made his choice. The Core training had seen to that. Noreela came first, and five years after running from that ethos, casting it aside and trying to purge it from his mind and soul, he realized that he had never really changed.

The small boat slipped from the mud into the fast-flowing river fifty steps above the rope, and Kel hurriedly strapped the punt to its side and took up the oar. He knelt on the downstream side and started paddling, turning the nose of the boat upstream in an effort to lessen the drag. But already he was being swept quickly down toward the broken bridge. The flow was much faster than he'd anticipated, slapping the boat and splashing heavily inside, soaking him in an instant with thick, stinking water. Something struck the hull and drifted by, and Kel stared down into the smashed face of someone he might have known.

He paddled harder, gritting his teeth as he searched for strength that wasn't there. The night and the waves had leeched it away. The boat spun beneath him, going sideways onto the water and starting to rock as the waves struck it. He paddled on, trying not to think about what would happen if the boat capsized.

"Fucking idiot!" someone shouted, and Kel grinned, because for a beat he thought O'Peeria was berating him from memory once more. But then he looked downstream and saw the boat he was heading toward, and the man and woman standing there holding the rope.

Kel plunged the oar into the water, trying to swing his boat around and avoid a collision, but the water was its own master that day. The oar either struck something just below the surface, or a current gave it a tug; Kel's shoulder wrenched and he lost his grip, watching the oar swept away beneath the rope line.

He sat down and held on.

The boats struck, timber cracking and splitting, and Kel was thrown to his right. His own craft was turning, its bow buried in the static boat, stern being swung around by the fast-flowing water, and it would be only beats before it was plucked free and swept down toward the ruined bridge.

Closer to those masts, that island.

"Come on!" the woman said. She was reaching for him, leaning across where the boats had crunched together, while the man held on grimly to the rope line. Kel knew them by sight, but not their names. The woman ran a stall on the harbor selling fresh catches, and the man was a fisherman. "Come *on!*" she shouted. "Unless you want to be there when *they* arrive." She looked past him toward the sea, and Kel was glad to see her fear. If there was fear, there would be caution as well.

Be afraid, Namior, he thought. And as he reached across and grabbed the woman's hand, hauling himself into their boat as his own tore free and was carried downriver, he remembered how fear on its own really held no power at all.

THEY EXIST IN the shadows. It has always been this way, and always will be, because the Core should not be. It is a left-over from a centuries-dead duke's paranoia, and the irony is that the paranoia was justified. There *are* things from beyond Noreela. The Core—a tight organization with no identifiable leader, and one clear mandate—has decided that this should never be general knowledge.

Especially as the Strangers are far from friendly.

And as well as existing within shadows, they watch from them also, because Kel and O'Peeria are hunters and killers.

Shadows are their friends. Darkness is their ally. So they wait, and the world goes on around them with no comprehension of the slaughter about to be wrought.

"Pelly and Rok should be here by now," Kel whispers. He's been sitting behind the remains of a tumbled statue for a while, and O'Peeria has become a vague presence to his left. His legs are stiff and aching, but he dares not move. *He* is a statue, until the time comes.

"Over there," O'Peeria says. She does not move, point or nod, but Kel knows where she is indicating. They have worked together for a long time, and they have a language all of their own. He looks past the stone remains and across Monument Park. He cannot see them, but he senses their presence, hunkered down behind the statue of a forgotten Voyager like just another part of the night.

There are thirty statues and pedestals in the park, placed at random amongst trees, between small ponds and around gathering areas that, during the day, attract hundreds of speakers, prophets, Practitioners, witches and magic-weavers. Several of the figures have been toppled in some hazy past, evidence of shifting allegiances and fading histories. There are also a few empty pedestals upon which figures *should* have been built, but perhaps their subjects had been shamed or uncovered as charlatans. Now they were empty, famous futures waiting to be told.

"He's here," O'Peeria whispers.

Kel cannot see the Stranger yet, but he does not question O'Peeria's pronouncement. She's a Shantasi, and he has long learned to trust her.

"Wait until he engages," Kel says. "Remember what happened last time?"

O'Peeria risks a small laugh. "Kel, you have no sense of adventure. You know how fast I am."

Yes, he knows. The Shantasi call it Pace. She has never told him how they do it, and he's decided he no longer wishes to know. They draw magic just like everyone else in Noreela, but he has come to believe that they craft it more confidently, and with greater skill.

The Stranger emerges from shadows, walking carefully along a path that leads through the undergrowth. The route opens into a wide clearing before them, and around its edges several pedestals stand, bearing famous figures from history: the First Voyager, Sordon Perlenni; the Widow's Peaks gate-keeper, Anselm Anto; the first Mystic of New Shanti, A'Kan Lone; and more. Kel does not recognize them all.

Core agents have seen the Stranger there several times be-fore, communicating with whatever strange place he comes from. O'Peeria believes he does it from there as a slight against Noreelan history. Kel is not so sure. But the reasons do not matter.

The decision to kill this one came quick and easy. There is no longer any doubt.

The Stranger pauses in the center of the clearing. He looks around slowly, turning so that he can scan his entire sur-roundings.

Kel holds his breath and relaxes, resting his fingers on the fractured pedestal before him, summoning the subtle screen-ing spell O'Peeria taught him. Magic tingles through his flesh and bones, coursing around his body as it merges with his blood flow, thumping in time with his heart, twitching in time with a muscle in his cheek, and he hates it as much as he ever has. He looks at his hand on the stone before him, and its outline grows hazy. This is one of the few times he relies on magic. Mostly, he has learned to trust himself.

The Stranger strips off his clothes.

That is always the moment when Kel feels most scared, and most justified.

The man sighs as he shrugs the shirt from his body, flexing his shoulders as the two long, thin proboscises emerge from just beneath his shoulder blades and taste the air. They seem to shift of their own accord, and the Stranger kneels and turns his face to the sky as the appendages cast spidery shadows on the ground behind him.

The sides of his neck gape where gills split the flesh. The skin of his stomach and hips is silvery, oily. The Core had long been trying to capture a Stranger for examination and dissection by some of their witches, but it is difficult. Dangerous. Usually deadly. If caught and interrogated, it is never long before they usher in their own deaths and the destruction of those around them. Kel knows ten people who have died fighting Strangers, and he has no wish for that number to increase.

The things on the Stranger's back curve around and meet above his head, forming the familiar, chilling silhouette that Kel has seen several times before. He starts to talk then—a low, continuous babble in a language none of them has ever been able to understand, and as his words tumble out, so the oval of night trapped within the appendages begins to grow lighter.

Kel feels the rush of fear that he always welcomes in. He swears it has saved his life many times before. His heart pumps, senses sharpen, hands grow cool and calm as they grab two short knives from his belt. His scalp tightens and balls tingle, and he glances to the left without moving his head.

O'Peeria has already gone.

The Stranger shouts. O'Peeria is a blur on the night, launching a throwing star at his face. Pelly and Rok, indistinct beneath their own shielding spells, are sprinting from the shadows across the clearing, and Kel thinks he sees his own thought echoed in their movements: *Damn O'Peeria, can't she wait?*

The Stranger falls to one side and the star snicks his shoulder. He screeches. As the thin limbs on his back part, there is a small explosion of pale light that diffuses quickly in the Noreelan darkness. *Connection broken*, Kel thinks. That's one good thing.

Then he sees the *bad* thing: the wave of weak light from the Stranger has wiped the camouflage spells from the Core members. They are no longer only shadows.

They adapt, he thinks. *Every new advantage we think we have over them, they adjust to it.* He stands and darts around the statue. And then he hears voices.

Many voices.

"What in the Black?"

"Something here, some animal."

Children.

"Skull raven. I heard they come out at night. I heard they peck holes in your head and steal your dreams."

"Stop talking sheebok shit, it's just a—"

"Don't talk to me like—"

"Look!"

The Stranger has stood and is facing O'Peeria. She darts to his left, almost too quick to see properly, but when she strikes with her short sword he is ready, twisting beneath the blow and kicking her legs out from under her.

Pelly launches her slideshock at the Stranger, whipping her arm forward and back so that the cutting wire swings around in a deadly arc.

The Stranger ducks beneath the wire and kicks with his heel at the weight secured to its end. The metal ball powers back at Pelly and strikes her cheek. Even across the clearing Kel hears the crunch of bones.

"Someone having a fight, or—?"

"We should fetch the militia."

"No, let's go. Let's *see!*"

Kel sees them now, a huddle of shadows emerging from his left. There are maybe eight of them, too old to remain at home but too young to frequent Noreela's taverns and drug warrens. Some of them carry bottles, and he catches the scent of rotwine on the breeze.

O'Peeria flips herself back up onto her feet and slashes at the Stranger again. He kicks her in the stomach and she bends double, winded, flitting from his right to his left side in a beat.

Rok closes in and fires a small crossbow strapped to his wrist. The Stranger grunts, staggers and runs.

"Get back, now!" Kel roars. The shadows of the youngsters change shape, standing up straighter as they crane to see who or what is shouting at them.

The Stranger's shoulder appendages begin to glow.

"*Now!*" he shouts again, still running, distracted by the children as he flings one of his knives at the fleeing target.

The Stranger plucks the blade from the air. He stops, grins at Kel, turns and throws the blade.

Kel hears the joining of metal and flesh, and Rok falls with the handle projecting from his throat.

"Rok!" Pelly shouts. She comes forward, holding her own face, her hand and arm black with blood in the moonlight.

O'Peeria is behind the Stranger then, swinging her sword at the glowing things and screaming to distract his attention. The man ducks, turns and falls on O'Peeria, and Kel hears the thuds and grunts of punching, kicking and biting.

He looks at the struggling Shantasi, across at the shadowy group of children, back to the fight. He should choose O'Peeria, not because of what he feels for her but because it will increase the chances of a kill.

But he goes for the children. Runs at them, shouts at them to scatter, to flee, and when he sees their dumb, frank fascination, he wants to slap it from their faces. It takes him a few beats to grab their attention; and then when they look at him they discern just how serious this is. As one, they turn to leave.

Kel sprints back to the fighting pair, sheathing his knives and pulling the small crossbow from a harness on his back. It is primed and ready, and he aims carefully.

"Kel!" Pelly shouts. She is kneeling beside Rok, who is making a pained, gurgling noise as blood pulses and bubbles from around the knife buried in his throat. "Kel, *help* me!"

Kel does not even look at her. Rok is dead already.

O'Peeria needs his help...but he begins to fear that he's too late. The Stranger's proboscises are glowing brighter than ever, emitting a weak light that reflects from the Shantasi's pale face.

He hears footsteps on stone, and he risks a quick glance over his shoulder. Rather than fleeing, the foolish children have come closer!

"Get the *fuck* away from here!" Kel shouts.

"What is that?"

"Those things on his shoulders, are they—?"

"Is he on fire?"

Boys and girls, not even old enough to dip their cocks or welcome a dipping, and there they are watching something that should not exist, and witnessing members of Noreela's most secret organization undertake their most deadly task.

O'Peeria screams as the Stranger does something to her.

I should have helped her! Kel thinks.

An arc of blue light stretches up from the things on his back, like lightning searching for somewhere to strike. It twists in the air, nosing this way and that.

Kel steps back. "Pelly," he says, quietly.

She looks up from Rok—dead now, blood trickling instead of bubbling—and rolls quickly away.

"Kill this fucking thing!" O'Peeria says. She screams again.

Kel steps in close again, feinting left, darting right when the Stranger lashes out with a sword, and he fires the crossbow almost blind. Instinct guides his hand, desperation his eye, and he hears the bolt strike home.

O'Peeria screams.

The Stranger grunts.

The blue light fizzles, dropping to the ground like a tired snake before fading away to nothing, leaving scorched stones behind.

Kel loads another bolt and goes forward. "O'Peeria!" The Stranger sits astride her chest, head dipped down, and Kel gasps with relief when he sees the bolt protruding from just below his right ear. He fires one more into the man's temple, just to make sure.

O'Peeria groans.

"We have to get away," Kel says, because he knows what will happen now, he's seen it all before, and they have maybe a handful of beats before the Stranger becomes more dangerous in death than he ever was in life.

They're driven by their wraiths, O'Peeria had said once, *lives ruled by the ghosts of their potential.* Kel is not sure he agrees, is not even sure he really understands. But he knows about survival.

"O'Peeria, come…"

Then he sees why his Shantasi friend, his occasional lover, cannot move.

The Stranger's fingers are buried in the flesh of her chest and neck. Her shirt is ripped open, and the dead man's left hand has pierced her above her right breast, and three fingers of his right hand are wedged in her neck up to their second knuckles. The wounds are barely bleeding. She's staring at Kel, her eyes wide with pain and terror, because she knows what is to come.

"Kill me," she manages to say. Her speaking makes the Stranger's arms move.

"No," Kel says, because he cannot. *I should have run to her, helped her!* He can't kill O'Peeria.

He senses the children behind him and he needs to tell them to go, but he cannot take his eyes from the Shantasi.

Pelly is by his side then, face still wet with blood and tears but tight with determination. "Away, now, before he—"

The Stranger's body convulses. Dead but moving, the protuberances on his back suddenly stand up straight, glowing no more but displaying a terrible unrelenting pressure from somewhere inside.

O'Peeria is screaming. She's pushing with her feet, trying to tear herself away from the corpse's grip, but her skin and flesh hold his fingers tight. She pulls a knife and starts hacking at her own chest, prizing her enemy's fingers away with the cool blade.

There are legends about the first time a Stranger was killed on Noreelan soil. They say that a Mourner tried to chant its wraith down, but the wraith crushed the woman to something the size of a fist.

"Kill me!" O'Peeria shrieks, still cutting, knowing it's useless, the agony so apparent on her face that Kel cannot look at her again.

"I can't…"

Pelly grabs his shoulder and pulls. He can hear her breath, fast and panicked, and the chatter from the children who should have never been there in the first place. That had been Rok's job; to check the area. Make sure they were alone. But Rok is dead, and there is no one left to blame.

There's a terrible splitting, ripping sound. Flesh tears, blood spatters the ground, bones snap and rupture, and a dark, thrashing shape emerges from the dead Stranger's cleft back. The long, thin limbs on either side go tense, then erupt in one final gush of bluish flame. It's not directed or contained, but it floats down like ash.

Sparks touch O'Peeria, and she screams.

That catches the wild wraith's attention.

"No," Kel says, and he raises his crossbow. But he has not primed it, and he cannot find his bolt quiver. By the time he's thought about drawing a throwing knife and trying to finish O'Peeria with that, the wraith has flowed down like thick water to puddle around its dead owner's corpse. It covers O'Peeria in something like a flowing shadow, but Kel can still hear her screams, and he hears the sounds as the wraith penetrates her body through every opening, expanding, tearing the last cry from her with one final surge.

The Stranger's body is melting beneath the drift of ash.

The youngsters are shouting and swearing and cursing, but he can no longer hear their words.

Pelly is crying as she grabs him beneath the arms and pulls him back between pedestals.

A Stranger's wraith exists for a few beats, if that, before being drawn down to wherever it is they go. If they run fast enough, perhaps...

But it is not coming for them, and he will never know why. It goes for the innocent, unknowing youngsters whose presence he has drawn to its attention. By the time Kel finds the courage to close his eyes, and the wraith is fading away at last, the eight lie torn apart across the ground.

THE MAN AND woman were holding tightly to the rope stretched across the river. But the impact had damaged their craft, and it was listing as water battered the damaged hull, one cracked board flexing and letting in water.

Kel stood in the unsteady boat and ducked beneath the rope, leaning on it from the other side. He did not look at the fisherman or the seafood vendor. He looked down the river, past the ruined bridge and harbor, out to where the masts came ever closer.

"Pull!" the man said.

Kel glanced at him. "I have to get to Drakeman's Hill."

"What? We've just come from that side. We're going across, away from the harbor and mole. Away from whatever comes."

"Scared?" Kel said, and the man saw something in his eyes that made him look away.

"Please help us pull," the woman said. She was kind, and afraid.

"No," Kel said. "I have to get over there, there's something I need in my rooms, then I have to get away. I have to—"

The man kicked out at him. Kel had not seen or sensed the strike coming. He bent over the rope to protect his stomach, and when the fisherman kicked again his knee caught Kel beneath the jaw.

His vision swam for a few beats, and he heard the woman berating her husband.

"S-sorry," the man said, reaching out to touch Kel's shoulder.

Kel knocked his hand aside and punched him in the face. The man fell back, Kel released the rope, and the woman instinctively came toward her husband.

The current caught the boat and dragged it down toward the bridge. They bobbed sideways down the river. The broken bridge was a couple of hundred steps away, and the boat would fetch up against the piles of debris driven against its uprights. From there, perhaps Kel could climb and make his way through the destroyed harbor, find a path up onto Drakeman's Hill... but the masts were very close. He could see a few militia gathering at the harbor, and a group of residents not frightened enough to flee, and he wanted to shout out loud that they should go, run, because everything was about to change.

He realized that when the mysterious ships docked, he would be there to see who, or what, they carried.

WHEN THE SMALL boat was driven against the huge pile of flotsam stacked against the broken stone bridge, Kel was faced with a choice.

The woman and her fisherman husband helped each other climb up, over shattered and uprooted trees, the remnants of smashed buildings and the dead things crushed in between. There were bodies in the detritus, both animal and human, and Kel caught flashes of pink and paleness. Some of them had hair, others fur, and some had broken shells and huge, serrated pincers. After that, he tried not to look too carefully.

When the couple reached the bridge parapet, they fell over onto the road, stood and turned right immediately. They could have gone left, negotiating their way across the wreckage jammed in the fallen arch, then along to the ruined harbor. They could have stood with friends and fellow residents of Pavmouth Breaks, waiting to welcome in whatever manned those boats. They could have joined in with the amazed conversation and excited pointing at the vessels, the island, the storm clouds still boiling away out to sea. But they chose escape.

Kel decided almost as quickly as they. Namior was to his right, but duty to his left. Duty to himself, and the Core he had abandoned, and the memory of friends he had seen die. And O'Peeria. He owed her everything, and the most he could do since he had fumbled his escape was to see what arrived.

He dropped onto the surface of the bridge nearest the harbor. From a distance it had looked ruined only in its shattered center span, but close up there was a lot more damage visible. The parapet was cracked and crazed, and the paving was missing great swathes of cobbles. Elsewhere on the harbor he could see that mud made up most of the surface, but where he stood the gushing waters had swept the bridge clean.

He looked out to sea. Past the battered mole, the craft coming in from the island were drawing very close. There were maybe thirty vessels, ranging from small sailing boats to a ship with three masts that looked set to dwarf the harbor, should it come in that close. Some of the smaller boats were driven by oars as well as sails, rising and falling with perfect synchronicity. They flew flags of many colors. The sails were a mixture of white, cream and blue, with one or two tattered spreads of dark green canvas here and there. They did not sail aggressively. They were grouped close together, not spread out like an attacking force would be. Kel could see no signs of weapons. He made out a few people here and there on the larger vessels, but there seemed to be no urgency to their movements.

He had never witnessed an invasion from the sea. No one had, ever, other than those ancient Noreelans who had watched the mythical Violet Dogs stream ashore. *Not far from here*, Kel thought. *A hundred miles north, that's where they lay claim to having suffered the Violet Dog invasion. Not so very far away . . .*

He walked carefully along to the harbor. Soon, he would be one of the crowd. He looked longingly up at Drakeman's Hill, but between him and the hill were dozens of buildings smashed down into alleys and roads, bodies floating in mud, and things washed in from the sea.

Most of those things were dead, but he saw movement here and there that he did his best to avoid. He'd spent five years living in a fishing village; he knew there were dangers out there. He had already seen the scarlet splashes of exploded sea anemones, some of them poisonous, and he feared that larger things could stalk the ruins.

The first of the boats, a small vessel, was swinging its bow so that it could edge against the seaward side of the mole. A few militia had gone as far as they could, stopping only where the first major wound in that huge construction prevented them from advancing any farther. They hung on to bows and crossbows. Swords and other weapons were slung haphazardly and hurriedly about their bodies. They did not look very intimidating. A dozen more militia waited where the mole reached the harborfront, and they had arranged a pile of debris before themselves as a rough barricade. But it would hardly stop a determined child, and from their stunned expressions, Kel knew that such defenses were symbolic at best. If there was to be a fight, it would not last long.

Two machines sat amidst the crowd of people on the harbor. One of them seemed motionless, but the other floated on thin tendrils of loosely hinged metal, each one lightly touching the ground. Kel could not see its Practitioner, but it seemed to have an air of readiness about it. He'd heard of machines being used in combat, though he had never witnessed it. He wondered what that one—which looked as though it had previously been used to load and unload heavy fishing baskets from trawlers—could do, were it called upon to act.

He drew level with the first of the people and went on, passing through the crowd so that he stood close to where the mole connected to the harbor. The machine stood before him, and a short, old woman was crouched beside it.

"What can it do?" he asked.

The woman glanced back at him and he saw fear in her eyes. "Maybe not enough," she said.

"Hold back!" one of the militia said angrily. "We can't assume *anything*. Hold back, Mygrette, or you'll be the cause of something unforgivable."

"Jus' being cautious," Mygrette said. Kel knew her—an old witch who lived up on the cliffs just beyond the village limits. She put more value in machines and the mechanics of magic, rather than the mind games played by Namior and her family. Kel was not sure which he trusted less.

"They see you and that machine ready to attack and—"

"If they're peaceful, they'll not be looking for a fight," Kel said. The man turned on him.

"And what do you know, wood-carver? You're not even one of us!"

"So we fight amongst ourselves because you don't want to fight them?" a short woman asked. She smiled at Kel, but he could see the anxiety there.

The whole crowd thrummed with a nervous energy. So much potential, so much history ready to change or be made. Kel still felt the urge to run, but the time for escape had passed. The best he could do was to find out more.

They all heard the thump as the boat struck the stone mole. Ropes were flung up from the vessel, and two of the waiting militia caught them and tied them on. Three others held back, arrows strung, glancing back at the crowd, then down at the boat.

Kel stretched, but he could see no more. The mole curved out around the harbor, and the visitors were still hidden from sight.

The watchers mumbled and whispered. Mygrette touched

the machine and hummed something Kel could not hear. He took a few steps forward.

They saw the first person climb one of the tied-on ropes and stand on the mole. It was a tall, thin woman with dark skin and pale gray hair, wearing dark slacks and a leather tunic. A knife was visible on her belt, but Kel saw no other weapons. She could have been a Noreelan.

She stood on her own, smiled at the several militia spaced around her, then looked past them at the ruined village. The smile dropped from her face. She looked north first, across the swollen river and past the broken bridge to the side of the village where Namior lived. Then her gaze swept slowly south, across Drakeman's Hill, down to the harbor, finally resting on the people assembled there.

Kel felt her looking directly at him and he stared back. He wondered if everyone gathered felt the same.

The woman's face crumpled for a beat, and Kel was certain he saw the glitter of tears. Then she gathered her composure and took two steps forward, bowing her head briefly at the militia and talking to them in subdued tones. Above the swell of the sea and the roar of the river, no one on the harbor could hear what she had to say. One of the militia turned and looked at the ruins of the harbor, but his expression offered no clue as to their discussion. The woman raised her arms once, slowly, but Kel could not tell whether there was any special significance to the gesture.

Then one of the militia broke away and trotted back along the mole, taking the arrow from his bow and slipping it back into the quiver slung at his hip. His companions were helping several other visitors up from the boat, and they stood in a small group around the tall woman. They all looked human. But then, Kel knew, so did the Strangers he had killed. Clothed, at least.

As the militiaman drew closer, so the questions began. *Who are they . . . what do they want . . . where do they come from . . . where's the island . . . what . . . when . . . how . . .*

The militiaman—whom Kel knew as Vek, a strong and capable soldier for such a small village—raised his hands and said nothing. When the clamor died down he made a point of scanning the crowd slowly, trying to catch everyone's eye. When his gaze slipped past Kel, Kel tried to read something in his eyes. *Is he scared? Is he excited?* But Vek betrayed nothing.

"Where is Chief Councilor Eildan?"

Kel looked around with everyone else, sharing the surprise that the head of the village did not seem to be present.

"Here!" a voice called. Eildan emerged from the wreckage of a building, shoving past the slumped, dripping remnants of a thatched roof. In one hand he clasped a large fishing harpoon, and he looked different from the way Kel had ever seen him. *Ready for a fight,* Kel thought, and his admiration for Eildan rose. He knew from village gossip that the Chief Councilor had been in the militia in Long Marrakash thirty years before, and there were rumors that he'd fought in some border skirmishes with the several independent states huddled in the mountains north of that once-great city. He certainly carried the scars of war, but he was always humble, quiet and secretive about his past. Here *is my concern*, he would say, banging a table or stamping a foot, marking the ground he did his best to control.

"Chief, the visitors request an audience with you," Vek said.

"Visitors from where?" Eildan said. He looked past the assembled Noreelans, past Vek, and out to where the unknown people stood on the ruined mole.

"The tall woman's name is Keera Kashoomie. She's an emissary. She says she has much to explain, but first of all she wants to offer her apologies."

Eildan looked back into the ruined building from which he had emerged. "There's a dead child in there," he said. "She looks perfect, her skin untouched, but her lungs are full of water, and her head...is soft...from where something hit her. She's a daughter of my village. Perhaps her parents are dead, too. Perhaps…" He swept his hand slowly before him, as though offering the people something in his palm. "Perhaps they're here." He rested the tip of his harpoon on the layer of mud coating the harborside, letting it sink in slowly. "I'm afraid," he said quietly. He spoke with great dignity and honesty, expressing what most other people felt.

Even Kel. Fear, yes, he felt that, cold and tense down his spine. But even if this was the invasion the Core had dreaded and fought against for centuries, he could not help but feel enthralled by what was about to happen.

Vek walked past the makeshift barricade to Chief Eildan, but when he spoke he made sure everyone else could hear. "She comes from the island, which she calls Komadia. She says her land is cursed. The only way her people have found to combat the curse is to repair the damage they do, and try to make amends. She says…" He trailed off, as though suddenly nervous at the many people watching.

"Yes, Vek?"

"She says they have many great technologies they can share with us."

"Let 'em have this!" Mygrette said, touching the machine by her side. It rose up on metal legs and several long, thin tubes suddenly sprouted from its back like spines, twisting and waving at the air.

Kel shrank back, thinking of the proboscises on a Stranger's back.

Mygrette gestured at the machine and the tubes vented fire.

"Mygrette!" Eildan said. He came forward, still hefting his harpoon, but Kel could already see that his mind was made up. "Not for now," he whispered to the old witch. "We need caution, but not this. Not yet. Let's see what they have to say first."

"Pah!" The witch squatted again, the machine resting down beside her.

Eildan turned back to Vek. "Bring her and those with her.

If we can find a room undamaged by the disaster they brought with them, we can talk. Tell her that the other boats stay out where they are. They can drop anchor, but I don't want another vessel docking in my village without permission."

"If they're here to invade, they'll do it anyway!" someone said.

Eildan smiled without humor. "Then we'll know the truth soon enough."

Vek nodded to the Chief and ran back along the mole. Kel saw him converse with the tall woman for a moment, then she nodded and spoke to her companions.

"They speak Noreelan," Kel said.

The man standing beside him, a tall farmer from the heights above Drakeman's Hill, laughed. He had his two little girls with him, but Kel knew his wife had passed away three years earlier. Pavmouth Breaks had closed down for a day for the funeral, and her ashes had gone into the sea. "Of course!" the farmer said. "They're *from* Noreela, somewhere. Out along The Spine, perhaps. One of the farthest islands."

"The Spine never ends," the younger of his girls said.

"Well, I don't know about that," her father replied. "But it *is* very long." He frowned then, looking out past the massed boats at the island they had sailed from. "Some magic, perhaps," he said, quieter. "Some cursed magic."

"I hope they *are* from The Spine," Kel said, but when the farmer questioned him with a raised eyebrow, Kel took a few steps closer to the edge of the harbor. The water was still several steps higher than usual, and filled with debris. A body floated facedown some way out, bobbing gently with the waves. Its hair was long, and silver scuttling things darted through it, climbing out of the water and sinking back in when they had what they had come for. The body's back was raw and red.

Kel knew what he must do. There was no use pretending, no point in waiting to see how this resolved itself. If these were

Strangers and this was the invasion, bringing the fight forward would change little. If anything, it might damage whatever plans they had. Perhaps they wanted to take Pavmouth Breaks subtly, forming a quiet beachhead from which they could expand out into Noreela. Make it difficult for them here, turn their trick against them, and maybe he would even create a chance at fighting them off.

If they were not Strangers, and this really was something else, then some small ignominy would be an acceptable price to pay.

Kel edged close to Chief Eildan, watched the visitors begin their walk along the mole, and when they stepped foot on Noreela soil, he prepared to expose whatever the truth might be.

HE TRIES TO chant O'Peeria's wraith down into the Black, but he has never been adept at such a task. His grief puts him at a disadvantage. Pelly has dragged Rok's corpse away and hidden it in some undergrowth, and she is kneeling a dozen steps away, crying, and holding both hands to her shattered cheek because the tears hurt so much.

Each chant Kel begins ends in pain. He tries to focus on O'Peeria's wraith, but his concentration is ragged, his perception poor.

He tries, and tries, but eventually Pelly nudges him with her knee. "Voices," she says, the blame in her tone obvious. "We have to go."

"I can't until—"

"Please yourself." She stumbles away into the night.

Kel looks down upon the dreadful ruin of O'Peeria's body, whispers an apology, and follows.

———

VEK CAME FIRST, two more of his militia walking on either side of him. These two still had their bows at the ready with arrows strung, but Kel had the unsettling impression they were to protect the visitors as much as the villagers. Behind them came the tall woman, Keera Kashoomie, and the four other visitors who had disembarked with her. There were two men and two women, and apart from their clothing, Kel could see nothing to set them apart from Noreelans. One of them even carried a swirling pattern of tattoos up the side of her neck and into her hairline, reminiscent of the body art he had seen Cantrass Angels excel at on one of his visits to the north. The clothes would have looked more at home in Noreela City than in a small fishing village such as this—leather jackets rather than hessian, canvas trousers, heavy leather boots. The quality was uniformly good.

They carried weapons, but nothing excessive. He saw knives, and the two women carried long, thin swords in elaborate sheaths slung from their belts and tied down their legs. They looked more ceremonial than functional.

The Core had found, tracked and killed as many women Strangers as men. Their distinguishing features had always been the same.

All five visitors wore jackets with high collars, covering their necks.

"Maybe you have gills," he whispered. *We'll all see soon.*

The visitors looked around at the village and its inhabitants, and the expressions on their faces were of stunned disbelief, mixed in with a tinge of guilt. If they were feigning their emotions, Kel decided, they were doing so very well. But Strangers always had been masters of deception, adept at blending in and being a part of the land they had come to spy upon.

He slipped his hand into his trouser pocket, through the tear in the pocket's side and around the hilt of the small knife he kept strapped to his bare thigh. This blade had once opened a Stranger's throat while O'Peeria and another Core member held her down. They had run, then, letting the wild wraith thrash itself down to nothing. The blood had been cool by the time he'd wiped it off, and when they returned, the Stranger's body had melted beneath the ash of its final exhalation.

He stood ten steps closer to the water than Chief Eildan, knowing that the militia's attention would be on the Chief when they got that close, not the people milling around him.

Vek passed and threw Kel a half smile. They had drunk with each other a few times in the Dog's Eyes. As Kel drew the knife and stepped forward, he hoped that they would drink together again.

The woman who called herself Keera Kashoomie offered no resistance, and neither did the other four visitors. The woman's swords remained in their sheaths. To the tune of mixed gasps and cries, Kel pushed Kashoomie aside, stepped behind her and clasped his arm around her throat. He held his knife ready to push between her ribs and into her heart. Then he backed toward the water, trying to make sure no one could circle around behind him.

"Don't do anything foolish," Eildan said calmly, and for a beat he was the only one to speak. Then voices rose in the crowd, a few apparently in support of what he was doing, and the militia emerged from behind their barricade and closed in, confused about which way to turn. Vek barked an order and several of them formed a barrier, cutting off Kel and the woman from everyone else. Vek himself came forward.

"Kel...now, we need caution, I agree. But they've done nothing yet that leads me to think—"

"Five beats, Vek," Kel said. "Then we'll see just how much our lives have changed."

Keera Kashoomie shifted slightly beneath his grasp, and he felt her swallowing in fear.

"This knife," he whispered, so only she could hear. "It has parted flesh like yours before. Let's see if it smells another enemy."

"Please, we've no choice in what we do. We're here because—"

"Hush," Kel said. He lifted the knife quickly to the woman's neck, using its thin blade to pierce her collar and open it with a sharp upward slice. Her skin beneath was dark and bare, showing no sign of gills or any other marks.

"What are you doing?"

"Jacket off," Kel said. "Make one move I don't like and I'll open your throat. Whatever you are, I'm quicker than you."

The two women visitors each had a hand on her sword handle, but Kel saw the slight shake of Keera's head that dissuaded them from drawing. If that happened, the militia might panic and attack. Confusion charged the air, and he could taste the tension.

Keera slipped the jacket from her shoulders and let it fall to the muddy ground. Beneath, she wore a wrinkled silk shirt, and Kel caught a waft of her body odor, earthy and somehow sensual ...

"Don't try to hex me," he said.

"Hex?"

He pulled her back against him with his arm around her neck, slipped the knife behind her shirt collar and pulled down. It took several slices to open the shirt all the way to her belt. She was bare beneath, her skin covered with a fine sheen of sweat.

There were no protuberances beneath her shoulder blades. No scars, no marks, no openings in the skin. Nothing.

Kel sighed and stepped back, dropping the knife. He started to shake, realizing only then how coiled he'd been, how ready to blow. If he had found a Stranger's proboscises, he'd have cut the woman's throat, and the harbor would have become a bloodbath. His plan had been to step back and fall into the filthy water, but he'd have been lucky to escape with his life, and the boats keeping a respectful distance would have sailed in and disgorged their invading army.

At the same time as relief washed over him, confusion and suspicion settled within him, and would not let go.

"Welcome to Noreela," he said. Keera Kashoomie glanced over her shoulder, and as Vek pushed past her and came for Kel, he was sure he saw the beginnings of a smile.

WHAT SORT OF fuckery was that?" Vek shouted.

"Just wanted to make sure they were like us."

"Well, they are, but now I have to wonder if they *like* us."

"Do you really care?" Kel asked. Vek stared at him, went to say something and shook his head.

Vek had shut Kel into a building at the foot of Drakeman's Hill, an old shop whose front had been ripped off by the tidal waves. There at the back, cut into the cliff, was the storeroom, already cleared of anything salvageable by the owners. A good cell. Difficult to escape. Feeling wretched and confused and filled with doubt, it suited Kel just fine.

"So how long do I stay here?" Kel asked.

Vek sighed and sat down. He'd come in without a weapon drawn, and for a second Kel had considered overpowering him and escaping. He knew he could. Break Vek's neck, steal his weapons, climb Drakeman's Hill to retrieve what he needed from his rooms, then past the farms and the hanging fruit vines and out into Noreela . . .

But something kept him there. Perhaps it was a result of exposing the visitor's neck and back and seeing nothing, but he thought not. He thought it was really all to do with O'Peeria. He'd failed her, and by escaping he would be failing Namior as well, fleeing when Pavmouth Breaks needed him most. Because even though Keera Kashoomie had no proboscises or gills, Kel still could not trust her. He knew far more of the world than most people in the little fishing village, and he owed them all so much.

"They're in with Chief Eildan now," Vek said. "When she came ashore, the woman was crying. She could hardly believe what had happened. Saw my weapons, started talking nonstop about how they'd help us rebuild, how they owed us, how they would suffer until our suffering was over."

"You think the suffering will ever be over?" Kel said. "I've seen at least twenty bodies myself. Do you really think Pavmouth Breaks will ever recover from this?"

Vek started to cry. It shocked Kel so much that, for a beat, he could not move or speak. He thought of going to comfort the big soldier, but he knew that would not be welcome. So he sat back and waited for Vek to speak.

"It hasn't hit me," Vek said at last. "All that's happened, it feels like a dream. I'll wake up in a minute. Too much rotwine last night, maybe. Too much stale fledge." Kel knew that many militia took fledge, procured through their contacts beyond the villages they patrolled. The drug was dangerous; mined from beneath the Widow's Peaks and transported across Noreela, its farseeing properties changed to nightmare the farther it traveled and the staler it became.

"We need to stay strong," Kel said. "There are plenty of people who'll need help today."

Vek looked at him sharply. "You're right." He stood and moved to the locked door. "You'll not do anything like that again?"

"I won't," Kel said, and he thought, *Not just yet.*

Vek produced a key from his pocket. "Keeping you locked up," he muttered. "Madness." He unlocked the door, swung it open, and stepped out into the ruin of the shop. Kel saw the soldier's shoulders rise and fall in a sigh, and beyond him he saw part of the ruined village.

Vek turned around. "Don't make me regret this," he said.

Kel went to the militiaman and slapped him on the shoulder. They looked together, and having emerged from inside, the enormity of what had happened seemed to hit them both afresh. Without another word Kel started making his way across the harbor, and back toward the damaged bridge that would take him to Namior.

Chapter Three

interference

NAMIOR'S GREAT-GRANDMOTHER was crying again. She sat close to the groundstone, but she had not touched it since dawn. She picked repeatedly at the eyelid of her good eye, as if to shift a speck of dirt, and rubbed at her good ear.

It's doom come! she had told them earlier. *A skip in the magic, an* interference.

"Please, Grandmother, you'll hurt yourself," Namior's mother said.

The old woman plucked at her reddening eye, swiped at her ear, and mumbled something beneath her breath. She had never descended so quickly and completely into one of her crazes.

Namior sighed and sat back against the wall, hugging her

knees and watching the same conversations swing around the room; alighting differently, expressed from alternate angles, but still always the same.

The people they had taken in had left, some to find their relatives and friends, others to make their way down to the harbor. One of them said he wanted to witness the moment that Noreela changed forever.

Namior stood, and her mother glanced at her with concern. "I'm only going outside to see," Namior said. "Down to the path. That's all."

Her mother nodded, her shoulders dropping. "But please, stay close. There are many who will need our help today."

Then why in the Black are we sitting around doing nothing? Namior wanted to say, but she smiled and nodded.

As she closed the door behind her and breathed in the heady scents of ocean and morning, she felt a weight lift from her shoulders. Her home was becoming clogged with bad feeling, and there was a miasma of fear from her great-grandmother that kept her constantly on edge.

She thought back to the last time she had touched the groundstone. Interference, the old woman had called it. Her hand had felt numb, and when she closed her eyes she traveled no farther than the inside of her own head.

She breathed in deeply. She never had been one for scrying. A gentle touch was the gift she took to magic, and her mother had always said she would be the village's healer one day. She still had much to learn, though, and sometimes she felt an incredible urge to leave and travel out into Noreela. There were so many places she had heard about and wished to visit. Noreela City, with its tall buildings, wide-open parks, street vendors, food, clothing and other goods imported from across the land, and the mix of cultures and people that made it a distillation of all Noreela. Long Marrakash, that ancient city awash with history that had once been Noreela's capital, and which was home to the museum of the ancient Voyagers from over three millennia before. Sordon Sound, the inland sea named after the First Voyager, Sordon Perlenni, filled with strange fish and bubble creatures, and skimming fraks, which patrolled the deeper waters and attacked any craft that ventured too close. New Shanti, the fantastical home of the Shantasi, rich in ceremony and tradition and, so some said, the purest race on Noreela—and the most familiar with the language of the land. The islands of The Spine, the wide-open plains of Cantrassa with their wild horses and wilder tribes, Kang Kang and its mysterious, dangerous environs...

So many places, and a thousand more besides. Noreela was a whole world waiting for her to explore. Pavmouth Breaks was but a spot in that world, and she already knew it so well.

She walked down the narrow alley and emerged onto the main path, looking out to sea at the island that had appeared during the storm.

Perhaps it's that, she thought. *Maybe this is the most amazing thing that has ever happened, and it's exposed the wanderlust in me.* She walked a little way until she could see down into the harbor. The visitors' boat was still docked at the mole, and out to sea were the other vessels, bobbing at anchor as if eager to sail closer. There were craft of many sizes and designs, and looking out to the island she wondered at the wealth of life it might sustain. Word had already reached them that the visitors were much like Noreelans, and in a way that had disappointed her.

But Kel's words came back to her as well. *We tracked and killed Strangers from beyond Noreela.* What had he been talking about? Had the waves shaken him so much that his mind had become unhitched? She thought not...but Kel was a wood-carver, that was all. Wasn't he?

She could not help doubting that. And she couldn't help hating him a little for planting that doubt.

A group of people came along the path, three of them struggling to carry a fourth. "Namior Feeron!" a woman said. "My boy, my *boy*!"

Namior tried to shake selfish thoughts from her mind, but they merely sank deeper.

As the group reached her, she took stock. The woman was a seed grower from around the headland, and the boy was Nerthan, her son. She knew the other people, but they were remote from what she was about to do. She blinked slowly and tried to feel the surge within her, the healing sense that she could usually summon at will. It was there, but weak. *Shocked,* she thought, *I'm still in shock.* But her great-grandmother's fears remained with her.

Interference.

The woman urged her helpers to put the boy down on the stone path. Nerthan moaned, which was a good sign, at least. Namior moved closer, the helpers backing away quietly, and knelt by the boy's side.

"He was coming down the stairs to tell me," she said, "because he'd heard the wave, or knew, or something, and then it hit and the top floor of the house…it's gone. And water poured down the staircase and washed him down to me, but his arm…his chest…" She started crying, and Namior tried to shut out the sound. It would do her no good to listen to the woman's grief, and neither would it help to hear the mother's opinions on what was wrong. Namior, for the moment, was on her own with the boy.

"Give me some space," she said. She sensed someone urging the mother to move away, and a few beats later Namior lowered her head and leaned in close.

"Nerthan," she said, "I'm going to touch you." He barely acknowledged her. His eyes were almost shut, and through the slight gaps she saw only white. His face was bruised and battered, a tooth had been knocked out, and a flap of skin had been clumsily sewn back into place across his cheek. She would leave that, because she knew there was worse to find. At least he'd have an impressive scar to show if he grew any older.

Namior closed her eyes and laid her hands flat against the

path, each fingertip sensing independently as she flexed and moved her fingers minutely. She felt grit beneath one finger, moss beneath another, the slick surface of a cobble beneath one more. She silently began to chant the words she always used. Her great-grandmother had passed them down the family line, and she said that they came from a hundred years before her, and though everyone who used them tried to improve or adjust, the original words worked best. It was something about their age, Namior believed, or perhaps a familiarity between the land and the chant. Sometimes she thought the magic was more aware of them than they were of it. That scared her, but thrilled her as well. She'd heard stories of fledge demons haunting those drug seams deep underground, and sometimes she imagined magic to be something similar. It would listen as she chanted to it, expel its powers, cast them upward through rock and into flesh and bone.

Namior opened her eyes again and ran her hands gently across the boy's body. She started at his head, working her way slowly downward. Her touch was so light that he seemed not to notice. When her right hand passed across his left arm there was a throb of heat in her mind, and as her left hand touched his shirt another warm burst. She continued down, feeling smaller flushes here and there, and then came back up to the arm and chest. She concentrated on the chest first, using both hands, moving them around just above his shirt. He moaned; she frowned. The heat was there, but she could not quite place it, nor see the shades of red and pink in her mind's eye that would usually tell her what was wrong. And she had to know that to be able to put it right.

"Interference," she muttered, and when Nerthan's mother spoke she ignored her and tore the boy's shirt open. His chest was already dark and swollen with bruising, and the right side was scraped raw by whatever had struck him.

Namior placed her hands directly on the boy's skin. It was hot from the pooling blood, but when she closed her eyes and pressed she sensed a different heat. Nerthan cried out.

Namior felt hands on her shoulders, but only for a beat. She was glad the others had pulled the boy's mother away. The wound was serious.

She sensed his ribs cracked and bent inward. One of them pressed across his heart, the sharp end having just missed piercing the muscle. Blood flowed where it should not, bone fragments blazed almost white in her mind's eye, and she felt the wall of potential building behind her ready to burst out. This was when it hurt the most, and this was the part she most enjoyed.

Now, she was with the land.

Namior took in a deep breath and tried to expand the burning zones in her mind. The boy's broken bones and torn flesh blurred in her vision, merging with her own hands, and she heard a gasp from those assembled around her. It never failed to amaze.

She opened her eyes. Her hands were in the boy's chest, fingers delving left and right as she sought broken ends, but where she pierced his skin there was no blood, only a soft light like fire. She kicked off one of her shoes and pressed her bare toes to the ground, keen to maintain contact.

"Nerthan," Namior muttered, and the boy's eyes fluttered open. He looked up at her, unable to talk or cry through the pain, but she had to warn him. "I have to hurt you to make you well."

He blinked once in acknowledgment, then clasped his eyes shut.

Namior tried, but something changed. A pulse passed through her and she felt the strength leaving her muscles, her flesh growing cool. She frowned and concentrated harder. Everything felt so far away! If she lost it, if her communication with the land was severed, she would be simply a woman with her hands buried in a dead boy's chest.

She screamed out loud, driving her mind and the magic closer together. The land spoke to her again and she grabbed those silent words with relief, bending to her task.

She had to be quick.

Namior fixed bones and stitched flesh, joined veins and tied nerves, and as she slowly lifted her hands out of the boy's body, the damage became less and less.

He cried out, and his mother was kneeling beside him, thrusting a large splinter of wood into his mouth so that he did not bite through his tongue.

The heat in Namior's mind lessened and shrank. The world twisted and flexed around her. She drew her hands out slowly, and by the time she parted contact with the boy's skin, the warm areas had faded back to a constant background hum. He cried some more, but she knew the pain would soon be gone. Even the bruises had faded to little more than a shade darker than his skin.

"His arm!" the mother said, and for a beat Namior wanted to reach out and slap her across the face. *Did you see what I just did?* she tried to say, but the words were only in her mind. *Did you see me save his life?*

She lost magic, and magic lost her. Interference.

When she slipped sideways, she was grateful to feel hands ease her fall.

NAMIOR WAS LIGHT-HEADED, but she did not pass out. She sat against the wall, feeling dampness chilling through her clothes, and watched Nerthan's mother.

"Set the arm," Namior said. "Splints. Come and see me again later."

"Thank you," the woman said, and she smiled her apology at Namior. Not everyone was a witch, and not everyone could access magic so deeply and effectively. Sometimes, so much was taken for granted.

"I just feel so tired," Namior said. "Last night…" She trailed off, and Nerthan was staring at her. *Did he feel the interference?* she wondered.

"Everything feels different," he said. The boy was only ten years old.

As he stood and his mother helped him walk away, Namior climbed to her feet and leaned against the wall. She looked down at the ruined harbor, the few people milling around down there, the mysterious boats and the large ship shifting with the swell. One boat was moored at the mole, and several stationary shapes stood guard. "Yes. Everything feels different."

"Namior?"

She closed her eyes and sighed, feeling the rush of relief at hearing that voice again. Anger welled, but so did the tears. "Forget something?" she asked.

"No."

She looked out to sea, curious as to whether the unknown island had changed with Kel close by. More threatening? Not so mystifying? But his presence altered nothing of what had happened, at least on the surface. As to what she *thought* about what had occurred . . . that would take some time to decide.

"So do they look just like us?" she asked.

"Yes." He stood behind her but did not dare touch her, not yet. She quite liked the shred of power that gave her.

"Are they your 'Strangers'?" He did not answer, and she knew it was time to turn around. "Kel, tell me you're just a wood-carver."

"I am a wood-carver."

"But tell me that's *all* you are!"

He looked tired, filthy and shocked by what had happened. Perhaps it had taken that long to settle on him, and his attempt to flee had been the result. "I can't tell you that," he said.

"Trakis?" she asked. "Mell?"

He shook his head. "I haven't seen them."

She suddenly wanted to hold him. Her mother was her bedrock, but Kel was the anchor she had found to hold her to that place. As she grew older and her training advanced, the wanderlust was turning into a passion, and it was only Kel's insistence that the village was the best place for them that kept her there. But there was a distance between them now, a lie — or a secret, which really amounted to the same thing — that felt as real to her as the magic pulsing through the land. She could almost see it, and for a second she was afraid to close her eyes, terrified that she would sense the heat of a fatal wound in their closeness. But she was a healer, not an empath. Old Mygrette was the one for that. Mygrette was good at *everything*.

"Was Mygrette down there?"

"Yes, with one of her machines."

"What did she do?"

"She was ready to fight. Eildan had to calm her down."

Namior nodded. Kel stepped closer but Namior turned her head away from him, only slightly, but enough to send her message. It pained her, but the reaction was natural.

Kel sighed. "There are lots of dead," he said. "And probably many more injured. Pavmouth Breaks . . . it's been on hold since the waves. Waiting. But now they're here . . ." He nodded down at the harbor, and the boats holding position beyond. "The time's come to start licking our wounds."

"You're not going to run off, then?"

"I haven't, have I?"

"I'm sure you tried," Namior said, and stared at him, seeking the truth in his eyes. *Tell me you didn't,* she thought. *Tell me you changed your mind and came back for me.* But it seemed he could no longer lie, even to please her.

"I couldn't reach my rooms to fetch what I needed. There's so much destruction. So I went to the harbor instead, and what I saw . . . changed my priority."

"So you don't want to track and kill them all, now?"

"No. But . . ." He frowned, looked over her shoulder and out to sea toward the new island.

"We'll be careful," Namior said, and she realized she was talking about Pavmouth Breaks as something separate from

Kel. He had become a visitor there again, even after living in the village for five years, falling in love, and changing her life. She wondered how long it would take for that to change once more.

"We *have* to be."

"We should go down there and start helping," Namior said. "I'll tell my family. And then you'll come with me?"

"Yes."

She brushed past Kel and, from the corner of her eye, saw him reach out for her arm. But she shrugged his hand aside and walked up the path, feeling him watch her every step of the way.

NAMIOR'S GREAT-GRANDMOTHER slept in the corner by the groundstone, twitching in her sleep and mumbling words none of them could make out. Her good eye was red, and her mother had bathed it while the old woman slept.

"Whether they're from beyond Noreela, or somewhere remote in Noreela itself, they're strangers to us here," her mother said. "Be careful, Namior. Mind everything you've learned. Weird times, these." She nodded, grunting to confirm her own pronouncement. She seemed more intense than she had in a long time, and yet her eyes were distant, as if there was more to be said.

"And?" Namior prompted gently, respectfully.

"Weird times. And in these weird times, I think you'll become a full witch."

Namior smiled and could not help the swell of pride that ran through her. She kissed her mother, promised she would return before nightfall, and closed the door softly behind her.

I think you'll become a full witch. The words hung with her, and the sky suddenly looked bright, the sea calmer. Her heart mourned dead friends, but her mind was thrilling with the thought of what might come.

She walked back down to Kel and leaned next to him on the path wall. He was looking out to sea again, and she followed his gaze.

"It looks like a normal island," she said.

"When's the last time you saw an island?" he asked, laughing softly.

"In books. Paintings. Images when I commune with the land."

"What images?"

"Part of my training, Kel, you know that. I stretch my mind to seek stories from across Noreela. A year ago, I spent some time stretching to The Spine. An amazing place."

"Never been there," Kel said.

"I can't make out much detail, but it looks..."

"Like it belongs," Kel finished for her.

Namior shrugged. Yes, it looked right. Not out of place at all, even though it had appeared from nowhere in the open sea. "I wonder where it came from?" she mused. "I wonder where it was before?"

"If it was somewhere close to land, we're not the only place facing this today." He nodded down at their ruined village. "We should go. I can lift and dig, and you can heal."

Namior turned to Kel, suddenly desperate to heal something between them before their brief moment alone was over. "Kel, tell me things will be all right."

"I can't tell you that."

"I mean between us."

He smiled. "I want them to be. And if you want them to be as well, then they will."

"Whatever your story might be?" *Strangers*, she thought, *tracking and killing strangers.*

"I never want to be a stranger to you," he said.

Namior smiled, but his choice of words unsettled her. She had many questions, and they had far to go. But Nerthan came to mind again, the pain on his face and the breaks across his body, and she was suddenly angry. Everything she was feeling was far greater than Kel and her. It was about her village and people. She closed her eyes tight, leaned against the stone wall. If she really concentrated, she could stretch and sense blooms of painful heat all across the hillsides, and down into the wave-ruined valley.

"I'm frightened," she said. "There's so much to do."

"I'll help."

"Thank you, Kel. I love you for that. But I think I'm frightened of you as well." She started along the path, heading for the Moon Temple and the many who needed help.

THE MOURNER WAS still at the Moon Temple, and the line of bodies outside had doubled. There were at least twenty dead, and Kanthia looked tired and drawn, her old face made older, her skin gray as though leeched of life. She turned to Kel and Namior as they approached through the Temple's ground. She was still obviously blind, but her eyes were even more haunted than usual.

"So many confused wraiths today," she said. "A lot of them died in their sleep."

"But you're chanting them down," Kel said. "Putting them at peace."

"It's never easy breaking the news of death to the dead."

"I'm here to fix the living," Namior said. The Mourner always unsettled her. She came closer than anyone else to talking with the dead, and chanting them into the Black seemed to leave a bit of the Black in her soul.

Kanthia gestured toward the Temple. "The lucky ones are in there."

Namior passed by the dead and their Mourner, and as she neared the Moon Temple she smelled blood and shit, and she heard the groans of those in pain, and the screams of those in agony. Kel touched her arm and held her hand, and she gave him a thankful squeeze.

"Namior," he said, "this is your place, not mine. I can't do any good in there, other than carrying out the dead, and I've seen enough of them already today."

"Of course," she said. "Yes, Kel. I'm sorry..."

He came close then, and she let him. "You have nothing to apologize for," he said. "That's all up to me. I'll come back later, and we can talk. I'm going back to the harbor, to see if I can find Mell and Trakis."

When she leaned her head on his shoulder, it felt just like before. He even smelled the same.

Kel kissed the top of her head and pulled away. "Take care," he said, his face stern.

It's a disaster, not a war, she almost said. But she nodded instead, because she could see the seriousness in his eyes. "Of course."

He touched her cheek, then turned and trotted down through the Temple grounds. Namior watched him climb the wall and disappear onto the washed-out path, and as she entered the Temple she saw everything she could smell from outside, and knew who was doing the moaning, and who screamed.

KEL LOOKED DOWN the swollen river for a while, past the ruined bridge at the masts spiking beyond the harbor. They were still at rest. The mast of the boat moored at the mole was just visible, and there were several militia milling around it, apparently talking to someone still aboard.

Beyond the harbor, beyond the masts, the new island basked under the Noreelan sun.

The sight was amazing. And for the first time since the previous night, Kel experienced his first doubt that it was anything to do with him.

There were a group of men and women working at a house upriver from where he stood. One whole façade had collapsed when its footings were washed away, bringing down the roof and internal floor structure as well, and the people were digging at the ruin with their bare hands. A machine stood to one side. It was as tall as a man, square, resting on three spherical wheels, and was lifting heavy stone blocks with its several flexible appendages. Kel wondered which one of the rescuers was its Practitioner. A woman glanced up and saw him watching.

"My father," she said, and though they were thirty steps away he still heard the pain in her voice.

He considered going to help. He could add one more set of hands to the rescue; more blocks removed, more timber beams shifted aside, more injured people or corpses uncovered and carried to the Moon Temple. Or he could try to protect Pavmouth Breaks from dangers yet to come. He had seen no gills or spine-limbs, but he still had difficulty finding any trust for Keera Kashoomie and her visitors.

Doubt was no good to anyone. He had to be *certain*.

Kel looked up at Drakeman's Hill. *Mell and Trakis*, he thought. But he could look for them on the way. He would remain in Pavmouth Breaks, for Namior and for himself, but to do so there were precautions he had to take and preparations to make.

The woman was still looking at him as she dug for her father with her bare hands. She was sweating, turning the dust on her face to dirt, and her eyes held a silent appeal.

Kel pointed across the river, as though indicating someone else he had to help. Then he turned away, and did not look back as he trotted along the ruined path toward the stone bridge.

THE RESCUE HAD begun in earnest all across Pavmouth Breaks. The bodies visible in the river, on the mud plains on either side, and piled against the bridge were being left alone for the time being, because it was the living that needed help.

But even as Kel picked his way across to the washed-out section of the bridge, he could see the things crawling through the debris to get to the fresh meat. There were crabs, some of them as small as his hand, a few the size of a small child, and their pincers were more than capable of stripping flesh from bone. Several varieties of sea snakes had left their slithery marks on the mud, and they curled through corpses' hair in search of moist morsels. He could even see the prints of a sea wolf beneath the bridge, massive webbed pads splayed across the mud to offer the beast support. He could not see the dangerous creature itself, because if it was still up from the sea, it would be hiding away in shadows and ruins. But he could only guess at the damage it had already done to the village's dead. He had heard about such animals; he feared that when the dead started to rot, it would move on to the living.

Kel climbed carefully across and through the debris bridging the missing span, then followed his earlier route to the harbor. There were still many people gathered there, most of them digging around in the dozens of ruined and tumbled buildings, though he guessed that the chance of finding survivors was slim. A few machines dug with them, using limbs splayed into paddles to shift large clots of muck and filth from between any remaining walls. These were constructs more used to rolling nets and shifting crates of newly landed fish, and the hard work was already evidenced by the scrapes and bumps across their surfaces. Their Practitioners stood close to them, ground rods punched deep through the mud and between the stone blocks of the harbor.

Several machines were at a standstill, their Practitioners sitting beside them exhausted, pale and bereft.

A shout went up, and Kel dashed across to the wreckage of the Blue Ray Tavern. The front wall stood to waist height, front door opening still evident, but a sidewall seemed ready to topple at any moment. Two militia were there, along with several members of the landlord's extended family, and as Kel

drew closer he saw a little girl kneeling in the mud and tugging at a human limb. The fingers were clawed and stiff, and
Kel turned away again before the inevitable wailing began.

Thirty steps away, Mygrette was standing close to her machine, guiding its actions as it probed the deep silt with a long,
thin limb. Its movements were jerky and hesitant, belying the
old witch's mastery of the machine and the magic that drove
it. She touched its stone shell, frowning and mumbling to herself. Then she looked out at the mole, across to the base of
Drakeman's Hill, back again. He could see the swirl of tattoos
across her cheeks stretched into a terse, tense expression.
Some said the tattoos were reflections of a witch's soul.

"Mygrette," Kel said as he approached.

"Wood-carver."

"My name's Kel."

"And what's in a name, today?"

"What do you mean?" Kel asked. The old witch looked at
him, and there was a lifetime of experience in the creases
around her eyes. Some called her mad, but Kel had seen
plenty of mad people. She was no more insane than he.

"The wind's still blowing," she said, "and the storm's still
here."

Kel looked up at the clearing sky, the stringy clouds, the
seagulls and salt birds gliding on the subtle sea breeze.

"Not up there," Mygrette said, and her tone added, *Fool!*
"In there!" She pointed to the foot of Drakeman's Hill where
Eildan, his council and the visitors were obviously holding
their talks. "Out there!" She thumbed over her shoulder
at the ships waiting patiently out to sea. "And here." She
stamped on the ground and looked down, and her machine
gave a pained, creaking sound. "The language of the land is
confused today." Mygrette stroked the machine's shell and
gave it her strange commands. It probed the mud again, and
Kel had never seen a machine that looked so unwell.

"The storm did that?" he asked.

"The continuing storm." She glanced at him, then looked

down at her feet again. "Like I said...ain't over yet. Plenty more to come."

"Maybe," Kel said.

"Huh!" The witch turned and walked to the edge of the harbor. The machine sighed to a halt, and Kel followed her. She stared down at the filthy water swelling against the ancient stone, filled with broken parts of Pavmouth Breaks, human, animal and otherwise. "You think like me; otherwise, why did you come talk to me?"

"I'm cautious, that's all."

"Cautious, eh? Wood-carver?"

Kel smiled. *She knows more.* On his travels with the Core he'd heard of witches who had learned how to supplement the innocent gift of magic with a combination of herbs, exotic minerals and animals extracts, giving themselves mysterious, sometimes unique abilities that they shared with no one else. He'd heard of them, but he'd never met one, not until he'd come to the quiet fishing village. Most there thought her mad, because they looked with eyes that had seen little else. But Kel had witnessed more than most Noreelans ever would in a lifetime.

"It's good to know not everyone will just accept this," he said.

"Right!" Mygrette laughed, surprisingly light and infectious. "Good that not everyone's blind, eh?" She laughed again, and turned back to her machine.

The Core often called their continuing mission the Blind War. *Does she know so much more?* Kel thought. He resisted the temptation to turn and watch the witch walk away. But he knew that, if things went bad, he had at least one ally.

He started walking along the mole. He had not intended doing so, but it seemed the right way to go, taking his suspicions to the visitors. He watched his footing. There was immense damage there, with huge stone blocks cracked, crazed or missing altogether after the great waves' impacts. The visitors' boat had moored just before one large section of mole that had been washed away completely. There were two members of the militia there, and one of them came toward Kel.

"Hello, Kel," the militia member said. Luceel was a regular at the Dog's Eyes, usually accompanying the militia captain Vek. Kel knew she and Vek were good friends, but nothing more, and he was glad it was she out there and not someone he didn't know.

The second militia member stood back, hand on his sword. *I could take that and stick it up through Luceel's chin before either of them could blink,* Kel thought. He frowned, trying to shake the image. He did not like the way his past was surfacing, swimming up from the depths in which he had, for a while, believed it had drowned.

"Quite a night," Kel said, glancing past Luceel at the boat.

"Not good."

"Are your people well?"

She nodded. "Up on the farm at the top of Drakeman's Hill. I saw Mell climbing the Hill on my way down this morning."

"Mell!" Kel felt a rush of relief, so fresh and wonderful as it washed away his concerns for a beat. "By the Black, I was sure that second wave got her. It *should* have."

"Dog's Eyes regulars," Luceel said with a smile. "Hard to kill."

"Trakis was with her?"

Luceel frowned and shook her head.

"Well, I'm glad you're okay too. So..." Kel nodded past her at the boat. She seemed to stiffen a little, as though suddenly remembering her job.

"I've been told not to let anyone close," she said.

"Why?"

Luceel blinked but said nothing.

"Can't I see?"

"It's just a boat, Kel."

"Really?"

She frowned. "Of course. They're just like us."

"Their island appeared in our coastal waters and caused tidal waves that wiped out half our village. And you think they're just like us?"

"Kel, they're devastated. Really. One of the women with the emissary told me, this happens to them once a generation, sometimes longer, sometimes more frequently. She said they live under a curse from before history. Usually the island comes to rest somewhere far out to sea, or close to uninhabited coastline. They can barely speak, they're so traumatized and shocked by what's happened, and what it's done to us. And they're going to help."

"Help how?"

"Help us rebuild."

Kel looked back along the mole to the harbor, the Noreelans digging there and the terrible ruin that much of the village had become. "You really think they can help us any more than we can help ourselves?"

"I really think so, yes."

"Already under their spell, eh, Luceel?" He smiled at her but without humor, and she did not return the smile. "So, can't I have a look?"

Luceel sighed and stepped aside. "Like I said, Kel, it's just a boat."

He walked past her, eyeing the militiaman. He knew the man's face, but not his name. He looked down at the hand on his sword, back up, and grinned.

The militiaman glanced away, and his sword hand went up to pick his nose.

Glad to see I've still got it, Kel thought.

As Luceel had said, it was just a boat. The sail had been folded and the boom tied straight, and it was secured to the mole fore and aft. The mooring posts had been ripped out, but the militia had tied ropes thrown by the visitors onto the ripped remains of two metal ladders on the mole's seaward face. The vessel was old, battered and obviously well used.

The deck had several areas where new boards had been nailed in, the cabin that stood toward the stern was sun-bleached and pocked, and the ropes scattered across the deck were ragged and worn. There were two hatches leading below, both of them closed but not obviously locked, at least on the outside.

Kel was not all that familiar with boats. True, he lived in a fishing village, but he had never taken a keen interest in sea-faring. He often talked to the fisherfolk who frequented the village's several taverns, and he had befriended many, but he was more likely to listen to their tall tales than ask questions. And all fisherfolk had good tales to tell. There were giant sea lizards and pirates of renown, missed catches and surreal sea monsters, humanesque rock dwellers singing their songs to lure boats to destruction, wraith ships crewed by the ancestors of those now living in Pavmouth Breaks, and occasional stories of loves lost to the waves and found again. So he tried to view the visitors' craft with an innocent's eye, rather than the gaze of someone who saw boats every day but had no interest in them. He was looking for things that seemed wrong, or perhaps things not there at all.

He walked along the mole for the length of the boat, then back again. He was aware of Luceel and the militiaman watching him, but when he glanced up it was Mygrette he saw, casually touching her machine as it probed for survivors, yet her attention was fixed on Kel.

It was a sailing boat, sail now tied. It was obviously used for fishing, as it had a few nets folded in a wooden box toward the bow, long ropes trailing from them and wrapped around a rope drum. The cabin's windows were of rough glass, and he guessed that any image viewed through them would be badly blurred and deformed. *They offer us a gift of wonderful technologies*, he thought, *and they can't cast glass?*

It was a working craft, not one built for leisure and pleasure, like some vessels he had seen when he spent a difficult few moons in Long Marrakash ten years before. There, some people virtually lived on the river, spending their free time afloat and only coming ashore to work. They harnessed river rays and used them to tow their craft, competing to see who could go fastest. Kel could not imagine this boat ever building up much speed.

He strolled back and forth a few more times, then headed back toward the harbor.

"Keep your trust precious," he muttered to Luceel as he passed her by. She did not respond. He hoped that was because she was considering what he had said.

Mygrette was waiting for him, as he knew she would be. She still stood by her machine, but her gaze called him over, and she began to question in lowered tones.

As he started lifting splintered roof timbers from the silted guts of the fish market, he told her what he had seen, trying to make clear things he had not seen as well.

"Just a boat," he said, lifting a chunk of masonry and seeing the dreadful paleness of a hand beneath. He sighed, caught someone's eye and stepped back for them to see as well.

"Just a boat?" Mygrette said. "Huh!"

The rescuers talked in low tones, working to uncover the body. Kel stepped back. He had started shaking, unexpected and frightening, and he had to fight the urge to run. Back to Namior, back to her home with her mother and great-grandmother, and away from death for a while.

"And what was this boat's name?" Mygrette asked.

Kel frowned, hugging himself to bring the shaking under control.

"Every boat has a name," the witch said, leaning in close so that no one else could hear.

He recalled walking back and forth, looking at the boat's hull, the cabin, the squared stern and pointed bow. He shook his head. "It has no name."

Mygrette stared at him, then turned away and went back to her machine. She touched its smooth back, and it grabbed a tumbled timber-framed wall in its delicate limbs and lifted, something inside creaking with the effort. Then it froze, and it took several touches from Mygrette before it would move again.

Beneath the wall, a corpse with sea worms squirming in hollowed eye sockets.

"*Mother!*" someone screamed, loud enough to wake the dead.

Kel looked up at Drakeman's Hill, misted with the smoke of a fire lit to defy the sea. It was time for him to climb.

AS KEL MADE his way to the base of Drakeman's Hill, he was amazed that anyone had survived at all. But he saw two people being dragged out of flooded cellars. They had survived the destruction of their homes, falling masonry and roofs, the scouring power of the waves, drowning, the deluge of mud and the cold of the night. The look on a young boy's face as he saw the sun lit a fire inside Kel's chest, and he turned away as his eyes watered. *Noreela can be so strong!* he thought, and felt a sense of proud responsibility that had been missing for so long.

When he had fled the Core, it had taken him a long time to come to terms with that desertion. Such dereliction of duty did not sit well with him. But once gone, he could not go back, and he had slowly come to believe that he had done the right thing. He'd been involved in a botched mission that had caused two Core and eight civilian deaths, and after that he could surely never be as sharp, prepared and brutal as was sometimes required.

But things were changing.

As he neared the foot of Drakeman's Hill, he saw in more detail where the waves had undermined the ground. A great wedge of land had gone, taking many buildings and paths with it and leaving behind a bare earth cliff between twenty and thirty steps high. In several places in the new cliff were un-

earthed hollows, each the size of a person and speckled with
the glint of crystals. Perhaps they had been precious once, but
not now. Not when their exposure came at such a cost.

Against the cliff, people had already built a rough pile of
rocky debris and strung a rope ladder. It was busy, with survivors being helped up the ladder and rescuers taking turns to
come down. Those coming down bore waterskins and food
parcels, medical supplies, and tools to aid in the rescue—
shovels, hammers and nails for shoring, lanterns. It was not
until he'd been watching the ladder for a while, waiting in
queue to climb up, that Kel noticed how many people also
descended armed.

He felt a swell of confidence, a flush of pride. *Yes, Noreela*
can *be strong.*

Glancing back at the harbor, he saw the masts of visitors'
boats waving in the swell once again as they turned and sailed
in toward Pavmouth Breaks. Walking out along the mole, visible even from a distance, he saw Chief Eildan still carrying
his heavy harpoon and Keera Kashoomie walking tall beside him.

The talking was over. The landing had begun.

HE CLIMBED THE paths up Drakeman's Hill, and the gradual change was striking. At the bottom, many of the buildings had shattered windows, wrecked doors, stripped roofs,
and sometimes blocks missing from wall corners and window
surrounds. He could see into many of the buildings, and most
of them were all but stripped of character. Furniture was broken and strewn across the street, clothing mixed in, and here
and there thick pools of mud and silt had collected. Some of
the pools were crawling with sea things, though most of the
creatures washed up with the wave were dying. Their deaths
added to the stink.

Around one corner, a boat had been deposited between

two houses. The path there was narrow, and the boat—hull holed, mast missing, wheelhouse gone—was resting across the two roofs. It had crushed the roof structures when it hit, burying itself in the buildings as though they were sandbanks. Kel had to duck to pass beneath the shell-encrusted hull, and he splashed through a puddle of seawater.

There was an old man sitting beside the path just beyond the boat. Kel recognized him as a farmer from the plains atop Drakeman's Hill—one of the oldest men from the village and someone trusted and revered. He leaned back against a stone wall, looking at his hands as though they were guilty of a terrible crime.

"Kel Boon," the man said. "I like your carvings. They are always fine and detailed, and more importantly, they have soul."

"Thank you," Kel said. He waited, expecting more, but the man went back to staring at his hands, as if waiting for them to act.

Kel considered asking whether he needed help, but the old man did not appear to be in distress. Not of the physical kind, at least. Emotionally... Kel was still too concerned about his own state of mind to start worrying about others'.

He went on, panting with familiar exertion, pressing down on his knees to help the climb. The path twisted and turned between buildings constructed at varying points during the village's history. Stone houses stood between timber constructions, and here and there were old mud-and-seaweed homes, their thick walls still standing solid. The stench of the sea lessened so far up, and he realized how sickening the smell of mud and death was down in the ruins.

He passed people going down, glanced at them all, and saw a mixture of shock, concern and wonder in their faces that did not sit well with him. All were emotions strong enough to cause change, and change was always dangerous.

Here and there, where the spaces between buildings offered views down to the harbor, he paused to see what was happening. Some of the visitors' smaller craft had moored along the mole, and from so high the movement of people disembarking was little more than a blur. A few boats had passed around the end of the mole and entered the harbor proper, but they seemed to have anchored away from the harbor or mole walls. The harbor was full of debris and dirt, and it moved like thick soup instead of seawater.

The larger ship was moving closer under oar power. Waves broke against its hull as it headed in. As Kel watched, the huge booms started to swing around, the ship began its turn, and launches were lowered all along its port side. The launches were full of people.

How many? Kel wondered. *A hundred? More?* Pavmouth Breaks had maybe two thousand inhabitants, both down in the harbor and valley, and up on the hills surrounding them. The waves had killed many, though it would be a long time before they knew the exact numbers. But the odds still seemed stacked in the Noreelans' favor.

Is this the way I should be thinking? Kel leaned against a wall to catch his breath. *Could they really be here to hurt us?* He closed his eyes and welcomed the cool breeze coming in from the sea, and he noticed a hint of something mysterious and unknown—a fruity scent he did not recognize. As he looked out to the island the idea crossed his mind, for the first time, that it was a place he had to visit.

A chill of anticipation went through him, a thrill of excitement.

He turned and started climbing again. The closer he drew to his rooms, the calmer he felt. There was even a selfish, dreadful part of him that still entertained the idea of escape.

No, not escape! Retreat. *But only to come back stronger.*

Yet as he reached the door to his rooms, in the long, low stone building where eight others lived, he realized that he did not yet know enough to run.

He unlocked the door and entered, and inside, last night had not happened. The sculpture he was carving for Namior sat covered by its blanket, and the unlit fire was speckled with wellburr shavings. He paused for a moment and breathed in deeply, relishing air untainted by the disaster beyond the door. Glancing at the voice carrier tucked away in the corner of his room, he thought of Namior, working at the Moon Temple to heal people injured by the waves, perhaps thinking of him, wondering where he was and what his intentions were. Wondering *who* he was. He had said too much, but not yet enough, and they had plenty to talk about when the time was right.

Kel sat at his carving table and pulled the cover from his latest work. The cliff hawk was beautifully wrought, yet it meant nothing. What was such a copy, when he could walk up to the top of Drakeman's Hill and see the real thing? What was the purpose of trying to capture nature in art? Was it appreciation, or arrogance?

"So many dead," he whispered, and the hawk stared back at him with unfinished eyes. He thought of the cries he had heard that day, the tears he had seen, and the sun was barely at its zenith.

Kel rubbed his face and looked at the dirt on his hands. There had been blood there many times before. As recently as that morning, he had been ready to spill some more. And if the situation called for it, he still was.

He had lost his knife, but no Core soldier was ever far from his or her weapons.

The floorboard beneath his carving table came up with a brief squeal. He drew out his weapon roll, the weapons wrapped in oilcloth, sharpened and cared for regularly since he had been there. Beneath the roll lay the bag of things he liked much less. He picked up the bag, opened the sealing string, and carefully pulled them out.

They were communicators, but far more effective than Namior's voice carrier. Perfected by the Core's greatest witches, they looked like small, thumb-sized nuts trailing long, sinewy tails. When the tails were breathed upon, they grew incredibly hard and sharp, and their tips could pierce stone. Once plunged into the ground, the magic of the land flowed into the round head. Crushed, a signal would be sent to all Core members across Noreela, as though the nut itself had taken root and bloomed a desperate call for help.

None of the weird devices had ever been used, but every Core member was in possession of several of them. *Use one of those fuckers, and Noreela's at war,* he remembered O'Peeria once saying. Even she had been afraid of them.

"I pray to the Black, the moon gods, the Sleeping Gods, and every cursed deity anyone in Noreela chooses to call their own that I don't have to use one of these," Kel said. But though faithless in religion, he had even less faith in himself. The prayers felt like nothing.

He rolled the tails away, tied the three objects back in their bag and slipped it into his pocket.

It took him a while to stow the weapons about himself. A knife into the sheath on his thigh, throwing knives tucked into the belt on the inside of his trouser waist so that their hilts were hidden, acid dust in leaf pouches in several pockets, and in his jacket pocket went the small crossbow he had used to kill his final Stranger. When he blinked, he saw O'Peeria dying beneath the thing's disintegrating corpse.

The only weapon he could not hide was the short sword he hung from his belt. No one would question that. He had seen many people descending into the valley armed, and if questioned, he could claim a fear of what had been washed up with the sea. *I saw sea-wolf tracks,* he would say.

The final thing he picked up was the carving. It was not finished, and not quite perfect, but he liked that. It spoke of potential in a safe future to come.

As he closed his door and prepared to go down into Pavmouth Breaks once again, Kel thought of O'Peeria, and how she had never assumed any future at all.

———

HE'S ABOUT FIVE hundred years old," O'Peeria whispers. "He *must* be. He knows so much, and he stinks like a fucking corpse."

Kel cannot help smirking. They have been drinking rotwine together all afternoon in a rough old tavern on Conbarma's waterfront, on the northern shores of Noreela. Frequented by fishermen, rage-shell dealers and visitors from the islands of The Spine, the most essential item of clothing is a knife. O'Peeria draws a certain amount of attention because she's Shantasi, but she is able to deliver a stare of such withering strength that they are left alone.

Somewhat drunk and tired and with Kel almost certain he will try to make love with O'Peeria later that night, they have to gather their senses to listen to the oldest Core member still alive.

They are sitting on the deck of a large, seagoing sailing boat. The old man lives on one of the distant islands of The Spine, so it's said, and it's alleged that he's watching for Strangers from the north. He has stated that this is his last-ever visit to the Noreelan mainland, so the Core has brought as many members together as they can to benefit from his experience.

It's the first time in his life that Kel has ever been on a boat, and the sea's gentle movement does not sit well with a stomach full of rotwine.

"I'll share your joke, Shantasi," Verrin says. Rumor has it he's changed his name sixteen times in his life, each change following his killing of a Stranger. He is bald, his scalp scarred with a network of fine, spotted wounds. His eyes are a piercing green. He claims to be over a hundred years old, and as Kel swallows his laughter, he can well believe that.

"My name's O'Peeria," she says, "and the joke's on you."

Verrin smiles. "I've suffered much worse. But I'm here, O'Peeria, because I know more about Strangers than all of you chunks of sheebok shit combined." A murmur passes through the dozen Core soldiers sitting on the boat's deck.

"No whispering," Verrin says. "And nudging your neighbors. I've earned the right to call you all what I want, although... you know I don't mean it." He sits on an upturned box before them, like a teacher facing a room of unruly children, and holds up his hands. "There's blood on these." He points to his head. "Bitterness in here." He sighs and looks down at his feet, and after a few beats Kel starts to think he's fallen asleep.

The Core soldiers are completely silent. No sense of mockery remains, because Verrin has begun, and they all know his history. There are no books, no images, no poems or songs in print, because nothing can hint at the Core's existence. They are people who all know too much. *Noreela is not alone...* The four words that would change their world forever. But word is always passed down, myths have their own impetus, and Verrin has become a legend among those Core members active across Noreela.

"You've all killed a Stranger," he says—a statement more than a question. He can likely see the truth of that in the eyes of those before him. Kel says nothing. "How many?" Verrin points to a woman to Kel's left.

"One," she says. "And another I wasn't sure about."

"If you still weren't sure after the killing, then he or she wasn't a Stranger." He points at O'Peeria. "How many?"

"Two," she says. "Definitely Strangers."

Verrin nods. Then he points at Kel and raises his eyebrows.

Kel thinks of lying, but Verrin is glaring at him, the old man's eyes home to so much more than Kel will ever likely know. "None," he says. "But my time will come."

Verrin grins. "It will. It will come, soldier. And you already have the look of a killer."

He laughs a little, then looks up over their heads, as though addressing someone much farther away.

"They look just like us, with their clothes on. Hide their gills and those cursed things on their backs, and sometimes you can spend days with them without becoming suspicious.

They'll just seem like someone from a long way away, who perhaps isn't aware of local customs, religions or laws. Noreela has many travelers and rovers, and this is not so unusual. But more often than not, a Stranger *will* give himself or herself away to those looking for them, even with the very subtlest of signs. You've all met someone you feel is just . . . out of place. Someone who unsettles you. They have a strange manner of communicating, gesticulating oddly as they speak. They look at you for too long after pausing in their conversation, or too intensely, or not for long enough. Their eyes can be cold, as though whatever unknown distance they've traveled to reach Noreela has affected their stare. And the one constant I've learned, the one thing that has kept me alive and killed so many Strangers, is this: trust your instincts." He falls silent, still staring away over their heads.

"*You* unsettle me," O'Peeria says.

Verrin's eyes droop, hooded by the threat of violence. He touches his collar and starts to pull it back.

The Core soldiers gasp. All of them. Kel can't help himself, and he is instantly sobered. He reaches for the short knife on his belt, as yet untainted by a Stranger's blood.

Verrin tilts his head to one side and shows them the side of his neck. It's brown as an old saddle, and just as worn. No gills.

Verrin smiles, and the soldiers' laughter is painfully nervous.

"Trust your instincts," he says directly to O'Peeria. "Though also trust that sometimes, they might be wrong."

Then he looks at the woman who killed someone she believed to be a Stranger but who evidently was not. "You can't afford to take the chance."

Chapter Four

only steam

PEOPLE BEGAN TO claim the bodies of their loved ones. They came singly, in couples or family groups, most of them dirty and disheveled, bloodied and bruised from digging through rubble or hauling mud by the bucket or shovelful. They approached the Moon Temple slowly, looking at that extravagant building with new gravity and uncertainty. For some it was a regular site of worship, for others simply a place they passed day after day without a second thought. In Pavmouth Breaks, as in most of Noreela, the choice of which deity to worship, or the decision to worship any at all, was still a free one.

As they came in through the gate in the wide stone wall, each of them looked the same: haunted. The wraiths haunting these villagers were not the ghosts of their dead relatives but the hope that they were not dead at all. The village had been shattered in the night, and missing people could just as easily be helping dig at a collapsed building, or buried beneath one still alive, as lying dead on the grass in the Temple gardens.

Like most ghosts doomed to roam, hope was a wretched thing.

Most of Namior's work had happened in the Temple itself. The worship mats were spread in concentric circles around the central marble moon image inlaid in the floor. That marble shone yellow or white, depending on which moon was in the ascendant, but now it was splashed blood red and mud brown, and the worship mats were beds for the wounded, and the dying. She had not become used to the smells or sounds, and the sights she would dream about forever. Namior had watched three people she knew die, one of them beneath her own hands as she tried in vain to heal ruptured organs and stitch smashed bones. She saw four people she did not know pass away as well, and Mourner Kanthia moved back and forth across the Temple like a disembodied wraith herself, her chants an almost constant counterpoint to the crying, sobbing and occasional screams.

Once, Kanthia leaned on Namior's shoulder when she was sitting at the rear of the Temple, trying to take a break. "So many sad spirits," Kanthia said. "I hope there's room in the Black."

"The Black is endless," Namior said, because that was what everyone believed. The Black was everywhere and everywhen, and Noreela was a speck of grit compared to its enormity.

"Endless," Kanthia said, and she uttered a sob as she went in search of another wandering spirit.

Namior was exhausted. As the sun began its journey down toward the watery horizon, she was working in a fugue, letting necessity guide her rather than her own observations. To begin with, when the language of the land spoke in terms she did not quite understand, she had put it down to her tiredness. But it happened several times during that long afternoon — times when it took longer than it should for the healing urge to take her and the power to touch her fingertips strongly enough for her to begin. *Interference,* her great-grandmother had said, and Namior's mind kept flitting back to the strange new island that had appeared in their waters.

With the Moon Temple full, Namior at last began to feel she had done everything she could. Several carers were administering potions to the sick and injured, and another trainee healer was going about fixing minor injuries, concussions and shock. Namior saw the boy's unsettled look as well, but she did not talk to him. Enough had gone wrong without making their fears solid.

What she craved most was a return to her home, some of her mother's fishtail bakkett, then sleep. But she knew that was selfish, and unlikely. However tired she felt, events would not let her rest, and the more she healed and the more weary she became, the stronger her sense of duty to the people of Pavmouth Breaks.

When three men arrived, pulling a cart loaded with several injured people, they told her that the village's main healer had been killed in a landslide upriver. That settled Namior's mind. After checking that the men were healthy, and assessing the wounded in the cart as all bearing minor injuries, she set off down toward the harbor. People had come from there telling of dozens of wounded, and hundreds more searching the ruins for any survivors. That was where Namior was needed most.

And then, there were the visitors. Scared though she was, her unrelenting sense of curiosity was urging her to go and see them.

So tall, one woman said, *and their clothes are so fine!*

Streaming ashore, another report came. *A hundred visitors now, some of them digging and searching for survivors, others already starting repair work to the bridge and some buildings.*

Machines! one young boy gushed. *Machines like you've never seen before!*

That boy's enthusiasm stuck with Namior, and disturbed her. As Noreela's magic seemed to be disturbed and drawing away, so the visitors had apparently brought their own. It chilled and terrified her, but it fascinated her as well.

"Mourner Kanthia," she said. The Mourner was sitting outside, staring at the row of dead bodies as though waiting for them to stir once more. There were several gaps in the line where families had claimed their own, and Namior could already smell the unmistakable scent of funeral pyres rising across the village.

"Namior. You've done your family proud today."

"Thank you, Mourner Kanthia." Kanthia always spooked her; she would likely chant Namior's poor great-grandmother's wraith down into the Black someday soon. But her pronouncement made Namior tingle with gratitude. "Your eyes...?"

The Mourner waved a hand. "I see nothing. A blow to the head did that, but perhaps it was a blessing. There's little to see now the sea's washed us away. And the wraiths..." She raised her face and looked up at Namior. "In blindness, I see them clearer than ever."

"Perhaps it will fade," Namior said. "But now, Mourner Kanthia, I feel I'm needed down at the harbor."

"Yes," Kanthia said. "Of course. Plenty of work for you there, girl. But don't wear yourself out."

"I can keep healing."

"I'm sure. But magic is hesitant today."

"Hesitant?" Namior asked. But she already knew what the old woman meant.

Kanthia's dour face was even more serious than usual. And she shook her head, as if to say anything more would be unwise.

Namior left, following in Kel's footsteps from earlier. On the undermined path, there were people going back and forth with food, water and tools. When she stopped one of them, the man looked startled, as if he had not even seen her.

"What's happening at the harbor?" she asked.

"They're here," the man said. He pointed downriver at the broken bridge. "I can see them there, building and mending. One of them smiled at me, I think. But I'm staying on this side, helping down at the seafront. I don't feel . . ."

"Safe?" Namior asked.

"Ready," the man said. "They look just like us, but I don't feel ready to meet them yet."

Namior nodded and went to say more, but the man turned and continued on his way. He wore a set of backpack straps hung with several full skins of water, and he was sweating under the load.

She followed him along the path, heading toward the bridge. She kept pace behind him, noticing how he walked with his head down, avoiding looking across at the harbor, the destruction, the visitors. Two women hurried from the opposite direction, passing the bridge from the northern shores. Each carried a small baby in a sling across her chest, and the man ignored them both.

"How bad is it around there?" Namior asked when they drew level. One of the babies was crying, but she was glad to see that neither was hurt. Both women had also been crying.

"Just like here," one of them said, nodding across the river. "But none of *them* are there yet."

"I'm going over," Namior said.

"You're the healer witch, aren't you?" the second woman asked.

Namior nodded.

"You and your family . . . what have you seen? What do you know?"

"About the visitors, very little. The storm and the waves have made things difficult. The land has suffered a blow, and its language has become confused."

"Magic is confused?" the first woman said, skeptical. "The waves did that?" Her child stopped crying and looked at Namior, as though silently asking the same question.

"They're helping," Namior said. She looked at the babies again and smiled. "Take your children somewhere safe. They look tired."

The women left, but she could feel the air of suspicion and uncertainty they had left behind. She breathed in and it tasted of the sea. Dead things decaying.

Where the bridge began, Namior paused for a moment and watched what was happening across the river. It seemed that, more than ever, the waterway cut Pavmouth Breaks in two. On the near side was destruction and death, with the residents hurrying around like frightened insects as they tried to start the recovery process. On the other side the destruction was even worse, but already there was an air of organization. And as she looked along the bridge at the smashed span, she caught her breath with surprise.

Three visitors were there, tending to the wounds in the bridge. And they had their machines with them. Two of them floated way above the ground, obviously not in contact with it at all. The size of people, the machines were shiny and light, as though made of glass, and every now and then they vented some clear gas at the air with a small *hiss*, audible from that distance even above the flow of the river. They dipped down at the mountain of debris piled against the bridge and lifted out branches, rocks and parts of buildings as though the detritus weighed nothing at all. Their arms were made of the same material and also vented gas.

The third machine worked on the bridge's surface. It was larger and more solid-looking, but still it vented at the air, more frequently than its flying counterparts. It ran on wheels connected by heavy chains, and its body seemed to be formed from sleek, smooth metal. There were several lifting arms, all of them working in concert. Wreckage had been pushed aside against the bridge parapets, and the machine seemed to be laying a series of long, metallic supports across the ruptured span. It was not clear where the supports had come from, and they were forged from a bluish metal Namior did not recognize.

The visitors each concentrated on one machine, and in their hands they held small devices that reminded Namior of the voice carriers she and Kel used to communicate. Their fingers moved, though from where she was Namior could not make out exactly what they were doing, and small puffs of gas issued from the undersides of these handheld objects. *Controlling their machines like our Practitioners*, Namior thought, pleased at her leap of logic. *It's like they're using voice carriers to tell their machines what to do. But…such machines! Just who are these people?*

She had never seen such machines before. They seemed independent of the land, and she saw no ground rods in sight. So where did their magic originate?

One of the visitors saw her watching. The woman was dressed in fine-looking attire: leather jacket and woollen trousers, with polished buttons and clips.

Namior offered a hesitant smile.

The woman beamed back at her, lifting a hand from the device and waving. One of the floating machines drifted slightly to the side, tilting and almost dropping the heavy branch it carried. The woman rolled her eyes skyward and quickly touched and tweaked the thing in her other hand. The machine vented two spurts of gas and righted itself.

It's all magic, Namior thought, *though they use it differently. Just magic.* Trying very hard to convince herself, she took her first hesitant steps out onto the bridge.

The silt and muck deposited on the bridge's surface had developed a thin crust, and most of the way she walked on it without breaking through. In those few places where the surface did rupture, she cringed at the smell that wafted up. It was not quite rot, though she knew she would be smelling that soon, but a heady reminder of the sea.

Closer to the break in the bridge, where the backwash had cleared all the muck away, she saw the bodies placed carefully on the other side. The visitors must have lifted them from where they were tangled in the mess, placing them gently on the bridge with their hands crossed on their stomachs. There were four corpses, mostly naked, battered, torn. Namior hoped she did not know them.

A floating machine hissed clear gas, lifting above parapet level with a twist of broken metal in its grasp. Hinged limbs hung from the ruin, and Namior recognized it as a part of a dead machine. Its fleshy parts, once existing beneath the limbs and around the shelf of its stone shell, were already swollen with rot. The visitor's machine lifted it delicately aside, then dipped down below the bridge once more.

Namior stopped a few paces from the gap in the bridge, spanned now by several long metal struts. The crawling machine working across the collapsed section ground to a halt, as if in deference to her, and a visitor lowered his hands and briefly bowed his head.

"It's safe to cross," he said, looking up at Namior again. He swung the controller box by his side and smiled softly. Namior was surprised to see nervousness in his expression. It gave her a burst of confidence.

She looked down at the space where the bridge had fallen away. The river raged ten steps below, still heavy with silt and wreckage, and there was no sign of the blocks of stone that had been smashed away by the waves. The new struts were spaced a step apart, and each one was just wider than her foot. She could walk across two adjacent struts, and if she stumbled, she would be able to spread her arms and land safely. But if that failed and she *did* slip through, the angry river would carry her into the harbor, and perhaps out to sea. She looked in that direction and saw several of the visitors' boats bobbing at anchor.

"He's right, I've walked it myself many times." This came from the woman who had waved to her. She had long raven hair, tied in a bunch across one shoulder. Her jacket was beautifully stitched, trousers well fitting, and she wore fine brown gloves. She waved her fingers slightly across the controller in her left hand, and one of the motionless machines rose and snapped two long arms at the air. "And if you *did* fall, I'd catch you."

"You speak perfect Noreelan," Namior said.

"Of course!"

"Those machines... I don't recognize how they work."

"Come across and I'll show you," said the woman. "It's only steam." She walked out along the metal struts, placing her feet without even looking down. When she got halfway she turned, performed a small bow and walked back.

Namior could not help smiling. Whether they were reassuring her or making fun, she got the message. She walked across, moving fluidly but carefully, placing her feet on the struts and feeling a surprising amount of grip. The metal seemed to display many colors as the sun reflected from it, like a boat's lamp oil spilled into the sea.

When she reached the other side, the woman was holding out her hand, her machine hovering in a haze of steam. Namior took it.

I'm touching a visitor, she thought. *And it feels no different from touching a Noreelan.* The two other visitors, both men, threw curious glances her way, but they continued controlling their machines.

"What's that?" Namior asked, pointing to the smooth box in the woman's hand. "Do you control them with that? What's the steam for? How can they still work without touching the land?"

The woman laughed, but it was a restrained sound. "It's as much as we can do," she said, "but it's nowhere near enough."

"Where are you from?" Namior asked. She looked over the woman's shoulder at the island, and back again.

"The island," the woman said.

"I don't understand."

The visitor shook her head, smiling softly. "We'll do our best to change that," she said, "but that must come from our emissary, Keera Kashoomie. This has...happened before. Trying to explain to individual people simply lets rumors loose, and the details get changed in the telling."

"It's a terrible thing that's happened here," the man controlling the crawling machine said. He looked down at the controller in his hands, then up again at Namior. He almost seemed to be crying. "But you have to believe this: we mean no harm. We're cursed, and—"

"The emissary," the woman cut in, glancing at the man. "She has been talking with your village Chief. I'm sure by now they'll have decided how best to address everyone."

Namior looked upriver to where the landscape of the village had changed so terribly. "You mean us no harm," she said.

Seeing the shamefaced way the men and woman averted their eyes, it was something she could believe.

SHE WATCHED THEM working for a while. It soon became clear that the visitors possessed the intentions and ideas, and the machines were simply the tools they were using. It was much like the use of Noreelan machines, except that the constructs had every single movement controlled directly through the devices in the visitors' hands. If one of the controllers' fingers slipped, the machine would skip sideways or turn the wrong way. The machines also looked very different; they were made of metal, with no stone, wood or flesh-and-blood parts visible at all. Their joints were fine, their surfaces smooth. Namior guessed that they were metal through and through.

The steam they issued was odorless, colorless and tasteless. She had no idea how it was heated. For the moment, she simply watched.

They lifted and moved aside debris from against the

bridge, and the crawler slid more metal planks out across the gap, pulling them together and fixing them with dabs of molten metal from its longest limb. Their controllers were calm, silent and concentrated, and though aware of Namior's presence, none became talkative.

Soon she started to wonder what would be occurring closer to the harbor. She bade farewell, and the man and woman who had talked to her both nodded formally and returned to working on the bridge. Already they were chiseling and shaping stones plucked from the riverbed by the floating machines, placing them atop the new metallic supports and forming a repaired surface where the bridge had been washed away. How permanent it would be Namior did not know, but it would bring the two sides of the village together once again. And in the aftermath of the worst calamity ever to befall Pavmouth Breaks, that was important.

As she walked from the bridge and onto the harbor side, she paused for a beat. The harbor had become a completely different place. Most of the buildings were gone, and those that remained in some form were all but unrecognizable. A layer of dirt and silt coated everything. People worked everywhere, digging and lifting and crying, and close to the sea was an area of cleared ground where the bodies were being placed. One of the village's more strident worshippers of the Sleeping Gods sat beside them, and Namior could see his lips moving as he tried to chant their wraiths down into the Black. But he was no Mourner. Pale and weak, he looked close to collapse. *So where are your Gods?* she thought, perhaps unfairly. It was said that the Sleeping Gods would return at the hour of Noreela's greatest need, but they had yet to come.

The visitors were everywhere. Small groups of them worked here and there, guiding their strange steam-venting machines to lift, drag and dig. The survivors from Pavmouth Breaks were searching just as hard, but now two groups worked together. The shock was great, Namior knew, and trust would be hard-earned.

Out along the mole, visitors worked at the smashed stonework, readying it for more of their boats to dock.

She looked for Kel, but he was nowhere to be seen.

"Namior!"

"Mell!" She ran to her friend as she emerged from between two tumbled buildings, and as they hugged, Namior could feel the tears burning her eyes. They streamed down her face, and she slumped into Mell's strong embrace, taking selfish comfort in the knowledge that her friend was still alive. She smelled of sweat and the sea.

"Trakis?" she asked. "Tell me he's safe, tell me you and he—" But she pulled back and saw the terrible truth in Mell's face.

Her gaze was drawn back to the pile of bodies.

"Not there, Namior," Mell said softly. "I don't know where he is. But not there. Kel?"

"Down here somewhere, thank the Black. Your parents?"

Mell nodded over her shoulder. "I took them up to one of the farms. They'd found their way up onto the foot of Drakeman's Hill, somehow, and I wanted them away from here. Those boats, that island. Didn't like the look of them."

"And now?" Namior asked. She stood on her own again, and only then could she see the need for comfort in Mell's eyes as well.

Mell looked around at the visitors and their machines. "Now I'm not so sure."

"How did you and Trakis get split up?"

"Just before the second big wave hit. We managed to get across the smashed bridge, climbing over the trees and debris already jammed against it from upriver. The river was wild. Mud, trees, bodies, animals, and there were lots of things washed up from the sea back then, both living and dead. I'm sure I saw the *Fiddleback*."

"The trawler?"

Mell nodded. "I know, it went down ten years ago. But it came in on the surge and went out again. Battered and broken, and it could do with a dash of paint, but..." She smiled weakly, shaking her head. "Anyway, we heard the second wave coming in. I thought we were dead, but Trakis insisted we run. We waded through mud, swam through pools of water where there used to be buildings, and we reached the Rettaro Fish Market."

"The basement?"

"It was flooded, but Trakis pulled me down. Next thing I knew the metal door was shut and I was down there, breathing in an air pocket, and it sounded like the whole world was ending above me. It went on forever. The impact was so heavy that there were waves in the basement, and there were a thousand fish down there with me, dead and living. The stink of it, the feel of the place... But the door held. And when I calmed down enough so that I could think straight again, and I managed to get back across to the door, I couldn't find Trakis anywhere."

"He didn't get in with you?"

"I *thought* he did." Mell looked past Namior and out to sea, staring at the island. She was frowning. "I *thought* I'd seen him drop in, turn and fight with the door clasps. But now, I think not. Maybe he couldn't pull the door shut from the inside, there was lots of mud and..."

Namior held her friend, and this time she was the one comforting and stroking hair as tears came from someone else.

"It was quick," Namior said. "Think that, at least."

"But he's gone... swept away... What of his wraith?"

"We'll find him. We'll chant him down together."

"I don't know how to do it."

Neither do I, Namior almost said, but Mell did not need to hear that just then.

As she hugged her friend and looked around for any sign of Kel, she saw a group of people emerging from the razed buildings around the altered base of Drakeman's Hill. Several militia accompanied them, and there were at least as many visitors, armed with long swords strapped to their legs. In their midst she saw Chief Eildan and a tall, striking woman walking by his side.

"Something's happening," Namior said. "Maybe now's the time for answers."

Mell wiped her eyes and looked. "I hope so. And I hope the answers are good ones. Though if they're not, there's really not much we can do about it."

Namior knew that Mell was right. The visitors were digging and rescuing, searching and helping, using their machines to rebuild essential structures like the bridge and mole. But they were present in numbers that could effectively subdue whatever remained of the Pavmouth Breaks militia, if the need arose. And the full capability of their strange steam machines was far from clear.

She wondered where Kel had gone. She was certain that he'd want to hear this.

EILDAN USED A whalebone horn to call attention. He and his entourage stood on the harborside, twenty steps along from where the dead were laid out beneath the scorching afternoon sun. The Chief was standing on the back of a machine, its stubby legs extended to give him its full height. He still held his harpoon, its blunt end resting on one of the machine's wooden shoulders. It sat motionless beneath him, metallic components streaked with mud, fleshy parts shimmering wet.

For a while the digging had stopped, machines rested, and people gathered around. Namior noticed the visitors listening as well, though they kept a respectful distance. *Or they're keeping us hemmed in*, Kel would probably say. She looked for him again but saw no sign, then the Chief began to speak.

"People of Pavmouth Breaks. The sun is out and blazing hot. The sea breeze is cool, but not too cold. I'm told that the cliff hawks have left their nests and gone out to sea, so the fish shoals are many today, and close to the surface. But our village..." He looked down and rubbed at his eyes with his free hand. Even from thirty steps away, Namior saw his other hand tightening on the harpoon shaft. His knuckles grew very white. "Pavmouth Breaks has suffered a disaster the likes of which it has never felt." He looked up again, seeming stronger now that he was into the grim subject at hand. "We dig. We shift the fallen buildings, save the living, recover the dead. The language of the land helps us, as always and evermore, and our machines work while we tire. And they will keep working so long as there's a Practitioner to guide them. Our healers heal, our Mourner chants the wraiths of those lost down into the welcoming Black. We move on. Because Pavmouth Breaks is a family. And though today we have lost some of our family members, they would want us to continue."

Namior looked around to see who else was there. She knew many of them by name, and most of the others she knew by sight. And though many shed tears, it was the missing ones who broke her heart.

"The machines stagger," a voice muttered. "Magic holds back." It was Mygrette, and Namior did not like the look of the old witch. She was tired, covered with mud and streaks of blood, and she seemed somehow lessened. Her machine sat beside her, motionless and cool. *Interference*, Namior wanted to say to her, but it felt like something secret. She started making her way through the crowd, but then Eildan continued, and she paused to listen.

"This is Keera Kashoomie, of the island Komadia," Chief Eildan said. "She has her own story to tell, and her own words of comfort to offer." A murmur rose through the crowd then, anger and confusion vying for the tone, but Eildan slammed his harpoon shaft on the machine's back. "Before she speaks, I'll say this, and I ask you to hear me: Keera is an emissary from Komadia. Her grief over what has happened is deep, her sorrow consuming. And as you can already see from what is happening around you, her desire to aid us in any way possible is plain to see."

"But those machines!" someone shouted. "Not normal. Not *natural*!"

"They dug me out!" someone else called, a voice Namior did not recognize, and for a few beats other voices rose, a verbal contest of accusations and exhortations.

"Calm!" Eildan shouted. "Calm, now!" The voices faded, and the surge of the sea was the only sound awaiting Eildan's next words. "I know suspicion," he said. "And I know caution. I've told Emissary Kashoomie that we have the right to both. She agrees. But let me also say this: I am your Chief because I am a good judge of character. I am your Chief because I have seen much beyond this village. You all granted your trust in my wisdom. And I trust Keera Kashoomie."

He held out his hand as though to invite her up onto the machine with him. She smiled, took his hand and stepped up, apparently confident in standing on something that must seem strange to her.

"Emissary Kashoomie," he said. And Chief Eildan jumped down to the silt-covered ground, leaving the attention of his people on the visitor.

KEL BOON STOOD hidden away in the remains of the Blue Ray Tavern. Two walls still stood at one corner junction, almost as high as his head, and he leaned there and watched what was happening beyond. To his right there was a hollow in the muck and debris where a body had been found and recovered. A sad place now, a dead place. He'd drunk in there many times, but listen though he did, there were no echoes of happiness and laughter to be found.

He'd arrived here just as Chief Eildan emerged with his militia and the visitors. After what had happened earlier, Kel decided to stay hidden away, able to see and not be seen, hear and not be noticed. The feel of his weapons was comforting, but doubt pricked at him again. There were so many people waiting to hear what the emissary had to say, and so many visitors helping in the rescue, that the villagers' weight of suspicion seemed to have been lessened by a combined aim.

He could see Namior and Mell, and the sight of them settled his heart. Trakis's absence bit at him. But the time for discovering what had happened to his friend was not now.

Now, it was time to hear the visitors' story.

Chapter Five

broken spine

A TALL WOMAN, made taller by the machine she stood upon, Keera Kashoomie wore sadness like a cliff hawk wore the wind. She looked over the heads of the assembled Noreelans at the destruction that surrounded them. She gazed northward first, past the broken bridge and across the river, then turned slowly until she was staring at the washed-out foot of Drakeman's Hill. She might have been crying, or perhaps it was the sun casting curious shadows across her eyes. From where he watched Kel could not be sure. What he *was* sure about was the weight of expectation that held the crowd—perhaps three hundred people in total—in rapt silence.

"This has happened before," she said, "and we can never

be more sorry than the last time. If you'll allow me to tell you about ourselves, and why we're here, and how it happened, I hope you'll then accept our offer of continued help and support. This is a dreadful day for Pavmouth Breaks, and a sad day for Komadia, and we Komadians are so sorry for what has happened. But before I say anything else, I want to tell you one thing. I want you to be *sure* of it. This was not our fault. There was no intention in this."

"An accident?" someone called, scoffing.

Keera blinked, then shook her head. "No accident," she said. "No act of the land, no slip in the balance of things. But not our fault."

"Then whose fault was it?" the same voice called. The speaker was keeping himself hidden, perhaps looking at the ground so that he could not be singled out.

"We no longer know. The past for Komadia is a hazy place at best. There are scholars among us who attempt to transcribe our history, from stories passed down through families, parchments discovered in abandoned dwellings in the deepest parts of our island, and vague memories from our oldest people. But history does not like Komadia. Once recorded, it seems to change. We are never at peace, and who or whatever cursed us so long ago seemed to desire that. *None* of us are *ever* at peace."

She brushed both hands back through her hair, the sun casting a halo around her head. Kel gasped; she was beautiful. He'd never let himself see that before, even when he was cutting the shirt from her back in his search for a Stranger's proboscises. He sighed angrily. He could not let himself be distracted by that beauty. Was she using it now? Fanning her hair to bewitch the men in the crowd, and some of the women, too? But after running them through her hair she cracked her fingers, an unbecoming gesture, then looked around again.

"From the best of our knowledge, our island's origins lie beyond the farthest extremes of what you now know as The

Spine. We were once the last island in that chain, before endless seas stretching west, north and east. We were the northernmost tip of Noreela, and there's a place on our island now, on the coast, that we call The Outlook, which used to be the most northerly tip of land in our world. It has the ruins of a lookout post, and on those ancient walls are paintings of deserted, lifeless seascapes. It's a much-studied place because it hints at our origins. But even the wisest amongst us knows little. There is writing there that cannot be read, and images of things that cannot be understood."

"Land's End is the last island," someone said. Kel stretched to see who was speaking, but the crowd made single voices anonymous. That was good. It meant that people could speak their minds.

"It is now," Keera said, "and it has been for much of history. Sixty years ago, we were situated to the south of that place for a time. Thankfully, it was all but deserted then, as now, I suspect. The ripples of our arrival spread out and touched land, but there was no one there to see."

"*Ripples?*" someone shouted. Other voices rose, angry and disbelieving, but Kel also saw a few people looking around quietly, perhaps embarrassed or uneasy in their belief of the woman's outlandish tale.

Chief Eildan raised his hands and slammed the harpoon down onto the harbor stone. "We will let Emissary Kashoomie speak!" he roared, and the crowd shuffled their feet, voices lowering and mumbling in apology or acceptance. "There will be time for questions later if our visitor will entertain them?" He turned to Keera, who smiled and nodded her assent.

Eildan stepped back again, and Keera Kashoomie waited until the agitated audience settled.

"Your loss tears my heart and tortures my soul. But I wish you to hear these words, because Komadia suffers also. It is a land cursed with uncertainty. The periods between our shifting from one place and being deposited elsewhere can be a few moons, or sometimes many, many years. I have lived through five shiftings. My mother, still alive back on the island, has seen twelve.

"History has hazed the reason for such a curse, or who or what caused it. But as with any facts lost to the vagueness of time, there are stories. Some tell of a storm that came in across the sea from the north, driven by an insane water-god. The god was doomed to eternal drowning, and it craved life on land. But it could not breathe the air, and the touch of soil on its flesh was a torture. So it coveted what we had, and drove waves at the island that were so tall that they almost touched our highest hills. When the tempest abated, the island was moved into the middle of an endless ocean. Komadia's survivors sailed out, and those that found their way back had traveled a moon in every direction without seeing land. Our people felt exiled, banished by the land, and they developed a very strong sense of community in order to survive.

"Other tales tell of an ancient magician who tried to tap in to the land, many centuries before the Year of the Black gave true magic to Noreela. He opened doorways that should have remained closed, and—"

"Your machines aren't driven by magic!" someone called. Kel saw Mygrette stepping forward, her tatty robes muddied where they dragged along in the silt. "And I see no magic in you, Emissary."

"That's true. And if you'll let me finish my story, lady witch, more will become clear." A ripple of laughter spread through the crowd and Mygrette turned away. Kel was amazed at how easily Kashoomie was playing her audience.

"Back then, so it's said, this magician practiced magichala with things from the sea: creatures, spices, rock salts and toxins from some of the more poisonous inhabitants found in the waters around The Spine. He suspected a great power in the land, and he yearned to learn its language. But when he tried to speak that language, the land reacted. Komadia was cursed by magic even before magic showed itself to Noreela."

"Cursed by magic!" Mygrette spat.

"There is no magic on Komadia, you're right," Kashoomie said. "At least not as you know it. We cannot speak Noreela's language; it remains silent to us. Instead, there is technology that our engineers have developed over time, and the heat of steam drives much of what we use."

"The heat of steam?" Mygrette said. "Sheebok shit! How do you even know of magic if you've been cursed to live without it for so long?"

"Because we travel," Keera said, and her voice dropped so low that the audience had to hold their breaths to hear. Her words appeared between the hush of waves, as though singing a song in concert with the sea. "Komadia has seen many parts of Noreela down though its long history. And it has also been beyond."

She trailed off, leaving those last scintillating words hanging in the air.

Beyond, Kel thought. *Where the Strangers come from?* He shook his head. She was fabricating these tales, blinding Pavmouth Breaks to her island's real aims...and yet, if that were the case, why attempt to do so with such outlandish stories? Some would believe, because incredible legends had the power of entrancing many who saw or knew of them. But many more would go to their beds that night even more suspicious of the visitors.

Maybe it was because the truth was even more incredible.

"What's beyond?" someone asked.

Keera Kashoomie sighed. "Sea," she said. "Oceans so wide that they cannot be crossed in a lifetime. Places where islands of living creatures are the only things breaking the watery monotony. Sea, sea and more sea. You should remember, the history that I'm relaying to you can never be known for sure. Each shifting seems to distort the past, as it twists the geography of our place in the world. All but two of the shiftings I have lived through have found Noreela's coast within a moon's sailing of our own. Those remaining two...just water."

"And why would that be?" Kel called out. He stepped around the wall, exposing himself to the stares of hundreds of people, yet remaining focused on Keera. He saw Namior turn to face him but he did not acknowledge her, not yet.

"Ah, the admirer of my clothes," the emissary said.

"Why, when there is endless ocean for you to be shifted to, is Noreela more often than not so close by?"

"We can't know the reasons for sure," she said. "But our belief is that the curse is finally fading. With every shifting that happens, we begin to hope it may be the last one."

The last one, Kel thought. *And if that's the case, and any of this is true, they'll want to ensure their safety out there. Make sure there's no competition from the mainland.* He looked at Namior and returned her unsteady smile. He nodded gently, and mouthed, *Soon.*

"So we might be neighbors for a long time?" someone said.

Keera nodded. "We hope forever."

"And our dead?" someone else said. "What of our dead? Who will be their neighbors, lost in the Black?"

Keera's face fell and she clasped her hands together before her chest. "We suffer every death with you," she said earnestly. "And we've already started helping. You've seen our machines, and we promised you a share of our technology. This I will ensure comes to pass. If you will permit, more of our people can come across from Komadia with larger machines, able to dig faster and move more. And as well as technology, we have knowledge that can help. Ways to find those buried who might still be alive."

"What ways?" Kel asked.

"Tame creatures, trained to smell out trapped people."

"Because this happens a lot?" Chief Eildan asked.

Keera nodded. "We have experience and knowledge of such things, because this happens too much." She slipped down from the back of the machine, holding up her hand to fend off the press of people and the rush of questions that filled the air.

She's leaving? Kel ran forward, still carrying the blanket-covered carving beneath his arm. But he saw the emissary's guards, the women with long swords, and their eyes were on him. He had threatened Kashoomie already that day, and they would not let him close again.

"Let us visit!" he shouted. "Let some of us come to the island if you've nothing to hide." And even in the commotion, his question was heard by the crowd, and by Keera herself. Some of the villagers gathered there shouted their agreement. The emissary paused, held up her hand and looked directly at Kel.

"That cannot yet happen," she said. "Not until we're sure it's safe. We have no wish to share our curse." She walked away then, Chief Eildan strolling quickly behind her. They headed back toward the mole, and the combination of militia and visitors' guards held the crowd back.

Kel watched the emissary go. She seemed a sad figure, a woman of sorrow dressed in fine clothes.

"Kel!" Namior called. She shouldered her way through the crowd to him, Mell following, and he hugged her in with his right arm. "Kel, I wondered where you'd gone."

"Up to my rooms to fetch some things."

"That?" she asked, touching the blanket.

"For you. But later. Now, I want to see what happens next." He smiled at Mell, then looked around at the crowd, trying to assess their mood, their fears, their beliefs.

An island from The Spine? He supposed it was possible. He had once traveled as far as Rockfield during the long pursuit of a Stranger, and if he looked out at Komadia, he could see similarities in geography; a craggy coast, low hills. But an enraged water-god? A magician who had preempted the Year of the Black and magic's introduction into Noreela, sixteen centuries before?

An island that moved itself?

"What do you think?" Namior asked. Kel heard excitement in her voice, as well as fear.

"I think her story is so unbelievable that many will believe." And he hugged Namior tight to him, enjoying the feel of having someone so close.

MELL TOLD HIM her story, and the three of them spoke some sad words about Trakis, shared memories, remembering their friend beneath the heat of the sinking sun. This most terrible day in Pavmouth Breaks' history was drawing to a close.

"Dusk soon," Kel said. "The tide's coming in. We can't dig through the night."

"They'll help," Mell said. "If there's anyone left buried alive, their animals will smell them out. Maybe even Trakis, somewhere under the Rettaro Market. They're here to make amends." Kel saw an almost zealous glow in his friend's eyes, and he wondered how much of that was restrained tears over Trakis's loss.

"We need to judge on actions, not words," Kel said.

"So now you come here with your sword and you're a hard man, wood-carver?" Mell said, but there was affection in her voice.

"Cautious." Kel turned to Namior, huddled beside him and starting to shiver now that the sun was dipping toward the sea. "You're cold. And your eyes . . . you need rest, Namior."

"And you?" she asked.

"I want to think about what they've said." He had watched the visitors and Chief Eildan conversing out along the mole. They had both glanced back at the harbor, as though trying to weigh how her words had been received, and the sight of everyone returning to their rescue efforts seemed to relax them both. Eildan handed his harpoon to his militia captain Vek to hold, and Keera Kashoomie climbed back down to her docked craft.

Namior leaned into him again. "And let's not forget our little talk."

Kel grunted. *Maybe. Or maybe I should keep my past to myself, as always.*

"What are they doing?" Mell asked.

"Perhaps they're—" But an explosion stole Namior's words away. A blazing light rose on a column of smoke from the emissary's boat, powering high into the sky, exploding in a shower of green sparks that continued burning as they started a slow float back down.

Kel gasped, looking around at those distracted from their search once more. While they stared up at the guttering explosion, he looked past the mole to the island that was even then being sent a sign. *So here it comes,* he thought. *Aid, or invasion. We'll know soon enough.*

The weight of the communicators in his jacket pocket was a comfort, and a terror.

MELL GAVE THEM both a hug and went back toward Drakeman's Hill. She needed to return to her parents, she said, and tell them what had happened with Emissary Kashoomie. Though exhausted by what the night and day had brought, there was an enthusiasm to her voice that troubled Kel greatly. Mell was never quick to judge, and trust came slow to her, perhaps the result of being born and brought up in such a small place. It had taken her a long time to take to Kel. But here she was, keen to spread the words of the visitor to her loved ones, and apparently willing to accept what Kashoomie had said.

Kel told her to take care, and she nodded with a soft smile. "You too, wood-carver."

Namior was almost asleep standing up. Her hands were as cold as winter storms, and Kel pressed them together and covered them with his own.

"Kel," she said, "I need to see my family."

He nodded and hugged her tight. Every instinct told him that he should stay and help; though some people were drifting away, many more were still searching and digging, working beneath the bluish glow of floating fireballs raised by the visitors. Machines flowed here and there, both Noreelan and Komadian, and he saw Mygrette the doubter still directing her own machine against a mound of rubble, dirt and seaweed.

But he was one man with only two hands, while back with Namior's mother and great-grandmother, perhaps he could find out more about what was happening. They must have been in their home all day, aiding wounded who were brought by, and her mother attempting to scry for what might come. And while he had doubts about the magic of their land, the fact that the visitors seemed lacking in that magic hopefully put Pavmouth Breaks at an advantage. He would grasp that advantage and make sure he was prepared for whatever might happen next.

They'll sail in, help us rebuild and we'll live peacefully forevermore, he thought. *That would be nice. That's what everyone wants.*

"Then let's go back over," he said, starting to lead Namior toward the damaged bridge. He could see that the visitors had already repaired it adequately enough to make it safe, and two of them were still there, their machines venting steam at the dusk.

"I'm not sleeping yet, though," Namior said. "When we get there, you need to show me what's under the blanket."

"A gift for you." But it felt so pointless, so indulgent, in the face of what had happened. *Can I still ask her to wed me, after all this?*

"That's nice," she said, sounding unconvinced. "And after that, you need to tell me why you have a sword on your belt and other things hidden away beneath your jacket." Her voice went quieter, and when she looked up at him her eyes were as sharp as ever. "I'm not *sure* what they are. But I *think* they're weapons."

They started for the bridge, and Namior led the way.

NAMIOR WAS BEYOND exhaustion. She had practiced her healing more that day than ever before, struggling with a temperamental magic; and the emotional impact of what had happened to her village was circling and waiting to strike. She was wary of that, and she was wary of Kel Boon as well. *I still love him,* she thought. *But I no longer know him.* Piled on to the changes wrought over Pavmouth Breaks, the changes in him were almost unbearable.

She talked briefly to the raven-haired Komadian who was still repairing the bridge. One of the floating machines had moved on, but the restored span was easily negotiable now that shaped blocks had been laid across the metal struts. She sensed Kel's unease when she talked to the visitor. She wanted to ask about the machines, exactly how they worked, what the steam meant, what powered them, and the metal the visitors had used to bridge the washed-out gap. Where it was visible beside the stone blocks, the dusky light colored it gray, not the blue she had seen earlier. But tiredness made her vision hazy and dulled her senses, and the desire to see her family was stronger than ever. Perhaps it was familiarity she needed most.

They crossed the bridge and walked up toward her home, avoiding the route through the Moon Temple gardens. Neither of them had any wish to see the dead again.

Namior stumbled as they approached her home, and Kel's arms were around her, steadying and enfolding her with a warmth she could not help welcoming.

"Come inside," she said.

"You're sure?"

"Of course. I want to know what my gift might be." She

smiled at him, shocked at the way the rising life moon reflected in his eyes. He held a deep sadness that she had never noticed before. "What is it, Kel?"

"I'm lost," he said. "Lost and confused."

She touched his face and felt stubble, grit and tears. "Come inside."

Namior went first, opening the door and sighing as the usual smells of cooking washed over her. Her mother was at the rear of the main room, stirring several pots where they hung over the fire pit. When she turned and saw Namior, her smile was wide and welcoming.

"Namior!" she said. "Been a busy girl, so I hear."

"So many hurt," Namior said, and she thought to add, *So many dead.* But it did not need to be said. "How's great-grandmother?"

Her mother's smile slipped a little, and she nodded at the door leading to the staircase. "Up there. She's very tired. I've not seen her this bad since . . ."

"Ever," Namior said.

"Yes." Her mother sighed. "This craze is a strong one, and she picks at her eye, rubs her ear. As if she's trying to blind and deafen herself against what's happening."

"She'll come through. She's strong. But Mother, can I smell fishtail bakkett? Can Kel stay for some?"

"Assumed he would. Enough for everyone."

"Thank you," Kel said. The woman looked at him and offered a brief smile.

"What else is wrong?" Namior asked.

Her mother waved one hand as though at a worrisome fly, but this time she did not turn away from her cooking. "Hard day. Lots of pain around today, plenty of grief, and the wraiths of people we know waiting to be chanted down. Many died in their sleep . . . don't know they're dead."

"That's not fair," Namior said. She sat on a large cushion, and Kel knelt beside her, leaning in until their shoulders touched.

"We'll lead Mourner Kanthia to them, once she's chanted down the ones she knows about."

"And what else?" Kel asked. "What did the groundstone show you today?"

"Taking an interest in our old magic now, Kel?"

"The visitors have told us their version of where they came from, what's happened to them, why they're here. I'm just curious if it's the truth."

"Curious." She stopped stirring and looked Kel in the eye. "Just curious?"

"It's a terrible day," he said.

"And why would I know the truth or lie of it?" She sounded suddenly defensive, and Namior started to rise. Her mother sighed and waved her down. "Rest, girl. It was difficult to scry today, that's all. Hazed. Lots of interference."

"You think maybe the visitors—?"

"The land's suffered an injury. That island . . ."

"They call it Komadia," Namior said.

"Whatever they name it, it's bruised our land, wounded it. And it'll take time for it to recover."

"You talk as though it's a living thing," Kel said.

Namior touched his arm and squeezed, and her mother glared at him. "You think it isn't, wood-carver? You cut the limbs from trees and make fancies from them, and you tell me the land isn't alive?"

Kel did not respond, and for that Namior was grateful. She was too tired to witness an argument.

The woman stirred her fish stew, testing it and dropping in a minute pinch of some herb or spice from a pouch on the wall. "So, we've had visitors all day long, and we've seen and heard much of what's happening. Did you see any more boats coming in as you came home?"

"No," Namior said, though in truth she could not even recall looking out to sea. The cobbled streets, the moss-covered stone walls, the undamaged buildings and herb-filled gardens had been so familiar that she had barely taken her eyes from them. Normality had struck her, warm and safe, and she had not wished to lose it again that evening.

"Hmm. They'll wait 'til morning, probably. Look too suspicious coming in through the night."

The conversation cooled, and they sat in silence as the stew cooked. Namior looked at the groundstone, smoothed by generations of her family's hands, and she resisted the temptation to touch it. She was tired, and the land was wounded. She needed food and rest if she was to face the morning strong and ready to begin healing once again.

"I need to wash and change," she said. "Will you call up to us when the food is ready?"

Her mother glanced from Namior to Kel, and back again. She nodded. "But I used the last of the hot water to clean the fish."

Namior stood, reached out for Kel and led him upstairs.

The stairs creaked slightly, but the house had been built strong many centuries ago, and they walked silently along the landing. Her great-grandmother's door was open a crack and Namior glanced in, keen to see the old mother's face one time before resting for the night. She lay on the bed with her hands twisted on her chest, her mouth slightly open. She mumbled in her sleep. A rush of love hit Namior, and a familiar sense of the fragility of things. So many people in Pavmouth Breaks could not look at their loved ones' faces tonight, and there were many mothers whose children were dead. But she was too tired to cry.

She led the way up the narrow staircase to her attic room, and once inside she closed the door, lit the oil lamp and sat gently on the bed. Its creaks were familiar to her, and many times she and Kel had stirred those creaks together. But that suddenly seemed so very long ago.

He stood inside the door, awkward, and her sadness deepened at the realization that he too felt this new distance.

"So what have you made me, Kel Boon?"

The wood-carver sat on a chair in the corner of her room, placed the gift on the floor and pulled the blanket from it.

Namior gasped. *Beautiful,* she thought, and for a moment the cliff hawk seemed to shift. She glanced at the oil lamp to see if the flame was steady, and when she looked back the carving was motionless again. She blinked, but there were no tears. *Tiredness is fooling me.*

"Wellburr wood," Kel said, obviously keen to fill the silence. "It cuts cleanly, and the sap stays fresh for many moons after it's taken. It feeds itself. It likes the chisel and the knife. If you look at it in just the right light..." He picked up the carving and stood beside the oil lamp, turning it this way and that. "Can you see the shadows? The depth?"

"Beautiful," Namior said. "Very beautiful."

Kel shrugged. He'd always been embarrassed when she complimented him on his carvings even though he took great pride in them. "It's not finished. The beak's not quite right, the claws are thicker than they should be. The wing tips need to be more pronounced. I had a couple of evenings' work to do on it, but...today seemed like the right time."

"It did?"

Kel really stared at her then, and she could tell from his eyes that he was fighting with something inside. He clenched his jaw, then came to her and handed her the carving.

She took it, surprised at how heavy it was, and how cool. Maybe that was the sap, still fresh. She turned it this way and that, trying to take it all in, but Kel stood over her and blocked out most of the light. *Whatever he has to say, maybe he needs a little nudge.*

Namior looked up between the cliff hawk's spread wings. "So tell me who you really are."

Kel sighed, and all the tension seemed to drain from him. He backed up a couple of steps and sat heavily into the corner chair again, resting his head back against the wall. He seemed to be staring at the ceiling, and Namior saw the flicker of light and shadow play over the cracked paintwork. She and Kel would be seeing completely different shapes.

Kel popped the buttons on his jacket and opened it. He touched the handles of weapons she did not know, not threateningly, but so that she saw. Then he closed his eyes and took several deep breaths.

After a few beats, with his eyes still closed, Namior thought he'd gone to sleep. She put the carving gently on the floor and touched the hawk's head, running her fingers across the wonderfully realized bone crest across its skull. It was used to crack the shells of large molluscs, and each crest was unique, a distinct mark of identity. *This is a hawk that never was*, she thought.

When she looked up again, Kel was staring at her.

"I'm Kel Boon," he said. "I'm the man you met five years ago in the Blue Ray Tavern, carving a set of wine tankards for the landlord. You watched me all night, as I carved and drank ale. I saw you watching, and you knew that I saw, but we played the game of not noticing. I wanted you to come closer, and you were fascinated by what I was doing. Seabed Kine... a strange wood, that should never be able to grow beneath the waves. But it does, and it's the hardest wood there is to carve. Almost as hard as stone. And it has the remnants of things long dead set in it, as if they died and the wood grew around them, way down at the bottom of the sea. So each tankard is unique and has the polished sections of dead things cast into it."

Namior remembered that night, and she flushed with embarrassment. She hoped it would not show in the lamplight.

"You came to me at the end of the night. I'd finished three tankards by then, and the landlord had paid me with food and ale for the evening. A good trade. You told me you'd never seen me there before, and you asked if I was a sailor. I said no, I'm a wood-carver, I'm Kel Boon. We met and drank together the next night, and I started to fall in love with you. That's who I really am. I'm Kel Boon."

"Then Kel Boon," Namior said, because her flush had gone cold, and she was becoming sure that he was playing her emotions, "tell me who you were *before* you started carving those tankards."

In the soft light his eyes seemed suddenly lifeless. Then she realized that he was looking at something much farther away than her, and the room, and what they had both been through that day. He was searching for himself in the past, so that he could introduce that person to his love here and now.

"I've killed people," he said. "Those I've killed directly weren't from Noreela, and they wished us harm. Some I've killed indirectly, or let die because of my actions, and they *were* Noreelans. They were the people I was trying to help, and some were people I cared about. And that matters more." He touched his thigh, tapping something metallic beneath his trousers as though drawing strength from it. "And that's the worst you need to know about me."

"The worst?" Namior said. The words he had spoken were gaining weight. "What could *be* any worse?"

Kel frowned, leaned forward and rested his elbows on his knees. His hands hung limp, still filthy from the work they had done. Perhaps they were stained with blood.

"I'm going to tell you a secret, because I love you. I could be killed for telling you this, but the Core want me dead anyway because I deserted them. I left because of a mistake I made. I was too weak to deal with it, and I thought that abandoning my cause...leaving behind everything that had meant so much to me, everything I was passionate about..." He shook his head, as though shuffling thoughts so that he could find a place to begin, or perhaps somewhere to end.

"Tell me about the Core," Namior said. She no longer felt tired.

"We number only in the hundreds, all across Noreela. We hunt down, follow and eventually kill people from beyond Noreela. We call them Strangers, because we have no other name for them. We know no more of their origins now than the original Core did four hundred years ago.

"Duke Melkar of Cantrassa formed the Core, because he and his witches had come to suspect a steady ingress of people arriving from beyond the seas. They'd disembark at Conbarma, usually from ships incoming from The Spine, then fan out across the Cantrass Plains. He created a group of thirty men and women—soldiers, Practitioners, witches—to find out more. When one of the Strangers was killed in a fight at the Conbarma harbor...Well, with the mystery of his death, a lot more became clear."

"What happened?" Namior asked. His mention of The Spine had struck her, but he did not appear to make any connection between what he was talking about and the story Kashoomie had told earlier.

"When a Stranger dies, his or her wraith bursts from the body. It's visible for a short time, and during that time it's deadly. It destroys anything of flesh and blood it touches. Then it settles over the Stranger's body and burns it away to nothing."

"And they look exactly like us?"

"Almost. There are...differences." Kel rubbed his face with both hands, glancing at Namior between his fingers. *Seeing whether I'm believing this,* she thought. *Whether it'll change anything between us.* She nodded for him to continue.

"That first death started a purge. Duke Melkar expanded the Core from thirty to three hundred, every one of them sworn to complete secrecy. He said that if the truth of what they had found got out—that there were people, *things*, from beyond Noreela—it would change everything. He was right then, and the same applies now. Can you imagine if the truth were known? Most Noreelans exist in their own small world, and even those who have open minds rarely think beyond the island. There are the Shantasi, but Shanti was close by and known about, even when it was destroyed many centuries ago.

Other than that . . . ? Everyone thinks we're alone. Noreela is a big enough world for most people."

"And the Core is as big as it ever was?"

"Bigger, if anything. When the purge began, over a hundred Strangers were tracked and killed, then the duke was murdered in his bed. The killer never caught. Quite apt.

"The Core members vowed to continue their mission, and through the years there has always been a cabal that ensures the numbers are made up. They found me when I was eighteen. I was traveling through the Pengulfin Woods at the time, on my own, heading nowhere. I witnessed a Stranger's execution. The woman who performed it, a Shantasi called O'Peeria, jumped me and held a knife to my throat. And she gave me a choice."

"Not much of a choice."

Kel smiled. "At the time, I thought I was one of the luckiest men alive. I'd always respected the old Voyagers, read a lot about their journeys and discoveries. And I was already starting to despair of finding anything that would equal that for me. This . . . the Core . . . To begin with, I thought it was an adventure." His eyes were distant again, and Namior could sense that he still carried the name of the Shantasi O'Peeria inside. Perhaps she'd ask him about her one day . . . but not yet.

"You don't think the Komadians are the Strangers you've hunted? I heard about what happened at the harbor, what you did to Kashoomie."

Kel raised his eyebrows.

"It's a small village, Kel. And I've lived here all my life."

He smiled sadly, fidgeting in the chair. "She's not a Stranger, no. But at the same time . . ." He shrugged. "For me, her story just doesn't carry the ring of truth. What they've done, what they're doing here now . . . I can't help being suspicious."

"But there's no sign that they're connected with your Strangers?"

"Nothing overt. But then, they say their island has been doing this for a long time. Have you ever heard of it? Any legends, stories, rumors of an island that appears from out of nowhere? Back in the main library of Noreela City, I spent a long time one summer studying old maps and charts, some of them drawn up by the ancient Voyagers. None of them *ever* mentioned another island beyond Land's End in The Spine. Not one map taken as accurate, and not even any of those assumed to be fanciful. And I know from people far older and wiser than I that much of Noreela's history is documented in that library, and much of its mythology originates from there. If her story is true, there'd be some evidence somewhere, don't you think?"

Yes, Namior thought, *you're right*. But he was talking about the Core, and she knew there was more.

"And in all these years of the Core, the truth has never emerged? No one has spoken?"

"Oh, they have," said Kel, his tone growing darker still. "People have tried to leave the Core and spread the truth. But the Core cabal have their own separate group of mercenaries, and they pay handsomely to have any absconders hunted down and killed. And if it takes a moon or two to find them?" He waved his hands. "Any stories they have told are usually treated as fabrication, myth, madness. Campfire tales is what O'Peeria once called them."

"And now you're an absconder?"

Kel nodded. "Pavmouth Breaks seemed such a safe place," he said. "Isolated, self-contained, small. Nine out of ten Noreelans have probably never even heard of us. And the more time goes by, the more I've started to think—to *hope*—that they've forgotten about me. It's not as if I'm shouting to anyone who'll listen about invaders with gills and lightning-sparking spines growing from their backs."

"Not everyone. Only me."

"Only you."

Namior lay back on her bed and looked at the ceiling,

trying to absorb what Kel had told her. *I believe every word.* She wished she did not, because it terrified her utterly.

"Do you want to contact them?"

"I've thought about it," Kel said. "I have. And though I can't contact them directly, I have the means to call them here."

Namior sat up, and however serious their conversation, she could not hold back a wry smile. "Magic, Kel Boon?"

"Magic." He tapped his jacket pocket, and she wondered just what he carried in there.

"So why don't you?"

"Because if I'm wrong, and Keera Kashoomie's story *is* true, I'll bring the Core here for nothing. And if I'm still here when they discover it was a wasted trip, then they'll definitely kill me."

Namior nodded. "And me."

"Only if they know I told you all this." He leaned forward in his chair, hands clasped before him like a worshipper beseeching the moons. "So don't repeat *anything* of this to *anyone.* Not your mother, not Mell. *Anyone.*"

"Just in case your suspicions prove wrong."

"Just in case." He nodded and sat back.

Namior's mother called up the stairs, and the smell of food seemed to follow her voice. Namior heard her great-grandmother stirring, and Kel sighed as though happy the conversation was over.

Or almost over.

"So how are you going to settle this?" she asked.

He stood and came to her, hoping she would also rise and be close to him. But she did not think she could do that, not yet. He was a different man, and though she loved him, and love involved learning, she'd been given too much in one fell swoop.

"There's only one way I can," he said at last. "Tomorrow, I'm going out to the island to see for myself."

THEY ATE THE fishtail bakkett, and it was wondrous. Kel
didn't trust magic, but he always trusted witches to know how
to cook. They were in tune with the land, and the fruits,
spices and herbs it offered up were a vital part of a witch's
training.

Namior's mother asked about what had happened that
day, most of her questions directed to Namior. Kel had the
feeling she already knew much of what had occurred, and
that she was simply enjoying the communication with her
daughter.

The older woman sat with them, ate with them, but her
good eye was bloodshot and distant. She paused frequently
and muttered something at her soup. As soon as she was finished, she closed her eyes and snored softly at the table.

After eating, Namior and Kel went outside for some fresh
air. Namior filled a long bone pipe with aromatic leaves and a
blend of dried roots, and she smoked it while the two of them
leaned against a wall and looked down at the harbor. There
were lights on down there, though not nearly as many as there
would have been only a night ago, and most bobbed in the
darkness. Kel guessed they were on the backs of Komadian
machines. Farther out to sea he could see the shipping lights
of the visitors' boats, though there was no sign of any more
vessels coming in. The island was silhouetted against the horizon, and he could see the speckled lights of settlements along
its coastline. The hills at its heart were dark.

"How will you get out there?" Namior asked, her gaze following his.

"I don't know. Most of Pavmouth Breaks' boats have been
smashed, but perhaps I'll find some upriver that are still seaworthy."

"If you sail down the river and out to the island, you'll be
seen."

*It should be so easy. But as well as crippling the village, the
waves stranded us as well.* "I'll find a way," he said. "Find a
boat, drag it overland, launch from farther along the coast."

Namior puffed at her pipe and offered it to Kel. He had never smoked. *If you smoke, you stink*, had always been his mantra. But if he took a considered breath just then, he knew he already stank of sweat, grime and the muck of disaster.

"I can help," Namior said.

"What?"

"I can cast a concealment spell. It won't make us invisible, but it'll deflect attention from—"

"Us? You're not coming with me." He cringed at his tone. But he had no wish to place Namior in peril.

"Why?" she asked. "Too dangerous for a woman?"

"You know I don't think at all like that, Namior."

She sighed smoke. "I know. But what's your reason for me not to go?"

"I'm the soldier."

"Oh. And just a while ago, you were the wood-carver I met."

"I still am. The cliff hawk should show you that."

Namior was silent for a while, smoking and looking down at the harbor, then up at Drakeman's Hill facing them across the river. That place at least looked as it had before the disaster, though there were more lights than usual at that time of night. Not many people could sleep, it seemed.

"All things considered, Kel, I'm more trusting than you are. I've seen no harm in these visitors, and the thought of going out to the island ... it excites me, it doesn't scare me. And I *can* help you get out there. If there's danger, we come back and you save me. Big soldier saves little woman."

Kel could not help laughing softly. "Stop with that, will you?"

"Well ..."

"What of the interference?"

"Hopefully that'll be settled by tomorrow," she said, and Kel saw smoke rings parting and interlocking again before her.

"In the morning," he said, "we'll go back to the harbor

together and see what's happening. Maybe with a night between us and the disaster, it'll be easier to judge."

"Time cures all?"

Does it? Kel thought of O'Peeria, and the children he had seen slaughtered, and he knew that was not the case at all. He blamed himself for their deaths as much as he had the moment he had witnessed it happen.

"The morning," he said.

"Very well," Namior said. "But you'll stay here tonight?"

He bowed his head and leaned forward, resting his forehead against hers. He was glad that she did not pull away. He smelled the familiar evening smoke on her breath, but for a change it was exotic and forbidden. *Time sometimes doesn't heal, but with every beat it changes.*

"Thank you, witch."

"Don't mention it, wood-carving soldier."

THEY WERE BOTH exhausted, physically and emotionally, and he thought they'd quickly fall asleep. But they stripped beneath the gaze of the unfinished cliff hawk, washed each other with water warmed by a spell from Namior, and the cleaner they became, the more their tiredness evaporated. Their breathing grew shallower and faster, and Namior took Kel in her hand, stroking and teasing as she pulled him to the bed.

He knelt and kissed her between the legs, and in her sighs of pleasure he heard an acceptance of the new Kel Boon, soldier *and* wood-carver. When they made love, everything but the two of them vanished.

Afterward, as they drifted to sleep beside each other, Kel thought of what he had intended asking Namior when he gave her the carving. But, the time for that had passed.

Chapter Six

containing the curse

SHE'S A FUCKING teacher," O'Peeria says. "Has been for ten moons. Who knows what shit she's been forcing into those children's minds? Curse her, this one hid *really* well."

They're riding a transport machine through the streets of Melute, thirty miles south of Long Marrakash. They're due to meet four more Core members to prepare for the killing. The air is heavy with snow, and the wheels wash through a sludge of icy mud and horseshit. It's so cold that Kel can feel the skin of his face hardening every time he exhales.

They share the transport with several other people, none of whom seem to know each other. The Practitioner sits at the rear of the machine, apparently comfortable in a haze of heat issued from vents along the construct's back. Kel wonders why the heat can't be shared. The Practitioner looks at him with hooded, yellowed eyes, and he recognizes the gaze of a fledge addict.

"We need to get the children away first," Kel says.

"Of course," O'Peeria says, as though it's a minor concern. For her, catching and killing the Stranger is the only important factor. She's said before that a few innocent deaths is a small price to pay. Most Strangers are there to infiltrate and collect information, as far as the Core knows. But it's ones like the teacher, who have been there for some time and insinuated themselves into a Noreelan community, that trouble them the most.

With O'Peeria, it is pure hatred.

Kel glances at her. There's a fine frost collected on her eyelashes and the light hairs across her upper lip. She's very beautiful, and he remembers her from the previous night, squatting above him and guiding him inside her. She had unbraided her dark hair and let it fall across her pale Shantasi body, and though she rode him, there had been a vulnerability about her that made him love her, just a little. They have known each other for six years, and last night was their first time.

This morning she rose, washed, dressed, and strapped on her weapons without saying a thing about what happened, and now she is the usual stern O'Peeria once again.

"O'Peeria . . ." Kel says.

She turns to him, and the ice is reflected in her eyes. "Later, Kel. After I've slit the throat of this sheebok-bitching Stranger." And she looks more excited and involved than she ever did with him.

When they reach the school, it has already begun. Children are streaming from the long, low building, running terrified in all directions, and Kel tries to guide them across the street into a leather store. O'Peeria curses and runs for the school, pulling her sword. The windows blow outward, and the familiar, dreadful blue light sizzles, crawling across the timbers and melting ice.

Kel follows O'Peeria inside. He can hear screaming.

As he enters the school and sees the blood, he discovers that those Strangers who infiltrate deepest, fight hardest.

WHEN THEY WENT downstairs the following morning, Namior's mother was at the groundstone. She rested one hand against it and chanted softly, and when Namior sat, her mother offered a pained smile. Namior looked troubled as she kissed her own hands and reached out for the stone.

Kel felt like an intruder, so he stepped outside and wandered down the path to the stone wall. He was keen to see what dawn would reveal.

There was already activity at the harbor. People worked at the ruins, Komadian machines helping, and from that distance it was difficult to distinguish between Noreelans and visitors. The bridge had a complete new surface where the central span had been washed away, and people were crossing in either direction, pausing to examine the repaired section. Several more Komadian boats had docked, though after a quick count Kel decided that no more had sailed out from the island. Between the buildings lower down the hillside, he caught glimpses of a small, squat boat moving slowly upriver.

That troubled him. From what he'd seen yesterday, there were no boats surviving in Pavmouth Breaks' harbor, so it was undoubtedly a Komadian vessel. The sight of one of their craft cruising inland felt almost like an intrusion. Previously, they had been moored at the mole or anchored in or beyond the harbor. Now they were sailing into Noreela itself.

He turned away, frowning, and Namior was walking down the path toward him. She carried two steaming mugs of bondleaf tea.

"Anything new?" she asked.

"The mud and silt look a shade drier. It'll be harder to dig out. And someone is sailing upriver."

"Komadians?"

"Must be."

Namior warmed her hands around the mug and drank her tea. "So what's the plan?"

"You mean, do I want you to come with me?" Kel said.

She glanced at him across the top of her mug, steam obscuring her eyes.

"I'd like you to," he said. "But . . . it might be very dangerous. These people could be what I've spent half my life trying to fight against."

Namior looked back down at the harbor, then out to sea. The island was almost unreal in the early-morning mist. It looked as if it floated above the sea, a ghost island, an image thrown across the ocean by strange effects in the air. Kel had heard about such mirages from sailors and fishermen.

"It really doesn't look like an invasion to me," she said.

"What of the groundstone today?"

Namior blinked and took another sip of tea. Frowning.

"Namior?"

"Still . . . strange," she said. "I can't feel it or hear it at all this morning. Neither can my mother. Interference, my great-grandmother called it yesterday. And Mother says when she touched it this morning, her craze grew deeper still."

"Interference. And what do you call it?"

"I don't deign to know magic."

Kel laughed. He couldn't help himself. "You sound like a Sleeping God cultist living in fear of her deities."

"But we all know for sure that *magic* exists," she said, a little coldly. "I respect it. Who knows how it's been altered by that island appearing? Maybe it's . . . I don't know . . . wounded."

"It's an energy we use, that's all. The island could have drained it, perhaps. Or maybe the Komadians have interrupted it on purpose."

"They don't even *use* magic. Their machines have steam."

"And just how in the Black does *that* work?" Kel asked. "They puff steam here and there, yet still they float, fly, lift loads most of our machines couldn't touch, even when there *was* magic to work them! It's a play, that's all."

"Or their application of the same magic," Namior said. "And why do you trust it so little? It tells us how to build machines, powers them, shows us things from afar. It helps me to heal. It's more than just an energy, it's a *living* thing. It *talks* to us." Namior's anger turned into passion, and Kel cringed inside. He had no wish to trouble or hurt her. Especially not after the previous night. That had felt something like acceptance, and he needed that. He might be Core, but he still felt weak and uncertain.

"Living," he said. "Maybe that's why I still fear it." Namior smiled, and he was glad to see it.

"My paranoid wood-carver."

Kel drank some of the tea and sighed as its heat coursed through his body. He'd seen Namior's mother making bondleaf tea many times before, and she usually used magical heat, not water warmed by fire. This drink was different, because this morning there *was* no magic. He appreciated the irony in the fact that it did not taste as good as usual.

"How far out do you think it is?"

"Three, four miles." Kel looked out at the island, the smudge of settlements along its coast, the wooded hills at its center. Maybe it was two miles. Maybe it was ten.

"Long way for two nonsailors," Namior said.

"I can rig a sail and ride the wind," Kel said.

"Currents? Tacking?"

He shrugged. She smiled.

"A real adventure," Namior said, and the excitement in her eyes could not help but transfer to Kel.

"I don't think you should tell your family."

The excitement faded, and her face grew sad. "I've thought about that. I hate lying to them, but I think I'll say I'm staying with you tonight. Just in case it takes more than a day."

And there was much more left unsaid, which Kel thought about but dared not express. *And what if we don't come back?*

For all her bluster, bravado and exhortations of trust, he could see that possibility shadowing Namior's mind as well.

SHE TOOK THEIR mugs inside to bid her mother and crazed great-grandmother farewell, while Kel leaned on the wall and looked out to sea, trying to make out more of the island than distance allowed. She returned surprisingly quickly, her step light and the usual half smile back on her face.

"Ready?" he asked.

Namior nodded as she walked by. He asked her no more, and they headed down toward the harbor.

Someone had strung charm ropes across the remains of the washed-out path, one end fixed into the wall, the other tied to sticks wedged into cracks in the surface. The ropes were dyed various colors, and threaded onto them were the dried bones of several unidentifiable animals, each of these painted a different color as well. Some ropes had the bones gathered together, and on others they were strung out at equal or random spacings. They could just about step over the ropes without disturbing them.

Namior seemed particularly troubled by the charms, and she did her best not to touch or disturb them at all. Charm breathers bowed to powers other than magic and the worship of gods. To Kel, they had always been just another cult or faction, but witches and charm breathers nursed an ancient tension between their two practices.

"It's only in honor of the dead," Kel said.

"What can false charms do for the dead?"

"Not for me to say. I don't believe in charms."

Namior stepped over another rope. "Foolish things." But Kel could see that she was unsettled at their presence.

When they reached the repaired bridge, a group of residents were crossing from the other side. They were covered in filth, faces streaked and hair awry, and they looked exhausted.

"What news from the harbor?" Kel asked.

"No one left alive," a woman said, her voice devoid of emotion. Her eyes looked very far away. She had a tattoo of a sea serpent on one cheek, fighting to be seen through drying mud.

"You've been digging all night?" Namior asked.

"Since daybreak. And it's the Komadian machines that have been digging. We've just been stacking the bodies." The woman tried to smile but it came out as a grimace. She and her companions went on their way.

As Kel and Namior started across the bridge, the woman called after them. "Take care. There's something in the harbor."

"What?" Kel asked. He turned, and the woman alone had stopped. The others were still heading home.

"Don't know," the woman said, shrugging. "I've only seen the ripples."

They walked on, and as soon as they left the bridge Kel's eyes were on the surface of the harbor. There was still plenty of debris floating on the surface, clumping together here and there and added to by the sea: smashed wood and seaweed; tangled clothing and dead fish. The water swelled and moved slower than normal, as though the slick of wreckage weighed it down. He saw nothing stirring there.

"Could be anything," Namior said. "You told me you saw a sea wolf's tracks, maybe it's still here."

At the harbor they saw Mell, working at the remains of the Rettaro Fish Market. Mygrette was with her, watching the search efforts, one hand stroking the back of her motionless machine. The old witch looked lost.

Mell looked up when they approached, tired but determined. She even managed a smile.

"Any sign?" Kel asked.

"Nothing." She pointed down at a hole in the mud where steps used to lead down into the basement. She had escaped from there the previous day, and now there were signs of fresh digging. "Been down there, looked around. It's still flooded, but he's not there." She nodded past the hole at where several low walls met. "The back of the market, where it met the dwelling next door. He's not there."

Mygrette was looking at Kel, leaning on a thick length of wood she'd found somewhere.

"Are they helping?" Kel asked her. He was aware of the activity around them, the movements of fit, well-dressed people across the mud and between the ruins, the sharp exhalations of steam from their floating, crawling, digging machines.

"They're doing more than we can," Mygrette said, slapping the back of her lifeless machine. Kel saw fear behind the violence. "They pulled a live girl out just before dawn, took her up there to the Healing Hall." She nodded at Drakeman's Hill. "Floated her up on a machine, because she was barely awake. Cleaned her lungs first, with some metal mechanical thing one of them wore around his belt. Steam drove that, too. So yes, they're helping. And I've not heard one of them complain." She glanced around as if to make sure no one was looking. "But I still don't trust 'em a spit."

"Why?" Namior asked.

Mygrette grinned, gap-toothed and cold. "Young witch, you are. Confident in your touch, but you only hear what magic tells you. You don't read it, you just listen. I've learned over the years to let it run through me, not into me, and when it runs no more, that's to be read, too. And our visitors, our Komadians, have something in their eye." She nodded and looked from Namior to Kel, because maybe she saw more in him. "You look. Next time you meet one, you look, and see if I'm wrong."

"Don't need to tell him," Namior said. "He's suspicious enough already."

"Good for you, wood-carver."

"They're doing more than digging," Mell said, leaning on a shovel handle. "They're building, too."

"The bridge is good," Kel admitted. Mell stared at him, and he knew she meant something more.

"Tell them," Mygrette said.

Mell gestured at Drakeman's Hill with her head. "I went up yesterday evening, spent the night at a farm with my parents. The farmer put us up in his barns and grain stores, maybe fifty survivors. Gave us milk, grain biscuits, a little rotwine. We were all exhausted, but I couldn't sleep. And when my parents slept, I went for a walk."

She came closer. "I like it up there. Always have. Away from the sea for a while, it's a different world. Still Pavmouth Breaks, but beyond the familiar smells and sounds. I walked across the farmland and out to the old Throats."

Kel knew of the Throats. They were the first part of Pavmouth Breaks he had come across five years before, a network of deep tunnels and caverns that led a treacherous path from the top of the cliffs, all the way down to the sea. Some said they were formed during the Season of Storms, a mythical time before life began on Noreela when the land itself was being shaped by the breath, fire and might of those gods now sleeping. Others suggested they might have been machined into the land by smugglers bringing artifacts by sea from Kang Kang. Kel believed neither, but he liked the fact that they attracted such stories.

"Dangerous in the dark," he said.

"That's just it," Mell said. "It *wasn't* dark. At first I thought it was the life moon, but there were clouds last night, and the moon was a smudge. And then I saw that the light was a glow coming from the other side of Steep Hill."

"Beyond the Throats?" Namior said, confused. "There's no one living out there."

"That's why I went to have a look. And I saw a group of Komadians and their machines. The light came from three of the smaller ones." She paused, frowning, and Kel saw that she was trying to describe what she had seen.

"And they were building what?" he asked.

"I'm really not sure." She glanced around, then put her

shovel down and stretched. Kel heard her knees pop and her fingers click.

"What did it look like?" Namior asked. She sounded worried, and Kel guessed it was the challenge of her trust for the Komadians, as much as what they might be building.

"It's not what it looked like that troubles me," Mell said. "It's black as the ink from ten-leggers. Square, thirty paces to a side, maybe as tall as me. I couldn't see windows or doors. And the stuff to build it was coming out of a machine."

"What sort of stuff?"

"It flowed. The machine was bigger than any I've seen down here, and it walked on eight thin metal legs. Steam came from several openings in its body, and water dripped to the ground and sizzled when it touched. The black stuff came from two vents in its stomach, and it was runny, soft. Soon after coming out it grew hard. And the machine went back and forth, layering the stuff and making the thing higher as I watched."

They stood in silence, save for Mygrette, who hummed some silent agreement.

"And they didn't see you?" Kel asked after a while.

"I don't think so. I left quickly, came back to the farm, and didn't sleep all night."

Kel looked at Namior, and she surprised him by offering no explanation.

"You should go and see," Mygrette said to Kel.

"What good would that do?"

"I don't know," the witch said. "What good *could* it do, wood-carver?"

"I don't want to see again," Mell said. "I'm digging. I'm still digging."

Namior hugged her friend and whispered something in her ear, and Kel saw a single tear mark a trail down Mell's filthy cheek.

Then Namior turned to him and smiled. "I'll go with you.

We can pass by the Healing Hall, and I'll see if they need my help."

"Care, both of you," Mygrette said.

"Take a rest," Kel replied.

"Tsk!" The witch waved him away and reached for her machine, slapping its side once again. "Magic rests, so we've to be on our guard ten times stronger."

Walking away, Kel asked Namior what she had whispered to Mell while they hugged.

"I told her to keep believing until there's no longer any hope."

"Poor Trakis," Kel said. *Hopeless*, he thought. *It's a miracle she survived down there, but up here . . . ? Hopeless.*

"Mygrette has suspicions about you," Namior said.

"She *is* a witch."

"So am I."

"But she's old and naturally mistrustful," Kel said, hoping he had not hurt Namior's feelings. "And sometimes I think she has the eyes of a cliff hawk and the mind of a skull raven."

"So how much do you think she knows?"

"I don't think she believes that I'm just a wood-carver." Mygrette had long been a worry for Kel, and he was glad that no one else seemed to see the way she looked at him. Perhaps that was the reason he and the old witch had formed a cautious friendship; she because she wanted to know more, and he because it made him feel like the person he had once been. He had a hatred for that person, but deep down, he sometimes missed the life. There had been excitement as well as danger, wonder alongside fear. Mygrette had seen some of that past in his eyes and, for all he knew, read it somehow from his mind.

"Well, you *are* a wood-carver," Namior said. "Even if it is only one of your many talents."

He raised an eyebrow. "Talking about last night?" But Namior did not honor him with a response.

They walked across the hardening layers of silt, passing between the sad remains of tumbled buildings and holes dug by those searching for lost loved ones. Where the rope ladder had provided temporary access to Drakeman's Hill, there was a set of rock steps held in place by heavy metal struts. A group of Komadians and their machines worked beside the rough ramp, piling more rocks against its side and fixing the metal with loud *thuds*. A few Noreelans milled around them, but they seemed to be redundant. The steam-breathing machines were doing all the work.

"Kel." Namior grabbed his arm, and they halted. "Do we really need to go up and see? Shouldn't we just do what you planned?"

"I've thought about that," he said. "The island's our goal, but I need to look at the thing Mell saw. It could be relevant. Could give us a clue."

"Maybe it's just something to do with how their machines run."

"Way up there?" He nodded at the steep slope before them, buildings clinging like the massive limpets that rode their larger trawlers. "Beyond the village? They are obviously trying to keep it a secret. There's something wrong with it, but—"

"Is it familiar? Have you ever seen anything like she described?"

"None of this is familiar to me, Namior. That's why I have to be certain, one way or the other."

"And you can't just...?" She touched his jacket pocket where he kept the communicators. He had debated telling her how they worked, just in case anything happened to him, but Core secrecy was deeply ingrained.

"I've told you why," he said, awkward. Speaking the words again would be difficult. *Because if I call them, they might come here and kill me for desertion.*

Namior stared up at Drakeman's Hill. Smoke came from a few of the buildings, and halfway up the hill they could see the long, low structure of the Healing Hall. "Then if we're stopped, that place is our excuse," she said.

Surprised by how quickly she had embraced their covert aims, Kel smiled and followed Namior toward the ramp.

They passed the Komadians without comment, returning smiles from the visitors and using the structure they must have erected while much of Pavmouth Breaks slept. Kel found something vaguely distasteful about their smiles and good humor, expressed as they were above a sea of mud that imprisoned scores, perhaps even hundreds, of dead. They should have been contrite and humbled. They should, if their need to help was honest and pure, have averted their eyes from the people for whom their arrival had caused so much suffering.

When he glanced at them, he was searching for something that set them apart. *Something in their eye,* Mygrette had said. Many worked in open-necked shirts, and they had no gills on their necks. A few had even removed their upper garments, sweating in their labors, and no strange appendages waved from beneath their shoulder blades. They were as human as the Noreelans.

Am I just too suspicious? he thought for the hundredth time. But he followed Namior up through the narrow alleys of Drakeman's Hill, and her own willingness to question what was happening urged him on.

They passed several buildings with dirty, torn and soaked clothing nailed to the front doors: the garments of the dead. It made Kel sad, but at least these families had retrieved the bodies of their loved ones. There would be many others mourning those who would never be found.

When they reached the narrow path that led to the Healing Hall, Namior told him to sit and rest while she went to visit. She promised she would not be long. He wished she would pass by the Hall and carry on with him, but he respected her sense of duty. So he sat on a bench beside the path, looked out toward the harbor and the open sea beyond, and it was from there that he saw the first of the big ships coming in.

It was a three-master, sails billowing grandly in a breeze

that Kel could barely feel. From that distance it looked like a well-built craft, and it rode the waves with grace. Two more were following, one of them halfway from the island, the other having just left. He was not surprised, but the sight sent a chill through his bones, part fear, part anticipation. As the potential danger increased, so he felt as if he were coming alive again.

The first ship anchored a hundred steps from the mole and commenced to lower sail. By the time Namior appeared again the ship was disgorging several launches, all of them apparently packed with Komadians. It was hard to see clearly from so far, but they appeared no different from those already working in the harbor.

"A friendly invasion," Kel muttered. He touched the package in his jacket pocket and wondered whether he was putting too much importance on himself.

"There's a young healer here," Namior said. "Barely a teen, but she's doing well. She knows potions and mixes, and doesn't seem concerned that magic is distant today." She sat next to Kel. "The badly injured are dead now. The girl's taking care of the rest. I offered to help, but she said she was doing fine on her own. Young pride." She rested her head on Kel's shoulder, then noticed the ships for the first time. "Oh."

"Shall we go?" he asked.

"Do you think—?"

"The signal was sent last night. I can't see anyone at the harbor about to contest their landing. So let's go and find what Mell saw being built."

"And then?"

"And then I'll decide whether to call them here or not."

Namior tapped his pocket again. "Whatever you have there . . . It sends its message by magic?"

Kel slowly closed his eyes as realization dawned. *Fucking idiot*, he heard O'Peeria mocking, *you've left it too late! Waited so they could mess things up, block things, and now—*

"I can find somewhere," he said. "Outside the village. If I

need to, I'll find a way." But fear was settling into him, a fear that magic's disruption was far more than an accident.

If I need to, I'll find a way.

NAMIOR COULD SEE that Kel was suffering, indecision and fear combining to press him into action. But she could also see a look in his eyes that she had never noticed before. He was excited, and he looked *alive*.

They passed his home with barely a glance and climbed the last few hundred steps to the top of Drakeman's Hill. The paths began to level, and the buildings became more spaced out. Between some were large gardens bearing vegetable crops, fruits trees and swathes of herbs, soil-planted or hanging from elaborate herb nets. Other spaces were untended, given over to wild growth. It was there that Namior would find plants useful for her studies, given time, but Kel marched them quickly along the paths, possessed by greater purpose the farther they walked from the harbor.

Namior remembered Kel once remarking on how strange it was that the steeper the hill, the more buildings were constructed there, almost as if the builders had relished the challenge. Namior had smiled, and nodded, and said that Pavmouth Breaks had always weathered hardships, which were reflected in the architecture of the place. Why build somewhere flat and out of sight of the harbor, when a steep slope such as Drakeman's Hill offered a far more complex challenge?

She rarely came up so far. While she was trapped in the village for the duration of her studies, she did not like to see what she was missing. And as Mell had said, the heights above Drakeman's Hill were a whole new world.

She could hear the sea between gentle gusts of wind, and perhaps she always would, however far inland she traveled. And she could still smell it, when the wind carried the scents her way. But if she looked inland, she could no longer *see* the sea, and it was easy to imagine that she was somewhere else entirely. There were two farms visible from where they stood, the closest being where Mell and her parents had spent the previous night. The farmstead consisted of several larger stone barns, a house built of timber and mud, and some smaller buildings, a few of them tumbled into disrepair. The fields around the farm were divided by low stone walls topped with the spiked airthorn plant, so named because it seemed to consist entirely of thorns. Some fields were home to wandering flocks of sheebok, the versatile cattle that provided meat, clothing, guts for fishing line, lamp oil and obscure and questionable medicines. Others held several larger, lumbering choes, while unoccupied fields were planted with great swathes of grain, root crops and hanging fruit vines. An old machine sat close to a wall nearby, and Namior knew it had not moved for at least ten years. Its flesh-and-blood parts had rotted away to nothing, and its metallic limbs and skirting had rusted to the color of the soil it was slowly sinking into. No one seemed sure of what had happened to the machine, but some said that the farmer himself had destroyed it, suddenly eager to dispense with magic's help. It was not something that Namior had ever understood, but since meeting Kel she had come to realize that there were those who did not trust magic as completely as she did.

Beyond the farm were gently rolling hills, more airthorn-topped stone walls, a few small copses of trees, a lake surrounded by tall, lush undergrowth. Past the lake rose Steep Hill, green and tall and shielding the wilds of Noreela from view.

Namior had climbed the gentle slopes to its summit several times before, and each time the large expanse of countryside beyond had both thrilled and terrified her. Steep Hill had always been the notional border of Pavmouth Breaks, a natural divide that generations of fisherfolk and farmers had treated as the extreme southeastern limit of their village. As such, beyond Steep Hill there were the wilds; no buildings, no differentiated fields, no planted crops or maintained woodland, and no signs of civilization. One rough trail led along the far base of Steep Hill toward the River Pav valley to the north, but even that was often overgrown, or shielded from view by the wild undergrowth that grew rampant across the lower slopes of the hill.

There's the rest of the world, Namior had thought the first time she stood atop the hill. *And one day I'll get to see it.* The concept had been exciting and intimidating. Now, looking at the hill as she and Kel walked toward it, she was suddenly more afraid than ever.

What would the Komadians be doing so out of sight?

And how did they even get there?

"We should go south first," Kel said. "Skirt around the Throats, climb the shoulder of the hill from that side."

"Trying to stay hidden?" she asked.

"If *they're* hiding something, it's the route they'll least expect anyone from the village to take."

They followed the line of the sea cliff for a while, never walking too close to the edge. There was a rough path there, worn by villagers who liked to come and collect gull eggs, or the more rare cliff-snake skins. The skins were tough, transparent and flexible, and were often used to coat and waterproof the large hats worn by fishermen. But the path only went as far as the second farm's extremes, and past that point Kel and Namior had to forge their own way through thickets of gorse, wind saps and hardy stone heathers.

As they approached the place where they would turn to head east, Namior saw a fluttering movement from the corner of her eye. She paused and looked out to sea, and hovering a hundred steps from them was one of the several cliff hawks that nested along that part of the coast. Its wings barely flapped, feathers rippling in the updraft, and it seemed to be looking directly at her. She gasped, held her breath and went slowly to her knees. She was aware of Kel paused to her left, but she did not want to turn her head in case it changed the moment. *I don't want to move on*, she thought. *Here and now is fine, I can live like this for a while. Whatever is to come . . . that can wait.*

The graceful bird dipped slightly, then rose again with one gentle flap of its wings. It hovered in the same place, staring at her, and Namior wondered whether it was thinking the same thing. Perhaps even in a cliff hawk's life there were some moments that seemed to matter more than others.

"Namior," Kel whispered, but she did not move, could not respond.

A breath of wind ruffled her hair, she blinked, and the bird was flying directly at her, wings folded back and cruel beaked head thrust forward.

She barely had time to draw breath before the hawk struck the cliff face six steps to her right and a dozen down. It was out of view for a beat, and then it dipped away from the cliff again, something small and squealing grasped in its big claws. *It's almost as if it didn't see me*, Namior thought. But she knew that was not the case at all.

"Come on," Kel said. "We need to climb Steep Hill now."

"Did you see that?"

Kel smiled and nodded. "I didn't get the head quite right, I know that for sure."

"You did well, wood-carver." She took his outstretched hand and followed him inland.

THEY CLIMBED THE shoulder of Steep Hill, and all the way up Kel's hand rested close to the handle of his short sword. *He's not the man I fell in love with*, Namior thought over and over, and everything she saw of him now was strange. The weapons he wore, the way he stalked up the hillside, hand on his sword . . . she recognized none of that. Yet in truth, she was seeing the real Kel for the first time. And behind the tough new veneer that he had revealed, she perceived his desperate hope that she would love him still.

She might well be a witch, but she was too confused right then to know what she really thought. All she could be certain about was that she had to stay with him.

Steep Hill was aptly named. In parts they climbed quite easily, breathing coming harder and shins burning with the exertion. At other times they went on hands and feet, almost holding on to the hillside as if it were doing its best to cast them off. It was not a particularly high hill, though, and soon Namior could see its summit cutting a hard line across the sky just above them. Kel had paused, lying flat to the hillside and holding his left hand behind him, palm up, signaling her to stop. He crawled forward slowly, and when he was high enough to see beyond the hill he paused and remained in that position for some time.

She wanted to call out and ask what he saw. She considered crawling up beside him. But he was so utterly motionless that she did not want to be the one to move.

At last he turned his head, very slowly, and looked back down at her. For a beat his face was blank, his eyes distant and dark. Then he focused on her, blinked and motioned her to join him.

"What is it?" she whispered as she crawled. But Kel turned away without speaking, lying flat on the hilltop once more.

The urge to rush was overwhelming, but she kept her movements slow and considered. To her what they were doing was exciting and terrifying in equal measure. *Is this how he always lived his life before Pavmouth Breaks? Before me?*

When she could see down the other side of the hill she settled into the grass and moss, all the strength going from her. "What in the Black is that?"

"They should be guarding it better," Kel whispered. "If they don't want it seen, we'd have never got as far as we have. So why here?"

"But what *is* it?"

Kel's only response was to hum softly.

The black structure Mell had told them about was being built at the foot of Steep Hill's eastern face. Its base was as Mell had described, square and about thirty paces to a side. But it was much taller than when their friend had seen it the previous night. The structure rose from the square base, its far edge curving inward almost imperceptibly, near face leaning outward, and Namior thought it would not be long until it cleared the highest part of Steep Hill. At its summit, where the machine worked, it was a perfect rectangle, thirty paces wide and maybe twenty across.

And the machine Mell had described was still there, huge, holding itself to the black structure with eight spindly metal legs, crawling back and forth like a giant slayer spider and exuding a black fluid from vents in its stomach. The material slumped onto the rectangular surface and found its own level. By the time one of the machine's legs stepped that way, it was solid.

On the ground around the structure's base was a group of Komadians, perhaps fifteen in total. One of them stood forward from the others, looking up at the machine and controlling it with a small box in his hands. They were too far away to make out details, but Namior saw the pale blur of his hands moving, fingers lifting and shifting.

A burst of steam issued from the machine's back, startling Namior. Kel's hand was already on her back, holding her down.

"What do you think it is?" she asked. The structure ate the sun. Nothing reflected back, it did not shine, but neither did it have depth. It was like a block of nothing being built up out of the ground and reaching for the blue sky.

"I don't know," Kel said. "I've never seen anything like it."

Namior looked at the Komadians clustered around the base of the hill, trying to make out faces, see if there was anyone there she recognized, but her gaze was dragged back to the black column growing out of the ground. *That's just what it looks like,* she thought. *As though the ground has sprouted that thing.* Its base appeared set deep, the ground around it apparently undisturbed.

"Are you going to try to send your message?" she whispered. She feared that Kel would say yes, but it was her own fear that drove her to ask.

"Maybe," he said. "Maybe not yet." He shook his head, frowning deeply as he stared down the hillside. "But just what in the Black *is* that?"

"We could go down and ask," Namior said. And as she spoke those words, they seemed to make sense. The Komadians had only helped them so far, apparently shocked at the damage the waves had caused, using their machines to dig for survivors, repair the bridge, build the ramp against Drakeman's Hill . . . "They promised technology," she said. "Perhaps this is it?"

Kel glanced at Namior in surprise, then back down at the industrious visitors. He shook his head. "We can't just go and ask, not yet. Whatever that thing is, they can't be too concerned about people from the village seeing it; otherwise, it would be better guarded. But still, I don't trust them."

"The island, then," she said. "Let's do what we said we'd do."

"The island," Kel said.

Taking one last look at the black structure, they slid backward down the hill.

A M I A *coward?* Kel thought. *Should I take out the communicators and try one now? Breathe on it, stick it in the ground? The consequences don't matter. It's Noreela that matters, it always has been, and I can never run away from that.*

But behind everything else was the certainty that the Core would kill him if they came there, even if the Komadians were Strangers. And if he did manage to make a communicator work where magic had become uncertain, it would likely end in conflict and bloodshed. *Use one of these fuckers, and Noreela's at war,* O'Peeria had said. He felt the weight in his jacket pocket—so much potential in such small things.

He had been responsible for enough innocent deaths to last many lifetimes.

He led the way again, reversing their route back toward the cliffs. Namior moved quickly and quietly behind him, and he was glad that she was with him. She might claim to trust the visitors, but there she was, spying on them and agreeing to go out to the island with him. Surely she had her doubts.

At the foot of the hill they turned toward the cliffs, passing through a small wooded area, and Kel concentrated on the grasses they had crushed on the way there, the small bush branches their legs had snapped, the splashed droplets where morning dew still clung to plants as yet hidden from the rising sun. And looking at the ground was why he almost walked into the man standing before him.

"Calm morning," the Komadian said. He was smiling, hands free of weapons, a dark-skinned man with long hair tied with metal braids, a small scar across the bridge of his nose, and a light leather jacket slung over his shoulders. "Lovely day for—"

Kel moved before he could really consider his actions. Perhaps it was instinct—the training drummed into him by the Core—or maybe it was an eruption of pent-up stresses and suspicions. Later, he thought that anger at his own clumsiness had a lot to do with what happened next.

He pivoted on his left leg and drove his right foot up toward the man's chin.

The visitor was quick, but not quite quick enough. He twisted to one side, but Kel's heel caught him on the jaw. He grunted and turned, facing the other way.

"Kel!" Namior said, and he silently cursed the volume of her voice.

He stepped in close and threw one arm across the man's

throat, pulling tight to prevent him from shouting. The man gurgled something and went stiff in Kel's embrace, both arms coming up and trying to shift Kel's arm from around his neck.

"Move away!" Kel whispered to Namior. He plucked a short knife from his belt and pressed its tip into the Komadian's back. *Now we'll see*, he thought. *Now we'll know for sure.* "Get back, Namior, you've no idea what—"

"What the fuck are you doing?" Namior said. She was trying to stay quiet, at least, but the amazement on her face gave Kel pause.

What am I doing? The man struggled, but did not fight, not really. He was groaning and gasping, trying to talk.

Kel pushed the knife a little harder, feeling it pierce the jacket and part the man's skin. The Komadian grew stiff and motionless, hands clawed in the air before him.

And if I kill him, and no wraith rages out of the wound . . . ?

He could feel the man's heartbeat, rapid and terrified.

I'm already a murderer.

Kel dropped the knife and tugged hard at the man's throat, and when the visitor went limp he eased him to the ground.

"Kel, I don't know, I don't think I can—"

"Quiet!" Kel moved across to Namior and pressed his hand over her mouth. "Please, just keep quiet." He nodded at his woman, his love, and when her wide eyes narrowed slightly and she nodded back, he took his hand away.

With everything he did next, he felt Namior's eyes boring into him. But she said nothing. He was glad for that, but he also knew that things had changed. She would stay, or she would go, and he could no longer have any influence over whatever decision she might make.

He went back to the man and began searching through his jacket pockets. *Weapons first, then evidence, but leave no sign.* The Komadian was carrying a short knife in a sheath on his belt. Kel glanced at it briefly before throwing it aside; well cared for, rarely used. He found no other weapons. Pulling the collar wide, he saw the smooth neck, and when he turned the man on his side and thrust his hand down the back of his shirt, he felt damp, hairy skin and nothing more.

The man groaned and stirred, and Kel prepared to run. *I could hit him and force him under again.* But he glanced at Namior, and knew he had committed too much violence already.

The Komadian sighed, eyelids fluttering half-open. Kel flicked his finger at the man's left eye, and when he did not blink Kel went through his clothing some more. In one deep pocket on the thigh of his trousers there were a few crumbs of fledge, stale and old. His eyes had not seemed tinged with the drug... but then the realization that the man carried something that came from Noreela, but not Pavmouth Breaks, hit Kel hard.

"Fledge," he said, flicking the crumbs from his fingers.

"So?" Namior asked. Her tone and stance were confrontational. Kel did not look at her, afraid that her eyes would take off the back of his skull.

"So, they've visited somewhere else in Noreela."

"Which is just what their emissary said."

Kel nodded, then went through the unconscious man's two shirt pockets. One contained a mass of dried root of some kind, and the other held a few strands of shredded, colored rope. He threw the root to Namior.

"What's that?" he asked.

She closed her eyes, sniffed the root, and frowned. "I don't know."

"Rope charm," Kel said, turning the rope strands over in his hand. "What's left of one, anyway." He nodded at the root. "Keep that."

"Why?"

"Because we don't know what it is."

"Don't tell me what to do, Kel." She stared at him, hard and harsh, and his shoulders slumped. The tension was still there, and there was a weight pressing him down as well.

"Please," he said. "I can't make your mind up for you, but

I need you to stay with me, for a while at least. Just until I'm sure."

"Sure of what?"

Kel shrugged. "I really don't know, Namior. But that thing they're building back there…" He pointed past her up the hillside, but did not have the chance to say any more. The man at his feet rolled from his back onto his front, elbows rising as he groggily placed his hands against the ground ready to shove.

And then Kel heard the sounds of people coming through the undergrowth.

He dashed to Namior, grabbing her hand and breathing a sigh of relief when she let him lead her toward the cliffs. Once they were out of sight of the fallen man he paused, holding his breath as he listened. Footsteps, the swish of clothing against undergrowth, a few subdued words and a burst of laughter. Whoever was coming had no reason to be cautious.

"Can you try to hide us?" he whispered, mouth pressed close to Namior's ear.

She nodded and pulled him down into a patch of bracken. From the pocket of her slacks she produced a long ground rod, the metallic sliver all witches used when trying to draw on the magic in the land for some purpose. She slid it into the soil between bracken roots, then clasped one hand around the metal end, holding Kel's shoulder with her other hand. She closed her eyes and started to chant quietly, and Kel looked away.

They were coming closer. He counted six people at least, making no real effort to keep quiet. And then, hissing through the morning air but barely interrupting their conversation, the gush of steam erupting from a machine.

He looked back to Namior and she was staring at him, panicked.

"It won't work!" she said.

That was all Kel needed to hear. He glanced around, saw that they were in as much cover as they could hope to find anywhere close by, and pulled Namior down beside him. "Keep as still as you can."

He moved only his eyes. He could see too much of the trees above them, too much sky, too many clouds. Even if the Komadians did pass them by without seeing them, as soon as they met their winded and bruised companion the search would be on. Namior's magic had not worked, and the two of them would have only one way to go: to the cliffs, then back toward Pavmouth Breaks.

They would be trapped.

I should have slit his throat, he thought, then a shadow fell over him, and he stopped breathing.

NAMIOR STARED DIRECTLY at Kel, trying not to blink, trying not to breathe, trying not to see this stranger lying before her.

The night before he had given her a gift and they had made love, but only moments ago she'd watched him readying to shove a knife into a man's back. Now he was lying there before her, staring just past her shoulder at whoever walked by, his jaw clenched and his right hand holding something cool and sharp across her leg.

If we're seen, he'll fight, she thought. *No matter that he found stale fledge in the man's pocket, and part of a rope charm, which are both things of Noreela. He's focused on his Strangers.* She blinked and tried to catch his eye, but his own eyes shifted only slightly, following shapes she could not see as they walked by.

The Komadians chatted softly, making no effort to keep quiet. Whatever they were doing there, surely it was of no harm? She heard the soft hiss of a machine venting steam.

Kel's eyes glittered. She had yet to see him blink.

Namior closed her hand around the ground rod piercing the soil between her and Kel. She shut her eyes and breathed softly, deeply, inviting the flow of the language of the land through her, but it was barely talking in echoes. It was like listening to someone speaking from a long way off, their words stolen by the breeze, meaning lost to the lazy sunshine bathing the ground between them. She listened harder, but the interference was strong. *It's never been like this before,* she thought, and that was true. Even as a little girl, when her mother first taught her to commune with the magic in the land, she had been able to sense its flow. Understanding had come later, but magic had always been available to her.

When she opened her eyes again, Kel was looking at her. He put a finger to his lips. Namior nodded.

When Kel slowly sat up and watched the Komadians walking toward the hill, she remained where she was, working the ground rod out of the soil. She ran it between two fingers to clean it off, then slipped it back into the sleeve in her pocket.

Kel leaned over her and pressed his mouth to her ear. So quietly that she could not even feel his breath, he said, "We have to leave now."

They stood and dashed through the undergrowth, lifting their legs high to avoid making too much noise. After a few beats Namior caught up with Kel and grabbed his arm.

"What did you see?" she whispered.

"Eight of them," he said, still moving. "And a floating machine I haven't seen before. It had tubes projecting from it, but they didn't steam. I think it was a war machine."

"How can you know that?"

Kel did not answer.

"So what now?"

He held up a hand and they stopped. Kel tilted his head sideways, listening, turning so that he could discern direction.

"What?" Namior asked.

"They've stopped walking and talking," he said. "They're trying to be quiet now, which means they've found him. So we have to go."

"Where?"

Kel's eyes darted here and there, and for a moment Namior was afraid he was losing control. She was surprised at how much that worried her. She feared him and what he had done, but somehow he was still very much in charge. *I'm no soldier*, she thought, though she could not hide the sick excitement that had seeded itself deep down.

"The Throats," he said. "Come on." They started again, emerging from the small wood and rushing through heathers and bracken toward the area where the first of the holes broke the surface.

"That's mad!" she said.

"They go down to the beach, yes?"

"Some of them, but no one ever goes in there. You *know* that. You know *why*!"

"Dangerous. But not as dangerous as returning to Pavmouth Breaks."

He's still set on the island, she thought. She looked left, past the cliff edge and out to sea, and the island sat there as though it had been there forever.

Someone shouted behind them. Namior did not turn around, afraid of what she would see.

"Here!" Kel slid behind a slight rise in the land and she followed him, skidding down on the gravel and wincing as it scratched her legs.

"Are they coming?" she asked.

Kel lifted himself up, then dropped down again quickly. "Not yet. Maybe they won't. But they can't know where we're going. They see us go down into a drop hole, they can block both ends and send in their machines."

"By the Black, Kel, can't we just get back to the village?"

"I need to see for sure," he said, his voice suddenly calm and full of reason. "They're not the Strangers I know, but I need to see the island. And you really don't have to come with me, Namior."

"I don't want to go back on my own."

"Well, you've always wanted an adventure." He actually smiled, and she was amazed to feel herself smiling as well.

"True," she said. "But I thought of traveling across Noreela to find it."

"What's better than an adventure in your own village?" He looked over the small rise again, then nodded. "We can go. Not far to the holes. Do you know which is the best one to go down?"

Like many children of the village, Namior had explored the Throats when she was a child, a mixture of curiosity and dares from other children encouraging her descent. And like most children who went down, she had never gone very far beyond the influence of sunlight. For people from a fishing village, being underground felt similar to being beneath the surface of the waves: it was not a place they were meant to be.

"They all lead down, and I've heard they all join up at some point."

"So let's go down the closest one to us," Kel said.

"I've never been all the way through."

"As a friend of mine always said, there's a first time for everything."

Namior liked that, but it did little to dispel the frisson of fear. Most children had started down the holes, yes, and few had gone far. But *everyone* in Pavmouth Breaks had heard the stories and rumors. Ancient, angry wraiths, deadly dark-snakes, poisonous fumes from the land's mysterious innards . . .

She took one more look at the island. Then Kel stood and ran for the first of the Throats.

Trying not to hear her mother's voice berating her foolishness, and her great-grandmother's confused tears, Namior followed.

Chapter Seven

beneath the ground, above the sea

THE HOLE STARTED as a bowl-shaped dip in the land. There was a rough path that led into it, worn over time by sheebok and the occasional daring child from the village. All the way down Kel felt horribly exposed, and when the sun was blocked out by the edge of the dip, that feeling only increased. As the hole, and escape, drew closer, the prospect of being discovered grew even more terrible.

The entrance to the Throat was dark and forbidding, sitting in one wall of the dip and curtained with trailing plants spotted with sharp, bright red flowers. Several bird corpses were speared on these hard blooms, their fragile bones a stark white against the petals. A sheebok's skeleton lay partially hidden beneath heathers in the bowl's base, and the ground was soft and boggy. The sun rarely seemed to touch the place.

Namior was standing back, looking at him uncertainly.

"It's the best way," he said. "If they *are* looking for us up here and in Pavmouth Breaks, we can be down onto the beach and out to the island before they realize we've gone."

"*If* we can find a boat that wasn't smashed by the waves."

Kel smiled and nodded, but said nothing. She was right. The chance of finding a seaworthy craft was negligible.

He went first, lifting the undergrowth aside, taking care not to touch the birds' bodies. A faint smell of the sea wafted from the hole, brine and decay brought up from far below. Beneath that he smelled other things he could not quite identify—a stale spicy must, and something rich and meaty. He took a deep breath and entered the tunnel.

Namior came in behind him, lowering the plant tendrils carefully so that they formed a perfect cover across the tunnel entrance. They shut out a lot of the light, and Kel felt a brief but intense moment of panic.

He breathed deeply, and Namior stood close behind him, her hands on his shoulders. "We'll need light," she said. "Have you even thought of that?"

"Of course," he snapped. Namior stepped away, and Kel sighed. "Sorry. I'm sorry."

"I'm going." She turned and lifted the trailing plants again, and in the silence between them Kel heard the clatter of hollow bones.

"Namior. Please come with me." The desperation in his voice was not false, and as he spoke he realized just how lost he felt. All the Core training could not change that, and it was because he had found a home and a love. He had settled, and the first thing the Core did to its members was to make them wanderers—homeless and adrift. "If you leave me here, I'm not sure what I'll do."

"You're the soldier," she said, but there was no aggression in her voice. "You're the Core fighter, trained for this."

"I've changed."

"Looked to me back there that you've never changed."

"Fighting someone is easy," he said. "Killing, more difficult. But without you, I think I'd only end up fighting myself."

She looked at him, truly staring, as though she were trying to see inside him, past the surface where lies and inconsistencies could exist and down deep to his soul.

"I might be able to give us some light," she said at last, and Kel breathed a huge sigh of relief.

He moved on, and a few steps into the tunnel the floor sloped gently into the drop hole, rough stone walls curving down like the insides of some waiting giant's throat. It looked dark down there, and every few beats there was a breath of stale air, and the sound of something roaring in the distance.

"The sea," Kel said.

"Maybe." Namior stood beside him, looking down into the darkness. "Maybe it's something *before* the sea."

"Everywhere like this has stories and legends," he said, realizing with a smile that he was almost whispering. "Maybe adults start them to frighten their children, or maybe children make them up to scare themselves."

"And what about frightening the adults?"

"It's just a network of caves leading down to the sea. And we need to move. If they're searching, they might just look into the mouth of the hole."

"Give me a beat," Namior said, and she knelt on the rough stone floor.

"I thought the magic . . . ?"

Namior looked up at him, the poor light shadowing her smile and making it darker. "There's magic, and there's magic." She held out her hand. "I assume you have a knife I can use?"

Kel handed her a blade and watched, fascinated, as she gave them light. A sprinkle of something from a pouch in her pocket onto the knife's keen blade, a dribble of spit, a rough scrape of the metal against stone, and the whole blade began to glow. The light grew, expanded, and when she held it out they could see down into the sloping tunnel. It did not illuminate far, but Kel could see enough to make out the floor, walls and ceiling close by.

"So if that's not magic . . . ?"

"The eggs of fire kotts. They live on beaches. Usually only hatch when something heavy walks over them. Then they attach themselves to whatever woke them, burrow in, and eat it."

Kel stepped back slowly, even though he knew Namior would have an answer.

"We soak them in rotwine for three moons before they're ready for use. Makes them . . . sleepy." She stood and held out the knife. He could see vague movement on the blade, as though the metal itself were flexing in extreme heat.

"Very clever," he said, smiling.

"I'm not a *slave* to magic."

Kel leaned forward and kissed Namior on the cheek, so glad when she did not back away. She tasted of fear, and excitement. It was a taste he knew of old.

IT WAS MORE a series of small caves than one long tunnel. Sometimes the floor was almost flat and they could walk, stepping over or around ridges, taking care not to break their ankles in holes or the open throats of crevasses that seemed bottomless. Other times they had to climb down steep inclines, and the rock was so rough and unweathered that its sharp edges scraped their skin and drew blood. There were no signs that anyone else had ever ventured so deep. With the pressing darkness, the breaths of breeze, the rhythmic roar that rose from far below, and the smells—still strange, still strong—it felt like somewhere removed from the world.

Kel had once ventured into the beginnings of a fledge mine in the Widow's Peaks. He had heard many tales about the drug miners who preferred to live their whole lives below-ground, and rumor had reached him that a Stranger had hidden herself away in one of the mines. But he had not gone deep. He'd heard talk of the creatures that supposedly lived in the lowest seams of the drug. Some called them fledge demons, others had named them Nax, and it was said that when they were woken, none of the miners involved ever escaped. A foolish myth, he had thought, one born of minds driven mad by the pressures of such depths and darkness. And half a day after entering the first crevasse that led to a deep mine, he heard such terrible sounds echoing up at him that he immediately raced for the sunlight. There were screams, made ghostly and inhuman on their journey through the mines, caves and cracks in the land. And there were roars.

The path they followed felt the same. The smells were different—none of the distinctive fledge taint—but the weight of Noreela around him was dreadfully familiar. After the fledge mine he'd had a series of terrible dreams, perhaps brought on by the drug fumes he had inhaled, or maybe by what he had heard and imagined happening down there. The dreams had convinced him that the Noreela that was meant for humans was the surface of the land. Deeper down, in the cracks and caves and crevasses, lay other things.

He could not share any of his thoughts or fears with Namior. They were foolish, like the superstitions of someone who knew nothing of the world.

The roar that sang up to them . . . it was the sea, washing against the beach and cliffs below.

The strange smells . . . minerals found only underground, degrading in the darkness.

He tried hard to see beyond the weak light issuing from the knife. But the darkness before him was deep.

HOW LONG WILL the light last?" Kel asked.

"It takes a while for the kotts to die. Maybe a day."

"Long enough," he said. *If we're down here for a day, it's because we're the dead ones.*

They came to a sheer drop, and though Namior leaned out with the light knife, the bottom remained in darkness. The thought of climbing down into something they could not see disturbed Kel, and it was with a jolt that he realized he was afraid of the dark.

"Do you have any of those things left?"

"A few." Namior took a pouch from her pocket and opened it, showing him the tiny, pale pink kott eggs.

Kel pulled a throwing knife from his belt and handed it to Namior. She went through the process again, and when she scraped the knife harshly across the stone, the sound echoed both up and down. Kel held his breath: the atmosphere in the caves suddenly seemed loaded, the echo fading into silent expectation.

"I feel like I'm being watched," Namior said.

Kel tried to smile at her, but she turned away, and he knew it had been a grimace.

Namior dropped the knife over the ledge. It soon clattered from protruding rocks and hit the bottom and, comforted that it was not too far down, Kel sat, turned around and edged himself onto the rock face. There were plenty of handholds. He started down, slow and methodical, and glanced up to make sure Namior was following.

Something touched his leg.

He gasped, almost losing his footing as he kicked out at whatever was there.

"What?" Namior whispered above him. She was still just leaning over the ledge, holding the light in one hand and aiming it down at Kel. He reached for it, shook his head, not knowing what to say.

Namior handed him the knife.

The thing touched him again, a soft, provocative caress on the bare skin between his trousers and boot. He did not kick out this time, but moved the shining knife quickly down, realizing just how useful a light that doubled as a weapon could be.

There was nothing there. Only the rock face, and the darkness that surrounded it, driven back grudgingly by the weak glow.

"Maybe it was my trouser leg, a breeze," he said, but he heard Namior draw a sharp breath.

"You felt something?"

"I thought something touched—"

"There are wraiths down here."

Kel leaned against the rock face, breathing hard. "You're going to start telling me all the old stories your mother and great-grandmother told you?"

"All the wraiths from Pavmouth Breaks that haven't been chanted down, and those that existed here even *before* the village began." She climbed down carefully, pausing beside Kel and waiting until he looked at her. "So they say." She smiled. But he could see her doubt, and her fear, and she was staring at him too fixedly for comfort. *She doesn't want to look down.*

He felt a sudden chill, and his surprised exhalation condensed in the air before him. No breeze, no sign of where it had come from, but the air in the cave seemed to drop sharply in temperature.

"We should keep moving," he said. And when Kel resumed his descent, he left the cold spot behind. He was not even sure that Namior had felt it.

Holding the glowing knife in one hand, it was difficult to maneuver from one handhold to the next. But lower down there was a slight slope to the rock face, and when he leaned in against it, he could relax his weight.

Arms and legs aching, using muscles that had grown lazy and weak, he continued down. A touch against the back of his neck, a kiss of cold air against his stomach . . . He climbed through them, breathing hard, concentrating on counting each step closer to the bottom.

The light exuded by the dropped knife drew him down.

By the time he reached the base of the small cliff, he had seen nothing that could explain the sense of being touched. He held the knife up for Namior, and while she finished her descent he scanned the rock, looking for cracks in which cave creatures might live, or the waving fronds of strange, dark-loving plants.

Namior jumped down beside him and picked up the second knife. "They'll avoid the light," she said.

"It was just these!" Kel grabbed his loose trouser leg and shook it, waving it against his shin. But even through his anger, he knew that touch did not feel the same.

The rhythmic sound washed over them again, a distant roar, or breathing from close by.

The drop hole sloped steeply down, the ceiling dipping very low and the walls opening outward, changing from a tunnel to a wide crack. Even with two knives smeared with glowing fire kotts, the illumination reached neither extreme, and Kel and Namior descended in a bubble of light. The floor was difficult to negotiate. There was no erosion there, and whatever violent forces had made the holes had left them filled with danger. The edges of cracked rock were sword-sharp; the spaces between promised broken ankles for the unwary. Kel even saw the unmistakable rancid smears of rock rot. He'd seen a man die from rock-rot poisoning in the rainbow-passes of Marrakash Heights, and he had no wish to go that way.

Namior paused to his left, lying sideways on the slope and looking at something in the rock. "Kel . . ." she began, but she seemed speechless.

There were fossil traces in the rocks around them. And when Kel went to her and looked, he saw the petrified remains that had caught her attention: curves of huge shells; the cracked dome of a skull, long and unidentifiable; a clawed seven-fingered hand that could have enveloped his head. He found them unsettling, but they were not what troubled him most. His fear was reserved for the unnatural things buried and fossilized with them. The hardened leather of a fighting helmet. The rusted metal of something that must have been a weapon.

"How old?" Namior said quietly. "A thousand years? Ten thousand?"

Kel grabbed her arm and tried to haul her upright. "Namior, there's no time now—"

"But this could be—"

"Whatever they are, they'll still be here tomorrow."

Namior nodded, and as she stood she ran her hand across the stone curve of a fossilized thigh.

They had to hurry. The sighs or roars from below were marking the passage of time, and he knew that, if his suspicions about the Komadians were correct, the search would be spreading.

Between blinks, something stroked his cheek.

Kel slipped, scraping his leg on a spur of rock and dropping his knife. He went down on one hand, breaking his fall, but driving a spike of sharp stone into his palm. He gritted his teeth and groaned, Core training keeping his pain silent.

Namior was beside him, lifting his hand and checking it in the light from her knife. "It needs healing," she said, her voice flat. She could not heal without magic.

"Something touched me." He wiped at his face with his other hand, expecting to see a spiderweb or some other physical trace. But there was nothing there . . . only the memory of the touch. So intimate.

So *intelligent*.

Namior bent across him, and for a beat he thought she was trying to protect him from something, and he drew in a sharp breath. Then she knelt up again, shaking her head.

"Knife's fallen too far."

Kel saw that his dropped knife had slid into a crevasse in the floor, and leaning sideways he could stare straight down. The crack was barely as wide as his hand, and the knife was at least a dozen steps down. As he watched, the light from its coating of fire kotts was blanked out.

"Its light has gone," he said, climbing unsteadily to his feet.

"The kotts last for—"

"It's *gone*. Swallowed. We have to move quickly." He started down the slope again, crouched so that he did not strike his head on the sharp stones of the rough ceiling. Blood dropped from his fingertips, and he wondered what could smell it, what could taste.

"Kel!" Namior called, her voice a harsh whisper. She caught up with him and grabbed his arm, but all she wanted was contact.

They moved together, taking it in turns to hold the light before them. Kel glanced back only once, and wished he had not. The darkness behind seemed to be pushing at them, advancing with every forward step they took, testing the weak light from the remaining knife as though ready to consume it, as it had the one he had dropped.

He tried not to blink, but his eyes stung.

He thought Namior was panting, but then he realized that she was whispering something as they moved, an urgent chant that echoed from sharp rocks and filtered away into caves no human would ever see. *It'll do us no good!* he thought. *They've done something to the magic, and nothing she's learned can help us now.* But when Namior looked at him and smiled, he realized that her chant was doing *her* some good. Perhaps sometimes, that was what magic was all about.

The tunnel twisted suddenly to the right and opened up into a wide, tall cavern, shockingly illuminated by weak light filtering down from several cracks in the high ceiling. Somewhere up there, other holes led from the cliff top and down into this hidden place.

"I think we picked the right Throat," Namior whispered. Her face shone with perspiration, her hair hung awry, and her eyes were wide. She grinned.

He glanced back into the tunnel from which they had emerged, little more than a crack in the cavern's vast wall. Darkness waited there, but filtered daylight held it at bay. Whatever might have been following them, rolling and billowing with the darkness, had reached its extreme, and Kel felt a brief rush of exhilaration at having escaped.

"Just the dark, Kel," Namior said. He nodded and said no more, because that was all they would ever know.

A terrible smell wafted by, carried on a slight breeze issuing from a hole ahead of them. He knew rot when he smelled it, and the scent of older death as well, musty and mysterious. Beneath the smells hung a red, meaty scent, almost strong enough to chew.

"That way?" He pointed across the cavern into the mouth of a large, conical tunnel. A roar filled the cavern then, and with it came the unmistakable smell of the sea.

"Any way where it doesn't smell like this."

Kel held up his hand, urging Namior to remain still and silent. He exhaled slowly through his mouth, listening for any sounds or signs of pursuit. He heard only the rhythmic growl of the sea.

They started across the cavern, and as they passed below the rents in the ceiling, they saw where the smells were coming from. Several corpses lay across the ground—sheebok, wild goat, and something that could have been a foxlion. A couple were little more than hide and bones, but the foxlion body was fresher, still rotting away and giving home to a legion of larvae and flesh-crawlers. The creatures must have ventured into Throats on the cliff tops, explored down, then slipped, falling through the openings above and dying there in the weak light. Their demise and rot was a hidden affair, and Kel felt like an intruder.

"There's something else," Namior said, and Kel knew what she meant. The red smell of exposed meat did not issue from there.

There were mosses growing across the cavern floor, pale green plants that huddled in the few patches where daylight from above splashed across the rock. There were also several pools of water, deep, black and rippling from small, unknown things moving beneath their surfaces. Kel tried to imagine what could exist down there, and he felt that flush of wonder that had left him so many years before.

They entered the new tunnel, and their senses were immediately assailed afresh. The roar of the sea was much louder, its smell stronger, and they could taste brine on the air. And that other smell, as well. Sickening, heavy, rich.

The floor sloped steeply again, none of it smooth or easily negotiable, but the light from the knife was supplemented by a vague glow creeping up from below. They must have been closer to the bottom of the cliff than the top, and Kel felt much more at ease.

They climbed down, helped each other past fissures in the floor, ducked under sharp protrusions pointing down from the ceiling, and all the while Kel feared reaching somewhere impassable. A narrowing of the tunnel, perhaps, through which they could not pass. A drop into a deep hole, sides too smooth and sheer to climb. An unfordable chasm, a flooded part of the tunnel . . . but all his fears were contradicted by the growing light from ahead. The brighter it grew, the louder the sound of the sea.

But the terrible stench also grew stronger. And rounding a corner, Kel saw the boat, and what they would have to do to launch it.

I CAN'T DO *it*, Namior thought. *No matter how dangerous it would be to go back, I can't do it.*

The smell was appalling. Kel had tried to attribute it to the animal remains they had found in the large cavern, but she had seen the lie in his eyes, and he couldn't have thought she was naïve enough to believe that. She had lived in a fishing village all her life; the smell of insides was known to her.

I don't know what he thinks of me anymore. She looked at him, her lover, the soldier, and she was glad she saw the same doubt in his eyes. *Maybe he can't face this either.*

The tunnel ahead of them was straight, sloping slightly downward and opening up into a wide cave that disgorged onto the rough shale-and-rock beach below the cliffs. Water dripped from the ceiling, and for the last thirty steps of their descent the rock around them had been wet and slick, draped here and there with things of the sea: seaweed, slime, the rotting bodies of fish. But the smell did not come from them.

Directly before them was a rowboat, probably snatched from one of the wrecked Pavmouth Breaks trawlers by the sea. It was wedged in the tunnel. Two paddles were still clipped along its gunwales, and it appeared to be seaworthy. One of the waves must have driven it in there, the water powering past it and forcing up the tunnel behind them, depositing the seaweed and fish that had made their final descent so treacherous.

Beyond the dinghy, dead people covered the cave floor. They were swollen, exposed skin pale and gray and split, puffy flesh gray and bloodless. Some still wore shreds of clothing, torn and tattered by the violence of being driven into that narrow place. She saw faces and looked away, because she would know some of these people. There were men and women, and here and there she saw the slight form of a child. She guessed at twenty dead, though perhaps there were more beneath.

Dead for just over a day, the decay was taking hold, the many wounds they had received quickening the process and allowing what remained inside to leak out.

I can't walk across a floor of dead people.

She tried to look away—at the walls, to see if she could climb across; past the cave mouth at the beach; beyond, out to sea, where she could see the southerly tip of the strange new island—but her eyes were always drawn back to the dead.

"Pushed in by the sea?" she whispered, glad when Kel took her hand and nodded.

"We can take the boat," he said. "Oars are still clipped inside. Can't see any holes. It's barely noon, we can—"

"I can't walk across there!" Namior said, aghast.

Kel held her upper arms, pulling her close until their foreheads were touching. "We can't go back," he said.

And she knew he spoke the truth. There was no way they could go back, and it wasn't only that the visitors might still be looking for them. It was that place they had come through. Her skin crawled thinking of it, and she wondered whether whatever was in the darkness back there still roiled, excited by the unexpected visitors it had received and let slip through its grasp.

I'll get in the boat, she wanted to say. *You can climb over, pull it across the bodies and down to the beach, and I'll sit inside and unclip the oars and get ready to start . . .* But there was no way she could say that. She was strong, she had come with him, and she had to be willing to help.

"They're dead people," Kel said, holding her tight.

"I'll see faces I *know.*"

"Just flesh and blood."

"And their wraiths? They'll be lost, wandering, I have to try to—"

"There's no way to chant them down now, Namior. Even if you *can,* we don't have the time. They'll be found. We'll send Mourner Kanthia this way, and they'll be luckier than those lost to the sea."

Namior closed her eyes and nodded, trying her best to see the sense in what Kel said. If they were to get out to the island and back before darkness fell, they had to leave immediately. The fact that they had found a seaworthy boat was miraculous, but that miracle was terribly balanced by what they must do to get it to the sea. It was like one of the ni and noy philosophies of the life- and death-moon worshippers, people who believed in the balance of their gods: caring and uncaring, good and bad, omniscient and blind. Namior did not ascribe to such beliefs—her own faith was earthbound and buried deep—but she knew what her friend Mell would say. *You've been given a gift and a curse.*

"I won't look down," Namior said.

Kel smiled and hugged her tight. "Neither of us needs to look down." He let her go and went the final few steps to the boat, climbing in, ducking low to avoid the cave's ceiling, and testing its integrity as he walked to its stern. Then he lowered himself onto the carpet of corpses covering their route out to the beach.

Namior closed her eyes, but she could not deny the fresh waft of rot.

And when she opened her eyes again and looked past Kel, she saw the metal man.

KEL WAS STARING down at his feet. His left boot had found space between the head of one body and the knee of another, but there was nowhere for his right foot to go, so he placed it on a chest, closed his eyes, and relaxed his weight from the boat. The corpse exuded a bubbling belch, and Kel breathed out slowly through his mouth to try to avoid the stench.

They're not people, he thought, seeing the hollow where a woman's eye had been picked out by something from the sea.

He heard the scrape of metal on stone. He frowned and looked to his waist and arms, trying to make out where his weapons were touching rock. He did not move, and the sound came again.

The light around his feet changed, and Kel turned and looked up. Something had moved into the mouth of the tunnel, fifteen steps away across the mass of bodies. It was shaped like a person, but there was little human about its movements, its sharp silhouette, or the way its knees and elbows flexed as it crouched into a fighting stance.

What in the Black...?

It was a metal man, its outer shell a dull, dirty gray, movements as fluid and unnatural as those of the machines the Komadians had brought ashore. As it came for him, the only sounds it made were the soft squelch of footsteps on dead bodies, and an occasional scrape as spikes on its metal shell touched rock and drew showers of sparks.

"Kel?"

"Stay back." Kel drew his sword. There was no doubt in his mind whence this thing came, and no hesitation in drawing the weapon. He recognized the way it was coming at him, and it was not to hug and offer a friendly greeting. *So where's its controller?* he had time to think, then the metal man drew a short, stubby tube from a cavity in its leg.

Kel drifted to one side, stepping lightly, ignoring what was beneath his feet. Something gave beneath his left foot and he shifted right, countering before he fell.

A sound thumped at his ears, a terrible blast that left him deafened for a beat, the sounds of the sea and Namior's scream drifting back in from a vast distance. He felt shards of rock speckling his head and right shoulder.

The metal man was five steps away, holding out the short tube. Steam rose from it in a small spiral. The thing's face was a confluence of curved metal plates, small deep holes where its eyes should have been, and for an instant Kel was sure he saw an expression of confusion flit across its solid features.

Kel plucked a throwing knife from his belt and launched it at his metal attacker. It glanced from its face, scoring a deep scratch, and as the thing's head flipped back Kel ran, driving forward with his sword and searching for a weak spot. He could see none.

The thing deflected the sword with its arm, bringing the other hand around in a wide, high punch. Kel ducked just in time to avoid receiving a metal fist in his face, but it passed over his head and struck his left shoulder, driving him down and back. His feet went from under him and he fell, wincing at the terrible softness of his landing. He kicked out, both heels connecting with the thing's right knee.

The metal man grunted.

Kel's eyes went wide with surprise. He glanced at the mouth of the cave, searching for the Komadian with his or her controlling box, but there was no one else there.

His attacker came again, aiming the steam-spewing tube, and Kel realized at last what he was looking into. Its circular end pointed at him like the mouth of a tunnel, deep and black. It was a projectile weapon, more complex than a simple crossbow. And he was looking directly into its business end.

He delved into his pocket and threw the acid pouch in one fluid movement. The pouch hit high on the thing's forehead and burst, scattering acrid dust across its shiny face. Kel squeezed his eyes closed and exhaled, but when he looked again a beat later the metal man was before him, closer than ever, coughing slightly, but otherwise seemingly unaffected.

The weapon's barrel was three steps from Kel's face.

Something blurred through the air above him, knocked the steam-tube aside just as it fired, and struck the metal man across the face. The projectile hit the tunnel ceiling, and chunks of rock pattered down across the trampled corpses.

"Kel!" Namior shouted. She'd dropped the oar, but she already had the second one in her hand, ready to throw.

The metal thing staggered back. It had dropped the tube, and both hands went to its hips, drawing small throwing stars, which it lobbed at Namior. She fell into the boat, screeching slightly as one found home.

Namior! Kel braced his wounded left hand against the body beneath him, tensed himself and pushed, shoving hard with both feet. He held the sword before him, aiming it at the thing's throat where the metal was lined with joints.

The metal man turned just in time to take the sword in its

neck. It grunted again, driven back against the tunnel wall. Its hands came up to knock the blade aside, but Kel leaned on the handle with all his weight, digging both feet into whatever lay beneath them and pushing.

Metal screeched against metal, the thing's throat plates parted, and a startlingly red gush of blood pulsed between folds.

Kel paused for a beat, then pushed harder. He heard choking as blood bubbled between the sword and the metal suit. And then the stricken thing let out a terrible, familiar screech.

Kel gasped. He let go of the sword and stumbled back a few steps, barely keeping his footing on the uneven surface of corpses.

The metal man fell to its knees, both hands clawing at its throat, scratching long scars into the suit's surface. It tipped forward, then steam trickled from two rows of holes on its back, metallic sounds snicked and whined, and a series of plates folded back to reveal what lay inside.

Two long, thin limbs rose from the body, flexing as though glad at their release. Blue fire sparkled along their lengths, sizzling the air and countering the stench of rot with the tang of burning. As they curved in toward each other, ready to touch and form the perfect arc, Kel swallowed his shock and acted.

A throwing knife in each fist, he raised his hands over his shoulders, took one step forward and launched them both. His aim was perfect. One limb flipped away, completely severed, while another slumped broken to one side.

"Run, Namior!" He heard her struggling over the side of the boat, landing on the bodies and dry-heaving. "Up and run, out, *now*!"

Kel never took his eyes from the Stranger. He no longer saw its metal suit...all he saw were its limbs, and the blood still pulsing from where he had stabbed it in the neck. As he went forward, he kicked the metal tube it had been firing at him. It was surprisingly light.

He grabbed the sword handle in both hands. The Stranger squealed. Kel lifted, bringing its head up so that he could look at its metal mask, searching out the eyes. "You may be here at last," he said, "but it'll never be easy for you."

The Stranger growled, or laughed.

Kel pushed on the sword, shoving it through the Stranger's neck and severing his spine.

Then he turned and ran.

NAMIOR WAS OUT onto the beach before she saw her own silhouette thrown before her. The blast of light was brief, but staggering, and the dull thud that accompanied it sounded like something rearranging itself in the land.

She resisted the urge to turn and look, because she heard Kel coming after her. She knew it was he because with every pounding footstep on the shale beach she heard him saying *Run, run, run.* She was not sure whether he was talking to her, or to himself.

She turned left, instinctively heading away from Pavmouth Breaks as the pounding sea forced her to make a choice. Fear prevented her from registering anything of her surroundings: only the need to flee.

"Namior!" She slowed and turned at last, and Kel was reaching for her. "Down behind this rock, this should be safe enough."

"Safe enough from what?"

"One of *them,*" he said, explaining nothing. He carried a golden tube in his hand, the same thing she had seen the metal man firing at him, and she flinched away. "Don't worry," Kel said. "It's dead."

They slipped behind a huge rock that had tumbled down from the cliffs above, and Kel was up leaning against its face, looking over the boulder and back the way they had come.

Namior stood next to him, for comfort more than anything, and that way she saw what emerged from the cave. A dark thing thrashed out onto the narrow beach, spinning, hissing, sizzling, crunching rocks beneath it, sending shards spinning through the air to splash in the sea or ricochet from the cliff face. She had the terrible impression that it was *searching* for them, but it flitted this way and that, as though possessed of a terrible indecision.

"Stranger's wraith," Kel whispered.

Namior reached out to him. *He was right*, she thought, and the idea was terrible. What evil had touched Noreela at the very place she called home?

"Can we run?" she asked. With the little Kel had told her about the Strangers, she assumed that to be the end.

"No," he said, ducking down and pulling her with him. "No, but it won't last for long. They never do."

They sat there behind the rock, squatting on pebbles and smashed-up wreckage deposited by the terrible waves, and listened to the thing raging behind them. Namior had sensed many wraiths in her life, and she had even seen some, when the light was just right and there was a cool, calm mist in the air. But she had never imagined anything like that creature.

A Stranger. A mad wraith. This can't be of Noreela. And they claim no magic, though their steam things astound me. She leaned in close to Kel. "They're from somewhere else, aren't they?"

"We've been sure of that all along," he replied, touching her face with one hand. "We just don't know where."

The sounds of violence lessened behind them, and Kel stood slowly to peer past the rock. He slid back down, landing with a gasp, and his head dipped forward, sweaty hair hanging on either side of his face. He was holding the metal tube in his hands, but he seemed not to notice it.

"Kel?" Namior stood slowly, and when Kel did not reach to stop her she knew the wraith was gone. The air on the beach seemed to shimmer before the cave, as though a great heat was issued from the opening, but of the raging dark thing there was no sign. Patterns of disruption scarred the loose shale. The sea came in, hushed against the shore and pulled out again, unconcerned, eternal.

Kel stood quickly, reaching into his jacket pocket for the small bag of things he had shown her before. "I have to call the Core," he said.

"Will it work here? Through stone?"

He smiled and shook one of the nutlike objects into his palm. He handed it to her while he tied the bag and put it away. Namior ran her fingertips across the thing in her hand, feeling the ridged shell spiked with delicate fronds, and touching the coiled tail that protruded from one end.

"One way to find out," Kel said, and he took the nut from her. He stared at it for a moment, his face going slack. "I've dreaded ever having to do this." Then he leaned forward and breathed out directly into his palm.

The stringy tail flexed slightly, shifted, and started to unravel. It turned around and around, its coil becoming wider, and while the nut remained in his palm, the tail stretched out over the side of his hand and grew strong and straight parallel to the ground. When it finished growing and changing it was as long as a person's arm.

"One of the Core's greatest witches made these," he said. "A charm, a spell, a wish, and a series of words tied up in a moment of time. Every Core member has taken a vow allied to those charms, and every single one will hear its call."

"How many are there?"

Kel shrugged. "Perhaps three hundred."

"Against this?" Namior gestured out at the island, thought of the ships sailing in and docking, and the man dressed in a metal skin carrying the steam weapon. And she wondered if perhaps Kel was mad.

"The Core will bring an army." He placed the tip of the tail against the ground between his feet and pushed.

Namior was amazed. The plantlike stem pressed between

two pebbles and pierced the ground, sliding in smoothly as Kel pushed down with little effort. At the point where its whole length entered the ground was a drizzle of sparks.

"I never thought I'd see you using magic," Namior said, and even after everything she managed a smile.

"I haven't used it yet," Kel said.

What if he can't? What if the interference stops that as well? But Namior could not think like that. Whatever angle the Core's witches used to approach magic must surely be mindful of such problems.

Once the nutlike object was pressed close to the ground, its long stem deep in the land, Kel knelt and used the Stranger's weapon to crush it and send the signal. That was poetry in justice, if ever Namior had seen any.

The nut shattered, shards of it speckling her feet. Kel stood up and backed away.

"What now?" Namior asked.

He frowned and shook his head.

The nut issued one thin tendril of bluish smoke, then its shattered shell rose rapidly from the ground, carried up by the stiff stalk. Once clear of the ground it fell sideways and shattered across the rocks, stem breaking into a hundred pieces as if made from the finest blown glass.

"Even this," Kel said, and his face fell.

"It didn't work?"

"No. Interference, your family called it. I call it poisoning. The Strangers are here, and they've poisoned the magic, made it easy for themselves. And this . . ." He held up the tube, examining it more closely. "*This* is their magic. And it doesn't rely on some vague language that few people know." He threw the tube down and kicked it away. "It doesn't need witches to chant, or a drawing of power, or Practitioners to run it. All it needs is steam." He stepped forward and kicked the tube again, sending it clattering across the beach toward the sea. "Steam! And how that fucking Stranger back there didn't kill me, I'll never know."

"There's room for luck in any belief or religion."

"Luck?" He was shouting, though his rage was directed outward across the sea, not back at Namior. "I feel so lucky now, that's for sure. I'm the luckiest Core member in Noreela right now! Here I am, at the heart of everything I've been trying to escape for five years. Right at the center of things, the place and time the Core has been agonizing about and fearing for hundreds of years. And what? I'm on my fucking own!"

"You're not on your own."

Kel looked at her, and his eyes were watery. He wiped at them and came to her, glancing around as he did so. They were still alone on the beach.

"This is so dangerous," he said. "This could be the beginning of the end, and . . ." He held her shoulders and looked intently at her face, as though trying to imprint her image on his memory.

"I'm not leaving you now," Namior said.

Kel nodded, went to say something, then turned and looked out at the island.

"We could go back," Namior said. "Try to get past them, go inland to where the magic might still be working."

"They could have done this everywhere."

"We should find out!"

"Back through the Throats?" he said.

"It'll take time, but—"

"No," Kel said. "Out there. To the island. They'll be expecting people to flee inland, and they'll have set up guards to prevent it. We might get past, but if we don't and they catch us . . . well, we know for sure they're looking for me now, at least. But out there is the last place they'll expect anyone to go."

"And maybe your signal will work from the island."

"Magic?"

"The Strangers are doing something to it. But if they truly don't use or even have magic, why do that same thing on their own island? And their island is in Noreelan waters, now."

Kel grinned. "You're a genius, Namior Feeron."

"Glad to help, wood-carver."

He seemed about to speak again, but he glanced past her at the cave, face growing grim.

"I'll help." Namior thought of the corpses she had run across, the feel of them giving underfoot, the smells and sounds... "Two will be quicker than one."

She expected him to protest, but he only nodded. And whatever it was he wanted to say, he kept inside for another time.

THE STRANGER'S METALLIC shell was twisted and distorted, and in places it seemed to have melted and re-formed in strange, fluid shapes. His body was all but gone, and a foul-smelling smoke rose from what was left. Namior saw smears of soot around the tunnel's wall and ceiling from where the Stranger had... ignited? Exploded? She was not sure exactly what had happened, and it was not the time to ask.

Namior Feeron walked across the bodies of dead friends to help those that were still alive. That was what she kept telling herself, at least. She ignored the sounds and smell and concentrated on the faces of those she loved: her mother and great-grandmother; Mell, searching for Trakis, digging against hope; Mourner Kanthia, so brave and vulnerable even though most regarded her as too close to death to be comfortable. And Kel Boon, the wood-carver who had turned out to be a soldier as well. And it was the "as well" that kept her eyes on him, the realization in all the confused, intense moments that he *was* still the man she had fallen in love with. The wood carving, the move to Pavmouth Breaks, had not been falsehoods on his part, nor the attempt to hide from whatever had happened. It was perhaps the most honest thing Kel had done. He was a soldier, but he was still a wood-carver and her lover as well, and as long as that remained so, she would be there to help.

Kel climbed past the boat and picked up one of the oars she had used to strike at the Stranger. He wedged it beneath the hull, tested the flexibility of the wood for a beat, then shoved.

The boat slid free, scraping across rocks then sliding onto the corpses.

Namior pulled, eyes half-closed. She concentrated on the sound of the waves behind her, timeless and familiar. She had been born with that noise in her ears, and every moment of her life so far had sung to the same tune. When at last she felt cold water lapping around her feet and pouring into her boots, she opened her eyes again, felt the sun on her face where it had just cleared the cliff, and climbed into the boat.

Kel pushed it out past the breaking waves, then jumped into the bow. He and Namior sat side by side and took an oar each. The swell toyed with them for a time, rocking left and right, but they eventually maneuvered the boat so that the bow pointed out to sea. Then they started rowing, cutting through the breakers and finding the gentle swell of the ocean, and watching the cliffs as they slowly fell behind.

The impact of what they were doing suddenly struck home. But Namior did not stop rowing. The exertion felt good, the perspiration on her back and beneath her armpits was cooled by the breeze.

"We'll be back," Kel said.

"You can't say that." A mile to the north, Namior saw the Komadians' ships at dock before the mole and inside the harbor. She hoped that from that far away, their rowboat would be indistinguishable from the waves. But with magic distant to her, there was nothing she could do to camouflage them.

"I can!" Kel said. His certainty shocked her, and she did not reply.

They rowed on, the boat lifting and dipping in perfect rhythm with the great sea. As more time passed, so a greater stretch of the coastline was presented for their view. Namior could see scars on the land where the great waves had struck, but the damage was starting to feel more remote. It was only beats since they had left land, but it already felt like days.

"We're rowing somewhere else," she said at last. "We're leaving the whole world and going somewhere else."

Kel was quiet for a while, and she thought he was not going to answer. But then he stopped rowing. Namior stopped as well, and when she looked at him they were close enough to smell each other's breath.

"We could be the first from Noreela ever to set foot on another land," he said.

Namior surprised Kel, and herself, by laughing out loud. "They'll write songs about us!"

And to the tune of the sea, and the rhythm of the oars, Namior and Kel made their way to somewhere new, and terrible.

Chapter Eight

somewhere new

WHEN THEY PAUSED for a rest, Kel seemed unsure of which way to look: back toward shore, to see whether they were being pursued; or out at the island, revealing itself in more detail the nearer they drew. So he sat beside Namior, shifting view every few beats. He said nothing, so she assumed there was little to say. She knew that would not remain the case for long.

She dangled her ground rod in the water and closed her eyes, opening herself to the language of the land. What little she heard was confused. A vague shred of what she knew came through, but it was lessened by a terrible, growing distance. She attempted a light spark, the simplest feat of magic she could think of, but even that did not manifest.

"Nothing?" Kel asked.

"The closer we get to the island, the farther away the magic becomes."

"Your shoulder."

She touched the wound where the Stranger's throwing star had hit her, shook her head. "It's nothing. Your hand?"

Kel held up his left hand. The blood was clotting, the gash in his palm ugly but no longer bleeding.

"We should start rowing again," he said. They did, and though the currents seemed to be nudging them southward, Kel did nothing to correct their course. The sea carried them away from the direct path between the island and Pavmouth Breaks, and though they could see no boats traveling between the two, that could change at any moment. If they were spied out there, there would be no escape. Namior did not think Kel could hold his own for very long against a boatload of those metal-clad Strangers.

Though her arms and legs were already starting to burn with the strain, Namior found the rise and fall of waves and the rhythm of their rowing soporific. All her life spent in a fishing village, and she had been out to sea only twice. Both times she'd not enjoyed the journey, and soon into the second trip she'd been sick. Fighting nausea and tiredness, determined not to let him down, she started talking to Kel.

"The Stranger, that metal armor. Have you seen anything like that before?"

"Never the armor. But the Stranger inside, yes. They're people, but they have . . . Well, it's strange. Gills on their necks. And those long things on their backs, like limbs or tentacles. We think they use them to communicate. They always reminded me of beetles."

"I've heard about armor," she said. Talking helped; the nausea was dwindling already. And she sensed that Kel knew more.

"Nothing like that, though. I've seen militia on the borders of the Poison Forests wearing armor of sorts, but it's heavy, unwieldy. That looked almost..." He splashed his oar in hard, taking out his frustration on the sea.

"It was like he was made of metal," Namior said. "I thought that's what it was when we saw him. A metal man. One of their steam machines."

"Finely crafted, for sure. The joints were smooth; he could move well. Almost as if the suit was aiding him."

"But you still found a way in."

"Yes," Kel said quietly. Three oar-dips later, he continued. "I think that was a lucky strike. Wedged between two plates, and when he turned his head aside, it pulled the sword in. Lucky. That's all."

Namior stopped rowing. The boat turned slightly, and Kel backed water to keep them bow on to the waves.

"There might be hundreds of them on the island."

"We'll look from a distance," Kel said. "I'm not stupid, Namior. I've been doing this for a long time. I know how to be quiet, what to look for. I'm trained."

She looked at him, seeing the man she loved and the man she had never known, and both of them stared back.

"So, the Komadians? The Strangers? Who are they?"

"The people I've been waiting for all my life." He nodded at her oar, and they started rowing again.

"Maybe the Strangers are just their soldiers," Namior suggested.

"That's what I've been thinking. And if that's the case, the armor shows they're readying for a fight."

Namior's sense of adventure was quickly being overshadowed by fear. She had always wanted to travel, but her witch training had kept her at home. *Not too long,* her mother had said several moons ago. *A year, a little more, and you'll be ready. But training half-finished can be dangerous. A witch knows from her ancestors what magic can do, and if you're left with only that knowledge, and not the ability, it can torture you. So stay, be here with us while we tell you all we know. And then, if you must, you can go.*

Why didn't you go, Mother? she had asked. *And your mother, and her mother as well? There must be so much to see out there!*

We did, the woman had replied, surprising her. Namior had always imagined her family as bound to Pavmouth Breaks by unbreakable ties. The thought of them traveling, seeing the vastness of Noreela . . . it had opened her mind, but also unsettled her.

But you came back?

Her mother had smiled then, nodded, and looked across the harbor from where they sat. *When you see so much of the world that your sense of wonder becomes bruised, and your hunger for more lessens, home is always the best place to be.*

Namior had been unsure of what that meant, but rather than lessening her desire for travel, it had made her more ravenous.

At last the wider world was revealing itself. And it had teeth.

The sea lifted them gently up and down. Ahead of them, the sheer cliffs receded; the narrow beach at their base was little more than a white line of breaking waves. Along the shore to their left, Pavmouth Breaks lay nestled in the mouth of the River Pav. The damage was evident from there; areas of the village built on the hillsides were defined and sharp, while those close down to the sea appeared smudged and indistinct. The spikes of several large ships grew from the sea outside the harbor. They were too far away to see movement, but the village seemed dangerous to them, not like home at all. Namior squinted to try to make out her house, but they all blurred into one.

Kel rowed in silence. He was frowning, and he kept glancing over his shoulder at the approaching island. Namior could almost hear his mind working, and she kept quiet for a while, giving him space to think.

Her fear for herself was matched by fear for her family.

What she and Kel were attempting was painfully dangerous, but her mother and great-grandmother were at home in Pavmouth Breaks, still under the illusion that the visitors were benevolent. At least she and Kel knew the truth. They had come to Pavmouth Breaks, and they were building something beyond the village. The eventual outcome could not be good.

"There are settlements along the shore," Kel said. "High cliffs, and low beaches. We'll go around the southern tip, see if there's somewhere more remote to land. Let's just hope the tide and currents don't carry us out to sea."

"Oh, thank you," Namior said. "How comforting."

"Well, at least if they do, you'll have your desire for adventure satisfied."

"I'm rapidly starting to reconsider."

They rowed together, shoulders and arms touching now and then, and Namior realized just how grateful she was to have him with her. They were heading into danger, but Kel had been there many times before.

THE CLOSER THEY drew to the island, the more nervous Kel became. He rowed while trying to look behind him all the time, and his neck and shoulders ached. He was waiting to be seen, watching for the ominous signs of sails being raised and boats launching to intercept them, and for the first time in his life he was afraid of the sea. The sea's depths became apparent; if they had to jump from the boat and swim, they would have no idea of what might be lying in wait below. The water could be a dozen steps deep, or six hundred. He had seen the prints of a sea wolf in the muddy harbor, and a disaster so great, washing scores of dead out into the sea, would bring many more carrion creatures. He'd heard countless tales of sea monsters over ales in the Dog's Eyes, but until then he had regarded most of them as myth.

His weapons felt heavy around his body, but they were tied well. They made no sound. He had O'Peeria's influence to thank for that.

The island was a rugged place, its haphazard coastline made up of jagged cliffs, steep inlets and low, rocky beaches. He could see signs of small settlements spotting the coastline, but Kel hoped that the farther they went around the southern shore, the more remote landing places might be available. It was hardly a plan, but it was all he could come up with just then.

He wondered what O'Peeria would do in such a situation, and he answered that thought in her voice: *Go to the island, find the bastards' weaknesses, then contact the Core, however the fuck you can.*

"You're sure we're doing the right thing, Kel?" Namior asked, not for the first time.

"Yes," he said. It was not the time for uncertainty.

Their little boat drifted farther south, and it started taking on water. He had been noticing it for a while, how the sloshing water in the boat's base was slowly growing deeper, but he'd shut it out. One more thing to worry about. At last, it was becoming obvious.

"Namior . . ." he said, but she already knew.

"I'll bail, you row." She knelt before him and started scooping handfuls of water out over the sides. He shifted along the seat a little, grabbed her oar and started rowing again. They moved slower, but at least the water level soon seemed to drop.

They were south of the island by then, and Kel was quite certain he could see no signs of habitation there. So he turned the boat's side to the waves and started rowing against the currents and tides. His earlier joke about drifting past and being carried out to sea came back to haunt him.

The rowing was hard work, and with the sea battering the craft side on, looking back at the island was more difficult.

Namior glanced up now and then, looking for him. "Closer," she said every time. "Getting closer."

He could feel the weight of the island at his back, a dreadful gravity pulling him in. If he stopped rowing, it would work with fate to draw him on. They were set solidly on their course.

"We're almost there," Namior said at last. "Let me help again, we need to find somewhere to land."

Kel shifted along the seat and glanced back. That part of the coastline was heavily wooded, almost down to the shore in some parts, and there seemed to be no easy places to land a boat. That was probably why there were apparently no settlements there, and it would work to their advantage. He saw beaches of rock, mud and exposed tree roots, and Kel wondered what the island's constantly shifting placement would do to its geography. He had no comprehension of the mysterious forces involved in shifting something so huge, but the rough and random shorelines must be part of the result.

"It won't be easy."

"Sea's not too rough close in," Namior said. "We should spot the place we want to land, then try to row against the current for a bit, let it guide us in."

"So is this an expert talking?" he asked, smiling.

"No. Common sense." She grinned, and a wave broke against the boat, sending spray across her face. Spitting, Namior settled beside Kel and they started rowing again.

They saw a place where the spray seemed lower, and the waves less violent when they broke, and decided to head for there. Kel thought Namior's idea was a good one, so they turned the boat and struggled against the waves striking the island at an angle. After an exhausting time edging along the coast they turned again, giving their stern to the waves and trying to control their route with the oars. They managed to maintain their aim, and the craft rose and dipped sickeningly as it began to hit the breaking waves.

Kel looked to shore, scanning the tree line, searching the shadows beneath for glints of metal or pale faces. They still seemed to be alone.

At last they beached on a spread of muddy sand and tangled tree roots. They hauled the boat up the slope, out of the surf and away from the prying eyes of anyone sailing by. They had to move along the beach before they could drag it in amongst the trees, turning it so that the bow was aimed at the sea. Then they both collapsed onto the soft ground, gasping, sweating, and finally hearing the roar of the sea without suffering it.

Kel kept alert, listening, scanning the undergrowth, smelling the air. *There could be anything here*, he thought. *It's a new island, a new world . . . anything*. He stared into the treetops and saw no monstrous forms lurking up there. The trees themselves did not seem overtly alien, though he could not identify the species. Birds sang somewhere out of sight, and something scratched a constant song behind them in the jungle. It sounded loud and large, but it reminded Kel of the small, finger-length hoppers on Noreela that could make so much noise with only their hind legs.

On Noreela . . . The phrase sent a shiver through him.

"We're somewhere else," Namior whispered. She sat up, scooped a handful of wet, gritty soil, and sniffed at it. "Smells the same." She picked a frond from a low fern. "Feels the same." She stood slowly and looked around, staring up the gradual slope where the beach gave way to wild growth. "But it isn't the same."

Kel stood as well, so close to Namior that their arms touched. "No. Not the same at all."

There were no signs of habitation anywhere, current or historical. There was movement and noise, but the sounds of nature seemed undisturbed by their presence. Kel rested a hand on his short sword, but right then it was not needed. Nothing came at them from between the trees, no one called. They were alone.

Namior took out her ground rod and pressed it into the sandy soil. She knelt beside it for a beat, eyes closed, then looked up at Kel and shook her head.

"There's nothing," she said. "Not even a background whisper. It's as if magic never existed."

"Only here," Kel said, because he could see how disturbed she was. Her eyes were wide and her face had paled, and she looked left and right. "And we won't stay for long. Come on. We'll be careful, but we have to move. Along the coast, I think. Staying close to the sea until we reach one of their settlements, then we'll hide out for a while and watch."

"Are you going to try one of your Core communicators?"

He shook his head. He only had two left, and they were too precious to waste. *Noreela will depend on one of these sending its signal.* He touched the small bag in his pocket and felt less at ease than ever.

THEY MOVED UPHILL and inland, because the ground close to the sea was wet and boggy. Spray from breaking waves washed through the air, and occasionally a larger wave would surge higher than normal, sending a small swell of water up into the woods. The ground vegetation at the shore was sparse, and the few hardy plants that survived there had thin leaves and thick stems. Their stems were spotted with white boils, and Kel guessed it was salt absorbed through their roots.

It was no real coastline. There were no defined beaches, no dividing line between types of vegetation, and the trees close to the sea had their great root networks exposed by water action. The roots looked fresh, and on their way in Kel had seen the water muddied each time a wave struck the shore. It was a new coast, formed days ago when the island first appeared. Perhaps older coastlines had been buried beneath the sea. The idea that the island was shrinking with each movement or manifestation was troubling; Kel could understand how desperate the residents of such a place would become.

A hundred steps from the sea, in amongst the trees, the slope of the land lessened, and the air was free of spray. They headed east, back toward Noreela and the part of the island where they had seen settlements along the shore. Kel went first, senses alert, mouth slightly open to aid silent breathing and good hearing. If one of the metal-clad Strangers came at them, at least he knew what they were, and where lay the weak spot in their armor. If more than one came at them...

The reality of what was happening struck him, so hard that the breath was knocked from him and he went to his knees. Namior was beside him, holding his shoulders, asking what was wrong. Kel held up his hand.

"I'm okay," he said. "Thinking."

Thinking about his time in the Core, all the training, the scant information about Strangers passed down from generation to generation, the threat the Core believed the Strangers posed, the theories about where they had come from and why they were in Noreela, the long periods of waiting and the brief moments of excitement when a Stranger was discovered, tracked and killed. O'Peeria, and her strange Shantasi ways. She had been a very soulful woman, but brutal when the need arose, and she grabbed life by the hair and whipped it around to her own liking. There he was, discovering the Core's greatest fear, searching an island of Strangers and invaders for he knew not what, unable to contact and mobilize the Core because magic had been put to sleep...no one had ever expected that, nor anticipated it, because magic had been with them for so long, ever since the Year of the Black sixteen centuries before. It was as much a part of everyone's life as breathing.

For every Stranger they had found and killed, there must have been more that somehow returned to the island, bringing with them everything they had learned of Noreela, and all the vulnerable points that could aid invasion. *We rely on magic so much*, Kel thought. *And it's the first thing they take.* He realized that, much as the Komadians seemed to rely on whatever strange power drove their machines, to do what they had done must take some far greater magic than he or Namior could hope to understand.

Once back on Noreela he had to get away, and see if the abuse of the land's powers extended beyond the Komadians' beachhead.

"Kel?" Namior said again.

"We're at the center of everything," he said. "You and me, we carry so much weight. Can you bear it, Namior?"

"Together we'll have to."

"Yes, together." He thought of O'Peeria, and wished she were still alive. Her death had been his fault, and he would never convince himself otherwise. But if he failed Noreela, that death would have been in vain.

"We'll be fine," Namior whispered into his ear, and she kissed him on the neck. How she knew what he needed, how she was so attuned to his moods and thoughts, he did not know. But he was glad.

They moved on. Kel found new confidence in his step and new purpose guiding his thoughts. He was Core again, enemy of Noreela's enemy. And he had already drawn blood.

THEY CAME TO a small ravine, cut into the land by a stream gurgling down from inland. There was a gorgeous array of red, purple and yellow orchids there, as well as rushes that swayed and hushed with the water.

Kel paused in the tree line for a few beats, concerned at the open space they had to cross. It seemed silent enough.

"Good job," Namior whispered. "I'm really thirsty." Kel was going to protest at drinking water from an unknown land, but if the water was dangerous to them, then the air would be as well, and the gentle touch of plant fronds, and they would already be doomed. Besides, the thought of a drink was good.

They climbed down the ravine's side and approached the stream.

Namior froze. "Do you see it?"

Kel crouched and drew his sword, left hand hovering close to a throwing knife on his belt. He looked around quickly, but he saw no danger.

"What?"

"The stream. Something . . . strange."

He looked at the stream and all he saw was the running water, sunlight sparkling from its surface, flies darting to and fro above it, and lush grasses and reeds growing in clumps along its banks. Some of them swished in a gentle breeze. None of the flies spotting the air were larger than his little fingernail. Nothing else moved.

"I can't see," he said, frustrated now. "What is it?"

"Part of the stream isn't flowing."

"How can—?" And then he saw. Twenty steps from them, a stretch of the stream seemed painted and motionless. It was maybe eight steps in length, and above and below it the water surged and splashed, moving quickly in its race for the sea. It was like a painted version of the scene, perfect in every way, yet home to neither movement nor sound.

And then it *did* move. The stretch of water shifted sideways, revealing the true stream underneath. As it shifted it changed, transforming from the texture and color of water to the spiky, sharp edges of lush green grass. Still eight steps long, it seemed to flex across the ground and whip through the grass like a gentle wind.

"What in the Black is that?" Namior muttered.

Kel saw the eyes opening. Small, black, they appeared at the front of the shape, piercing through the image of motionless grass. They were lifeless and emotionless, and he had never seen their like.

"Namior—" he began, but then the thing opened its

mouth. The growl was unsettling, a low rumble that Kel felt in his stomach rather than heard.

It came at them, the images across its body flickering as it passed grasses, ferns and stones. Its mouth hung open, red and deep and spiked with long, sharp teeth. It had no need to camouflage its insides, nor its intentions.

Namior jumped to one side and Kel stepped into its path, launching a throwing knife and plucking another from his belt as the first struck home.

The creature roared and veered away, climbing the ravine's side and hanging there. It merged with the bare earth and occasional mosses, invisible but for the protruding knife and the blood flowing from the wound. Kel could hear its breathing, fast and heavy. He held the other knife at the ready.

"Let's go," Namior said.

"I should finish it off."

"It's a wild thing," she said. "And *amazing*!"

"And if it follows, it'll creep up on us amazingly quickly as well." He plucked the small crossbow from his belt, primed and loaded it, never taking an eye from the creature hanging on the ravine wall. He could just make out where its head was turned back, deep black eyes staring into him.

He aimed the crossbow between those eyes. The thing did not seem to flinch.

"Kel," Namior said, but she sounded resigned.

"We can't take the risk." He fired the crossbow. The animal shrieked, the bolt disappeared, then the creature slid slowly to the floor of the ravine, claws carving deep gouges in the earth and rock wall. As it slid and died, the colors and textures of its skin changed rapidly, passing through several states before resolving into an even, dark green.

"There it is," Kel said. "Would you really want that thing following us?" Dead, the creature was revealed. It was a long, wide lizard, almost twice the length of the tallest man. It had vicious-looking claws on strong legs, and across its back were hundreds of spiked, bony protrusions. Kel's throwing knife stuck from a fold of skin behind its head, and there was a wound just above its left eye where the bolt had penetrated. It had swirls and angular patterns on its sides, and they could have been painted there.

"Do you think it was wild?" Namior asked.

Kel moved closer, bending to look at the markings. It was difficult to tell whether they were naturally formed. "Don't know. We should move on quickly, just in case."

"Just in case its owner is out there somewhere?"

After Kel retrieved and cleaned his knife, they climbed the other side of the ravine and slipped between trees, continuing their journey toward the part of the island facing Noreela.

Kel tried to see everything differently. A branch swayed in a breeze, leaves fluttering shapes and colors down at him, and he paused, trying to discern the shape of the creature hanging there. But it was just a branch, and they were only leaves.

Namior said she was hungry, but though there were bright red fruits hanging from one particular species of tree, Kel did not want to risk eating any. He'd spent enough time traveling in Noreela to know that sometimes, plants gave out attractive signals to intentionally kill potential predators. In a strange place, caution was essential.

After seeing the lizard-thing emerge, they had not even dared drink from the stream.

"Are you keeping track?" Namior asked. "If we have to come back this way in a rush, will you be able to find the boat?"

"No problem," Kel said. "The Core—"

"Is there anything they *didn't* train you to do?"

"Wood carving." Kel grinned, as much in pleasure that he could still joke, as in response to Namior's own smile.

WHEN THEY HEARD the first voices, they were passing through a glade of pink-and-white flowering trees, the colors and hues seeming to affect the air itself. The grass there was long and soft, the trunks smooth and slender. Kel was looking for trees that were not trees, but he saw only beauty. An irrational anger simmered beneath his appreciation of the place. His friends were digging in mud for their dead relatives, yet on Komadia there were places of such splendor and peace.

The voices came from ahead of them, low and unconcerned. Someone laughed. Kel fell to his knees, trying to locate the exact direction of the voices, looking around to see where they could hide. Namior was down beside him, pointing away between the trees at a movement she had seen. She moved close to Kel and cupped her hands around his ear.

"I'm sure they're moving away."

Kel nodded, because he thought so too. He stood and ran, crouched down, to a thick-boled tree at the edge of the glade. He heard Namior following him.

Through the trees he saw four people walking along a path in the forest. The path had been worn down over time, a wide, smooth spread of dry soil, broken here and there by protruding tree roots. It must have been used frequently.

Two of the people were Komadian, indistinguishable from those who had stepped ashore in Pavmouth Breaks. Their clothes were similar, their faces pale, hair long and tied by several metal clips down their backs. Another had dark skin and short hair, and intricate black tattoos swirling across her bare shoulders and down her arms. She was quieter than the rest and walked with a graceful purpose.

The fourth person was blue.

Kel squinted, in case the sun was dazzling him and confusing his vision. But the sunlight was filtered by the many leaves and blooms above, landing around his feet in softened, gentle tones. And he heard Namior's gasp as she saw the short man.

His skin was a very light, pale blue, his hair blond and long, and he walked with the same casual gait as the rest. He laughed, talked, gesticulated with his long arms. He was not ill at ease, and the others treated him like one of their own.

But blue skin . . . !

Nothing else about him seemed so peculiar. He was shorter than the others, though not surprisingly so, and lightly built. He gestured at the air as he spoke, as though painting shapes on the atmosphere of the forest. Kel could hear his voice, and it was deep and melodious, the sort of voice that would attract attention around any campfire—

But his skin is blue.

Kel and Namior watched the people disappear along the path, drawing farther away with every step, then passing out of sight behind a fold in the land.

"We're imagining the same thing," Kel said. "We must be. *No one* has blue skin."

"No one from Noreela," Namior whispered.

Kel searched around for a reason: blue blooms on a tree they had not noticed; heavy spiderwebs casting a hazy blue light. But there was nothing.

Namior shivered and leaned into Kel, craving contact. "This is all so wrong. I just can't *imagine . . .*"

"It's harsh," Kel said. "But many of the great thinkers have said there must be more than just water across the seas."

Namior shook her head. "It's just more than we can think about, more than we know. Thinking they might exist and meeting them are . . . two very different things."

"I knew a Shantasi," Kel said.

"O'Peeria." Namior said her name with no inflection; Kel had never been open about his lost love.

"Even though she was Shantasi, and they bestow great importance on their ancestral heritage, she found the idea difficult."

"Shanti wasn't very far away, so the stories say."

"Close enough to sail to in ten days."

"Maybe we should leave," Namior said, but when Kel looked at her he knew she did not mean that. There was fear and dread, but her eyes also glittered with an excitement he knew was reflected in his own.

"We must be close to a settlement by now," he said. "Once we've seen that, it'll be time to leave. I need to see as much as I can."

"For the Core?"

"And for myself."

"I can hear the songs they'll sing already," Namior said, smiling softly.

They moved on much more carefully, conscious that they were on land where Strangers were known to tread. Kel wondered whether the lizard was one of their own; a Komadian more unusual than simply a human wearing blue skin. He wondered so much . . . but safety was his prime concern. He could not risk Namior, and more important, he could not risk himself. The weight of Noreela's future pressed on his shoulders and weighed in his pocket, and he had spent too long losing strength.

At last the forest ended, trees fading away into a beautiful grassland that stretched along that flank of the island. To their left, perhaps a mile up the slope, more trees began, different varieties from those they had come through, the spaces between trunks clogged with a dark green shrub. To their right, down the slope, was the sea. And across the sea, for the first time since they had landed, they could see Noreela.

The sun was heading across the head of the island, and soon the grassland before them would be in afternoon shadow. A mile ahead of them, where the grassland ended and buildings began, a tall, dark structure curved up at the sky.

Kel saw movement, and halfway to the structure were the people they'd seen in the forest. The blue-skinned man was in the lead, following a rough path across the hillside toward the coastal village.

"What is that thing?" Namior asked, but Kel already heard recognition in her voice.

It was tall, perhaps a hundred steps. Its surface was a dull black that gave out no reflection. Its pinnacle was pointed, its base square, and it curved gently over the village whose boundary it seemed to mark.

"Protection?" she said. "From the things in the forest, maybe?"

"Maybe. But do you see what it is?"

Namior nodded. "Same as the thing they're building above Steep Hill."

"So what are they protecting Pavmouth Breaks from?"

Namior shrugged, barely able to take her eyes from the huge construction.

"Let's wait and see them pass it," Kel said. "They'll be there soon. Then maybe we can go up into the tree line there, curve around above the village, take a closer look."

"Closer," Namior said, nervous. But she did not object. She had not yet taken her eyes from the tall black structure.

The Komadians walked casually across the grassland, pausing just once when the blue-skinned man pointed out something on the ground. They gathered around, looked and went on. Just four friends out for a walk in the wilds. Kel had not seen any weapons, though it was possible that they carried knives and short swords beneath their flowing clothes.

As they approached the black monolith they climbed a set of steps, negotiating a ragged ridge in the land that seemed to mark the village's extremes, the levels beyond all slightly higher. Without seeming to acknowledge the tall structure, they disappeared into the village.

The sea shushed against the shore to their right, the beach out of sight. Below the village, Kel could see the edge of a harbor, and a few unrigged masts bobbed here and there.

"Some of those buildings seem strange," Namior said. "It's too far to see properly, but . . ."

Kel agreed, but he could not make out what made them unusual either. "We'll get closer."

They moved back into the forest, and when the trees and undergrowth were deep enough to hide their movements from the village, they turned uphill. They moved much more cautiously now, and the forest never felt safe. Things could be hiding from them, waiting to pounce. And Komadians walked here.

Everything was strange, and Kel felt that he should be noting things, remembering certain leaf shapes or plants' stem structures, consigning to memory the sweet birdsongs and scratching sounds that reverberated between the trees. But he was a soldier, not a man of study. If the time ever came, then the artists and book writers could make the place their own.

They came to a place where the land lay open, a deep wound dark with shadows and hazy with steam. Pausing at its edge, Kel felt a low rumble in his stomach, rising through his feet and legs from the ground. There was a rhythm there, like the signature of subterranean drums. He felt queasy, and Namior touched his arm, her face pale, skin slick with sweat.

Leaning over, feeling Namior grab his belt and pull back, Kel looked down into the pit. His view was mostly obscured, but between the mist and darkness, he caught a brief glimpse of glinting metal, and the orange glow of intense heat. Perspective was deceiving; it could have been ten steps deep, or something immense half a mile down.

"What can this...?" Kel could not finish the sentence. Neither of them knew what the crack in the ground could be, and whatever lay below was a mystery. The gentle mist rose, and where it touched Kel's skin it left a warm, slightly oily residue.

"I can feel it in my bones," Namior whispered.

"Let's move on," Kel said. "This might not be safe." They headed uphill away from the rent in the land, and the irony of his words was not lost on him. It hung with him like the echo of a warning.

This place is the greatest discovery in Noreelan history, he thought, but he could not welcome that idea.

There had already been bloodshed, and many deaths. And "greatest" could easily mean most deadly.

NAMIOR WAS AMAZED. Everything was new, and every few beats she wanted to watch a brightly colored butterfly, mull over a spiked seedpod on the end of a plant stem, listen to the birds. But with each new wonder came a feeling of dread, and her heart was confused.

Several times she pierced the soil with her ground rod, listening for the language of the land. Each time the result was the same: nothing. So she tried to open her perception, searching for a language she could not know or understand, but which she could hear and feel. Still, there was nothing. The land was dead to her, without magic, and that made her sick to her soul.

The blue-skinned man had scared her. The hole in the ground spoke of deeper mysteries. Everything she had ever believed was shaken, and the shaking continued with every step they took.

She could feel Kel's tension and the fear that kept his muscles warm and his limbs loose. But she could also sense his strength, and with every beat that strength seemed greater. He had a purpose in mind, a mission to perform, and she could almost taste his determination.

They edged uphill through the forest, pausing now and then to assess their surroundings. Namior looked for spreads of leaves in the tree canopy that did not move in the breeze, bark on their trunks that did not change shade as their aspect altered, and shrub limbs that remained motionless as insects and hand-sized butterflies lifted from their flowers. She felt observed every step of the way, but whatever watched kept to itself.

Kel altered their route slightly, peering down through the trees at the village and the monolith at its boundary. That terrified her. They were building its cousin across the sea, its base set in the Noreela she knew and loved. Protection, subjugation—whatever its intent, she feared it. The tidal waves might well have been unintentional, but the metal-clad Stranger was a thing of war.

Kel paused, and she almost walked into him. "Pond," he said. But even before she looked, she knew from his voice that it was so much more.

It was quite small, no more than fifteen steps across. Around its circumference several carved logs provided seating places, none of them occupied at present. Stout, long plants grew at its edge, hanging plump blue fruits out across the water. As Namior watched, a sticky limb erupted from the pond, plucked a fruit and disappeared again.

It was pink and slimy, and the width of her arm.

"What *is* that?"

Kel shook his head and stepped closer.

"Kel—"

He held up his hand, still not taking his eyes from the pond, and Namior had to follow.

The water's surface rippled, calming as they approached and stood at its edge. It was shaded by the tree canopy, its depths unknown, but here and there she could make out a pale shape huddled just below the surface, motionless. The sense that the pond was full of something other than water was strong.

Dozens more fruits hung just above the pond, and many more stems had been relieved of their burden, springing upright again and already showing the bulbous signs of fresh fruit growths.

There was an acidic odor, and the tang of something sour on the air. Namior was not sure whether it originated from the pond or the fruits growing above it.

Kel knelt and drew his sword, but Namior put a hand on his shoulder. "Don't."

Kel ignored her. Where the blade touched the water, ripples spread, and they were interrupted by ripples from elsewhere as the pond seemed to shift. There were several splashes that Namior was too slow to see—she witnessed only the disturbed aftermath—and she tried to focus on what Kel was doing.

I can run, if it takes him or hurts him I can run back to the boat and—

Kel probed deeper and lifted something with the blade. "Gills," he said. He stood and backed into Namior, turned and grabbed her arm, then started walking quickly away. His grip tightened, hurting, and she had to follow.

"What was it?" she asked.

"Gills. It had gills."

And when he let go she walked silently with him, because she remembered his description of the Strangers he had met and killed in Noreela.

As they fled up the slope, she heard the distinctive sound of something splashing in the pond behind them, its echo pursuing them between the trees like mockery.

SHE DID NOT mention the pond again. That would come later. There would be *plenty* to talk about later.

As they drew closer to the village, still hidden away in the forest, they began to make out the shades of other large structures in the distance. They seemed to match the first tower, though much farther away, and at first Namior thought they were tree branches close by. But it soon became clear that there were other tall spires around the village, and that some of them were connected.

"Chains?" Namior asked.

"Maybe. Or ropes, or wires. What in the Black could they be for?" Kel's concern was magnified in Namior, and she stayed close, enjoying the heat and smell of him.

Lines stretched across the village from one structure to the next. Some of them must have been many hundreds of steps in length, yet they did not sag.

"I see five," Kel said. "Can you see the tip of that one down there? Must be close to the harbor, or in it."

"Do you think they're building one on Pavmouth Breaks' harbor right now?"

"Remember the woman telling us they'd seen something strange in the water?"

Namior nodded, and realization came. "So they could be doing all this under our noses." A sinking feeling of defeat weighed her down.

"Yes, or beyond the sight of most villagers. And at the same time, they tell Chief Eildan that they come in peace, and offer samples of their steam technology that will blind most people to what's really happening."

"We have to get back," Namior said. She thought of her mother, suspicious but still open-minded, and her great-grandmother, subject to her worst craze yet. "We have to go, warn Eildan, tell *everyone* what we've seen here and—"

"What *have* we seen?" Kel leaned against a tree and wiped a hand across his face, dirtying his skin even more. "They're building that thing above Steep Hill, and they have the same here . . . but maybe they're sea defenses. Maybe, when the island shifts, Komadia is also under threat from its impact on the sea, and these things form some sort of barrier?"

"You believe that?"

"No. But hundreds in Pavmouth Breaks would. It sounds plausible, doesn't it? They destroy half our village, and think they can help by replicating the defenses they themselves use."

"Not everyone will believe lies like that."

"They don't need everyone's belief. And we can't fight this with half a village of survivors."

"What about the pond? Those things?"

Kel shrugged, his expression growing dark. "Unless anyone else has seen a Stranger, that means nothing."

"So it's all down to the Core," Namior said. "But what if you can't contact them, even when we get back?"

"We have to assume I will, somehow. And when the time comes, we'll need to tell them as much as we can."

She nodded, smiling with little humor. "I'm scared to shitting death, Kel, but yes. I want to see more. It's amazing and..." She shook her head.

"And horrible."

They moved nearer to the village, and when they were as close as they could go while remaining under cover of the trees, they paused and sat in the shadows.

Namior had never seen buildings like them. The walls seemed to be made of metal, colored and curved into many shapes and forms. The colors were mostly subdued, autumnal tones, and most were gently curved, not sharp and spiked. But there were exceptions. A building lower down the slope toward the sea was much higher than most others, its conical roof steep and spiked with vicious-looking arrowhead shapes. The roof was lined up and down with different-colored metals, and some of the colors hurt Namior's eyes to look at; not because they were so bright, but because she did not know them.

Her blood ran cold. She looked up at the sky, and it seemed just like any sky she'd see above Pavmouth Breaks. But when night fell on the place, she wondered whether she would know the stars?

"Namior, that temple in the middle..." Kel said, trailing off.

"It's just the light. The way the sun's striking it. I know spells that use the sun to dazzle and confuse, and change the way you see things."

"Spells? I thought you sensed no magic here."

"None that I know," she said, "but we know they have their own."

The closer Namior looked, the more she started to make out a few differently styled buildings. There were several two-story houses made of wood, their angles and edges lined with folded metal panels. Another building, close to the edge of the village, was a low, domed structure of mud and reeds, windows carved through its thick walls and surfaces bleached almost white by sunlight.

"I can't see anyone," Kel said.

"No. I have the image of movement everywhere I look, but…"

"Those things surround the village. They never quite intrude…always built just out from the village's edge." He pointed, drawing an imaginary line between the tall structures.

"Strange." Namior stared down the slope, across the rooftops to the sea. The ocean appeared as it always had, with no odd colors to confuse, no textures to scare. She concentrated on the swells and white-crests, taking comfort in the sea's constant existence. Then she looked up slightly, and across the sea lay Noreela. Pavmouth Breaks was a smudge in the River Pav's valley, and though she could pick out no individual buildings, still she could place her home. If she could see so far, perhaps she would meet her mother's gaze returned her way.

"We should go," Kel said.

"I thought—?"

"Down into the village. Just the edge. Go past those things, see what's different, see if they cast anything across the village that might help us."

"What if we're seen?"

"We need to make sure we aren't." His eyes softened, and he leaned forward to plant a kiss on her lips. Namior closed her eyes, shutting out the alien place for a blissful beat. Then Kel pulled away, and when she looked again he was pointing down the grassy slope.

"From here to that boulder," he said. "Then from there, through that long grass to the ridge just outside the village. Over the ridge, across to that domed mud-built building. Only a couple of windows pointing this way. Then we listen and watch, and try to get a feel for the place."

"I'm not sure I really want to feel it," Namior said. "It's not a place for us, Kel. Not for Noreelans."

"And Noreela is not for them," he said firmly. "It never will be. I need to know more, Namior."

She nodded slowly.

"You can wait," he said.

"No."

"Namior, I'm faster than you, and—"

"No! Someone's got to look after you." *And I don't want to be alone*.

"Right. Follow me."

Without any more talk, leaving no time for contemplation and doubt, Kel broke cover and ran.

TIME SEEMED TO flex. It took a while to work their way carefully across the open ground, but it felt like a few beats. When they reached the ridge that ran around the perimeter of the village, Kel climbed, using rock outcroppings and exposed roots as hand- and footholds. Namior followed, and as she cleared the top it felt as if they were climbing into the village from underground.

Resting flat against the dried-mud wall of the domed Komadian building, Namior looked up at the black structure curving high above. She expected to see the strange, graceful metal machines gliding across its surface, congregating at one place and pointing steam-pipes, goggle eyes and grappling claws down at the intruders. But all was quiet, and she felt a comforting breeze on her face.

"I can't hear anything," Kel whispered.

Namior shook her head and shrugged. Not only were there no voices, but there were no other sounds that she would normally associate with village life; barking dogs, whistling sweet birds on their homely perches, the purr and crunch of machines, the steady beat of a village living through its day. The sea was always a background, but Pavmouth Breaks was never silent.

Kel began edging along the wall toward one of the windows. Namior wanted him to stop, but curiosity also had her in its hold. That, and a sense of occasion. Her comment that they would sing songs about them in the future had been a joke, but this was truly something...

Maybe we're not the first, she thought. *Maybe the island has appeared many times before, as their emissary said, and had its visitors from Noreela, and they were caught and killed and—*

"Here," Kel whispered. He waved her over, and she joined him looking into the window.

The glass was thick, and so clear that it almost wasn't there. Namior had to reach out and touch its solidity to believe it. Beyond, the room was deserted, and she viewed the frozen moment of someone else's life. A low table in the center was scattered with bowls and glasses, colorfully woven cushions were scattered across the floor, and several thin, flexible pipes hung from the ceiling. They ended in complex-looking metallic constructs, large as a fisted hand and glimmering. One of them swung gently as though only just touched. Another seeped a puff of steam. Beyond the table and seating area were several curtained rooms, and beyond that a door that led out onto a street. The door was wide open, and they were offered a teasing glimpse of a wide thoroughfare, planted with short trees on either side and curving out of view. They saw the face of a neighboring building through the door, partially clad in a subtle green metal, with flowers growing in a narrow trench along its base. This building's door also hung open.

"Shall we go around?" Namior said, surprising herself with the suggestion. But the glimpse they'd had into the new world was so enticing.

Kel nodded and edged around the curved wall. They passed into shadows cast by a wood-clad house, and had to walk through a vegetable patch planted between the two. They stepped carefully, conscious not to crush any of the blooming plants. None of the vegetables seemed completely familiar.

They moved slowly, exposing themselves to view from several buildings and a dozen windows. But though doors were open, nobody seemed to be at home.

Namior saw that many of the buildings—dwellings, shops, and others that seemed to be gathering places, with wooden seats lined up both inside and out—had metal pipes curving up from their walls and protruding through the roofs. From a few pipes rose a trickle of steam, but most seemed dormant. They reminded her of the tentacle things she'd seen emerging from the dying Stranger's back. She shivered, and Kel looked her way.

"Seems like steam means a lot to them," he said.

"Where *are* they all?"

And then above the gentle hush of the sea, they heard the sound of a crowd's laughter. Like a wave it rose, broke and receded, leaving them awash with its humor.

"That way," Kel said. "If they're all gathered for something, I think it's important we see."

"Maybe it's a progress report from someone who's been to Pavmouth Breaks."

"Maybe it's a battle plan." Kel looked so serious, so anxious, that Namior had the sudden urge to hold him and love the fear away.

"I don't want to stay here much longer," she said.

"Nor I. I hope we won't need to."

They set off along the tree-lined street, trying to keep to the shadows cast by buildings, moving slowly at first, then picking up speed the more certain they became that everyone was gathered in one place. A slight breeze blew up from the direction of the sea, carrying the familiar smell and the foreign sounds of unknown voices laughing, speaking, and providing a hum toward which they could aim.

Namior wanted to stop and look at everything, but she was following Kel. And he only had one thing in mind.

Streets opened up wide, and soon they entered a part of the village where there was no apparent order. Buildings sat here and there, paved paths twisted between them, clumps of trees provided spreads of random shadow, and well-maintained areas of vegetable and fruit bushes gave a splash of green, purple and yellow here and there. It would be easy to get lost, but Kel was homing in on the sound.

The crowd.

Namior wondered whether some of them would be blue.

They passed between two tall buildings, then skirted around the temple-like place they'd seen from the tree line. They tried not to look up at the disturbingly colored spire. It had all the trappings of a place of worship, but there were several double doors that stood wide open, and inside there was a spread of pools, some filled with water, others apparently with steam. More of the flexible pipes hung from somewhere too high to see, and a mist made their view inside uncertain.

A roar came from somewhere nearby, the sound of many voices raised. Namior frowned. There were whistles and hums there as well, and clicks and pops. Perhaps part of the sound was being made by another of their steam machines?

They walked past the temple building, and Kel held up his hand. Then he pointed at a low structure to their left, its door open, insides bare but for a round, cushion-covered bed.

"We can't just—" she began, but Kel was already through the door.

For a moment she was alone. She turned her back on the building and looked around, past the tall-spired temple and back up the hillside to the tree line. She could not make out the exact place from which they had viewed the village, but she thought she saw a flash of movement, as though she and Kel were still up there.

"Namior!" Kel hissed from behind her. "Namior! We have

to go. Oh by all the *Black*, by all the fucking gods, we have to leave *right now!*"

But he did not reappear, and when Namior ducked through the door she saw her lover standing by the far wall, a couple of steps away from a long, low window that looked out across a square.

He could not move. He seemed frozen, apart from a desperate, hitched breath that jerked his upper body.

Namior skirted past the bed and stood beside him, and looked out, and everything dropped out of her world.

THE SQUARE WAS full. But not just with people.

At its center was a stone platform. A woman stood there, similar to Keera Kashoomie but even taller, hair shorter, and she waved her arms and smiled. She was speaking, but Namior could not hear her above the clamor of the crowd. And even had she been able to hear, the words would not have registered. Namior's mind had shifted to allow room for wonder, and disbelief, and finally fear.

Fear for Noreela, and herself.

Fear for her sanity.

There were people present, but they did not matter. The things *between* them were what Namior concentrated upon, trying to make sense but finding none. She saw a tall woman with feathered wings clutched behind her, a man with four arms, a diaphanous spirit that swelled and shrank the air around it. A young child disappeared from one place and appeared again elsewhere, three women sat conjoined by a thick fleshy girdle hugging their waists, and two men pierced each other with sharpened hands, kissing at the same time. A young girl floating above the ground called colored lights into being from her eyes, a man walked on insectile legs, a woman glided on one moist foot, and an androgynous person walked on air. Several people were gathered around a normal-looking woman riding a naked man, the couple reveling in their union, the audience darting reptilian tongues at their conjoined genitals. With each tongue impact the woman cried out, and the man groaned, and the people around them closed their eyes in shared ecstasy. A short person walked by, wiping at its beak with a clawed hand. A tall woman sat away from the edge of the crowd, her knees far higher than her head, and a hundred tiny crablike things were huddled across her back, suckling on red-raw teats on either side of the woman's spine.

The woman on the central platform raised her hands again and the crowd roared, squealed and cried. A man ran through the throng, carrying something above his head. It looked like a block of uneven glass, throwing off a rainbow of colors that Namior knew and some she did not. She shied away from the window, afraid that if one of the unknown colors reflected upon her, it would hurt. People cheered and hooted, and when the man reached the stone platform, he placed the glass object gently on the ground. Namior could no longer see it. Something told her that was good.

And then there was Trakis, her friend, the big man with whom she had been drunk many times and who, when they were young teenagers many moons ago, had kissed her behind the harbor and told her she was his first and last.

Two Strangers had him, each holding an arm, and they marched him through the crowd. They were not wearing their metal armor. He looked terrified; his eyes were wide, face bloodied, clothes tattered.

"Trakis!" she hissed. Kel's hand flashed out and grabbed her arm, preventing her from going too close to the window.

"We can't help him," he said quietly. "Whatever it is, whatever they're doing..."

"But that's *Trakis*! He was washed away, or buried!"

Kel said nothing, and Namior could hear his breath, fast and urgent. *He's thinking of something, some plan, some way to rescue him.* But of course, he was not, because there was nothing they could do. By coming there and witnessing the creatures at the gathering, they had made themselves Pavmouth Breaks' final hope.

And Komadia's greatest enemies.

The crowd parted for the Strangers. Trakis struggled, but one of them twisted his arm higher and he cried out, a human voice among the multitude.

They threw him down before the raised stone platform.

The crowd began to chant. Their voices were more serious, but still quite casual, as though they had seen such things many times before. The tall woman reached beside her for a long, flexible tube, and she pointed it down. Steam billowed out. A sharp crack rang out, and crystal shards speared through the steam.

What are they doing to us? Namior thought. *Is this some torture? Is this some game?* She heard a brief, terrible scream.

"No!" she said, and Kel's hand covered her mouth.

The observers stared down at what Namior could not see, wearing expressions of wonder and delight. Another scream came and it chilled her to her soul; they were doing more to Trakis than just killing him.

The chanting continued, more steam gushed, and at some signal Namior could not hear, it ended.

The silence was shocking, and more terrifying than the noise. One wrong move, one carelessly muttered word, and they would be heard.

Namior was holding her breath. It began to hurt.

And then someone shouted, and where Trakis had been thrown down, a shape slowly stood. It was the Trakis Namior knew so well . . . and yet there was something different. He did not hold himself like her friend. He seemed smaller, leaner. And he was no longer afraid.

The woman on the platform raised her hand, the crowd cheered, and Trakis smiled.

"What in the Black . . . ?" Kel said, and this time it was Namior who stopped him from moving closer to the window.

"I want to go," she whispered. "Kel . . ."

The audience quietened, and the woman on the platform said something to Trakis. She was crying. Namior's tears came then too, but she guessed their causes were vastly different.

"Now," Namior said. "While they're shouting, while there's noise, we have to—"

"Not yet," Kel said. "Not until we're sure."

Trakis turned from the platform and walked away. The crowd parted around him, some of them smiling, others reaching out to touch him with hands or whatever passed as limbs. He retained that gentle smile, but he was frowning as well, and Namior was no longer certain she knew that face.

The people and things let him go. Some watched after him, but there seemed to be a general agreement to leave him alone. *Giving him time to adjust,* Namior thought.

"Kel—" she said, meaning to tell him they had to leave, had to save themselves, because she thought Trakis was far beyond saving.

But Kel was already standing at the door.

"Kel!" she whispered, but he would not turn.

Trakis came directly past the building where they hid, walking uncertainly as if he felt lighter than he ever had before.

Namior left the window and went to Kel's side, terrified, but thinking, *If he has to see, then I'll see as well.*

"Trakis," Kel said.

The big man walked into view before Kel, a few steps from the doorway, and he paused, looking their way. He was still frowning through his uncertain smile, and for a beat Namior felt a sense of overwhelming relief, because he knew them. His smile widened. He half raised his hand as if to point . . . but then he looked away.

Trakis was no longer the man they knew.

Kel backed into the room, pushing Namior with him. He grabbed her hand and closed it around a knife. In his other hand he carried his short sword. "We run," he said, nodding at another door in the opposite wall. "We can't be caught. *Everything* depends on that."

Still shaking, still tingling with disbelief, Namior followed Kel from the building. They ran for their lives, and for the future of Noreela.

WHEN THEY REACHED the edge of the village, there were metal men in the tree line. Kel skidded to a stop and Namior almost ran into him, and if she'd done that he might have fallen far enough forward from the shelter of the domed building for the Strangers to see him.

"Down to the shore," he whispered. They stalked along the edge of the village, passing through the shadow cast by the tall black structure and using the sound of the sea to draw them along. They could not cross the open grassland, because the Strangers in their war suits would see them. They could not go up into the forest because of the risk of confrontation. Their only hope was the beaches and whatever might lie above them, hidden from the Strangers, hopefully, by the curves and folds of the landscape.

Namior could hear white-crests breaking against the shore, and smell the familiar tang of the sea that she had lived with all her life. But all she could see was Trakis falling, and that person wearing Trakis's face.

They only sent over people that wouldn't shock us, she thought. *None of those other . . . things.* And as the memory of the multitude of strange creatures they had seen rose again, she wondered just how many more there were.

Landing there, finding their way across the island, even tackling the huge lizard-thing . . . through all of that, Namior had felt in control. They were choosing every move they made, weighing the risks and assessing their next best course of action. Now they were fleeing, and she was terrified. The sky crushed down on her shoulders, the unknown ground pushed up with all of its force, and everything she passed—building, tree, timber fence—tried to press her into something so small that she would fade away entirely. There was so much more than she could have ever imagined. But rather than feeling amazed at what she had seen, she could only feel dread at what was to come. If they did not escape the island, they would be killed at the hands of things she could not understand. If they did escape, and made it back to Noreela, then they'd bear tidings that would change the villagers' lives forever.

Close to the sea, they left the settlement. There was something of a beach there, covered with coarse sand and scattered with scraps of fishing net, small cages and hollowed logs used as buoys. A couple of small boats were pulled up onto the shore, and Namior thought about stealing one. But Kel passed them by, and she knew they were still too close to the village. *They must not be seen.*

She had no desire to end up like Trakis.

The level beach soon faded away, replaced by boulders and rock pools gleaming with countless tiny creatures. She kept glancing to her right to see whether they could be spied by the Strangers. But though she could see the tops of the forest's trees, the land rolled down and seemed to provide natural cover.

She listened for sounds of pursuit, but heard nothing but the sea and her own panicked breathing. Either they had not yet been discovered, or the Komadians and their Stranger soldiers were closing in without a sound to give them away. That idea haunted her, and she expected the sun to be blocked any moment by a leaping shadow.

Kel moved quickly, crouched over, weapons so well strapped to his body that none of them touched each other. Occasionally Namior heard the scrape of metal on stone, but he would be quick to step aside or cover the offending blade or handle with his hand.

"Something ahead," he said. Looking before them,

Namior could see trees growing down to the shore. They were past the grasslands and almost back in the forest, and soon they would be darting from tree to tree. The forest would hide them better, but it could also provide cover for watchers or pursuers, or dangerous animal life they had yet to see.

"What is it?" she asked. The beach changed from fallen boulders and broken ground, to the tangle of roots and mud that they had encountered when they first landed. And then she saw the glow.

"Weird light," Kel whispered. "Come on, into the forest, we can go around and—"

"I want to see what it is," Namior said. The glow came from a dip in the land to their right, just within the influence of the trees. It looked as though a rainbow was sleeping there. She went toward it and Kel followed close behind, his curiosity evident.

They found crystals. They started close down to the sea, and some were broken, their sharp edges dulled by wave action. Many more sat in a gully that led up into the forest. The gully had once been a stream, but it no longer carried water. Perhaps the crystals absorbed it.

They seemed to be growing, most of them upright, though some were tilted slightly, like flowers following the sun. They were the same as the thing that the man had carried across the square, most around the length of a human's forearm and slightly thicker. They were beautiful, but somehow revolting as well. The light refracted from them felt unclean and the colors corrupt. Namior could think of no other way to describe them. She could almost taste the colors, and smell them, and they made her sick.

"Amazing," Kel said. He stepped past Namior and approached the edge of the crystal gully. She wanted to reach out and grab his arm, but through the disgust, she was amazed as well. There was something mysterious about them, perhaps magical in a way she had never encountered or imagined ever before. A large part of her training as a witch was the acquisition of knowledge, and not all of it was comfortable to have.

"What do you think they are?" Namior asked.

Kel did not answer. He froze for a beat, then started stalking closer, attention focused on one crystal close to the edge of the gully. She went with him, glancing back along the beach at where the village reached the sea. They had heard nothing since leaving—no more cheering, nor any sounds of pursuit. That troubled her.

"By all the gods," Kel muttered. "This is the same as . . ."

"It's what was carried into the square," Namior said. "What they used when Trakis . . ." She trailed off. The crystal was not still. For a beat, she thought the shapes dancing inside were caused by something disrupting the sunlight, and she looked up, expecting to see the Strangers in their metal suits bearing down upon them. But the only thing moving was the sea. It shushed and whispered to their left, speaking secrets they could never know.

"There's something in there," Kel said. "Something moving. Something *alive.*"

Namior went cold. The hairs on her neck and arms bristled, and a chill broke across her body. Sometimes while making love, Kel bit her neck and caused the same effect, but this was the exact opposite of lust and pleasure. It was disgust and pain.

It was not something solid, of flesh and blood. It was smoke and light, mist and color.

"A shade," she said. "But . . . different."

"A shade's the ghost of something not yet born," Kel said. "How can we see that?"

"Then maybe the wraith of something born and died." Namior bent and looked closer. Within the crystal's light-spreading mass, something dark seemed to roll and twist. Parts of it moved fast, thrashing massively in a space too small to contain it. Other parts rolled and billowed as slow as storm clouds. Every movement seemed pained, and she was sure she heard wretched screaming somewhere too far away to be true. "Or perhaps it's both. A trapped soul."

"I don't understand."

"We're living things, Kel. We're not *meant* to understand the dead."

"But when they brought that thing into the square..." He grew distant, looking out across the sea at their home, thinking. And then he slumped to his knees.

"What? Kel?" She reached out, and when she touched his flesh it was cold and hard, muscles tensed against a threat she did not yet know.

"All these years," he said. "They've come, and we've tracked them and killed them, and all this time they were trying us on for size."

Namior looked across the array of crystals, and all of them held the same sickly movements of something trapped for so long, awaiting a new, fresh body to call its own. A body like Trakis's. A body like her own.

"We have to go," she said.

Kel switched from despair to anger in the blink of an eye. He spat, kicked out at the crystal nearest to them and its base shattered, breaking from where it grew from the ground and hitting the dirt hard. The thing inside flipped and rolled some more, agitated by the movement. Namior closed her eyes, and something spiked at her ears like a cry too high to hear.

Kel took off his jacket and wrapped the broken vessel.

"You're *taking* it?"

"Yes."

"But—"

"But nothing. The Core has to see. Our witches might be able to use it."

Namior could see the sense in his actions, but the thought of traveling back with that thing in the boat with them...She shivered again, and the nausea was still with her. "It just seems so wrong," she said.

"All the more reason to take it back." His gaze softened, but he still spoke urgently. "Please, Namior. We need to go."

They walked through the breaking waves where no more crystals grew. Namior felt rough edges beneath her boots, and wondered whether they were walking across the broken roots of old crystals. What happened when the sea struck them? Why did they grow so close to the sea, rather than inland where...?

The possibility hit her that they had seen only a small portion of crystals. Perhaps inland there were many more. Valleys filled with them, hillsides spiked with their dreadful beauty. Maybe Komadia was home to a hundred thousand trapped souls.

She felt a brief moment of pity. But the memory of Trakis's final agonies drove it down, and the danger that her village, family and friends were in ensured that pity had no place in her heart.

Kel splashed through the breaking waves ahead of her, hugging the thing to his chest.

And then a high whistling sound rose up behind them, and a thousand voices called out in anger.

"THEY'VE SEEN US!" Kel said. He climbed a tangled bank of tree roots and rocks, holding the cloth parcel to his chest with one hand and finding handholds with the other. Namior followed, and soon they were in the forest again, following the coastline as they ran for their boat.

If it's still there, Namior thought. *Or if they haven't already found it and hidden their metal-clad soldiers behind it, ready for our arrival.* But she could not trouble herself with that at the moment. She had to run, watch her footing, jump over fallen logs and step around twists of tree roots seemingly reaching up to trip her. They had to manage their escape and survival step by step.

The whistling sound came again, and from somewhere inland she heard undergrowth crashing as something stormed through.

"When we get there," Kel said, "jump in and get ready to start rowing."

"But you—"

"I'm stronger than you. I'll throw this thing in and push the boat down to the sea." He was panting, but he spoke calmly, and she could not doubt his logic. They needed to be rowing away when the Strangers arrived at the shore.

Something cracked up the hillside, and she heard a cry of pain. Maybe one of the lizard-things had taken down a Komadian. Right then, she could not even smile in hope.

Namior leapt a fallen tree and found herself ahead of Kel, pumping her arms as she ran. She jumped over anything that looked as though it could trip her, snaked around tree trunks, ducked beneath branches and clasped the knife in her hand like a lucky charm. No charm could work if it had not been properly made, she knew, but the blade glinted, its keenness comforting.

"They're coming," Kel said. Namior glanced uphill and saw the glimmer of metal, way up between the trees. *They*, Kel had said. He'd almost died fighting just one of them.

And then she saw the boat. She resisted the temptation to throw down the knife and start pushing, instead doing exactly what Kel had said. She climbed in, dropped the knife and grabbed the oars, holding them along the gunwales in readiness to dip into the water the instant it was close.

We'll have to get over the breakers. Past the waves, across the white-crests, then back to Noreela, and they'll be chasing us all the way.

Kel hit the boat hard. The wrapped crystal fell from his hands and thumped down inside, and the craft was already sliding across tree roots and oily seaweeds, slicking down toward the beach with Kel grunting and straining behind it.

He'd jammed his sword into the boat's hull, just inside and still within reach.

Namior looked over his head and through the trees. She could see plenty of movement, but she wasn't sure how much of it was simply leaves flickering in the breeze. She saw a flash as something shiny moved from left to right, then all was still once again.

When she glanced back down at Kel, he was grimacing.

"They won't stop," he said. "I've never met a Stranger that knows fear."

"Lucky bastards."

Water splashed across Namior's back. She gasped at the coldness, then when she dipped the oars they were wet as well. She started pulling, watching Kel splashing through the breaking waves, looking behind him at the rough beach, his footprints, the twisted trees, pulling, pulling. The boat jarred up and splashed down, again and again.

Kel heaved himself in, landing with his face close to the wrapped crystal. He paused, just for a beat, then looked up at Namior.

"We might just—" he said, but the rest of his words were drowned by a flurry of explosions. Flashes burst from within the forest, Kel winced, something struck Namior in the chest, and she fell back. She tried to close her hands on the oars but they were gone. She felt around, waving her hands, confused at why she was not still rowing, why she saw sky and clouds instead of beach and water. Confused, too, at why the water in the bottom of the boat felt so warm.

Lying on her back, the late-afternoon sky suddenly seemed very blue and peaceful.

KEL BOON FELT something whip by his right ear and thought, *They're shooting at us.* Beyond Namior, past the bow of the boat, the top of a wave parted and spat spray at the sky. Another shot hit the boat's stern a hand's width from his head. Wood splintered, and he felt shards peppering his cheek and exposed neck. He grimaced in pain, looked at Namior, and something hit her in the chest.

Her eyes and mouth went wide. Blood sprayed the air before her, splashing into the water sloshing inside the boat. And she fell back, striking the wood and gasping, hands clawing at the air as though to catch a cloud. Looking at her chest Kel could see the meat of her, and the white flash of bone.

"No!" he yelled, and another volley of shots smashed into the boat and sea.

Every instinct was pulling him toward Namior, pressing his hand to her wound and his mouth to hers, looking into her eyes to make sure they still saw him. But if he did that, he would be dead.

If he turned around and tried to fight—crossbow bolts against projectile weapons—he would be just as dead.

So he reached into the boat and picked up the heavy crystal, shaking his jacket away so that the sun kissed colors from its angular surfaces, and held it up high.

The shooting ceased. There were four Strangers standing along the edge of the forest, two of them down on the beach and up to their knees in water. They all held golden tubes, steam venting from them, and their dull metal armor reflected the color of the waves.

The crystal was heavy.

Namior moaned behind him, hissing something wet at the air. *Not her, not here, not now,* Kel thought.

"I'll do it!" he yelled, though as yet he was not quite certain what "it" was. He heaved himself up into the boat, holding on tight because the waves were striking the bow, lifting and dropping it again and again. He dropped the crystal, rolled, and snatched it up, and when he looked back at the beach the Strangers had all advanced several steps.

"Stop!" Sitting on the cross seat, he placed the crystal in

his lap; it was warmer than he'd expected, as though the thing writhing inside exuded heat. Then he drew a weighted throwing knife and held it up, heavy handle pointing down. He had no idea how much damage he could do with that, but the Strangers exchanged glances and lowered their weapons.

"I'll smash it!" And he almost did. Namior was bleeding and dying behind him, and he came so close to indulging the only small, petty revenge he could muster. He wanted to feel the Strangers beneath his sword, part their necks as he had the one on the beach, watch their enraged wraiths spit and sputter as their existence faded away to nothing, not even the Black. But the greater revenge of denying them what they had come for . . . that was more noble.

And for that, he had to survive.

He put the knife down on top of the crystal in his lap, picked up the flailing oars and started rowing.

The Strangers watched. One of them walked into the sea, waves breaking around its stomach, then its chest. Kel dropped one oar and picked up the knife, and the metal-clad soldier halted.

He heard that rising and falling whistling from somewhere else on the island. An alarm? A scream of pain?

"Namior?" he said, not wanting to look back. He was still too close. If he turned away, they might try to get him with a lucky shot. So he rowed hard, feeling the muscles of his back and shoulders pulling but relishing the sensation. "Namior?" he said again, listening for any sign of acknowledgment.

She only hissed, and it sounded far too much like air venting from her ruined chest.

Up one wave, down another, topping the white-crests as they roared in to expend their energy on Komadian soil, and the Strangers watched them go. Kel glanced down at the crystal, at the shifting thing inside that could have been as big as his hand close-up, or the size of a mountain thirty miles away. *What do I have in here?*

He drew farther from shore, and when he was far enough

away he let the waves take him for a while. They drove the small boat along the southern shore of Komadia, and he could see the first buildings of the settlement they had visited. Behind it, up the hillside and closer to the forest, the curving black monolith pointed at the sky, obvious now that he knew it was there. Viewed from that distance and angle, it could have been a ravine split down into the ground, as well as a structure built up.

He turned and looked at Namior, and he feared that she was already dead. But he could not stop. The wound in her chest was wide, deep and pulsing blood, and there was nothing he could do for her without help. If he stopped, to hug and whisper as her life ebbed away, he would be losing whatever small chance she had to survive.

"Keep breathing, keep fighting," he said. He repeated those words over and over, and they became the beat by which he rowed.

The pains in his shoulders and back became so great that he thought he was on fire. He rowed harder.

The sun was setting behind the Komadian hills. It threw the shadow of that alien land across the sea after him, and he knew that in that shadow, they would come.

HE ROWED THROUGH the dusk, through his tears, and despite the certainty that his arms were no longer a part of his body. Once away from the island, he paused several times to go to Namior, but all he could do was to make sure she was still breathing. He tried pressing his jacket to her bleeding wound, but her breathing became harsh, and she thrashed in unconsciousness. She was withdrawn, fighting for survival inside her own mind. He hoped that would last.

Watching Komadia, expecting to see sails coming after him at every moment, the jagged silhouette of that strange place took on sinister proportions.

As the second love of his life lay dying behind him—a slower death than his first, yet weighing even heavier on his shoulders—he did his best to plan. The rhythm of the waves and the tempo of his rowing made it easier to concentrate, the physical side of things taking care of themselves.

The absolute priority was to contact the Core. The time they had always feared was upon them, and though it might not be exactly the invasion they had anticipated, still the Strangers had declared war on Noreela. Perhaps they would stay until every person in Pavmouth Breaks had been taken away and made a home for one of those things trapped in the crystals. And maybe there were many more such crystal fields all across the island, thousands of them, and their intention was to launch forays deeper and deeper into Noreela. Their weapons were deceit and stealth, and Kel knew that Noreela's realization about what was happening would be far slower than the Komadians' progress. They could sweep across the land, taking people, changing them and advancing again, and by the time any survivors realized what had happened, the wave would have moved on.

How to contact the Core? That was something else entirely. Land. Get Namior to a healer. Escape Pavmouth Breaks, plant the communicator, let it do its work...

Except there was something wrong with that scenario: the part about finding a healer for Namior. His Core training was urging him to leave her on the beach and escape. The fate of Pavmouth Breaks, and perhaps Noreela, was far more important than the life of one woman.

"I have to land and leave her," he said to the air. A wave hit the stern and splashed across him in response.

Kel stopped rowing for a beat and let the waves take him, urging the craft closer to shore. He bailed water for a while, looking back at the island. But there were no signs of pursuit on the dusky water. He turned and looked at the shore, surprised at how far he had come. He should be planning where to land, not just aiming haphazardly and hoping it would be somewhere safe. South of where they had left, farther along the beach, that would be best…except that would mean dragging Namior back up through the Throats, and he would never have the strength to take her all the way. She'd die in there, adding her wraith to the darkness. And he would be left mourning another dead love.

The Komadians and the Strangers must surely have communication devices, similar to the one Namior had foisted upon him. Those on Noreela could already know of their covert visit to the island, the theft of the crystal, and they would be ready for him.

There was nowhere safe to land. It was impossible. This was all too much for one man, especially a man who had shunned such responsibility long ago.

Namior moaned in pain, the sea urged him closer to home, and the sunset painted Komadia blood red.

Chapter Nine

leaving

KEL FELT THE crystal watching him. He covered it with his jacket. His arms were almost useless by then, and the tide and waves seemed to be carrying him toward the harbor. There was little he could do to correct their course. And in truth, he thought it as good a place as any to land. If he could drift past the larger Komadian ships in the darkness, beach the boat on the ruined northern shores of the village... It felt foolish and crazy, yet at the same time it just might work. They would be watching for him along the coast, not in the harbor. They would never believe that he would be mad enough to return there.

And Namior needed help as soon as possible. She had stopped moaning, and he took that to be a bad sign. He wished he could throw down the oars and go to her, listen to her breathing, check her wound, but he could not. Though he rowed little, he used the oars more to try to steer them, attempting to find the best route through to the harbor.

There were three large ships anchored in the waters outside Pavmouth Breaks. One of them was dark, but the other two were speckled with lights that did not look like candles or lamps. Some of the lights moved.

"Kel…" Namior moaned. *Too loud!* Kel turned and leaned over her, whispering.

"Namior, be quiet, we're almost there. Almost home."

"Kel!" she said again, almost shouting. "They're coming. *They're coming!*"

Kel hated doing it, but he reached out and clasped his hand over her mouth. She moaned and twisted her head, and he dreaded whatever dreams he was giving her. Then she went slack, head dropping to one side, and he could hardly feel her breath on his hand.

He sat up again and rowed, aiming between the darkened ship and the two with lights. That should take him through to the river channel, and from there he could aim for the northern shore.

Is the tide coming in, or going out? he thought, still not close enough to tell. He paid little attention to the rhythms of the sea, the ebb and flow of Pavmouth Breaks' life, and he regretted that. He regretted a lot of things.

Don't you die! he thought, wishing his desires could carry weight and import. Some witches, so it was said, were so in tune with magic that they could affect events by thought alone. But they were few and far between, and in Pavmouth Breaks their talents would be as useless as his.

It was not dark enough. They would be seen. The Komadians would be waiting at the harbor, at the end of the mole and around the river mouth. There would be Strangers, clad in their metal suits and wielding deadly projectile weapons or other as-yet-unseen methods of killing. He and

Namior would be killed quickly, their bodies weighed down and thrown into the harbor, surrendered to the sea as succulent food for the many creatures enjoying such fare since the waves.

It was not dark enough. They would be seen...

Kel lay down in the small boat beside Namior, hand resting on her shoulder in readiness to clamp down on her mouth should she wake. He held his small crossbow in the other hand, primed to fire, but if they *were* seen, he knew there would be no escape.

The sea carried them home. They were at the mercy of the ocean, and would go wherever it decided to take them.

The darkened ship passed by close to their starboard side, a huge, looming shadow that the dusky light barely touched. All seemed quiet on board, though Kel was sure he could hear a rhythmic *boom, boom* as they drifted past. The sound was so low and quiet that he could have felt it rather than heard it. He touched the boat's hull, its base sloshing with water, and felt a beat.

There's something in the harbor, the woman had said. *I've only seen the ripples.*

Kel raised his head, tried to correct their course with an oar, then lay back down.

Namior was still breathing, but he could also hear the terrible bubbling of air in her wound. It would take a lot to heal her... but he did not start crying just yet. Things were bad, but defeat was not yet inevitable.

The other two ships were full of life. Light globes floated across their decks or hung in the rigging. Voices carried across the water, some speaking Noreelan, others languages that Kel did not know. They sounded cheerful and unconcerned. *They would,* he thought. *Their love hasn't just been shot in the chest!* He looked up at the towering stern of the closest ship, almost wishing that he could see a head silhouetted there at which to fire the crossbow. A small act of revenge... but it would feel good. But he saw no one, and the rowboat drifted by.

The harbor was before him at last, bathed in false light. People were still digging in the ruins for the missing and dead.

Kel knew what had happened to some of the missing, at least.

He lay still, hoping that if they were seen, any watcher would mistake the boat for a craft set adrift by the storm and waves. As Namior didn't cry out in her dreams, perhaps they stood a chance.

But the crystal . . . ?

There was so much he didn't know that even the vaguest hope seemed naïve.

The rise and fall of waves lessened. Kel closed his eyes and tried to sense the drift of the boat, and when he heard the sound of breaking waves, he knew where they were. *We're going the right way!* he thought, amazed. *The sea has pushed us into the river mouth, and the tide is taking us toward the northern shore.*

No shouts came, no explosions of steam weapons, no splashes as the gilled Strangers came for them, and Kel dared hope.

Something nudged the boat. He caught his breath and held the crossbow at the ready. If a shape rose behind him over the boat's stern, it would stove his head in without his having a chance to fire. But if something came over the bow, or the sides, then maybe . . .

The wooden hull ground over something solid, and the stern started to swing around.

Beached!

Kel risked raising his head. The tide had driven them through the harbor mouth and against the northern shore, at the place where Pavmouth Breaks had sustained the most damage from the waves. The gentle hillside above him was scoured almost clean of any sign of habitation. No houses remained standing, and what few walls jutted from the ground were piled with debris. He would have to cross a large expanse of mud and filth, climbing steadily, before he reached the first of the unaffected areas. He could see a few houses higher up the hillside, damaged but still standing, and around the curve of the hill heading inland were Namior's home and the Dog's Eyes.

"Namior," he said. "I'm going to have to move you soon. We're almost home. Do you hear me?" She said nothing, did nothing that hinted she had heard.

He looked across the river mouth at the harbor. There was plenty of activity there, illuminated by floating light balls. He wondered why they were still pretending to search for survivors. Maybe they weren't ready to make their final move just yet.

They're waiting until they've finished building. It was not a comforting idea, because he did not know how long that could take.

After everything he had seen, Kel resisted the temptation to try another communicator. He only had two left, and he could ill afford to lose another to a place empty of magic.

And then he realized the tough choice he had feared was upon him. Namior would need carrying, if he could find the strength. Slung across his arms would be best, her head resting against his left shoulder, because if he tried slinging her over his shoulder it would crush her wound and maybe kill her. Whatever that thing had fired might still be inside her, and any movement could prove fatal.

That would mean leaving the crystal behind.

The alternative was to take the crystal and try to leave Pavmouth Breaks immediately. Smuggle it out, beyond whatever cordon the Komadians might have established, using all his training and stealth to slip by. The Core's witches would want to see it, study it, and hopefully learn from it. Beneath his jacket lay one of the most important artifacts on Noreela.

But if he left Namior there, she would surely die.

Kel closed his eyes, but there was nothing to make the decision for him.

He sat up slowly and looked down at Namior, his love. He

touched her face, and she was cool, and when he lifted her hand and let go it flopped back down beside her. A tear squeezed from his eye but he rubbed it away.

He grabbed his jacket, wrapping it around the bulky shape of the crystal, and jumped from the boat. He could not look back. Wading through the mud, lifting his legs high to take the next step, and the next, he *would* not look back, in case Namior had lifted her head and was watching him leave her there. So he strode onward, sometimes slipping in the muck and almost letting the crystal go.

A shadowy shape on the mud resolved itself. Kel paused, breath caught in his throat and the moment frozen. But the sea wolf was dead. Its flippered legs were stretched around it, torso slumped across the muck, and its head was tilted to one side, blind eye staring out to sea. A slick of insides had spilled from a terrible wound in its underside. Its several layers of teeth were clearly visible, and various claws and spine appendages were wilted in death.

Something had killed it. He'd seen the sea-wolf prints in the harbor soon after the waves, and they were viciously territorial creatures; it was unlikely there'd be two in the same place. He thought of those Strangers with their gills and steam weapons, and the woman who had seen ripples in the harbor.

Kel walked on, and when he reached the remains of an old stone wall, he started digging. He scooped out handfuls of dried mud, streams of sand and chunks of broken masonry, and when he thought he'd gone deep enough he lowered the crystal into the hole and buried it.

He hoped that whatever lay trapped in there found it darker still.

Namior was moving when he returned to her, writhing slowly in the water at the base of the boat. She opened her mouth but nothing came out. Her chest and stomach were completely soaked with blood.

Kel paused for a beat and looked across the wide river mouth at the harbor and mole. There were several boats within the harbor, all of the Komadian, but no one seemed to be looking his way, and if they did, they were not concerned at what they saw. Could it be that the Komadians on the mainland did not yet know what had happened? It seemed unlikely, but he could see no signs of panic or a search, and letting the boat drift in had been easy.

Or could they be so confident that they did not care?

"Come on," he said, leaning into the rowboat. "Namior? I need to lift you. It will hurt, but don't shout, don't scream. Can you hear me?" She said nothing. He sighed, then tugged the soft sheebok-wool lining from the inside of his shirt. It was damp with sweat. He held it in both hands and spun it tight, then placed it across Namior's mouth, careful to keep her nose free. He lifted her head and tied it behind her neck. It might not be enough, but it would have to do.

Hopefully, the pain would be bad enough to keep her unconscious.

"Don't die!" he said, suddenly shaking and sobbing, then forced himself under control. It was not the time. Later, perhaps safety would offer the opportunity for grief. And if she died, all he would have would be hatred, and revenge.

Revenge for O'Peeria, as well.

He had spent a long time trying to shed such bitterness.

Kel leaned into the boat again, left arm under Namior's knees, right arm working around the back of her neck and moving down, lifting her torso, grabbing beneath her armpit and pressing against her chest close to the wound. His arms and shoulders were weak and numb, but he gritted his teeth and stood.

Namior squealed, and Kel felt the sound come from deep inside. Then she was still again, and as he started working his way up the muddy incline he could hear breath bubbling through her wound once more. He was amazed that she was still alive.

He slipped several times, but never let her fall. The slope increased, and he had to negotiate his way around fallen homes, everything covered in a layer of dried muck from the sea. He felt the dampness of Namior's blood soaking through his shirt, and a cool sea breeze chilled him.

"Don't die," he exhaled with every step.

He walked and climbed and slipped, thinking at every beat that his strength would leave him. As he struggled, night fell across Pavmouth Breaks.

IT STARTED TO rain. Kel had made it up from the ruins by then, and into the winding streets above. But the rain made the cobbles slippery and chilled his overworked muscles, and the time would soon come when he could carry her no far-ther.

Namior was silent and unresponsive, head hanging back, mouth slightly open as if to catch the rain. On a few occasions he thought she was already dead. But he could feel her frantic heartbeat, and blood still ran from the wound.

He heard the woman before he saw her. "Druke! Druke!" The name echoed along the path before being swallowed by the worsening downpour. She called again, and it had the sound of a name oft-repeated. Kel guessed she had been look-ing for a very long time.

The woman rounded a corner before him, a study in ab-ject misery. Her clothes were sodden, slumping down from her shoulders, sleeves hauled past her hands by the weight of water, giving the impression that she was melting. Her hair was long and lank, only adding to the image, and her mouth hung open, flexing only as she called that name again. "Druke! Druke!"

She noticed Kel, and Namior in his arms, but her expres-sion did not change. She looked past him. Kel stood aside to let her pass.

"Have you seen Druke?" she asked.

"I don't know Druke."

"He was here, but now he's gone."

"Lots of people have gone," Kel said.

"No, no, he was here today. And today, he's gone. Down at the harbor, helping the Komadians dig, and he never came home again. Never came home to me . . ."

"Perhaps he's in a tavern," Kel said, and he went to pass by.

"Not my Druke," the woman said with utter conviction. "He wouldn't do this to me. It's *them*. They've done something to him." She came close and leaned across Namior, pressing her face up to Kel's, tears mixing with raindrops on her cheeks. "Don't trust them for a minute," she said. And then she was on her way, calling into the rain and receiving only the echo of a name in response.

Kel staggered on. Namior's weight pulled him down, and with each step he had to force his knees not to buckle. He passed windows lit by weak oil lamps, and every corner promised capture, every dark doorway could be hiding a Stranger, metal suit discarded but still just as deadly. If the time came, he was not sure he had the strength to fight.

Other dwellings he passed were empty and dark. There was something ominous about that, but he tried to concentrate on walking. That was all that mattered: move on, never stop.

He heard other names being called in the night, and eventually he heard a voice he knew.

"Namior!" It was coming closer, and Kel groaned as he hurried forward to meet it.

Namior's mother emerged onto the wider footpath, and the first thing Kel noticed was the glint of metal in her hand. *She stalks the night with a knife*, he thought, and he was thankful that she recognized the danger.

"No!" She saw them and ran, sheathing the knife and helping ease Namior down when Kel's knees gave out at last. "No, Namior, no . . ."

"She's alive," Kel gasped. "But she needs help. A healer."

"The last healer's gone," she said, never taking her eyes

from her daughter. "I don't know where. She left the Moon Temple and never returned. What happened?"

"Komadian soldier...shot her."

"What with?" Namior's mother was already pulling the sodden clothing away from her daughter's wound, expertly exploring the extent of the injury.

"Projectile weapon of some sort."

"Where?"

Kel did not answer. And it was nothing to do with the Core, or secrecy, but everything to do with guilt.

The woman looked up at Kel, then glanced over his shoulder and nodded out to sea. "There?"

"Yes," Kel said.

"Help me. We need to get her home. Magic's gone, the land talks no more, but I know some of the old magichala ways."

"She's going to be—" Kel began, trying to convince himself, but her mother cut in and cried her first tears.

"She's going to die!"

Kel shook his head but he could speak no more. He helped lift Namior and carry her through the rain, heading uphill toward her home, and the air between him and her mother was thick with unasked questions.

She's not going to die, he wanted to say, but he could not speak out loud. He had lied enough.

NAMIOR'S GREAT-GRANDMOTHER was sitting close to the groundstone, but not close enough to touch it. She was shivering beneath several layers of blankets, only her gray-haired head visible, and her face looked older than was possible. Kel could see little in her one good eye save blankness. Even when she blinked, she gave away nothing.

"Grandmother?" Namior's mother said, but the old

woman slumped to her side, muttering and spitting as her hands clawed at the air.

Kel felt so helpless. He knelt beside Namior and closed his eyes against a sudden faintness. Her mother thrust a thick crust of bread into his hand, and he bit into it with a passion. It was seeded with nuts, and he felt the energy nestling in his stomach as soon as he swallowed, ready to spread out through his body. "Thank you," he said through a full mouth.

"Right now, don't even talk to me," she said. She squatted beside her daughter and started feeling around the wound. No questions about the island, what he had been doing there, what they had seen, how Namior had been shot, how they had made it back...

He finished the crust and watched the woman work. First she stripped Namior's blood-soaked clothing and washed her chest, exposing the wound just below her right breast. There was no matching wound on her back, which meant that whatever had been fired at her was still inside.

She lit several candles and placed them close around Namior, and to begin with Kel thought they were for some sort of ancient magichalan ceremony. But then she placed a wooden spoon between Namior's teeth, poured a mug of strong rotwine over the wound, and when the injured woman's writhing and moaning had subsided she went to work with a knife.

"If you can't touch magic..." Kel began, but he did not want to finish. *How can you save her?*

"There's nothing you can do here," she said. She never once stopped what she was doing. Her knife was in her daughter, and she sprinkled some sort of powdered herb around the bloody wound. "She's mine to look after the best I can. But you need to go, Kel Boon."

"Please don't say that," he pleaded. "Not after what we've seen. I'm not sure what I can do." And that was the painful truth. He still had the two communicators in his pocket, but to use them was impossible when the land no longer spoke and could not listen.

Namior's mother glanced up, and her eyes bore a heavy sadness rather than hatred. She opened her mouth to say something, hesitated, then returned to her operation. The knife twisted and flicked, and something slicked from the hole in Kel's love's chest. She gasped and groaned, and more wine was poured around the wound.

Her mother picked the object up, rubbed it against one of the blankets around her shoulders and held it to the light. Her eyes went wide, her mouth hung open, and she asked, "Just what *have* you seen?" It was a small crystal, the size of Kel's thumbnail, and it caught candlelight and threw a sickly rainbow around the room.

Namior's great-grandmother screamed. She rolled into the groundstone and flinched away again, as if afraid it would burn. Her hands covered her eyes, and her almost toothless mouth was twisted into a pained grimace.

"Grandmother?"

The old woman sat up. She stared at the crystal, its splash of light emphasizing the redness around her remaining good eye. When the crystal swayed, its reflection caught her across the throat. "I only hoped..." she said wretchedly, but whatever she hoped for was never spoken. Instead, she stood unsteadily and came to them, shedding blankets like veils of madness. When she reached them she wore only her loose dress.

She took the crystal from her granddaughter's hand, holding on to it as gently as a dream. Then she looked at Kel. "Core?"

"What?" he gasped, astounded. What could that simple word mean coming from this madwoman's mouth? Was she ex-Core herself? One of their old witches, fled?

"Here." She gave the crystal to Kel. "Maybe you can use their magic against them."

"Grandmother, I don't understand why—"

"Hush, girl." The old woman never shifted her eyes from Kel Boon. And even beneath the mask of startling change, Kel could make out madness still simmering. "There must be people you need to contact."

"But—"

Then the old woman sat beside Namior and started crying. It was not a slip back into her craze, but her demeanor promised that she had nothing more to say. At least, not right away.

"The Komadians are our enemies," Kel said to Namior's mother. "I promise, I'm doing what I can." He looked down at Namior, wanting to kiss her, whisper into her ear, but content that she was with those who loved her, and if she could survive anywhere it was there. "Tell her I love her. And I'll come back for you all." Sparing one last confused glance at the mysterious old woman, he went for the door.

It was still raining outside, and he held out his hand to let the water wash the last of Namior's blood from the crystal. Then he dropped it in his pocket, checked his weapons, and headed into the night.

HE HAD TWO communicators left, and he could not risk trying one again until he was beyond the village. He had to travel past the Komadians' influence, outside Pavmouth Breaks and across the plains.

He made his way down to the river first, moving slowly, always cautious of what was around the next corner. He moved from shadow to shadow like a wraith, footsteps silent and hands always ready to pluck a knife from his belt, every sense playing a part in examining his surroundings. Core training ran deep.

Close to the river he paused in the shadow of a ruined house, settling on a pile of rubble and hiding from the moons. Work still continued across in the harbor, with rescue teams now digging farther inland along the course of the river. Lights hovered in the air above their heads; Komadian technology. Puffs of steam erupted here and there, and every time he heard one Kel was reminded of the hard coughing of the Strangers' mysterious weapons.

He saw Noreelans digging with Komadians, and the trust the visitors were abusing made him feel sick. While some dug for missing villagers, other Komadians were building the strange black tower above the village.

And where there was one tower, perhaps there were more.

Trakis's screams of agony came to him again. *Do they want us all? Is that the fate for everyone in Pavmouth Breaks?* He had certainly seen plenty of the large crystals, and if every one contained one of those trapped things . . .

Perhaps this was just a bridgehead. Capture the village, use its inhabitants to restore their dead to life again, then move inland. Farmsteads, villages, bands of rovers traveling across the landscape. And then the cities: Noreela City? Long Marrakash? New Shanti?

Though Kel was desperate to know more, he already knew enough. To travel across the bridge would be foolish. Perhaps the visitors on Noreelan soil really did not know about his and Namior's trespass, but risking capture was the last thing he should be doing. His priority was to leave the village and contact the Core. He was important.

He was Pavmouth Breaks' only hope.

Kel turned his back on the harbor and started inland. The footpaths and one narrow street followed the river valley, rising steadily and disappearing at the last of the houses, almost a mile in from the sea. There, he would have to go overland, either following the course of the River Pav or climbing out from the steepening valley and moving across the plains. Somewhere on his route, he would find the place the Komadians considered the village boundary. What he would discover there, he did not know, but he could hazard a guess:

a Stranger, clad in metal and told to kill anyone trying to leave.

There would be more conflict before he could attempt to contact the Core.

The rain eased off as quickly as it had begun, and walking away from the harbor, Kel heard someone else calling the name of a missing loved one. He could not make out the name, nor whence it came, but it gave the night a melancholy air, like low music played at a child's funeral. The voice went on for some time. It died away eventually, fading in volume rather than ceasing altogether. Kel knew that the caller would remain unfulfilled.

And if they *did* meet their missing loved ones in the dark streets, they could be someone or something else.

At one of the path's junctions he followed the course of the river and, walking down from the house-huddled hillside, he found a dead militiawoman. He paused twenty steps away, squatting and lifting his small crossbow from his belt. He primed it with a soft click, then looked around, hoping that his night vision would be effective enough to see anything hiding away in the shadows. The life moon did its best to illuminate the scene, and the death moon was peering over the head of Drakeman's Hill. But darkness still lay heavy in the valley.

Nothing moved. A mist of rain came down again, drifting across the scene like shifting wraiths.

The militiawoman was slumped against a wall where two paths joined. There were rats on her stomach, chest and splayed legs, and several more gnawing at her throat. Rain was beaded on her sword's blade where it lay several steps from her hand.

Kel moved forward. The rats heard him and scattered into the night. He paused and waited for the attack, but it did not come. He moved closer, taking a deep breath in preparation for what he was about to see.

It was Luceel. He'd drunk with her at the Dog's Eyes, and now her throat was open to the bone. Her head was tilted back to one side, her eyes collecting rain, and he could see her spine.

"Are you *all* gone?" he whispered. He thought of the rest of the village militia, Vek and the others, lying dead across Pavmouth Breaks. What had happened? Had the Komadians taken control, under cover of darkness and the falling rain? There were still people digging down at the harbor, searching for bodies more than survivors, but was that all a show?

He knew that he should chant Luceel's wraith down into the Black, but last time he had tried such a thing it had been O'Peeria—a painful time, with guilt haunting his every breath. And truly, he did not have the heart.

"I'm sorry," he whispered, "but you'll find your way there eventually." He closed her eyes and covered her head with her jacket, hoping it would keep the rats from her face.

Then he moved on, more cautious than ever, and aware that the dangers in the darkness were more real than he had feared.

AND IN THE darkness, O'Peeria is his guiding light. He follows her through the gaps between buildings, the crawlways beneath floors, the gaps under and around foundations. She knows all the spaces outside what and where people know, and she sometimes asks why he doesn't, as if it's the duty of a Core member to understand the shadows and echoes of a world, as well as the world itself. But then, she always has been more committed than he.

The Stranger they seek entered the underground several days before, and the Core is sweeping in from the outskirts of Noreela City toward its center. O'Peeria seems confident that they will have their kill soon. Kel is not so sure.

"There are a million places to hide," he says.

"So what? Places like this, the hunter has the advantage over the hunted. This fucking Stranger is trying to hide, he has to be lucky and stay unseen all the time. We only have to be lucky once."

"Do you really love this?" Kel asks. The question has been bothering him for some time, because his own thoughts about being Core are becoming more and more confused. He feels that the Core as a whole is doing good, but he is doing bad. They kill the enemy, and that's what they're trained to do, that's *his* whole reason for being. But somewhere deep down, something is starting to feel wrong.

"Fuck me, no!" she says. "I *hate* it. I'd much rather be back in New Shanti, hunting sand deer in the desert or fishing from the coral spines outside New Drymouth." They're following a forgotten underground canal, and she pauses by its side, pale face illuminated by the light ball at her shoulder. She has always been more comfortable and confident than Kel when it comes to using magic.

"Then why do it?"

She shrugs, as if the answer is obvious, then smiles sadly, realizing it is not. "Because I know I'm good at it," she says. "And I'm hoping that'll help it end soon."

"After this one?" Kel asks. "Or the next? You really think it'll ever end?"

"Yes," she says. And she surprises him by touching his cheek, a brief show of affection that he is becoming unused to. There is sex and groaning and licking, but there is so rarely any real love. "One day they'll make their move, and soon after that it'll be over."

"But who—?"

"Who'll win?" She shrugs again, and her eyes turn hard. "The less they know, the more likely it'll be us."

"Then the more Strangers we kill, the better."

"Right. Ready?"

"Yes," Kel says, but he knows his eyes say "no."

They travel deeper, and come across the site of the kill

beats after the Stranger's wraith has flailed down into nothing. Three other Core are there, and they talk briefly before melting away again into the underside of Noreela City.

That night, after several bottles of rotwine, there is sex and groaning and licking. It is only when O'Peeria is asleep that Kel tells her he loves her.

HE WAS THINKING of Namior when they caught him. He had told her that he loved her many times, and every time he meant it more. He hoped that when Namior awoke, her mother relayed his message.

It was a woman he recognized. He did not know her name, but she ran a shop down at the harbor selling the day's catches for the fishing families of Pavmouth Breaks. She emerged from a doorway thirty paces ahead of him and approached, and to begin with he crouched down and held his crossbow at the ready. When he saw her smile, he stood and smiled back.

"Not a nice night," he said, and then he saw the strangeness in her eyes. She did not recognize him at all.

"It really doesn't hurt," she said. "And you won't remember, or forget anything."

As he lifted the crossbow again, something flashed beside him and struck it from his hand. He turned to face a Stranger in metal armor, projectile weapon pointing at his face. Perhaps the one that had killed Luceel.

The Stranger spoke, and the metal mask made its voice androgynous. It was a language that Kel had never heard.

The woman nodded, her smile gone, but her eyes still glittering.

The Stranger grabbed Kel's arm, squeezing so hard that he cried out in pain. It started dragging him along the path, so fast that he had to run to regain his feet and keep pace with it. He looked over his shoulder at the woman, but she had already turned her back on him, and she soon disappeared once again into shadow.

He could reach for a knife and try to find the weak spot in this Stranger's neck armor . . . but it would rip his arm off in a beat. Whether it knew who he was and what he had done, or thought him just another catch, Luceel's body was testament to the fact that they were not averse to killing.

Kel began to panic, weighing what he must do against the chances of success. He could let himself be led away, and every step he took would lessen the final chance he had of communicating with the Core. Or he could fight and risk death, seeking that small chance at escape.

O'Peeria told him to fight. Namior urged him to go calmly and await a better chance.

But the decision was taken from him. In the beat when he decided to reach for his knife, another Stranger appeared from behind a pile of smashed trees and fractured buildings washed up onto the hillside. It grabbed his free arm and held on just as tightly.

Kel cried out again. And the Strangers exchanged something that could only have been a laugh.

Chapter Ten

transition

THEY PASSED THE last of the buildings and started uphill, out of the river valley and toward the plains above. The Strangers were dragging him in the exact direction Kel wanted to go, and every step increased his dread.

If their intention had been to kill him, they would have done so already.

He walked quickly between them. Their grips on his arms loosened a little, but they were still tight enough to hurt. Neither Stranger spoke, and though he considered saying something, their inhuman metal masks encouraged only silence.

The landscape was lit by weak moonlight, and their route up the hillside was treacherous. *I could fall*, Kel thought, *and roll, and take them with me, and hope the weight of their suits increases their impact.* But that was desperation more than a plan, and he put the idea to the back of his mind. Upriver slightly was Helio Bridge, a hundred steps high and four hundred long, spanning the river and the narrowing valley from side to side. *If I can slip from their grip . . .*

But he had been lucky fighting one of the things, once; he doubted that the same luck would hold with two of them. They would catch him and throw him from the bridge.

Up, out of the valley, and he wondered whether they were beyond the scope of the magical interference. For the first time, he wished he was more welcoming and in tune with the language of the land, because perhaps then he could sense it well enough to know. And if it *did* speak back to him up there, he'd struggle free and plant a communicator before they killed him. But there was no whisper of magic, and such sacrifice would be pointless unless he was certain.

He thought of Namior and pleaded to the Black that she still be alive.

The Strangers hauled him up a steep bank, and as they neared the top Kel saw a glow from somewhere beyond.

"No fighting," the Stranger to his left said, his voice heavily accented. "Do what's told you. You're a good one. Strong. Don't make us kill you." They reached the top of the bank.

The first thing Kel saw was another one of the black towers, identical to the one being built above Drakeman's Hill and those he and Namior had seen on the island. It was fifty steps high and tapering, curving inward toward the village below and behind them. A machine crawled across its flat upper surface, slowly making it taller. It seemed to swallow moonlight, giving off nothing but a dull blackness.

At the foot of the tower lay the source of the glow. Several light balls floated above a flat area, giving faint illumination to the people gathered there and the fence that kept them contained. To the left of the compound, a long, low building seemed to squat like a huge beetle ready to leap, several legs on either side propping it upright. A Komadian entered the building, and Kel had the distinct impression it was a machine acting as a temporary shelter.

The people in the compound were from Pavmouth Breaks. He knew some of them by name, recognized others. They sat huddled together on the heathers and grass, sharing blankets and warmth. Some slept. Others simply stared past the fence that imprisoned them.

"What are you doing?" Kel muttered, but the Strangers nudged him on without responding.

They headed down a slight slope toward the compound, and every step of the way Kel knew he could not go in there. Once trapped, his options were drastically reduced, and the two communicators seemed to gather weight in his pocket. He looked left and right, but the Strangers were keeping close, and they'd see it the beat he made a break. They'd shoot him down. And dead, he'd be no use to anyone.

As they neared the fence, Kel saw that the heavy chains strung between uprights were of uneven construction, and there were small, boxy machines at irregular intervals along their runs. The chains extruded from their surfaces, and weak light glimmered around their sharp edges. The machines themselves were keeping the people trapped.

"In," one of the Strangers said. A section of chain before Kel dipped, just low enough for him to step over. He felt expectant eyes upon him.

"No," he said.

One of the Strangers leveled his projectile weapon, the other pulled a sword.

Kel drew a short knife from his belt. The Stranger stopped, and its shoulders started to shake. Then it laughed.

"In!" it said. It charged at Kel, knocked the knife aside with its metal forearm and lifted him, dropping him over the lowered chain and onto the ground.

By the time he'd sat up, the chain was raised again. He stared across it at the two Strangers, but they were already walking away. One headed back toward the village, the other walked along the fence to the low building beyond. He wanted to shout at them. Wanted to call one back and try, just try to find that weak spot, desperate to feel the warm flow of blood across his hand and arm once more.

"Fuck!" he shouted, scrabbling to his feet, reaching for the barrier.

"No!" someone shouted, but Kel was angry, and it was too late for him to take heed. He grabbed hold of the black linked chain. And his world exploded.

HE WAS SITTING in a chair in the Dog's Eyes. His head throbbed and swam, consciousness expanding to encompass the world, then contracting to a point too small to know. Expanding, contracting...

A million tiny insects crawled across his skin. He could feel each of them individually, and every one of their legs pricked him. It was not painful, but uncomfortable. The discomfort kept him pinned to the world like a moth gatherer's display. He was there, in the Dog's Eyes, and the world grew larger and shrank down to nothing, again and again.

Someone was sitting across the table from him. He couldn't quite make out who it was, but he knew that he was being watched.

Kel reached for a shape on the table, but the movement unbalanced him and sent him spinning. Floor and ceiling changed places, and his surroundings faded to a level blankness, speckled here and there with bursts of bright light.

The insects had finished crawling, but he could still feel every single one of them standing still. They stood like a threat. *Touch the chains and we'll start moving again.*

Chains? Kel shook his head and reached for the ale tankard. Neak's Wanderlust ale would always calm, soothe and settle him in those moments when panic overtook him.

And those moments still came. He knew that Noreela was not alone, and sometimes that knowledge was too much for one person to bear.

"Take a drink," a voice said from a hundred miles away.

Kel smiled. "Trakis," he drawled, though the voice was not quite the same.

"Take a drink."

Kel grabbed the tankard and drank. It was water, not ale, and it coursed through his body and drove away those millions of tiny insects. They lifted from him in waves, and he sighed as his skin settled, his flesh stopped quivering and his head ceased its interminable spin.

"Better?" the voice asked.

Kel took in several deep breaths, and his world expanded outward again, farther than ever before. He looked. A man sat across the table, and Kel did not recognize him. They were not in the Dog's Eyes at all, but a low, long building with several tables set against one wall and a pile of canvas-wrapped packages along the other.

"It may tingle for a while, but there'll be no lasting damage. Not this time. But the chains remember; touch them again, and next time the pain will be worse. Again, and your muscles will knot and cramp for days. One more time after that, and you're dead."

"Then I'll be dead," Kel said.

"I don't want that." The man lifted a mug to his mouth and took a long drink. He smacked his lips and sighed.

Kel looked around, and he realized where he was. From the outside, the building had looked like a parked machine, and the inside only confirmed that suspicion. There were pipes and ducts, wheels and spindles, and steam leaked from several places where joints had worked loose.

"Why am I here?" Kel asked. Ignorance was the way to go . . . at least until he could see how much this man knew.

"Because you were trying to escape from the village."

"I was going up the valley to see how far the damage went. Not beyond. I've no reason to go beyond."

The man stood and reached down behind his chair. He lifted Kel's sword and placed it on the table, followed by his knife, crossbow and throwing knives.

Kel eyed the weapons, then glanced around without turning his head. Two metal-clad Strangers shifted in the shadows, just enough for him to see them. He sighed. *Not yet*, he thought.

"Strange tools for a fisherman," the man said.

"I'm a wood-carver."

"Then wood carving in Noreela must be a dangerous business. My name is Lemual Kilminsteria. You can call me friend."

"Does everyone out there call you friend?" Kel asked, nodding outside. "I saw *my* friends, before I touched the chains that keep them here."

"Their own safety," Lemual said.

"I don't understand." *Ignorance, ignorance.* "You're helping our village, and I thank you for that. We've suffered such a terrible loss. My own friends . . ." Kel looked down at his hands on the table, and at the edge of his vision lay a throwing knife. When he shifted slightly he heard metallic movement behind him, but also felt the weight of the two communicators in his trousers pocket. *Can they not know what they are? Can they not know who I am?* Hope touched him, and he did his best not to let it show.

"It doesn't hurt a bit," Lemual said, standing back from the table as though inviting Kel to reach for a weapon.

Kel looked up. "What doesn't hurt?"

"What you saw today, on Komadia. What you know. We're lost and in pain and our island is cursed, but nothing has ever made us *monsters*."

Kel stared at the man, the Komadian, and all the while he was aware of the two armored Strangers watching. He remembered O'Peeria dying beneath one of their kin, and Trakis out on the island, taken over by whatever the thing in that crystal had once been. He remembered his friend's screams. No, of course, not monsters.

"Fuck you, friend," Kel said.

"Let me tell you!" Lemual said, and the appeal in his voice could not have been feigned.

"Tell me what?"

"About us. About the island, and what happened to us."

"So you know that *I* know what you do," Kel said, "and you're wanting me to feel *sorry* for you?" He began to stand, but one of the Strangers closed in, quickly and quietly. He could see the projectile weapons, their smooth snouts both pointing at his head.

Lemual looked at him for a few beats, frowning, then sighed and shook his head. "I just don't want you to fight," he said.

"So tell me," Kel said, sitting back in his chair. *Perhaps this will be the truth*, he thought, *or perhaps not. Whatever, it will buy me time. And it might be priceless to the Core.*

Lemual glanced up at the Strangers. "You can leave," he said. The metal-clad men did not question him, but obeyed like soldiers listening to their commander. They left the strange building, and Kel knew one more thing about them.

"You're not afraid of me anymore?" he asked, looking down at his weapons displayed on the table.

"I never was. I'm from a land so far away that you people can't possibly imagine, and I can move faster than you blink." His smile remained, perhaps meant to be calming, perhaps superior.

"Then maybe I won't blink at all," Kel said.

Lemual sighed. "I hate trouble. I hate killing. I hate it every time Komadia moves somewhere else, and we face the whole cursed process one more time."

"I know what you're doing to us. To my friends. The curse is on us, not you."

"Komadia can't just die," Lemual said. "We can't just give in, let our land cease to be."

"So you're fighting for your future, and you don't expect us to fight for ours?"

"Every time The Blighting shifts us somewhere new, we *expect* the people there to fight. I'm one of those who chooses to try to stop the conflict before it begins, because it never does any good. We always win. I'd rather we grow and restore, then move on, without losing too many people."

"Don't like it when your soldiers die, is that it?"

"They're animals," Lemual said, waving his hand over one shoulder. "Born from slime, they'll return to it, unless they're..." He trailed off, looked away, and Kel thought of that strange pool back on the island, with things growing and shifting just below the surface.

"I've killed them," Kel said, frowning as he thought of the Strangers he had killed or witnessed killed over the years. Certainly not animals, they were intelligent, sly and fast, possessed of a cunning which often meant they evaded capture by the Core for many moons.

Lemual's face darkened, then the smile broke out again. But this time it was sad. "I've told you everything, yet still you cannot understand."

"I've got quite an imagination," Kel said. *Maybe you can use their magic against them*, Namior's great-grandmother had said. He looked down at the table and saw the nugget of crystal from Namior's chest, but he did not require that. He possessed his own source of power.

"If the woman dies," Lemual said, "it's because of your anger, and your fight. If she survives, we'll take her."

Kel tried to hide his surprise at how much Lemual knew about him. "You'll take her, drive out her soul, give her body to something else."

Lemual looked away. "The core of her will remain." *That's the first thing he's told me without looking me in the eye*, Kel thought. *And the first time he's betrayed his lies.*

Kel reached into his pocket and brought out the communicators.

Lemual tensed and opened his mouth, ready to call the soldiers back in.

"Nuts," Kel said. "I'm hungry. If I could kill you with one of these, they'd be on the table before you." He picked up one communicator, held his breath and put it into his mouth, tucking in into his cheek. He pretended to chew. The moisture would keep it wound.

"Where is the crystal you took?" Lemual asked.

"So that's it," Kel said. "Why? Friend of yours?" He held the other communicator in his hand.

Lemual glanced aside.

Kel let the first communicator drop from his mouth, and as he raised the other one in his right hand, he reached for a knife with his left.

The man had not lied about one thing; he *was* very fast. Before Kel's fingers had even touched the blade, Lemual was pressing his hand to the table.

Kel breathed on the communicator, letting its curled tail unfurl and harden along his forearm.

"I told you—" Lemual said.

"—only what you want me to hear." Kel tugged, trying to free his hand, and when Lemual looked down again he struck.

The tip of the communicator parted the man's skin at the nape of his neck. Kel pushed hard, and it cut through flesh and bone like the sharpest of knives.

Lemual coughed blood. He tried to stand, but Kel kept his hand on the communicator. He leapt across the table, turning the man as he went, then pushed him to the ground.

No alarms sounded, no steam vents gushed, no Strangers streaked into the building.

Lemual was moaning softly, his hands reaching beneath him where the spike protruded from his stomach.

Kel kicked his legs from under him, driving him down to

the ground. He felt the impact through the communicator's head as Lemual struck the hard soil, then he pushed with both hands.

This is when I live or die, Kel thought. Because he could not leave. He had to wait and see whether the communicator worked, and if this man died the same way as the Strangers, his wraith would rip from his body and tear Kel apart. But there were no arcing limbs streaking white lightning on Lemual's back.

"Work," Kel said quietly. "*Work!*"

"What...?" Lemual whispered, but talking hurt him too much.

"You're not getting us," Kel said. "All the other worlds you've visited, all the people you've taken, they're nothing to Noreela and Noreelans. We'll fight until we're dead or you're dead, and fuck you both ways." He touched the communicator head, twisted, then jerked his hand away.

It was growing hot.

It's working!

Lemual vomited. It was a violent, unexpected action, and Kel stepped back in surprise. There was a lot of blood in there. The dying man's arms thrashed, pressing at the ground to try to lift the communicator's tip from the soil, but whatever held him there was strong. His legs kicked, and Kel sat on them so that he did not make too much noise.

Kel reached up to the table, grabbed as many of his weapons as he could, and watched the communicator as it began to glow.

Then he lifted his sword, turned its blade flat and brought it down on the communicator's head.

It smashed.

There was an explosion inside Kel's mind; a rush of heat, an expansion of light, a blast of realization. It would have woken him if he was asleep, sobered him had he been drunk, and for a beat he felt a welcoming link to hundreds of other people all across their vast land.

He gasped, then fell to his knees beside the dying man.

"Message sent," he said.

"What ... have you ...?"

Kel did not even bother to reply. He shoved his sword into the prone man's back, piercing where he assumed the heart to be. Lemual's body stiffened and went limp. Kel withdrew the sword, then used the blade to lift the dead man's clothes away from his back. There were no proboscises, no gills.

His own sickness rising, Kel turned away and tried to calm himself. Killing was never easy. But the war had begun. He only wished O'Peeria could be there to fight it by his side.

HE HAD TO get away from the place as soon as possible. Strapping on his weapons once again, priming his crossbow, keeping the short sword to hand, Kel tried to imagine what was happening across Noreela.

If the communicator had worked as the Core's witches had intended, it would have sent a signal directly into the minds and dreams of every Core member. A warning, telling them that the long-expected invasion had begun, and planting a seed of direction that would bloom as soon as they set out on their way. Several hundred Core, many in Noreela City and others much farther out, would hurry there by the fastest means possible. They would ride their transport machines until they reached the place where Komadian interference interrupted the flow of magic and language in the land. Then they would walk, warned by the failings of magic that something momentous was happening, and that this was not a false alarm.

They would likely not be there that day, or the next. Help was coming, but it would not be quick.

He was faced with a stark choice: leave and await the Core, or go back into Pavmouth Breaks. But even before deciding that, he first had to find his way out of the machine-building, and the compound surrounding it.

Footsteps.

Kel held his breath and crouched, rushing to the sidewall of the large room. The doorway was a few steps from him, curtained by a fall of gauzy material, and the footsteps came closer, metal scraping stone. A Stranger . . . and all Kel had on his side was surprise.

The guard paused outside. Kel heard the very faint whisper of metal on metal. He thought of Namior, tried to imagine her lying in her house with her mother fussing over her. *Core?* her great-grandmother had asked Kel, and she obviously knew far more than she had ever revealed. Then he remembered O'Peeria, and though he wished her by his side, her mere memory aided him, making him angry and determined. *The time has come*, he thought, and he saw O'Peeria grinning, her pale face and dark hair beautiful in the strange light inside the machine.

Kel closed his eyes and breathed deeply.

The curtain shifted aside and Mell entered.

He could kill her within a beat, his crossbow aimed directly at her face. Mell . . . who he had yet to tell what he'd seen happening to Trakis, back on that damned island.

She looked at him, let out a huge sigh of relief, and smiled. "You made it!"

"Mell?"

"Who else were you expecting?" Her voice sounded flat. She looked down at the body, and it was just too dark for him to see how her expression changed. "You've been busy."

"Are you one of them?"

"Of course not. I'm Mell. You said so yourself."

"How did you—?"

"I heard they were keeping people here, came here to see if I could do anything."

"What's your favorite ale?"

"As if you didn't know." She smiled, but it was not Mell's smile. Too easy, and too wide, because she'd never liked her crooked teeth.

"*I* know," Kel said, raising the crossbow again. "But do *you?*"

Mell came closer then paused again, glancing across at Lemual's body. Kel saw such grief on her face that it knocked his guard aside, just for a moment.

A metal-clad Stranger breezed through the door, aiming its projectile weapon at his head.

"It doesn't hurt," Mell said.

Kel dropped to the floor before her. The Stranger would not shoot through her body, and he still desperately needed that surprise, that element of shock that would set him half a beat ahead of the soldier.

He aimed the crossbow at Mell's face.

She gasped and dropped to one side, and Kel fired past her left ear.

The bolt struck the Stranger's face and ricocheted into the gloom. His head flicked back and his weapon fired, the projectile passing above Kel's head and impacting the machine's wall.

The whole room shuddered, and a tapestry of weak blue sparks appeared across its surface before quickly fading away.

Kel rolled, priming and reloading the crossbow as he went. Back on his knees, aiming again, and he was already looking into the black tube of the Stranger's weapon. He gasped and looked up at the ceiling, glancing down again quickly, amazed that the Stranger had fallen for his deception and looked up as well, releasing the bolt, hearing the screech of metal turn into a scream of pain as it passed through the plates across the thing's neck. Its shiny chest glimmered as blood flowed, and it went to its knees, dropping the weapon and clasping both hands to its throat.

Don't die yet, Kel thought. He went to run past the

Stranger, but Mell—or who- or whatever had taken her body for its own—reached out and tripped him.

Perhaps she thought he would still be reluctant to hurt his friend. Maybe all their studies, their spies, their covert observations of Noreela had told them that Noreelans were so attached to friends and family that confusion would be his reaction, not action. But Kel was Core, and the past days had confirmed everything the Core had ever suspected.

As Mell crawled for him, he drew a throwing knife and launched it at her face. It pierced her left eye. In her right eye, as she died, he saw nothing of the Mell he knew.

The Stranger was gargling and croaking, blood spewing from its mouth and pulsing between the metal plates across its throat. It would die soon, and if he was still inside when it did . . .

There was at least one more outside.

Kel grabbed the thing's projectile weapon, surprised at how light it was, knowing he was a fool even to try using it. But it was much more powerful than knives and bolts, and though the Strangers had their soft spots, he had many more.

The weapon was as long as his forearm, and the back of it expanded into a bubble the size of his fist, its surface hot and damp. The front part of the tube was thin and pointed. It had fired once, and he only hoped there were more projectiles inside. Did it take the Stranger's magic to fire it? Was it a machine, like the thing building those huge columns, or a tool, like his crossbow?

He went outside to find out.

The other Stranger must have been patrolling around the chain compound when it heard its companion's weapon discharging. It was running, close to the chains, and it fired at Kel as it moved. That saved him; he felt the projectile pass by his head, close enough to flick up a tuft of his hair.

Kel steadied the tube against his hip and pulled the curved metal trigger. It jerked in his arms and spat a gush of steam, and the Stranger tripped and fell. In the poor light from the floating light balls, he saw the jagged hole on the back of its metal-clad head.

Dead, he thought, then the change began.

It was close to the chain compound, and Kel could see the shadows of people moving in there as they came close to see. He glanced up at the ever-growing column arching over them, saw the machine still moving up there, and wondered who or what was controlling it.

"Get back!" he growled, running a wide circuit around the fallen Stranger. He waved at those behind the fence, gesturing for them to move away, but their pale faces showed no comprehension.

"Wood-carver?" he heard someone say, and he almost laughed out loud, thinking, *Do I look like a fucking wood-carver?*

From behind he heard the vicious wailings of the first dead Stranger's wraith. And beside the compound, the metal man he had just shot burst open and the long limbs rose from its back, blue light sparking and arcing from tip to tip.

"Back!" he shouted again, retreating himself. He looked up at the tower again, and the machine up there seemed to have stopped, pausing on the edge as though gazing down. Kel ran up the slope, away from the compound and the rampaging wraiths. He could do nothing for those within the chained areas, not yet. Maybe when the mad wraiths went down...

The screaming began, and he fell to the heathers and covered his head.

KEL WATCHED WITH one eye. He had to, in case one of the wraiths came up the hillside after him. There was no way of telling whether the things had any memory of the existence they had so recently departed, but if they did, perhaps vengeance would be their prime motivators. But the one inside the building remained there, and the spectre outside raged and twisted and roared without apparent direction, as had all the others he had seen.

In the poor light, he saw those in the compound backing away from the mad thing. *Good*, he thought, *let them know the fear.*

Kel looked up at the flat top of the tower. The machine extruding the material to grow the tower remained motionless, and he knew that its controller must be watching from somewhere.

He scanned around the tower's base, then back past the chained enclosure and the raving wraith to the low building he had so recently fled. Three dead in there, and one more outside, and suddenly the impact of his escape hit him. He'd killed four of them to get out, two almost-humans and two of the deadly Strangers. He actually smiled, and heard a voice telling him that they'd write songs about him. O'Peeria or Namior; he could not decide.

But he could still not see the Komadian controlling the building machine.

The wraith struck the chains. Insubstantial, fleeting, it passed through with little more than a fall of weak sparks. The prisoners screamed, darting left and right as the thing scored across the ground toward them. Kel could have shouted, but they no longer needed warning. For them it was all down to luck, and fate, and whichever gods they chose to call their own.

And then he saw movement at the base of the tower. A shadow parted from its influence and moved closer to the chains, watching the wraith as it raged its way out of this world.

Kel knew that he did not have long. Hidden by the night, he ran across the hillside, circling the small dip in the land and edging around behind the tower.

Somebody screamed. The wraith had found flesh and blood. It would take a few more beats to die.

He hoped that the Komadian was fascinated enough with the carnage to have lowered his or her guard.

Kel ran directly down the shallow slope to the rear of the tower. He touched its surface, then jerked away, repulsed, *never* wanting to touch it again. It was unnaturally smooth and warm, like the chitinous shells of the fist beetles, which sometimes drifted down onto the village from the plains above. And it throbbed with an alien energy that made no sense.

He heard the wraith's final explosive demise, and more screams.

Edging around the base of the tower, cautious not to touch it, he came to the corner nearest the compound. Something steamed and spat on the ground within, and he wondered whether he had known him or her.

The Komadian was acting quite calmly. He took something long and thin from his pocket, waved it until a blue spark burst from one end, then brought it up to his mouth.

Kel placed the Komadian weapon carefully on the ground and buried his sword in the man's neck.

The object fell from the Komadian's hand, and Kel heard a voice crackling from it. He did not know the language, but he could sense the concern.

Shit! He stamped on the device and ground it into the dirt.

The man was still moving. Kel stood on his chest and pulled the sword free, and the Komadian cried out in pain.

"Not again, not again," he pleaded, and Kel knelt down to stare into his face.

"I hope you never find peace," he said.

The man blinked up at him, crying. Kel saw the terror in his eyes, and for a beat he felt pity. But only for a beat. "It hurts," the man whispered. Kel checked the unwounded side of his neck for gills, found none, then slit his throat.

He wiped his sword in the heather and picked up the

metal weapon. Walking away from another corpse, he felt a moment of sickness. But a cool memory grabbed his arm, and O'Peeria told him to be fucking strong, not weak.

Kel breathed deeply a few times, then looked up at the structure towering over him. He could not see its flattened top from there, but he was certain the machine atop it remained motionless. He could hear nothing other than the frightened whispers of his fellow villagers.

Doubts haunted him. He had killed Mell's body, even though it had not been her mind controlling it. But was there anything left of her? Had she known, at the last, what he had done?

Feel no pity for your enemy, O'Peeria had always told him. *That's the Core way, and the* only *way we can win. No pity for them. Only rage.*

But the enemy had never been like this. Kel looked back at the man he had just killed. He did not recognize him. The man had been terrified. *No pity,* he thought, but he was not so sure.

He began to shake, delayed shock stealing control of his muscles, but a shout from the compound brought him around.

"Kel Boon!" a woman called, and he knew that voice. "Is that you? Or are you something else in a wood-carver's body?"

Kel went closer to the chains and looked through. A woman stood facing him, a group of people behind her, and it was Mygrette, Pavmouth Breaks' oldest witch.

"They caught *you*?" Kel said.

"Aye, trying to escape this cursed place. Not as fast as I used to be. Spit on them all! And you, Kel Boon?"

He ignored the loaded question. "I'll try to get you out."

"These things," Mygrette said, waving at one of the boxes along the fence. "Chains came from out of them. Bastard machines, not honest ones like ours."

"Then this will be poetic," he said, hefting the metallic

tube. "Stand away." He waited until Mygrette had herded everyone to the end of the compound, then aimed at one of the boxes along the fence and fired.

The effect was not as severe as he'd expected. The projectile struck the box and seemed to be absorbed into it. The box sighed and slipped to the ground. A section of chain crumbled away, turning to grit and dust in the darkness, spitting a few sparks before fading to nothing.

When the prisoners filed out, they stood in small groups behind Mygrette. The old witch had sometimes been an object of ridicule, and even derision, but Kel was glad that they perceived her strength at a time like this.

"So tell me, wood-carver—" she began, but Kel cut in. An urgency had settled over him, inspired perhaps by the fight he had just won, but also prodding at him with a sense of time passing and doom closing with each breath.

"Not now," he said. "Just believe me when I tell you I know some of what's happening. The whole village is in danger, Mygrette."

"Ha! *There's* news."

"Get far away, if you can." There was a muttered chorus of disapproval.

"My husband!" someone said, and "My child!"

"Help is coming," Kel said. "But you can't go back, not now. It's too dangerous. You'd never get to your loved ones, and if those things catch you again, they might just kill you. So run, hide on the plains, and you'll see your families again soon."

"When?" someone else asked.

Kel tried to hide his doubt, but it felt like a lie. "When it's over."

Mygrette stared at him for a few beats, and he felt like a sheebok being examined by its buyer. Then she grinned. "You never were the best carver I've ever seen."

"I'm still practicing," Kel said. He stepped closer to Mygrette and held out his hand. "Do something for me.

When you're far enough away, and you're certain you hear the language of the land once more, breathe on this, plant it, and when the head grows warm, shatter it."

Mygrette's grin faded. "There's much about what's happened I don't understand. But this, I don't like."

"It's just to be sure."

"That help is comin'?"

"It *is* coming," Kel said, remembering the communicator shattering across the Komadian's bloody back. "But there's no harm making doubly sure."

The old witch looked at the curled object in her hand. "Breathe, plant, smash."

"That's about it."

"And you?"

"I have to go back. Slow them down, if I can."

"Nothin' to do with a woman you've left back there, then?"

And Kel's sense of urgency suddenly formed into something else. Doors opened and closed in his mind, barriers fell, and some sort of understanding hit him. *Core?* Namior's great-grandmother had asked. "Something to do with her, yes," he said. "And the old woman who lives with her."

Mygrette grabbed his hands. "There's an old Voyager blessing I know," she said. "Good travels."

"Good travels, Mygrette."

Kel watched the witch working her harsh charm over the others. Then they left, heading away from the coast, the only place they had ever called home, and the many loved ones they had left behind.

Help is coming, Kel thought. But he had a weight of dreadful responsibility resting heavy on his shoulders. And before it could crush him to the ground, he started to run.

Chapter Eleven

such sights

THE LIFE MOON lit his way, and with every step he expected to see it reflected from the armor of a waiting Stranger.

Kel moved quickly, working his way back over the small hill, across the plain and down into the valley of the River Pav. The lights of Pavmouth Breaks were still out of sight along the valley, but he could already smell the ruin that had been visited upon his village. Being away and coming back again had made the stench of mud and death even more oppressive.

Leaving the dead behind, Kel started to feel good. He had abandoned the Komadian weapon by that tower, and he was glad. His sword felt good back on his belt, the weight of his crossbow familiar. His heart hurried, his senses were heightened and alert, and he felt like a shadow moving through the night. He had killed, but they had been the enemy. The invaders. The body stealers. And when the occasional doubts still intruded, he remembered Mell's undamaged eye when she had died, and the certainty that there was nothing of her there. He had killed an invader inside his friend.

Mell was dead. So was Trakis. Murdered for their bodies, viciously and without any regard for the fate of their wraiths. He should entertain no guilt.

He saw the glow of Pavmouth Breaks farther along the valley, a haze in the darkness that indicated where people still dug through the hardened muck of the flood. He was not certain why the Komadians still allowed the search, but he saw it as a good sign. With them trying to keep up their pretense in the village, the opportunity for him to move about and talk to the people who mattered still existed.

That would not last. Perhaps the Komadians in command already knew of what he had done at the compound, but if not, he was certain that they would find out very soon. That tall tower had stopped growing, and whatever arcane use it was intended for had been delayed, at least for a while.

Moments beat by, and every beat carried the village and its people closer to their doom. If Kel knew the Komadians' plans, he could try to avert them. But for the moment, even though he knew more than anyone else, it would be like shooting in the dark. All he could do was disrupt them as much as possible until help arrived.

Unless Namior's great-grandmother was aware of more than she had suggested. She knew of the Core, at least. And even without that to draw him there, Namior's home was where he needed to begin.

HE USED HIS knowledge of Pavmouth Breaks' geography to keep himself safe. There were Strangers on the streets, but he heard their movements from many steps away and always had time to hide in a garden, doorway or side street.

The darkness was his ally, and when he moved through several areas where cold air sighed past him, he knew how troubled the village was that night. As well as Strangers, wraiths haunted its byways. He hoped that the time would come when a Mourner could chant them down.

He still heard voices crying out here and there, a sad song of the missing. Perhaps their loved ones were being held in other chained compounds elsewhere outside the valley. Or maybe they had already been taken across to the island, like Trakis and Mell. The order of things confused him, and the processes being carried out, and Kel was desperate to find out more. The more he knew, the more was mysterious to him. Knowledge would give him power. And when the Core arrived, he needed to tell them everything there was to know.

From the Moon Temple, where Namior had worked to heal the injured just the day before, Kel could see across the river to the harbor.

One of the big Komadian ships was moored at the mole. Its sails were stowed, and a score of light balls floated above the ship, mole and harborfront, shedding their flat illumination across the whole area. A few people still dug, though from what he saw, he was quite sure that they were all villagers. It seemed that the Komadians had tired of search and rescue.

But what turned him cold was what he saw along the mole. A line of people, maybe thirty in total, were waiting to board the ship. It was too distant to recognize anyone, but Kel could tell for sure that they were all Noreelan; stooped, tired, dirty and beaten, residents of Pavmouth Breaks who were willingly undertaking a journey to their doom. And some of them seemed to be laughing.

Keera Kashoomie, the Komadian emissary, stood at the bottom of the boarding ramp with several guards, shaking hands, swapping words and doing her best to lift their spirits.

Kel wondered what she was telling them. *Just for a while, a break from the ruin, and we have such sights to show you.*

"Surely this can't go on!" he whispered. He wanted to run down to the bridge the Komadians had helped repair, rush across to the harbor and shout a warning. Some would believe him, perhaps, though many would not. But at least a few could fight against the horror awaiting them. And if a few fought, the rumors of their fight would spread like a contagion. Pavmouth Breaks could stand and rail against what the invaders were doing instead of queuing up with a smile and a nod.

But though Kel might manage to seed a rebellion, he would be killed in its first real fight. And he was not about to sacrifice himself needlessly.

Not wishing to see any more, he edged his way through a narrow opening between buildings, kicking a gaggle of rats aside as he did so. He stepped through whatever it was they had been eating, and it stank. He tried to persuade himself it was a dead dog.

When he reached Namior's small, uneven street, he watched her house for a while. The soft glow of candlelight showed around the edges of curtains, and the place felt warm and welcoming, not dangerous.

"Please be alive," he spoke to the darkness, pleading with the Black. "Please."

Even before he knocked, Namior's great-grandmother swung the door open. Kel held his breath—he waited for the mad laughter, the confused tears. But her eye, though still bloodshot, had changed. "Been wondering when you'd be back," she said.

"Namior?"

"Alive."

"She'll be well?"

The old woman smiled, but it was humorless. "For now."

"I need to ask you—"

"In from the street, boy!" she said, waving him inside. "There's no knowing what's walking the darkness these days."

"Don't *you* know?"

The woman did not respond. Instead she went back into the main room and sat slowly by the groundstone, shrugging a blanket around her shoulders again, seeming to shrink down into herself. Kel watched for the craze, but the old woman was more in control than he had ever seen her.

"Just the two of us," she said. "The others are asleep. So now's the time for your questions and some truths from me."

"I want to see Namior first," Kel said, and that was suddenly the most important thing for him. The relief that she was still alive was soon masked by his growing sense of dread, but for that instant, to look on her face was his greatest wish.

The old woman waved one clawed hand at the stairs, and Kel went.

Upstairs, he stood by the open door to Namior's attic room and looked inside. Many times they had made love on her bed, trying to ease the creaking of its wooden frame and stifle their groans and sighs. They had made promises to each other there, as well, and he had lied to her, because lying was a large part of being in the Core. Namior lay beneath a thin blanket. Her eyes were closed, several candles burned on shelves around the room, and Kel could see the rapid rise and fall of her chest. She made small noises in her sleep, and the room listened to her groans of pain, not pleasure.

Kel went in and kissed her gently on the lips. She did not react. She smelled of the sea, and he realized how special she was, not just to him but to everyone. She knew what was happening, and if she died, that would make him the only one.

"Live," he whispered into her ear. "Please live, Namior." Her only answer was a small sigh. He touched her hand and squeezed, then backed out of her room, keeping her in sight until the last possible moment.

Halfway down the staircase, he leaned against the wall as heat and light blossomed in his mind. His perception widened then closed in again, the briefest glimpse at infinity, and he smiled. Somewhere inland, Mygrette had planted and smashed his second communicator.

Back downstairs, Namior's great-grandmother was sitting in the same position by the groundstone. She watched Kel enter the room and sit close to her on some floor cushions.

"Still sleeping," she said. "The body heals better that way."

"Your craze?" Kel asked.

She shrugged, and her good eye rolled in its socket, as if searching for her erstwhile madness. "Perhaps over the years, I've let my mind grow lazy. And a craze will feed on fear." She took in a deep breath. "But I saw you bring Namior in, and saw what my granddaughter dug from her. And now I have to fight my fear for the ones I love."

"You're Core." Kel knew there must be others like this, old members who had lost their way or left of their own accord, like him, hidden away here on the edge of Noreela. If there was one, there were many.

"Do I look like a soldier to you?" she asked, offering a toothless smile.

"Do I look like a wood-carver?"

"Appearances can deceive."

"First lesson of the Core."

"No, just common sense," she said, "known to everyone who leads a life of deceit."

Kel listened for noises from outside, but all was quiet. The only sound was the spit of burning candles, and the old woman's harsh breathing. It was strange conducting a conversation with her—usually her words were confused, and sometimes she never spoke at all.

"Tell me," he said.

The old woman sighed, and the weight of every year she had lived was expressed in that one, painful sound. "I'm a witch, like my daughter, and her daughter, and your Namior. Since you've been with her I doubt you've ever seen me leaving this home. But it wasn't always so. Many years ago I led a...colorful life." She smiled at old memories, then glanced up at Kel again. "Seen more of Noreela than you."

"I've seen a lot."

"Pah!" She waved her hand again, slapping his words from the air. "You've seen the parts of the land where people live. I spent the first thirty years of my witching times seeing the parts where people *don't* live. The Poison Forests. Mol'Steria Desert, dodging Shantasi scouts and living in catacombs deep beneath the sands. Spent six years roaming Kang Kang, east to west and back again."

"No one survives that long in Kang Kang," Kel scoffed.

"And yet, here I am."

"So what do you know of the Core?"

"Whispers," she said. "But I spent some time following whispers, tracking them, listening to them harder than others. Because all whispers start somewhere." She looked directly into Kel's eyes, judging his reaction as she went on. "I know the Core has been in existence for over a thousand years."

"Not that long," he said.

"Maybe they just don't tell you it's that long. And they're here to protect Noreela from threats from beyond."

"The threat's arrived," Kel said. "Namior and I went to the island and saw what they were doing. Stealing our bodies. Using them as hosts for...I don't know. Disembodied wraiths."

"I met three Core soldiers on my travels," she said, as if avoiding the subject of Komadia.

"How did you know they were Core?"

"I had a way of telling. One of them fled the moment I revealed my knowledge to him. The second, I killed. The third, I loved, and he became my husband."

Kel could only stare wide-eyed, mouth agape. "Does Namior know?"

"Of course not!"

"And the one you killed?"

The old woman lowered her eyes and shook her head. "Everyone's allowed their secrets."

"I have to go," Kel said, standing. "I've signaled them, they'll be coming, but if I don't do something they might be too late."

"A place of wraiths," she said. "That's what they'll find."

"No!" Kel said, and her lack of faith made him even more determined.

"He told me so much," she said. "About the Strangers, and what happens when they die. About the fears of invasion. The Core, their mission, their hunts. All the time, he thought he was sharing secrets, but I already knew it all. My husband died, and I never told him the truth." She started crying dry, bitter tears that shook her shoulders and caught in her throat.

"The truth?"

The old woman looked up, and Kel realized that she was afraid. Not of her crazes, or the Komadians, or the way magic was somehow being held from the land. She was scared of *him*, Kel Boon.

"Namior should go with you," she said, wiping her cheeks. "The two of you belong together, I've seen the love there. Leave Pavmouth Breaks before it's too late."

"How *can* she go with me?"

"Will you trust me?"

"I don't know what you mean." Kel stood. And with the old woman's fear, came a little of his own.

"I can make her better." She rose and shuffled away, heading for her small room at the rear of the house.

Kel had never been back there, but he followed her, unsettled by what she was saying and what it could imply. He stood in the doorway as she knelt before her bed and felt around beneath it. She drew out a small chest, dragging it across the floor with surprising strength.

"What's that?" Kel asked.

"My secret life." The woman stood and looked back at Kel, and he could see that she was excited. Scared, old, twisted with age...but still excited. "No one else has ever seen what's in here. *No one.*"

Kel nodded, but said nothing.

Namior's great-grandmother—witch, wanderer, Core killer and lover—opened the chest with a pendant that hung around her neck.

She took out a small blue box, weak candlelight shining from its metallic surface.

"We'll need water," she said, showing Kel the box.

"Why?"

"To make the steam."

Kel took a clumsy step back, hand on the hilt of his sword.

"You won't be needing that, Kel Boon." She had not changed. She was still the little old woman he'd seen in Namior's home a hundred times before. But she looked different to Kel, holding a device he did not recognize or understand, talking about the steam needed to drive it. And the crystal pendant caught his eye.

"You're one of *them*!"

"Not for a very long time."

He drew his sword, stepped forward quickly, and pressed its point to her neck. She stood still and calm, allowing him that moment, and when he used the sword to move aside her collar she turned her head so that he could see. There were no gills.

"And my back's just old, wrinkled skin," she said.

"You brought them here."

"No!"

"You've been here all along, planning, making sure Pavmouth Breaks would be just right, and—"

"No, Kel," she said, louder this time. "I left long ago, the same way my husband left the Core. The same way *you* left it."

"You know *nothing* about me and the Core."

"But you don't deny you're hiding from it?"

Kel said nothing.

"I've spent seventy years of my life on Noreela," she said. "I'm as Noreelan as you."

"You're from somewhere else!"

"I *left*! I've no idea what they've told you, what you think you know, but the island was cursed many generations ago. Komadia is from the far south, way past the Blurring. Legend has it we were visited by one of your Sleeping—"

"More lies!"

"The truth, Kel! All but a few Komadians were ripped from their bodies and imprisoned in those terrible things. You can't imagine the pain." She glanced away, staring into an incomprehensible distance. "Those few who survived, the Elders, invested all their rage and loneliness into building great constructs, buried deep, to shift the island. Take it places where they could try to cure the curse."

"By invading? Stealing?"

She shrugged, then looked down at his sword. Kel lowered it.

"The Elders' descendants gave me this body and brought me back into the world. And Komadians are *strong*, Kel. First the host's soul is cast aside, then with a strength born of frustration and rage, the changes to the body begin. Over time, the host's blood becomes Komadian blood, and Komadia's bloodline goes on. Mind alters body, Kel. It's more than any Noreelan witch can achieve. But I always knew this body wasn't my own, and I always grieved for its previous owner. Komadia's way was not for me; I left when we manifested close to The Spine. I swam for a day and a night to flee that place, and the island moved on two moons later."

Kel glanced down at the box in her hands. "You've kept that hidden all this time."

"It's not the only thing I brought with me, but it's all I kept. I was a healer before I left Komadia, and I've been a healer ever since. But never once with this." She shook her head. "I'm not even sure—"

"Don't say it," Kel said. "After all this, don't tell me it won't work."

"I'm slave to a new magic now, wood-carver." And her good eye looked haunted, and so very old.

UPSTAIRS, MOVING QUIETLY so as not to wake Namior's mother, they stood beside the wounded woman's bed, and watched her struggling to breathe.

"The impact shattered a rib and hit her lung," her great-grandmother said. She poured water carefully into a small hole in the top of the blue metal device. She spilled a few drops, and they dripped onto Namior's hand. She did not even flinch.

"Your magic will fix it?" Kel asked.

"No longer my magic." She held up the box. "This is old knowledge of mine, that's all."

The old woman swilled the box around, and Kel saw its color change from light blue to dark. Then she stroked its sides, and on its surface a swathe of small, domed humps appeared, pushing up through the metal until they protruded a finger's width above the box's top. She looked back at Kel. "Pray to the Black."

"I pray to nothing."

"All you Core people, faithless. You think with all you've seen and know, you'd *want* to believe in something more." She pulled back the blanket, opened Namior's sleep shirt and placed the box between her breasts, just above the dreadful injury.

Namior gasped, groaned.

"Stay back," the old woman said, even though Kel had not moved. "Trust me."

He did. Komadian she might have been in the past, but he sensed a kindred spirit in the old woman. She had left a place she grew to dislike, and made her home elsewhere. He had left the Core and tried to settle in Pavmouth Breaks. Both of them were somewhere they should not be, trying to belong, and perhaps both of them were lost.

She must know so much . . .

But right then, Namior was the center of Kel's world.

Steam hissed from several openings along the side of the

box. The woman pressed some of the nodes on its upper surface, stroked others, her fingers flitting across them as if she were playing a delicate musical instrument. She maintained contact with the metal for a while, her eyes half-closed and lips moving slightly as she muttered silent words. Then she nodded and took one step back, gaze fixed on Namior's ruined chest.

The steam formed strange patterns above the unconscious woman, twisting into shapes that were almost known, ideas on the verge of being seen. Kel could feel a breeze in the room from the badly fitted window, but the steam was untouched. It formed layers and swirls, waves and curtains of warm mist, then several thin metal legs sprouted from the sides of the box and dipped down into her wound.

Kel shifted forward, but only to look more closely.

He had seen Namior delving into broken flesh to knit bones and splice veins, her fingers working with a stunning dexterity. The machine did the same, only much faster, and its flexible limbs could reach into places where fingers would not. Namior's breath bubbled and spat for a beat, and a fine spray of blood came from her mouth as she uttered a soft cough. Then the machine rose above the wound, limbs flexing and twisting too fast to be seen, and Kel watched, amazed, as first her flesh, then her skin was bound back together.

The old woman gasped, swayed and had to lean on the bed to prevent herself from collapsing. Kel went to help, but he found that he did not want to touch her. Unreasonable, irrational, but she was still one of them.

"I'm fine," she said, sensing his turmoil. She chuckled, and for a beat he saw her craze showing through.

"But I need to ask you—"

"My heart, my old heart...I need rest. When she wakes, you can talk to me together."

"One question," Kel said, and he realized that he was unconsciously blocking the doorway. Could she move him? If she had to, if he forced it, could she *fight* him? The blue box was back in her hand, emitting puffs of steam and hissing quietly, and there was something strikingly eerie about it. Almost *lifelike*. And he decided that yes, she could fight him; but he also believed that she would not.

"One, then," she nodded, exhausted.

"Is there a way to stop them?"

The old woman stared at him, still breathing heavily, her eye never wavering from his. "I think maybe some can be saved."

"How?"

She waved her hand at him again, closing her eyes. "That's two questions, and I need to think on them. Bring her down with you, when she's awake, and by then I'll have an answer."

"Why didn't you say anything—?"

"I was hoping against hope," she said, the voice of a frightened little girl. "And my crazes weren't feigned."

A hundred more questions shuffled in Kel's mind, but he stood aside to let her pass. "Thank you."

"No need for thanks. She's my great-granddaughter, and I love her as much as life itself." The woman groaned and sighed as she walked slowly down the spiral staircase, careful not to tread on any squeaking floorboards in case she woke her granddaughter sleeping below.

Kel went to Namior's bedroom window and moved the curtain aside. The ship was still moored in the harbor, though there was no longer a queue of people waiting to board. A few villagers continued digging for survivors. Kel closed his eyes and wished he could un-see the whole scene, but he could not. *There's no one left alive under the mud,* he thought. *And even if there is . . .*

It all felt so useless.

One thing the Core had never decided upon was how to fight the invaders, if and when they came. There were plans and ideas, theories and schemes, but all of them involved magic, the one constant in the land that could always be relied upon.

But not there. Even if the Core arrived that night, the fight would be a short one.

He thought of the old woman downstairs, and what she had done, and the more he dwelled on it, the more confused he became.

KEL SAT FOR a while in a wooden rocking chair beside Namior's bed, desperate to do something but not knowing what he *could* do. As he'd come back into the valley from the stockade, he'd had vague thoughts of initiating some sort of resistance. He hoped his Core training would help him to move around the fishing village unseen, break into homes that might be locked and set traps in which they could capture and kill Komadians and their metal-clad Strangers. It had seemed like a hopeless plan even then, with no real end in sight other than eventual, inevitable capture, and now it seemed foolish to even consider.

At least he'd sent his message. Mygrette had planted the communicator he'd given her, and a message sent double would hopefully be heeded with twice the urgency.

He had no idea how long it would take for the first of the Core to arrive. But the more he thought about the near future, the more certain he became of his course of action. *I should be there to meet them. And yes, to warn them about how the language of the land has been stifled. And . . .*

And there was the crystal he'd buried.

He realized he'd been rocking in the chair, his eyelids drooping, and the movement and soft creaking noise inspired a memory: Namior naked before him, turning her back and lowering herself down as he sat in the rocking chair; sinking onto him, lying back, and both of them letting the movement do its work; her groaning, his hand over her mouth to hold in her cry.

Good times, yet even then he'd been concerned about things that had seemed so important at the time.

"I'll save you, Namior," he whispered, leaving the chair and sitting beside her on the bed. He waited there for a while, his tiredness closing in again, and he leaned back against the wall, Namior at his side.

IMAGES OF THOSE he had killed haunted his light doze; the Stranger on the beach, the Komadian interrogator Lemual, Mell and whatever had taken her body. They were all trying to talk to him, but however hard he listened he could not hear their voices. He was troubled, because he was certain they had something important to say, but all he could hear was a heavy, steady breathing.

And then he thought of O'Peeria, his other love and another person he had always assumed the guilt for killing. She walked into his dream and swept the other faces aside in that rough, confident manner she'd had. He held his breath, hoping he would hear her when she spoke, but she had nothing to say. She just smiled.

Then she looked down, and when Kel opened his eyes and followed her gaze, he saw Namior. Her eyes were open and she was watching him. "Breathe," she said softly, answering her own dream. "Breathe."

O'Peeria was gone but Namior was there, and Kel slid from the bed so that he could kneel down and press his face to hers.

"Am I awake?" she asked, and he laughed because he was wondering the same thing. He kissed her and held her face, looking into her eyes and reveling in her smile.

"How do you feel?"

She was looking around the room as if it was a strange place. "Don't remember getting back here."

"What's the last thing you *do* remember?"

"The boat. You, rowing. We passed a ship with no lights, then . . . nothing. I was dying."

"You might have been. I was terrified that you were."

She went to sit up, cringing against the pain that threatened to burst across her chest. Her shirt fell open and she looked down, gasping.

"Where . . . ?"

"Your great-grandmother healed you."

"The magic's back?"

"No." Kel sat beside her on the bed, desperate to retain physical contact now that she was with him again. "She's quite an incredible old woman, isn't she?"

"She is," Namior nodded. "But her craze?"

"There's lots to tell," Kel said. "And after that, there's something we have to do."

"Warn everyone!"

He shook his head sadly. "Too late for that. The Komadians are already gathering people and ferrying them out to the island. Some of them . . . some have even been sent back."

"Who?"

Kel shook his head again. *I can't tell her yet. Not Mell, not what I did . . .*

"I'm hungry," Namior said, seeing his discomfort. "And thirsty. But apart from that I feel . . . well." She propped herself on one elbow, stretched, ran her other hand between her breasts. "Do I look well?"

Kel smiled and stared at her chest. "Don't tempt me."

NAMIOR'S GREAT-GRANDMOTHER WAS waiting for them downstairs.

"I have to go out," Kel said, catching the old woman's eye. Namior objected, but he calmed her with a kiss and held her close. "Just for a beat. You and your great-grandmother talk. She's got something to tell you. And when I come back, we've got plenty to plan."

"I feel ready to go out there now!" Namior said. "Fight those bastards. Get back at them for Trakis and anyone else they've done that to. I'm ready, Kel!"

"Good," he said, laughing softly. "We'll get our chance."

He glanced across at the old woman again, and she was trying to offer him a smile. But the prospect of the lie she had to admit, the old deception about to be revealed, turned her smile into something else.

"I won't be long," Kel said.

"Where are you going?" the old woman asked.

"To collect something I left behind." He stepped outside and closed the door behind him before either woman could say anything else.

Kel stood motionless in the cool night breeze. He breathed in deep and let it out slowly, happy to be out of the dwelling and away from the pressures inside. There was so much history there, and the house was filled with such deceit, that he welcomed the honest darkness. He felt guilty for leaving Namior to discover those truths on her own, but it was a family matter. There was also a sliver of doubt and concern . . . but much as his strict training went against it, he trusted the old woman. Perhaps the five years since he'd left the Core had almost made him human again.

He remained in the house's shadow for a few beats, listening, scanning the darkness, sniffing the air for anything strange. There were voices in the distance—one calling the name of a lost loved one, the other laughing—but he could hear no one nearby. Three rats ran along the narrow path, pausing to sniff at his feet before sauntering on their way. Kel was certain he was alone.

He moved cautiously but quickly, down to the main path

and west toward the sea. In places he could see between buildings and across to the harbor. He scanned quickly, looking for the metal-clad Strangers, but he saw none there. It seemed that they were still keeping to the shadows and extremes, and for a while that was a good thing. He hoped it meant that they had yet to reveal themselves to the village as a whole. While the Komadians could still transport residents to the island of their own free will, things would go slowly and peacefully. And while Kel hated the idea of people willingly going to their doom without a fight, it made time for the Core to arrive.

But they would soon find the bodies of those he had killed. Time was short.

As he moved, it felt as if the village had been divided into two areas: the harbor, where nothing untoward seemed to be happening; and elsewhere, in the dark, where Noreelans called for their missing loved ones, Strangers prowled and the village militia lay dead. He was in the most dangerous part.

Kel reached the last of the undamaged buildings and started clambering down over the fallen walls. When he reached the place where he'd buried the crystal, he paused for a few beats and looked around. The sea hushed onto the broken shore. Waves broke around the ruins. The boat he and Namior had arrived in was still there, beached on a shelf of stone. Something called in the night, a sea doon floating somewhere above the waves and seeking a mate, or prey. But no shadows moved where they should not. Kel was alone.

He started digging. The muck and debris he'd piled in on top of the crystal came out easily, and he was soon making his way back up the broken slope, a bulky shape beneath one arm. Though his jacket was still wrapped around the crystal, he could feel a vague warmth bleeding through, like the sad heat leaving a just-killed body. But he guessed that its warmth would go on and on.

What he carried in his hands could be priceless. Whatever happened here at Pavmouth Breaks, the crystal would help the Core to understand so much more about the Komadians, their nature and intent. Whether or not they saved some or most of the village's inhabitants—and Kel was determined to do his very best to help as many as he could—he knew that the crystal *had* to reach the Core. It would be taken away and hidden deep, where no one could find it. And the Core had its witches. They would learn its secrets, and the secrets of the thing trapped inside.

Several times Kel almost dropped the object, so sickened was he by what he carried. One of *them*. One of Noreela's greatest enemies, and he was taking it back to the house of the woman he loved.

But in that house lived another of Noreela's enemies, now, perhaps, its friend.

Back through the streets, Kel paused at every twist and turn of the path, afraid of what he would find around the next corner. There were more rats, and a couple of wild-looking dogs that had muzzles blackened with dried blood. They both growled at him, but he growled back, and they scampered off into the night.

Close to Namior's home, a shadow came at him from the darkness.

"Kel Boon!"

Kel took several steps back and drew his sword.

"Kel Boon, it's your Chief Eildan." He gave the name grace and import, but his voice was tinged with fear.

"You're alone?" Kel asked.

"Alone, yes. And you?"

Kel nodded.

"There are *things* in the village," Eildan said. He still carried his harpoon, knuckles white where he gripped it hard. "From the sea, from the island, things come to kill. I saw my militia, many of them, dead in a hole upriver!"

"Pavmouth Breaks is in great danger," Kel said, remembering the Chief welcoming Keera Kashoomie unquestioningly and with open arms. "They're not what they tell us."

"I don't know where my wife has gone," Eildan said, a sob belying his previous strength.

"They're taking people to the island. And those who try to escape are corralled into stockades up on the plains."

"Stockades?"

"Chief Eildan, we need to be ready to move," Kel said. "Help is coming, but in the meantime we have to help ourselves. Fight when we have to, move when we can, and do our best to leave the village and get out of the valley."

"Leave? Don't be ridiculous!"

"Believe me, we've got no—"

"What have you got there?" The Chief had noticed the bundle beneath Kel's arm, and he stepped closer to see. He was pale and terrified, and it looked as if he had not eaten or drunk anything since the waves.

"Weapons," Kel said. "We need to go house to house, Chief, and tell people to prepare. The Komadians are not here to help us, they're here to…." To what? What could he tell the proud, ignorant Chief Eildan that would make him believe?

"To what?"

"Invade," Kel said. "Form a beachhead."

"And help is on its way?"

"I hope so."

"How do you—"

"Chief," Kel said, "I have to go. Many more homes to visit." Eildan was not used to being interrupted, and he stood up straight, ready to berate.

Kel walked past him and continued along the path.

"Kel Boon?" the Chief called after him, his voice suddenly very small.

Kel turned around.

"Have you seen my wife?"

"No, Chief," Kel said. "Maybe she's already made it out." He turned and walked away before he could see the hope in Eildan's eyes turn to doubt.

Chapter Twelve

old lies

NAMIOR WAS STANDING outside her house when Kel returned. She saw him emerge from the shadows with the thing still wrapped in his jacket, and a moment of panic seized her. *I've been cured by magic from that place, so does that make me closer to whatever he carries?*

Kel paused before her, and she could tell that he was holding his breath. He looked exhausted and afraid, but his main concern right then was her.

"She told me," Namior said.

"And?"

"And I came out here to wait for you."

"Does your mother know?"

"She says not." Namior looked down at her hands, clasped

before her stomach and twisting together. If she separated them, she was afraid that she'd hit something. So many lies, but she did not know where or how to begin considering them.

"Namior, she made you better," Kel said.

"I know."

"She says she feels as Noreelan as any of us."

"Yes, I know." She looked up, feeling a brief and irrational anger at him for trying to defend the woman. *She's lied to us all these years . . . and maybe her crazes are a result of the pain of lying, rather than old age.*

"She's going to help us, then we can—"

"I don't care, Kel." And she truly did not. The waves, the floods, the deaths, the island, the Stranger Kel had fought and killed, all of them had been terrible and terrifying, and yet when her great-grandmother revealed her secret, Namior's world had fallen apart. "I'm not Noreelan."

"Of course you are!" He came closer, lowering the bundle and resting it on the ground between his feet. He reached for her, but Namior lifted her hands, ready to push him back.

"I have Komadian blood in my veins," she said. "You can't deny that. And you *know* what we saw out there! Those things, not *human.*"

"But *she's* human."

"No, Kel. She told me about the curse, and the Elders who survived it. Wherever her body might have been taken from, her heart and mind were Komadian, and even her blood's been turned that way. I don't see how anything can change that." She pointed at the thing wrapped in Kel's jacket. "She was one of *those.*"

"Maybe," Kel said. "But it doesn't matter."

"It doesn't *matter?*" She could barely speak, so heavy was the weight of what she had just discovered. And the heft of that knowledge crushed her, because she could not consider telling her mother, exposing her, denying her history. "How can you *say* that? You've lied to me, and now she has too, and what of everyone else? Am I the only one who really knows who I am?" It was foolish, Namior knew that, an overreaction; but many things she had taken for granted were no more. Waiting for Kel, she had been trying to work out what proportion Noreelan she was, and what proportion Komadian. She felt tainted.

"She says she's all Noreelan and against the invaders, and I trust her."

"Why?"

"Because once out of her craze, she's only tried to help. And she cured you." Kel sighed and came closer, leaning against the wall of the house beside her. "While you were unconscious, I tried to get out of the valley to send a message to the Core. I was caught and . . . I killed some of them."

"Those Strangers?"

"Some of the others, too."

"Who were they?"

Kel seemed to pause, and she saw his haunted look as he stared up at the starry sky. "Just Komadians," he said. "So they'll be looking for me. And if she wasn't completely on our side, she'd have turned us in by now."

"She knows what you did?"

"Some. But come in with me now. This will be the proof." Kel lifted the crystal and walked past Namior, reaching for the front door with his other hand.

"Kel!" Namior said, too loud. "No!" But he had already opened the door, and as he went inside, Namior heard her great-grandmother's hoarse voice mutter something. And the old woman began to cry.

YOU HAVE TO wake your mother," Kel said. "Everyone has to go."

Namior stood inside, looking around the room. Her great-grandmother was sitting on a floor cushion, staring wide-eyed at the thing Kel had put uncovered on the floor before her.

Its strange colors were muted in the poor light. She was still crying.

"Namior?" Kel said.

Her great-grandmother looked up at her. "Do as he says. I know how I can help you, now."

"How?" Kel asked.

The old woman looked at the crystal again. "Where did you find this?"

"The island, of course," Namior said.

"*Where* on the island?"

"By the coast," Kel said. "There were thirty there, maybe more."

"You'll have to draw me a map. Komadia changes."

"What do you know?" Namior asked. She could not keep the anger from her voice, and her great-grandmother glanced up a with very old, very sad face. *She knows it can never be the same again*, Namior thought, and she felt a sudden, intense sense of loss for the love that had changed between them.

"These things only survive on certain parts of the island. Something about the ground they grow on; something that seeps up from below." She leaned closer and looked at the crystal, the dark swirls and shapes inside, the dull surface, sharp edges and the glimmer of something deeper. She was shaking as if in pain. "Unknown centuries I was trapped. I knew existence, and the passage of time...like one long craze." She reached out and almost touched the crystal. "I wonder who this is?"

"They're destroying our village," Namior spat, "stealing our *bodies!*"

"Never pity your enemy," Kel said, and the old woman glared up at him.

"I'll smash it," Namior said. She darted at Kel and reached for his sword, determined to swipe down at the crystal and break it open, casting out the sick thing trapped inside. But Kel caught her hand and held her, staring at her but talking to the old woman.

"How do we get it out of the village?" he asked.

"That?" the woman said, pointing at the crystal. And she shook her head. "I have no idea."

"You said you could help," Namior said. She looked at her great-grandmother, and she saw someone else. She remembered old times—myth singing, storytelling, the woman teaching her to cook biscuits and longgrass pie—and she could no longer associate such good feelings with the wretched old woman sitting before her. That unbearable sense of loss hit home again, and she almost went to her. But she did not know whether she would hug, or hit.

"And I will," the woman said. And Namior realized that the old woman felt the same sense of loss. "Namior..."

Namior looked away. She caught Kel's eye, and he glanced back at the old woman.

"Yes?" Namior said.

"Just because I'm from somewhere else, that doesn't mean I'm not me."

Namior fought it hard, but she began to cry. There was a warmth in her chest that could have been left over from her injury, or perhaps it was grief, and she clasped her hands before it.

"I love you more than you probably believe," the woman said, "and my deceit has no bearing on that."

"Not for you, maybe," Namior whispered, and it sounded cruel. She looked down at her feet and heard the rustle of clothing.

When Namior looked up again, her great-grandmother was standing by the door, holding the handle. In her other hand she carried the blue metal box, and a trail of steam issued from it and rose in the dimly lit room.

The old woman smiled. Namior could feel Kel's gaze upon her, the heat burning in her chest where her life had been saved. And it was a lifetime of love that helped her smile back.

With a contented sigh the old woman opened the door

and stepped outside. "Join me, Kel Boon," she said. Then she closed the door gently behind her.

"Where is she going?" Namior asked.

"To help," Kel said.

"How?"

"I don't know. But I suspect we'll find out soon."

Namior sank down next to the groundstone and reached out, touching the cool surface, feeling and sensing nothing at all.

"She saved my life," she whispered.

"Namior, wake your mother. We need to leave. I have to meet the Core before they come in, and—"

"And that thing?" She looked at the crystal and wondered who it was and what history it possessed. Did it carry the memories of lost loved ones? Had it spent so many centuries mourning those it knew might be dead? *Never pity your enemy*, Kel had said, and search though she did, she could feel no pity inside her for the trapped thing.

"I'll hand it to the Core," he said. "They have witches."

"I'm a witch."

Kel looked at her, and his silence asked, *Would you like to touch it, know it?*

Namior stood and stroked the groundstone one last time. *I'll be back*, she thought. *When all this is over I'll be back, and I'll talk with magic again.* She held back more tears but felt empty inside. "What do I tell my mother?" she said, looking up at the ceiling.

"The truth."

Namior met Kel's gaze. "You need to go to her now."

"I won't be long. Wake your mother, prepare her. We'll try to get out of the valley, head for the stockade I left earlier, with luck the Komadians won't have noticed what happened there yet. And if they haven't, that should give us a clear path up onto the plains."

"And if they have found out?"

"Then we go another way."

Namior watched him leave and close the door. She climbed the staircase and stood for a while at the top, absorbing the changed feel of the house. It was uneven, upset, and the realization hit her with a thump that she would never see her great-grandmother again.

"Yes, I love you," she whispered to the still air, too late. And then she went to wake her mother.

NAMIOR'S GREAT-GRANDMOTHER WAS waiting for him in the shadow of the house. For a beat he feared her, but when he drew close he saw that she was only the little old lady he had known. The craze had faded, yes; but the fear in her eye remained.

"I must get to Komadia," she said. "Help me find a way. And tell me where on its coastline you saw the crystal field."

"You can help from there?"

"Perhaps I can limit the loss."

"Then I'll come with you. I know a way, and I can—"

"No." The woman's voice sounded different—stronger— and Kel caught his breath.

"But you'll never make it there alone."

"Perhaps, but you can't be risked. After this, you might be the most important person in Noreela." Her voice softened, and when she reached out for his face, he let her touch him. "And for my sweet Namior, you already are."

He told her about the beached boat, and where they had come across the crystal field, and when the woman turned to leave Kel reached out and held her shoulder. He could not remember ever touching her before. Beneath the clothing, he felt her bones.

"What are you going to do?" he asked.

She began to cry. Real, wrenching tears that shook her shoulders and stuck in her throat. She looked past Kel at the house, up at the window of her granddaughter's room, then higher at Namior's window.

I need to know, Kel thought, but she was crying so hard that she could barely speak. She shrugged off his hand and left, walking into the shadows until the only evidence of her ever having been there were her echoing sobs.

Kel thought to go after her. But then the door behind him opened, and Namior's pale face appeared. He went to her and held her close.

"Mother doesn't believe me," she said. "And she's not leaving."

NAMIOR'S MOTHER SIMPLY shook her head at Kel, which had been her first reaction when Namior had told her the story. "The Core? I've heard of it. Its purpose is a myth. They're murderers and drug dealers, not protectors of Noreela. And you, Kel, a soldier? Carrying those weapons doesn't make you one. As for my grandmother being someone from . . . beyond Noreela? None of it makes sense, and none of it is true."

"If you had magic—" Kel began, but Namior's mother snapped in quickly.

"But we don't, do we?"

"And why do you think that is?"

"Kel?" Namior asked.

He sighed. "We have a little time."

What is she doing? What did she tell Kel out there? But it was not the time to ask. Namior raised her chin, indicating that he should go back outside. He sighed and did so, pulling the door to behind him but not closing it completely.

She turned to her mother again, desperate, frustrated and fearing for her more and more. "You *have* to believe me," she said. "You *have* to believe Kel. Look at that." She pointed to the crystal, unveiled on the floor between them. "Does that look like anything Noreelan?"

"He's poisoned your mind," her mother said. She looked down at the crystal. "So you've been out to the island and stolen something that might be precious to them . . ."

"They almost killed me, Mother! Yet look at me now."

Her mother looked away, and Namior felt like reaching out and shaking sense into her. Was she really so scared? Did she know more than she could possibly imagine admitting to?

"I'm leaving with Kel," Namior said. "I'm helping him." If she had expected a panicked response, she saw none. "Don't you care? Can't you even consider that I'm telling the truth? I saw that thing he killed on the beach, I saw people, *things*, on the island that were so far from human . . . And I saw what they did to Trakis!"

"And you were wounded, and Grandmother cured you without the use of magic." Her mother looked at the door through which Kel had passed with true loathing in her eyes. "What drugs?" she asked. "How did he do it?"

"Great-grandmother's magic healed me! *Their* magic! And now she's gone, and you don't want to know where, or why?"

"In her craze, she wanders," Namior's mother said, "and now you're leaving with a killer."

"So you *do* believe he killed something. Good. Believe the bad stuff about him, but not the fact that he's trying to save—"

"I'll always welcome you back, Namior."

"Mother. You're so afraid. But we're doing our best." Namior could see that her mother was not being unreasonable, or cruel. She was simply acting on the things she believed to be true, and denying all the terrible possibilities that she could not bear to believe. Perhaps the truth was that without magic she was lost.

She collected the crystal in Kel's jacket, and at the door she glanced back at the woman she had woken to tell something terrible. Perhaps she thought she was still having night-mares.

"Take care," her mother said.

"You too. And when the fighting starts, hide as well as you can." Namior turned away, opened the door and went outside without looking back.

I might never see her again.

"Namior—" Kel said, but she cut him off.

"I'm coming with you. Whether she believes or not, I'm helping her by helping you." She handed him the crystal, and whispered, "I can't carry that."

"Follow me," he said. "Try to copy my footsteps, stop when I stop, run when I run. Be my shadow."

"Kel…"

He touched her face with his free hand and stared into her eyes. "Your great-grandmother is returning to her people. And somehow, she's doing her best for us."

She nodded, wanting to know more but also dreading that knowledge.

Kel set off, hugging the wrapped crystal under one arm and bearing his short sword in the other hand. Namior followed, amazed at how silently her love could move, as if he were a wraith himself.

The suspicion and doubt in her mother's eyes had been painful. And the devastating fact that she doubted her own daughter's observations and opinions, blaming them instead on drugs used by Kel Boon to lead her astray, enraged her. After all the years of being trained as a witch—*listen to the land, heed your heart, love your family and help them when help is needed, look beyond what is known and be willing to accept the unknown*—her mother could display ignorance as profound as her knowledge of magic. Namior could understand her desire not to believe, but her mother's shunning of all evidence shocked her.

Perhaps it was all too much. Namior had learned the facts

slowly, exploring and identifying most of them herself or in Kel's company, seeing things when there was no magic to see for her. To be sat down and told every bad thing that was happening...perhaps she would have had trouble believing as well.

So all that was left to her was to love her mother and help her now that help was needed.

The village streets were dark and seemed deserted, and the fresh air felt good on Namior's face. She breathed in deeply, enjoying the exertion, and try as she might, she could feel no pain in her chest from the wound.

Kel knew the exact route he wanted to take, and he moved without hesitation. Left, right, over walls, between buildings, and she tried to follow with the same confidence.

They climbed the river valley, passing darkened homes and buildings, and they did not meet one person. Either everyone was inside, hiding away from threats known or suspected, or they were somewhere else. Kel had told Namior of the stockade he'd broken down. She did not like to think of others locked away like that, but the farther they went, the more likely she thought it to be. The village had never felt so empty.

He had also told her about the villagers boarding the ship.

The buildings became less frequent, the hillside steepened, and paths became slippery from the moisture in the air. Kel paused more often, listening to the darkness. Namior listened with him, but she heard nothing to set her on edge.

She wanted to ask more about her great-grandmother, but she could not break the silence.

A woman crossed the path ahead of them. She seemed to float rather than walk, and she was naked, her skin silvered by moonlight. There were several fine, featherlike tendrils drooping from her stomach and hips, stroking the ground behind her and leaving clear raindrop sparks, and she was beautiful.

When she turned and looked at Kel, Namior saw that her eyes were the color of the life moon.

Kel froze, and Namior dropped to her knees. The strange woman whispered a song that seemed to originate inside Namior's mind, stroking the recesses of her memory, planting fantastical new images as if they were old. Namior opened her mouth to join in the song, but then behind the woman a more familiar shadow rose.

"Back!" Kel said. He dropped the bundled crystal and darted forward, pointing at the woman, shouting "Back!" again as though talking to her, not Namior, and she knew what he was doing.

She dropped to the damp ground and rolled up against a cold stone wall. The shadows concealed her.

The woman faded away into the darkness, like a candle snuffed out. Beyond where she had been stood a Stranger.

Kel lashed out with his sword, but the metal man snatched the weapon from his hand, snapped it in half, and threw it into the night. It clattered down out of sight. Another armored soldier emerged from farther along the path, leveling its projectile weapon at Kel.

A punch in the chest, the coolness of air touching insides, the dreadful sense of weight as something shattered bone and tore flesh—

Given clarity of memory, Namior wanted to shout out. Then she glanced at where the crystal had rolled, and because she could not see it she thought it was still wrapped, still hidden. If it had fallen from the coat, death-moonlight would have found it by then, reflecting its dreadful colors.

Kel would not wish her caught; shouting could not aid him.

He struggled briefly with the first Stranger, but the element of surprise had already won the battle for the invaders. The first one held Kel's arms away from his body, while the second smacked him several times across the back of the head. He fell limply to the ground. The first soldier kicked him hard in the ribs, and when he did not react they settled down beside him and started drawing and disposing of his weapons.

Namior remained motionless, trying to breathe slowly and evenly, though her heart pummeled at her chest. *Already been shot once*, she thought, and she had to hold in a crazy laugh. She watched the Strangers rooting through Kel's clothing and pockets, casting aside every weapon they found with little concern about where it came to rest.

A knife slid across the stone path and struck her right forearm. She closed her eyes and remained motionless. Though the temptation to pick it up was strong, she was terrified that she would scrape it against the ground. *When they've gone*, she thought. *Though what good it will do me . . .*

The Strangers hissed and whistled. Perhaps they were communicating, or maybe just straining as they picked up Kel between them and dragged him along the path.

"Oh, Kel," she whispered, watching until she could see him no more. Then she grabbed the knife, eased herself upright, and prepared to follow.

But for what? There was no way she could fight the things. She'd be killed or caught, and Kel had taken the fight forward to them in an effort to protect her.

She took a couple of tentative steps, paused, then remembered the crystal. It took a few beats to locate it, but when she picked it up it was still wrapped against the darkness, still warm through the coat. She grimaced with distaste.

I have to take this to the Core. That was Kel's main aim, and . . . She cursed quietly and stomped at the ground. She was just a witch without magic! Whatever her great-grandmother would do to try to give them time, it needed positive action from her as well.

Desperate, feeling hopelessly entangled in events, and perhaps strangled by them, Namior slipped through an open gate into a porl-root garden and sat against the wall. The crystal gave her some warmth, and though she did not like the feel of it, she was too cold to push it away.

She closed her eyes and rested her head back against the wall. Her heart wanted to take her back home and wait there until the Core arrived and made things better. But she knew that would be turning her back on what was happening. And though her mother seemed content to do that, she was not. Not after what she and Kel had done, and seen.

And not after her great-grandmother.

So she had to move on. Escape from Pavmouth Breaks, resist the temptation to go after her love, and wait for the Core. She would hand over the crystal and tell them everything she knew. And then she would be their guide back into Pavmouth Breaks.

NAMIOR RARELY LEFT the village. To climb out of the river valley, to stare across the plains above to distant horizons, lit the flame of adventure in her heart. With her training as a witch muting that flame, it was painful for her to light it too often.

Kel's reluctance to explore had been a knife in her heart ever since she had known him. *I've done my traveling,* he would say, and though now she could understand some of his reasoning, that still hurt her. Maybe he *was* Core, maybe he *had* seen much of Noreela before fleeing and settling there, but she would have loved for him to have taken her wishes to heart.

So she walked and climbed on her own. Every footstep hurt her more than the last; she was leaving behind her family and her love. And every step took her farther into darkness, and increased the distance between her and everything she had ever known.

So here, at last, was adventure. And she was terrified. But deep down, she was also more excited than she had ever been. Maybe it was because she had been wounded and unconscious, removed from the world for a while, but she was able to place a strange distance between her and the danger she was facing. Even after seeing Kel struck down and dragged away, she went on with the conviction that it would not happen to her.

Perhaps because it already had.

She rubbed at her chest as she walked, feeling no better or worse. Her great-grandmother had truly healed her, and Namior would have given anything to be able to talk with her again. The old woman she had known all her life had changed completely, and Namior had not had the chance to discuss or explore any of that change with her. It would be a regret forever.

She's doing her best for us, Kel had said. Namior had no wish to dwell upon what that meant.

She continued along the valley, following the river and deliberately walking away from the direction in which the two Strangers had dragged Kel. *I won't be harmed*, she thought. *I won't be caught or stopped, because I've already been shot and come through the other side.* Such false conviction was foolish and could be dangerous, but it gave her courage, and she did her best to smother doubt.

She passed the ruin of an old stone house, a haunted place beside the river that local myth suggested had been built over a thousand years before by a Dagenstine monk. As a child she had often come there with friends, and they had dared each other to sneak within the fallen walls and try to guess the monk's name. It was said that whoever guessed his real name would resurrect him from the otherworldly un-death that the Dagenstines had believed in. Much as they had tried, none of them had succeeded. *We all needed something to be scared of back then*, she thought. *Now that something to fear has finally arrived, I wish I could go back to whispering names against old stone walls.* She passed the ruin with a nostalgic glance, and threw a few names at its walls: Trakis, Mell, Kel Boon. Nothing stirred, and its ancient builder remained absent.

Soon after the ruin she passed beneath Helio Bridge, moving slowly and glancing up often, wary of Strangers watching from above. The crossing a hundred steps above her appeared deserted. Though its central stone support bore impact scars where it grew from an island in the middle of the river, the damage appeared minimal. Perhaps the Komadians had used the crossing to move from one tower's location to the other, passing upriver from the village so that no one could witness their activities. She paused in the bridge's shadow, listening, sniffing the air. But she sensed that she was completely alone.

After Helio Bridge, the valley walls closed in and made the going much more difficult. The timeworn path disappeared. The time had come to climb up onto the plains above, so she started up the valley slope without pause. It was much steeper there than farther down toward the sea, but she hoped that the farther inland she came, the less chance she would have of bumping into a Stranger. But Namior had no real idea how safe she was or how far into Noreela the Komadians had penetrated. All she could do was to act on instinct.

The climb was difficult, but she went at it with gusto. Carrying the crystal made it more treacherous—both the object's weight and the fact that it kept her left arm out of action. But she leaned forward into the slope, pushed with her feet, and here and there grabbed on to thick grasses or small shrubs with her right hand, steadying herself and pulling when she could. The rain made the going slippery and slick, and several times she almost lost her footing. Her heart jumped, her knees hit dirt and she held on hard. But she never fell.

Halfway up the steep hillside, she reached a flattened area, home to a small shrine to the life moon. It was an old structure—a low, round surface whose sharp edges had been dulled by time, its upper surface pitted with the actions of rain and frost. Namior sat on it, mindless of the water soaking through her trousers and undergarments, and tried to catch her breath.

There was something above the hillside on the opposite side of the valley. It was a blankness rather than a presence, a space in the night blanking out clouds and stars, a part of the rainswept darkness that was missing. She frowned and tried to concentrate, looking to either side to allow her night vision a better view.

It rose above the valley wall, leaning down toward Pavmouth Breaks, and Namior thought of the huge dark sculptures they had seen on Komadia. Perhaps it was the darkness, and the loss of perspective, but this empty space looked much larger.

Something sparkled atop the dark shape. Namior rubbed rain from her eyes and stared, but she did not see the movement again. It had looked like the sort of spark that sometimes formed around a ship's mast during a storm. Or perhaps it had been the moonslight glinting off something metallic.

"They're building even more," she muttered. Kel had told of a construction on the plains above her, with the stockade at its base. Now there was another one across the valley from her, and also the one that they had seen in its early stages above the top of Drakeman's Hill.

Whatever the influence of the things, she was close to passing beyond it.

This must be how they've been interfering with the language of the land. That excited her, and she touched the outline of the ground rod in her pocket, thrilled by the idea that she might be able to commune with magic again soon.

Still tired, muscles aching and cramping, she ignored the discomfort and set off once more.

As she reached the top of the steep hill, and the slope shallowed as it turned from hillside to high plain, she was grabbed from behind.

She did not even have time to scream. A cold metal hand clamped across her mouth, and as she lifted her hands to try to pull it away, she dropped the crystal. It rolled away from her, shedding Kel's jacket and reflecting the sliver of life moon visible between clouds. Rain splashed from its surface, giving the impression that it moved of its own accord.

Namior kicked back, wincing as her heel struck metal. *It's one of them!* Failure consumed her, so shattering that all she could think to do was to fight. She kicked again, twisted, struggled, trying to worm her way loose of this Stranger's slick metal armor. It held her tight, then lifted her from the ground and took a step toward the dropped crystal.

The metal man paused. Even her kicking and struggling did not stir the Stranger, and it grew utterly motionless. *It's looking at the crystal.*

The Stranger dropped her, pushing her forward so that she almost toppled, still grasping her wrist. She was about to shout mindless, useless abuse at the thing when she felt the cold prick of something piercing the skin of her forearm. She drew in a sharp breath and bit her lip against the pain.

The Stranger released her. It looked down at its hand, where several long, very thin spines were withdrawing back into its knuckles.

Namior went for her short knife, but she held the handle without drawing it, knowing it would do no good.

And waiting. Because something strange was happening.

The Stranger looked at her, its immovable face soulless and mindless. It bowed its head slightly, glanced once again at the dropped crystal, then walked past her and disappeared into the darkness, heading back toward Pavmouth Breaks.

Namior stood there for several beats, confused, scared, and expecting the darkness to erupt in violence at any moment. But she was alone once more. The rain was so heavy, and the night so deep, that the Stranger's brief attack already seemed like a dream.

There were several small puncture wounds on the tender flesh of her underarm, and rain diluted the blood still seeping from them. *I have Komadian blood in my veins*, she had told Kel, and much as he'd tried to dissuade her from that idea—or perhaps he had thought it impossible—it had saved her life.

She scooped up the crystal, wrapped it once again in Kel's jacket and started running.

NAMIOR WAS SOMEWHERE unknown. She had been that far out several times before, the plains of heather and bracken higher above sea level than any of Pavmouth Breaks, but never in the dark, never in a rainstorm, and never with such dangers in the shadows.

But if she stalked every shadow, it would take her forever. If she stopped to assess each fold in the land, she would still be there come morning, and by then the Stranger might have spoken to other Komadians, and her strange nature would be known. So she threw caution to the darkness and assumed that she was alone.

She thought of her mother, hiding away from the truth in their family home, and of her great-grandmother, and whatever sacrifice she had made to give them time. And Kel? Caught, dragged away... dead?

But thinking on that could not help her. It was the Core that must possess her attention just then. An invisible army, an unknown group, existing for centuries amongst Noreela's communities, converging on Pavmouth Breaks to enter into a battle they had been training for forever.

And the only thing that stood between them and defeat, was Namior Feeron.

SHE WENT ACROSS the plains, farther than she had ever traveled. The wilds closed in around her. Everything felt different up there. And even when she plunged her ground rod into the soil, and felt the welcoming waves and whirls of magic extending into her mind, Namior's dread increased. She was away from Pavmouth Breaks—away from Komadian influence—and in a place where she had never been.

The darkness was complete. Thickening clouds hid the moons, and heavy rain blurred the air. Shadows became mysterious rather than threatening, and though she should have felt a sense of freedom and release, what she actually felt was alone.

The crystal exuded warmth, wrapped in the jacket like a newborn.

She headed east, needing to go farther inland before deciding which direction to take...and with that thought came the realization that she was lost. Kel had not hinted at where and when he expected to meet the Core, had not mentioned how soon they could be there, but he *had* seemed confident of the fact that he could leave Pavmouth Breaks and be able to find them. Perhaps he'd had something else in his pockets, some other Core magic that would guide them in. But Namior had been following him blindly, and with him gone, she was blinder still.

Taking shelter from the rain beneath an overhanging rock, she paused to urinate, then drank some water from a depression in the rock's upper surface. Beneath its shadow again, her clothes wet but her body slowly warming her, she slid the ground rod in and touched its tip with one finger.

Noreela spoke to her, and it was wonderful. She had never missed anything so much. The language of the land whispered of things near and far, and Namior had only to dip into that flow of expression to find hints of what she sought. Ten miles ahead it was no longer raining, the cloud front falling back toward the sea. Five miles farther, a giant hawk breathed its last into the soil upset by its landing, pressures slowly crushing its body. It was said that the huge creatures were born, lived and died above the clouds and out of sight, melting away on the winds up there, their gaseous bodies going to dust, and to find one on the ground was a rare occurrence. Any other time Namior would have run to it, eager to examine its bulk; instead she only noted its location in case she had a chance to visit in the future.

Of course I'll have a chance, she thought. *When all this is over and Kel has come back to me...*

She turned her senses back toward the sea, and there was a blank spot in her mind. She groaned slightly, frowning, eyes squeezing shut and turning left and right, as if to dislodge a smudge in her line of sight. But the blankness could not be dislodged, however much life and death it might shield.

Can't they feel this? Can't anyone looking this way through magic sense this, realize that something is wrong? She turned away and cast her awareness inland once again. The ebb and flow of magic calmed her, its implied taste, smell and touch a gentle caress upon her traumatized mind.

She listened for others riding the waves of magic nearby, but there were none. She tried to sense the whisper of the land where it powered machines, but the landscape around her felt deserted.

Namior withdrew the ground rod and cleaned it on the hem of her jacket. She was still soaked through, but warmer than before, and the thought of going back out into the rain depressed her. But sitting there could achieve nothing.

Tying the arms of Kel's jacket in a sling, carrying the crystal and eschewing its potential warmth, she went back out into the night and the rain.

The problem of how she would find any Core members in such darkness preyed on her mind. She tried to imagine how Kel had been thinking, which way he would have gone, what he would have done . . . but she was distant from him. So she walked on, worried that she would pass the Core by. And even more worried that they were not coming at all.

Maybe they had not even heard.

After several more pauses, and as the rain stopped and dawn began to draw a fine mist from the landscape before her, her worries were put to rest.

The Core found *her*.

Chapter Thirteen

slaves

KEL'S HEAD THROBBED. It felt as if the metal bastard was still hitting him, and each heartbeat was another blow. He tried not to groan, and he dragged his feet, letting the two Komadian soldiers drag him up the hillside using their own energy. They clicked and whistled at each other, but he could not tell whether the sounds constituted language. The Strangers he had tracked and killed with the Core were not like them; far from stupid, they were able to fit into Noreelan society almost seamlessly until magic found them out. But these metal-clad Strangers were different. *Born from slime, they'll return to it,* Lemual had said dismissively.

Kel tried to remain limp, pretending he could not hear, or

smell the slightly acidic odor emanating from them as they climbed.

And then it clicked, the truth pulsing in between throbs of pain: the armored Strangers *were* born of slime, out of the stinking pond he and Namior had seen on the island. Other Strangers—the one that had killed O'Peeria, the many sent to infiltrate Noreela down through the centuries—were slime-born as well, except that their primitive souls had been replaced by cursed Komadians from crystal prisons.

The realization did little for him. His shins were skinned on one ledge of rock, and he bit his bottom lip to prevent himself crying out. At one point, one of the Strangers tried to rush on ahead, still holding his arm and twisting it in the shoulder socket until Kel was sure he was going to scream. But the other soldier hissed something, and they returned to their original pace.

They climbed in the same direction he'd climbed earlier, but once out of the valley they turned left, heading back along the ridge toward the high cliffs half a mile north of Pavmouth Breaks. He'd been up there a few times, rooting through the sparse forests in his search for hardwood to carve and shape, eschewing driftwood washed up along the beaches because forest wood gave him more of a link to the land. It was a wild place, and more than once he'd seen evidence of people from outside Pavmouth Breaks having camped there. *Not now,* he thought. *Anyone camped here now will be killed or taken by* them.

The ground around their feet changed from heathers to bracken, bramble and small ghostly flowers, glowing even though the moons were hidden by rain clouds. Sparkle drops. They flowered once each year for several short days, their natural luminosity attracting insects to pollinate them, before the blooms faded and their seedpods burst to the air. Kel wondered how different Noreela would be when the new pods erupted.

The Strangers walked through the flowers, crushing them underfoot.

They dropped him to the ground. Kel turned his head slightly to the right as he fell, but the landing was quite soft. He kept his eyes closed. Rain splashed onto his face, surprisingly comforting, and he allowed his mouth to slip open so that some of the moisture touched his tongue. He was thirsty, and with that realization came a writhing hunger.

Heavy footsteps receded, and Kel risked opening his eyes.

Among the trees, a hundred steps from him, a giant structure rose into the darkness, deep black against the imperfect night. Around its base were the stacked shadows of felled trees, the flesh of their cut trunks pale. Turning his eyes instead of his head, Kel could not see the tower's summit. There was no sound of a machine working anywhere nearby.

Finished, he thought. *And so high! And the others aren't far behind. Whatever they're planning, and whatever these things are for, it'll happen soon.*

He saw one of the Strangers pass between the trees and disappear around the corner of the structure's base. The other was out of sight, but he could not hear footsteps. Perhaps it was motionless behind him, keeping watch five steps away. Maybe it knew he was awake.

Kel closed his eyes. The Core had trained him how to project his senses, concentrating on each one in turn in an effort to exaggerate the whole. He listened hard, breathing through his open mouth, but all he could hear were raindrops dropping on last year's fallen leaves. He inhaled slowly and deeply, smelling only damp soil and the clear tang of rain, the alien sourness absent. He risked touching the tip of his tongue to the air, but he tasted nothing he did not know. His sense of touch was dominated by the throbbing, pulsing pain from the bruises on the backs of his head and neck. He tried to blot it out, but even his extremities were possessed by its warm glow.

He scanned as far as he could without moving his head, and he saw nothing new.

I could get up, he thought. *I've killed those things before. I'd have a chance, at least, and—*

As if reading his thoughts, the Stranger standing directly behind him stood astride his body and touched his temple with the barrel of its projectile weapon. The metal felt oddly warm against Kel's skin. Primed with steam and ready to fire.

Kel shifted to show that he was awake and aware of the soldier's presence. Then he sat up, slowly. His head swam and he kept both hands on the wet ground, supporting himself. The Stranger backed away a little, still pointing the weapon at his face. *My reputation steps before me,* Kel thought, and he even managed a smile.

"Kel Boon," a voice said, "smiling at secret thoughts." A Stranger and a Komadian were walking through the trees from the direction of the structure. The Komadian's footfalls were almost silent, clothes dark against the night.

"Keera Kashoomie," Kel said, maintaining his smile.

"I knew you must be Core from the moment we landed," she said. "You held a knife to my throat and checked my neck for gills."

"Perhaps I should have made you some with my blade."

The tall woman stopped a few steps from Kel and smiled down, cool and in control. "And perhaps I should have had you killed that first day."

"Why didn't you?"

Keera shrugged. "Easier if the populace is compliant. But we win, either way. We always win."

"One of your friends told me that only recently."

"Lemual," she whispered, the smile dropping from her face. "I wasn't certain it was you." There was only hatred in Keera Kashoomie's eyes. That shocked Kel, and behind it he perceived a truth he knew he would grow to regret.

"Oh," he said. "You and Lemual."

Keera nodded at the Stranger by her side, and he stepped forward.

Kel barely had time to raise one arm in front of his face before the Stranger's metal-gloved hand struck. He fell back, feeling blood gushing from his nose, eyes watering, the pain and shock spreading through his head.

"Where is the crystal you took?" Keera asked.

"Why?" Kel said, wincing through the red mist. He could not see; pain had robbed his sight. "Another potential lover of yours in there?"

A pause, during which Kel imaged the woman nodding again, and then the Stranger behind him kicked him in the back. Kel cried out and fell sideways, one arm twisting around so he could press his hand against his back. It was a natural response, but it did nothing to ease the pain.

Keera Kashoomie came and squatted beside him. If he'd still had his weapons, he thought he could have killed her before one of the Strangers killed him. Even without them there was a chance he could rip out her throat, plunge his fingers into her eye sockets or break her neck, but the odds were not so great, and right then he did not relish the risk.

"Well then, let's try this one. Where is the woman who accompanied you to Komadia?"

"Dead. One of your slime-things shot her with its steam weapon, and she died when we returned." He held Keera's gaze, remembering the sight of Namior being shot to strengthen the lie.

"The crystal?"

"Hidden. I know where. I can find it for you." They cared deeply for their trapped people. Lemual had displayed that, and Keera also made it clear. Kel could use it to his advantage, but to do that, he had to stop trying to antagonize the woman. *She reminds me of O'Peeria*, he thought with a shock. *Gorgeous, strong, cold.*

Keera stared at him for a long time. The pain eased in his face, enough to reassure him that his nose was not broken, and the flow of blood into his mouth lessened. He sat up again, slowly, and still the emissary did not break eye contact with him. Kel could read nothing on her face, nothing in her eyes, and as the rain halted and the first hints of dawn touched the sky inland, he felt his life hanging in the balance.

"I buried it," he said, to break the silence.

"You're the first Core we've ever captured," she mused, her voice loaded with threat. The Core had tried many times to interrogate a captured Stranger, and in the early days, so it was said, many Core members had died doing so. Did Keera and her fellow Komadians know the fates of all those Strangers they had sent? Those spies, infiltrators, invaders? The Core had always assumed that the arcing proboscises were communicators of some kind.

He wondered whether revenge formed a part of their makeup, much as it often dictated events and lives in Noreela.

Perhaps all he could hope for was a quick death.

"The Core is coming."

Her grin broadened, and she prodded him in the chest. "Let them." Then she stood, backing away from Kel and still smiling.

Here it comes, he thought. *Whatever's going to happen, here it comes.*

"I could take you to Komadia," Keera said. "There are still many thousands of my people in their crystal cells. Interested?"

"I'll never let one of your things take my body," he said, desperate and hopeless.

"Don't think you'd have any choice, Noreelan. Choice is way beyond you. *All* of you." She leaned forward, her eyes glittering and her expression one of glee. "But no, that's not to be your fate. The thought of walking past you on Komadia as we take the island here, and there, and somewhere else . . . seeing your face for eternity, knowing what you did to Lemual . . ." She turned away, averting her eyes just as he saw the first glint of tears.

"What, then?" he asked.

"Like I said, you're the only Core we've caught. I'm sure with the right persuasion, you can tell us plenty."

Just kill me, he thought. And all the Core training in existence could do nothing to shelter him from the terror.

NAMIOR SAW WRAITHS in the mist. The dawn confused her vision, casting misleading light across shadows that refused to fade. The shapes made holes in the mist, moving slowly, drifting across the periphery of her senses, and as she focused on one so another would move more, as though to distract her attention.

She had seen wraiths before. They haunted the growing shadows of dusk and the retreating shades of dawn, sometimes visible through shimmering heat haze when the sea breeze was just right. Once or twice she had been touched by one, when her power as a healer was not enough, and the departing spirit gave thanks for her efforts. And all those times she had never been afraid . . .

Namior knelt on a small eastward-facing slope, staring out across the depression in the land before her and wishing that the sun would rise faster. That heat would burn away the mist, then she would no longer see what terrified her so.

She cursed the Komadians and what they had done. They had shown her things beyond her knowledge and magics she could not know. They had made her afraid when there should be nothing there to fear.

A sudden movement to her left drew her attention, and from the corner of her eye to the right she saw something quickly closing on her. She gasped and dropped to her side, drawing her knife, dropping the coat-wrapped crystal.

The swirl of mist beside her faded away, like a breath through smoke.

The crystal had come to rest against something. It should still be rolling, but it was motionless. The more she concentrated, the more ambiguous the mist seemed, curling around solids that were not there and filling voids just made.

"Put the knife down," a voice said.

Shock made her drop the blade and wince back against the slope. She brought her hands before her face and looked up, because the command had come from above.

A shape manifested from the mist, taking on color, solidity and weight. It was a machine the likes of which Namior had never seen before—a tall thing standing on three long metallic legs and topped with a cylindrical body. Sat astride the body was a man.

"Who...?" Namior said, but she could barely speak. *It's them*, she thought. *The Komadians. They went farther inland than we knew, guarding, expanding, exploring...*

The machine buzzed, and the man's hand rested on a series of levers sprouting from its metal back like stiff hairs. Namior saw no steam, nor did she hear its hissing anywhere inside. Several curled wires hung from the underside of the machine's main body, trailing against the ground. Its long legs were thick and heavily jointed, not slender and graceful, and she saw the slick of grease leaking from where they joined the torso.

"You look confused," the man said. "Never seen anything like this before?"

"Not quite," Namior said, then everything around her changed.

Four figures faded in from the mist. In the space of a beat they shimmered, sent shudders through the surrounding skeins of vapor, and took on color and mass just as the tall machine had moments before. There were two men and two women, one of the men pointing a large crossbow directly at her chest from five steps away.

"Core?" Namior said.

The man sitting astride the machine frowned, then barked an order in a language she did not know.

Two women and a man came at her, knocking her to the ground, grabbing her arms and sitting on them so that she could not reach for any concealed weapons. One woman pulled a knife and slashed at Namior's jacket and undershirt buttons, ripping them open and exposing her chest and stomach. Then the other woman and man rolled her over and pulled the clothes from her shoulders and down to her elbows. They pressed her facedown into the heathers.

Namior knew what they were looking for. "I'm not one of those fucking monsters!"

"She's clear," a woman's voice said.

"Test her anyway."

"I'm from Pavmouth Breaks, they've come and attacked our village, and—"

"Say one more thing before we're sure about you," the man on the machine said, "and we'll cut out your tongue."

Namior believed him. *So this is the Core.* She had so much to tell them, so much to show, but, silenced, she had to let them find their own way for a while.

They let her roll onto her back, then the two women knelt on her arms again. The one on her left had long, dark hair and pale skin, and Namior realized she was seeing her first Shantasi. Kel had told her a little about them, and Namior had so much more she wanted to ask. But the woman stared back without expression. In her left hand she held a knife pressed against Namior's throat.

The woman on her right was short and thin, and looked as if a gust of wind could break her. One side of her face was a mass of scars, and her left cheek looked as if it had been smashed and reset by an inexperienced healer. *Bone shattered,* Namior thought. *I'd have used a curve of reglet egg to reform that shape, rather than leave her . . .* The woman glanced at Namior as if she knew what she was thinking. Namior tried to smile. The woman looked away.

The man, his hair a startling mass of ginger with scarlet shells braided into its many twisted strands, sat astride her hips. Namior was aware of her exposed breasts, but he seemed unconcerned, picking through the contents of a small circular tin.

"Hurry!" the man on the machine said.

"Mallor, they're difficult to catch." He grabbed at something in the tin and held it up to dawn's first light.

An insect struggled between his thumb and forefinger.

"What are you—?" Namior gasped, but the Shantasi lifted her knife and laid its blade across Namior's lips.

The man nodded to the Shantasi woman, and faster than Namior could see, the woman sliced a small cut below her left breast. It took a few beats for the shock to pass and the sting to burn in, and by then the man had dropped the insect into the dribble of blood.

Namior felt it running across her skin and down toward her stomach. Then she heard a sizzle, a harsh spit, and all three Core members stood from her and backed away, eyes wide.

"Not Noreelan!" the Shantasi said. "But..."

"No markings, no gills," the scarred woman said.

"I *am* Noreelan!" Namior sat up and pulled her jacket shut. The movement caused alarm amongst the others. The Shantasi woman flipped a bow from her shoulder and strung an arrow, and the soldier bearing the heavy crossbow leaned forward. Namior could almost hear the tension in the firing mechanism, the creaking as his finger applied more and more pressure to the trigger.

The man on the machine, Mallor, passed his hands across its controls, and it took three steps back. Then its legs shortened and thickened, and a tubular appendage emerged from its belly aimed at Namior.

"Mallor, I don't know—" the scarred woman began, but Namior saw advantage in their confusion, and she knew she might only have a few beats left.

"I'm from Pavmouth Breaks. I'm a witch, a healer, and I came here to find you. You're Core, yes? I brought that to show you." She pointed at the crystal, apparently forgotten in the confusion, and she wished it had rolled out of the jacket so they could see.

"The signal?" Mallor asked from the machine's back.

"Sent by my lover, and now he's—"

"Your blood killed the pod beetle," the ginger man said. "Noreelan blood would nourish it."

"My great-grandmother . . . she was a Komadian. She fled them a long time ago."

"Komadian?" the Shantasi asked.

"The invaders. They're here."

The five Core were silent for a beat, all of them looking at her with a mixture of confusion and incredulity. The Shantasi took one step back, bow still raised, and Namior perceived a sudden calmness in her features.

She was going to shoot.

"Kel Boon sent you his message! He brought you here, and now they have him."

"Boon?" the scarred woman said, obvious recognition in her voice. The Shantasi glanced at her, then back at Namior, confused once again.

"Pelly," the ginger man said, "who's Boon?"

"He was with me in Springchain Park," Pelly said. "When all those children died. You remember that? When I got this?" She touched her face. "It was all his fault."

Mallor sighed, the softest sound. "I've heard of him. Everyone thinks he's dead."

"He ran away," Namior said, her voice low. "He's been living here for five years. I only knew . . . he only told me about the Core after the waves came."

"Waves?" the ginger man asked.

"Him," Pelly whispered, stroking the ruin of her cheek and looking somewhere far away in place and time.

"Deserted," the Shantasi said. "That's as good as dead, in my eyes."

Namior stared at the pale woman, past the arrow aiming at her face. The Shantasi stared back. It was Mallor's voice that broke the silent stalemate.

"U'Nam, keep her covered. The rest of you, ease down. And you . . . what's your name?"

"Namior Feeron."

Mallor touched the machine's controls and it lowered him to the ground. He was very tall, and older than Namior had thought at first. When he walked to her, she felt the weariness in his every step and breath.

"Namior Feeron," he said, "I'm Mallor, General of the Western Core. You need to tell us everything."

AS SHE TALKED, the sun burned the mist away, and the landscape was slowly revealed. She told them about the storm and the waves, the island that had appeared out to sea, the visitors. She told them everything, and she was disturbed at how calmly they listened to all that she said, even when she relayed information about their strange steam machines and the Strangers with their projectile weapons. She cried when she talked about her great-grandmother's revelation, certain somehow that the old woman was already dead. Her observers should have been standing in fear and shaking their heads in wonder. But these were Core, and she knew that they had seen and done more than most in Noreela. Theirs was a world within a world: their wider understanding of Noreela and what might lie beyond existing within the constraints of a blinkered and inward-looking land. Cynicism, she supposed, must come naturally to them.

When she explained about their sea journey to the island of Komadia, what they had seen, and what they had brought back, the ginger man and Pelly unwrapped the crystal from the jacket and gasped. Its surface was pale and dull, and Namior could see nothing of its depths. Perhaps beyond the scope of Komadian magic, the thing inside had died.

They quickly put it down and covered it again, wiping their hands on their clothes.

"We should go in," U'Nam said.

Mallor shook his head. "There are not enough of us."

"Even so, who's to say what's happening in there right now?"

"More's the reason to wait." Mallor raised one hand when the Shantasi went to protest some more. "U'Nam, you'll get your fight. But right now it's contained, and these Komadians seem only to be concerned in forming their beachhead."

"And the longer we leave them," Pelly said, "the stronger they'll be when we attack." She nodded at Namior. "You heard what she said about those towers, or whatever they are. They're building defenses. Leave it another day, and maybe we won't be able to break in at all."

"And without magic?" the ginger man said. He hefted his crossbow. "I'm as good as any hand to hand, but if we've no machines to back us, where's the hope?"

"We can't just sit here!" U'Nam said.

Mallor was quiet, staring past where Namior still sat toward the village beyond, hidden behinds hills and down in the river valley. Namior sensed a sad wisdom in the old man, and she wondered how long he had been preparing for that day.

"This is all new to us," Mallor muttered. "The Core has always known the day would come when we make contact with more than single, solitary Strangers. We've become efficient at finding, tracking and killing them. But this . . ." He nudged the crystal with his foot. "All new. So we send the news to the other Core, tell them all to get here as quickly as possible, and when we're strong enough, that will be the time to act."

"It's the whole village at risk!" Namior said. "My family, friends, and if you just leave them—"

"Your great-grandmother is one of them, you said that yourself!" Mallor did not raise his voice, but confusion was evident in his eyes. He was doing his best, feeling his way through the maze of new information and into an event he had, perhaps, thought would happen after he was dead. He was tall, confident and wise. But he was also terrified.

"She left them willingly, which means they must have

their weaknesses. If you can only *find* them, take advantage, then maybe—"

"And they happen to appear where your old relative has made her home?" U'Nam asked.

Namior looked down at the ground. "Maybe there are refugees from Komadia all across Noreela."

"Speculation," Mallor said. "That's not what we need. Caution is required here. If we expose ourselves now, they'll come at us with everything, and that will leave nothing between them and the rest of Noreela." Mallor's voice brooked no argument, and when he turned away Namior could find no words to call him back.

"Boon," Mallor said to Pelly. She blinked, wide-eyed.

"Kel's talked about you," Namior said, looking at the scarred woman. "His guilt brought him here."

"He's a fucking deserter and deserves to die," U'Nam hissed. "And when this is over..."

"He's been fighting them every step of the way!" Namior said. "When their emissary stepped off the first boat in front of the whole village, he was at her with a knife, checking her for gills and those *things* on their backs. She had none. But he could have been killed by his own people, as well as by theirs. We were ready to welcome them in, because they were helping so much after the waves, and they made themselves out to be just as much victims as we were, and we fell for every word. All but Kel. If he hadn't been living in Pavmouth Breaks, no one outside would know what's happening. None of you would have been called here if it weren't for him."

"No excuse for cowardice," U'Nam said.

Namior held her shirt and jacket shut and stood. The ginger man raised his crossbow and pointed, but she ignored him, taking three steps forward and standing nose to nose with the diminutive Shantasi warrior. "It's his failures that torture Kel," she said. "The Komadians have him now, and he won't say a word."

"He'll likely have no choice," Mallor said. "We have to assume they know the Core has been contacted."

U'Nam stared at Namior, but her words were for Mallor. "I'm not for sitting around playing with myself," she said. "So what do we do?"

"Very well." The old man sighed. He nodded at Namior. "You can help." When he smiled at her his eyes twinkled, and Namior thought she saw confidence in his expression for the first time. "You know Pavmouth Breaks, so you can lead three of us in to reconnoiter, ready for when the rest of the Core arrive."

Namior sighed, her shoulder slumping with both fear, and relief. *I can do something to help,* she thought. Ruined though her village was, and living through its darkest time, she could already feel it drawing her back.

"And Boon?" U'Nam asked.

"You don't know him," Pelly said. "I once did." And that seemed answer enough.

THE BEATING IS torture enough. Disparate pains meld into one, the world turns around him, confusing up and down, left and right, and the time soon comes when he wishes for death, craving an escape from the pain the two Strangers are subjecting him to while Keera Kashoomie watches, the bruises and cuts, and the sharp heat of other things they're doing to him; touches with steaming tendrils extruded from their metal forearms, and a scorching blue light that dances across the hairs on his arms and hands and is so cold it's hot. As yet, they have asked him nothing.

Torture enough, but the voice that mocks him is worse.

"Fucking weak and fucking useless," O'Peeria says. Somehow he can see her through the trees, sitting at the base of the Komadian tower and shaking her head as the beating continues. He's not sure *how* he can see her, because the Strangers are throwing him around like two foxlions playing with a sheebok before the kill. And besides, he's sure his eyes must be bruised shut, the skin and flesh around them weeping tears of blood. But still she's there, armed in her full weaponry as if she has come to help.

She can't help. She's dead. Yet she stares at him as if he's nothing, and he feels his body flipped around and dragged across the ground, and he cannot escape her gaze.

MALLOR AND THE others had been traveling all night, so they took time to eat, drink and rest. U'Nam and the ginger man had come from a village fifty miles to the north, and their machine had ground to a halt ten miles away, its internal gears and fluids seizing under the constant strain. No amount of cajoling or magical channeling could urge it onward, and they had left it in the shelter of a copse of trees. Pelly and the other man had come all the way from Pavisse, the mining town that gave the River Pav its name. It sat close to the source of the river, and Namior had heard many tales of the great machines run by the miners; digging things, swimming constructs, and machines that reached miles underground to bring mined goods to the surface. They had traveled by boat, leaving it moored down on the river when they'd come into contact with Mallor. The four did not seem overly familiar with each other, and Namior wondered whether they only met when pursuing or killing a Stranger.

And there was Mallor himself, the Core's western general, tending his machine and sending gentle whispers of magic into its internal workings. He revealed no origin and told Namior only that he had ridden across the plains. She imagined him wandering Noreela's western extremes, waiting, watching, bringing Core to him if a Stranger was tracked, living on his own in the wilds during those times when they sensed nothing of threat from beyond the land. A forlorn existence, but one she suspected he had lived for years. He seemed uncomfortable in company, preferring to sit beside his machine and share its magical drive.

They ate and drank in silence, Namior feeling suspicious glances thrown her way. The sound of the insect sizzling and spitting came back to her, and she shivered in dawn's growing warmth. *My blood did that.* But her blood had also saved her, when the Stranger had caught her and sampled it on the way out of Pavmouth Breaks. She hoped these Core understood how useful she could be.

When the silence grew uncomfortable, Namior asked about the signal that Kel had sent.

"A calling," Pelly said. The woman seemed intense and severe, and Namior was still uneasy about her comments concerning Kel. "It's something we're all trained to listen for, but none of us hopes to hear."

"What did it sound like?"

"Not as it should," Mallor said. "The first one, at least." He left the shadow of his machine and came to join the group. Even squatting down, he was almost as tall as Namior. "But the second was clear enough."

"Not as it should?" U'Nam asked.

Mallor shrugged. "There was something . . . askew. None of you heard that? None of you sensed it?" Heads shook.

"Guess that's why you're the general, Mallor," the ginger man said, and soft laughter fluttered around the group.

"He sent the first signal using their own magic," Namior said. "I'm not sure how. But the land back there is silent." She nodded behind her, back the way she had come, and for a beat Pavmouth Breaks existed in her mind as an unknown and unknowable place. The feeling soon evaporated, but it left her cold and afraid, with a hollow in her heart yearning to be filled.

"We've so much to learn," U'Nam said. "These are great times."

"Great?" Pelly said, almost a shout.

The Shantasi waved her hand. "You know what I mean. Important."

"You want them to write songs about you, Shantasi?" Namior said, but she immediately regretted the comment. She shook her head and looked down at her hands.

"I need to send word to the Core still journeying here," Mallor said, standing to go back to his machine.

"How many?" Namior asked.

"In the next day, perhaps a hundred."

A thrill of hope rushed through her. *A hundred! And all trained fighters, many of whom had experience killing Strangers. Maybe there's hope yet!* But then she thought of Kel, and wondered where he was and what was happening to him, and the hope dwindled to something negligible and unimportant.

"There's a vulnerable spot in their armor," she said, pointing at her throat. "Just here."

"Armor?" U'Nam said. The Core glanced around at each other, confused, unnerved, and Namior's hopes shrank some more as she realized she had plenty more to tell.

ONE OF THEM holds him down while another pours something into his mouth. It's hot and insubstantial, like steam, but has a defined taste that he cannot place. *Because I've never tasted anything like this before*, he thinks. At least they have ceased beating him, for the moment.

"Oh, that's right, just lie back and enjoy yourself," O'Peeria says. She's standing behind the Stranger leaning over him, poking toward the metal armor with a thick spike from her belt but never quite touching.

Then the stuff hits his stomach, and he wishes they *were* beating him again.

It burns, it melts, it seems to explode in a continuous,

everlasting eruption through his flesh and bones, breaking his skin and bursting out in showers of meat and blood and gristle . . . and yet nothing about him changes, not on the outside. The Stranger continues to pour, and when Kel starts to cough and gag, the other one grabs his chin and forehead and holds his mouth open wider still.

O'Peeria is saying something to him, but her voice is lost in the buzz of pulsing blood thumping at his ears. She seems keen to tell him something, pointing and prodding at the air with the spike, and she's just as beautiful as ever.

Kel glares at the Stranger close to his face, trying to see eyes behind the armor and hoping that he can appeal to him. But the soldiers are drones, simply doing what Keera Kashoomie tells them.

Still, no questions. *Softening me up*, he thinks.

Something flashes high overhead, and maybe it is in his eyes.

"What?" Keera says. He cannot see her. There's confusion in her voice. And then fear. "*What?*"

Kel cannot see very much at all. He feels impacts on the ground as someone runs, then his eyes are spiked with a bright flash once more. The Strangers seem unmoved; they hit him again, kick him, scratch.

The pain is exquisite. But with O'Peeria staring over the Stranger's shoulder, Kel no longer wishes himself dead.

NAMIOR LED THEM back to Pavmouth Breaks. Mallor had instructed the two men to remain behind and await the arrival of more Core, and to tell everything they knew about what had happened. He left the crystal with them, wrapped up in Kel's jacket and hidden away beneath a gorse bush.

The two women came with them. The Shantasi moved with a grace and silence that Namior had never witnessed, and though U'Nam was brash and surly, Namior could not help but admire her. Pelly walked with purpose in each step, as if every moment of her life was spent seeking revenge for her terrible scarring.

Namior had come several miles inland, and the first part of their journey was comfortable. They picked berries and ate while walking, U'Nam moving fifty steps ahead to scout for dangers. Namior expected a continuing barrage of questions from Mallor and Pelly, but they walked mostly in silence, all lost in their own thoughts.

She was desperate to return. Her mother needed her, and Kel was still down there somewhere, prisoner of the Komadians. The chance of her rescuing them both seemed preposterous, but she had nothing else to hold on to, and events had driven her to utter desperation.

She had fled the village during the stormy night, but returning in the calmer morning gave everything to view. As they mounted a small rise and heard the first faint sounds of the River Pav to the south of them, Namior gasped and fell to her knees.

Two of the tall, black towers were easily visible. The northernmost tower rose from the high, wooded cliff tops a mile from the village, the ground approximately at the same level as where they were. Its base was hidden by trees, and the tapering edge facing them was black in the morning sun. It curved to the south, toward where Pavmouth Breaks lay mostly hidden down in the river valley, looming over Namior's home as if preparing to fall at any moment. South of the village, another tower rose on the opposite hillside. The tip of another was visible farther along the southern hill-sides—the one she and Kel had seen on top of Drakeman's Hill, Namior guessed—and she could also see the top of another one peering out of the river valley.

"What in the Black are they?" Pelly whispered.

"What I told you about. Their machines built them. We saw them on the island, too."

"Something to do with their magic?" Mallor said. "Giant ground rods?"

"Their magic is nothing to do with Noreela," Namior said, shaking her head. "I think they're more likely the interrupters of our magic."

U'Nam remained silent, taking everything in, trying to process what she could see. Her expression was severe, and she had strapped a small crossbow to her left arm.

"That's the way I came out," Namior said, pointing south toward the river. "I had to climb, but the valley sides are shallower this far inland." She pointed west, toward the towering structure and the landscape between them and it. "That was where they took Kel. When he was captured the first time and put in the stockade, that must have been at the base of that thing there." She nodded at the monolith half-hidden by the folds in the land. "The one up on the cliffs . . . I didn't even know about that one. I doubt anyone does."

"They surround the village," U'Nam said. "All leaning in toward the valley. The whole village is down there?"

Namior nodded, trying to imagine everything she knew, and everything she had always known, hidden down there in a cleft in the land.

Mallor knelt and touched the ground, clasping a handful of heather and soil and closing his eyes. "This is still Noreela," he said. "But there's a shimmer even here."

Namior did not need to use her ground rod to know what he meant. The language of the land was repulsed by that place, pulling back like someone drawing away from a fire.

"Shouldn't we wait until dark?" Pelly asked.

A jagged slash of lightning arced across the valley, sparkling between towers for a beat before fading away. Namior caught her breath, then ground her teeth together. *Something else beginning.*

"No," she said, sharper than she'd intended. "We can't waste a beat."

Mallor nodded his agreement. U'Nam said nothing.

They went down into the valley.

THEY ALL FELT it when they passed within the influence of the towers. Magic pulled away, and it was a sickening sensation, leaving them bereft. Namior had lived that way for days, but she still cried out and put her hands to her face, trying to hold in the last echoes of magic dwindling in her mind. Even those soon fled, driven out by whatever the Komadians had done.

U'Nam produced a small, intricately etched metallic box from her pocket and concentrated, expecting it to do something it would not. Mallor knelt and clasped a handful of dirt, throwing it away and wiping his hand on his trousers as though it disgusted him. Pelly touched her scarred face.

"We're there," Namior said.

"We still have these." Pelly drew her sword. A tear sparkled on the hard scar tissue of her left cheek and she did not wipe it away. Perhaps she could not feel it.

"It's so *wrong*," Mallor said.

"We still have faith in magic, even though it's no longer there," U'Nam said, pocketing the box. "That's what makes us strong." She drew her sword and looked at the others, pale face betraying nothing.

"We should move on," Mallor said, staring at his hand. "We need to know the lay of the land, enemy strengths, concentrations of defenses. We'll penetrate as far as we can without being seen; any threats, we fall back. This is just scouting. Understood?"

"Yes," Pelly said.

U'Nam looked straight ahead.

"U'Nam?" Mallor said. "Understood?"

The Shantasi nodded.

"If enough Core arrive, we'll attack at dusk."

They descended the slope quickly and started following the course of the River Pav. When they passed by the ruined Dagenstine monk's dwelling, Namior waved at them to slow down. Soon, the trail would lead to a path, and after that the first buildings. The river hushed by a couple of hundred steps to their left, timeless and unconcerned at the fate of people, places or lands.

"This is the start of my village," she said.

Mallor nodded, and U'Nam took the lead.

Namior was impressed at their stealth. She'd heard tales of the Shantasi, and how they were possessed of unusual speed and a natural agility, but Mallor and Pelly also seemed to flow along the trail rather than walk. She felt clumsy in comparison, and she remained close to Mallor, expecting him to berate her noisiness at any moment.

She glanced up at the hillside to their right, wondering where Kel was, *how* he was, and whether she would ever see him again. *Of course I will!* She was angry at the direction her thoughts were taking. Maybe she should have guided the Core to the stockade from which Kel had already escaped once? But it seemed unlikely that they had taken him there a second time, especially after he'd murdered to escape.

Perhaps they'd just dragged him away and killed him.

Namior paused and closed her eyes, breathing deeply, listening to the sounds of the river. There was no magic about her senses, nothing tied in with the land; nothing but herself. And deep though her sense of doom had sunk, it still did not feel like a world in which Kel was no more.

Fingertips tapped her upper arm and her eyes snapped open. Mallor stood before her, eyebrows raised in a silent question.

Namior shook her head, and they went on.

The first home came into view, and the trail changed into a cobbled path. Soon they would be within the village's embrace, and they would start to see people preparing for the day. Some would be heading down to the harbor to continue in their rescue efforts, while others would be taking children to their teachers, looking to trade or—

But there was nothing, and no one. And she soon realized the foolishness of her thoughts, because Pavmouth Breaks had changed forever. The air was gloomy, the atmosphere dark, and looking up she saw that the sky was overcast again, and the sun she had seen rise up on the plains seemed unlikely to touch that place.

Storm's coming, she thought. She knew that the others would see little to suggest that, but she had lived there all her life. The direction of the clouds, the tang of sea on the air, the lazy quality of the light, all pointed to rough weather descending upon them soon. The last storm had brought them chaos; she hoped the next would be less harsh.

Mallor grabbed her arm and pulled her down. Namior looked for the other two, but they had melted away somewhere, finding hiding places where the path looked long, straight and clear.

Someone stepped from a doorway thirty steps along the path. It was a woman, her clothes grubby, hair awry, carrying a half-empty bottle of rotwine and mumbling to herself. Namior recognized Rhutha, the village drunk, who caused occasional problems at the Moon Temple and elsewhere. She was a worshipper of the old Sleeping Gods, one of only a few in the village, and most people treated her as an oddity who caused occasional annoyance.

Rhutha stumbled down the path toward the sea, swaying from side to side.

U'Nam emerged from behind a bush just across from them, and Namior was reminded of how the Core had manifested out of the mist, their magic-aided camouflage startling her into thinking they were wraiths. There was no magic, but the Shantasi had still merged with the land.

U'Nam glanced across at Mallor, who shook his head.

And if he'd nodded? Namior thought. *A quick blade across the throat for Rhutha?*

Pelly rolled from atop a garden wall a dozen steps ahead, and when Rhutha stumbled out of sight they continued on their way.

EVEN THOUGH HE is sure that Keera Kashoomie has gone, still the Strangers beat him. Kel curses them, *hates* them, but he can do little about it. The flesh of his legs feels as if it has been melted from his bones, his insides are fluid, and he's sure that blood is leaking from every orifice. The Strangers stand back as he flounders on the ground, and O'Peeria walks right between them and squats by his side.

Now that they've stopped pouring things into his mouth, he can hear her again.

"Feeling better?" she asks. She's resting her forearms on her thighs, hands dangling down, and he tries to reach out and touch her fingers. But she's not there. "Letting yourself get caught . . . really, you call yourself Core?"

"No," he croaks, and blood or saliva rushes down his throat.

O'Peeria seems surprised for a moment, but then she smiles and laughs softly. "Not surprised, really," she says. "But you're missing so much." She emphasizes the words and stares at him intently, glancing back at the Strangers without moving her head.

"What?" he says.

"Use your fucking eyes, Kel! Remember the Core training? It gave us . . . filters. We all see everything, but Core can sort it down to the useful, and everything else. Have you really been gone so long?"

"Thought so," he says, looking past her at the metal-clad men. "Thought . . . I'd left it all behind."

O'Peeria smiles sadly, and he realizes that he can see the approaching Stranger right through her face. She reaches out one hand and touches his cheek, and this time he feels it, little more than the kiss of a butterfly's wing but still there, still wonderfully there. "But it's all . . ." she begins, and he finishes for her.

" . . . come back to me."

He sees everything, filtered down to useful and useless, and when the Stranger kneels beside him, Kel's arm flashes out. He breathes slowly, not concentrating too harshly because he knows doing so will fracture his senses. His fingers close around the hilt of the knife tucked into the Stranger's metal boot, its color making it almost indistinguishable from the armor.

The Stranger freezes in surprise. Only for a beat, but it is long enough.

Kel rolls to the left, pulling the knife free, then rolls back again, thrusting up with the blade, hearing and feeling the scrape of metal on metal as it pierces the Stranger's armor at its throat and penetrates flesh and bone.

"Yes!" O'Peeria says, her image dispersing to the dank air but always, always there. "You're back."

The Stranger gargles something, his companion comes forward, and Kel, not trusting his legs for an instant, starts rolling away, pulling the knife with him.

The second Stranger runs past the first, dives for Kel and lands across him. Kel gasps, winded. But he continues rolling, knowing what will happen when the first Stranger dies and needing to be as far away as possible.

The metal-clad man falls from him, then kneels, grabs his head and presses its face up close.

Kel slashes up with the knife. The Stranger blocks it with its metal arm, pulls its head back, then slams it forward again into Kel's bruised nose.

He almost passes out from the pain.

The first Stranger is lying on his side, and his armor is beginning to melt, blue sparks flying, the two writhing limbs struggling to break free of their constraints in readiness for death.

The soldier pulls its head back ready to strike again. Kel

remains motionless, inviting the impact. And when its curved, hard nose connects squarely with his forehead, Kel thrusts the knife into the Stranger's throat.

The world explodes. He sees the redness of fresh blood, then darkness seeks him out and pulls him down. As he goes, he is calling out for O'Peeria, but if she is still watching, she does so silently.

THEY MOVED QUICKLY down into the village. Namior had thought she would be of help to them, knowing the geography of the place so well. She could take them through its hidden routes, she knew which garden went where, which paths led toward the river and curved up the valley sides. But it looked almost as if the three Core had been there before; they flowed through the streets and alleys, pouring down toward the harbor like so much floodwater. There was a comforting confidence in their movement.

Why did they bring me? she thought. *They'd have been even faster without me, I'm slowing them down, so why not leave me waiting with the others?* But she soon found out.

It was an old woman, walking slowly through the streets and calling a name. Her voice was hoarse from shouting, and her face was puffy with tears. Namior recognized the name she called, and when the woman saw them she froze, eyes going wide as she stared at their weapons.

"No problem here," Namior said softly, stepping forward with her hands stretched out, palms up. "It's—"

The woman's face lit up. "Are you here to save us?" she asked, childlike wonder pulling her creased skin into a smile.

"You can't tell anyone about this," Namior said.

"Are you going to rescue my son?"

Pelly moved past the woman and squatted by a wall, motionless and alert. U'Nam had already retreated to cover their rear, and Mallor squatted at the edge of the path, listening.

"Where is he?" Namior asked, fearing the reply.

The woman's smile faded quickly, replaced by confusion. "I saw him down at the harbor," she said, "but he isn't really *there.*"

"What do you mean?" Mallor asked, and the old woman gazed at him, eyes resting on his drawn sword and the crossbow on his arm.

"He's not himself anymore. He was for a while, after I found him. But then he just...went away. Right before my eyes. And he hasn't spoken to me since."

"Did anyone else see?" Namior asked, but the woman ignored her.

"So I'm looking for him everywhere else," she said, delusion welcoming back the smile. "He must be *somewhere.* Maybe he's lost. Since the wave, everything has changed."

"It has," Namior said. Some of it looked the same, but it felt different, as though they breathed air from somewhere other than Noreela. "Please, don't tell anyone you've seen us."

"Changed so much, and now there are *things* in the streets."

"Things?" Mallor asked.

The woman grabbed Namior's arms. "But you'll find my son, won't you? If I can't?"

"We will," Namior said.

"Swear on the Black?"

Namior caught her breath, because she could do no such thing, and the last thing she wanted was to upset the old woman.

"I swear on the Black," Mallor said.

The woman looked at him again for a beat, then seemed to decide something for herself. She nodded and went on her way.

"Move on," Mallor whispered, and they continued stalking down toward the harbor.

He's cold, Namior thought. But if that would help them do what they could for Pavmouth Breaks, so be it.

Pelly led them down toward the river, and soon they came to the first signs of destruction. The Core paused for a moment, evidently shocked, standing beside a house, beyond which lay a landscape of ruin right down to the water's edge. There were signs of digging here and there, desperate excavations to search for impossible survivors. The river sighed by.

Namior looked up at the sky, depressed by the mud and water, but what she saw there did little to alleviate her mood. The clouds were gathering thick and heavy, and they seemed to be so low that she could have reached up and touched the lowest of them. They were streaming in from the sea, thickening all the time, cutting out the morning sun and giving dusk back to the village. The breeze was increasing in strength, sweeping exotic smells in from across the water. Namior closed her eyes and experienced a brief but intense flashback to her time on the island. She shivered.

Mallor clasped her arm. "What is it?"

Namior shook her head, but she saw Mallor glance up at the clouds. Lightning thrashed again, reverberating around the valley.

"Sea storm?" he asked.

"They do come this quickly, sometimes." She saw the shades of clouds in his eyes.

"I've told Pelly to work us along to the harbor. I need to see what the situation is down there, then we'll get back out, wait for the others to—"

"My mother."

"That's not why we came in, Namior, not this time. Soon."

"I'll be going to her, even if you're not. I've guided you in."

Mallor looked ready to object, but he sighed and turned away.

Pelly led them parallel to the river, slipping over garden walls, through stone arches, and along narrow alleys where rats and mud-blights scampered and slunk through the shadows. Namior knew every place they saw, and many should have been nostalgic to her: the garden where she'd had her first kiss; the small courtyard where her father had died, bent over a table with a glass of rotwine in his hand and still laughing from some joke; the house where once lived a boy she'd thought she'd loved, long before Kel. But she passed the places and felt nothing, and that upset her more.

This is my *village*, she thought, but the clouds collecting above her were doing their best to deny her that certainty.

U'Nam and Pelly paused at a bend in the path, frozen into invisible shadows. Mallor touched Namior's arm. The two of them dropped, and Namior listened for the step of metallic feet.

Pelly dashed back to them. "Bodies ahead."

They went on, and Namior prepared herself, but she could never have been ready for what she saw.

Chief Eildan was pinned to the front of a house with his own harpoon. It had been driven through his chest and buried deep in the wooden lintel above the building's front door. His feet were a step above the ground, and blood and shit pooled around the door, the puddle extending through the gap beneath. His face was slack and bloody from a beating, and his eyes were missing.

As Namior gasped and dropped to her knees, she heard the chitinous scampering of many-legged sea things running away.

Eildan had grasped her attention, but when she looked down and saw what U'Nam was doing, she could not help uttering a cry of shock. There were several more bodies piled along both sides of the path, broken, holed and bloodied, and slimy, finger-sized things crawled over them, eating. But it was the weapons that U'Nam was inspecting, not the corpses of people Namior had known.

She made herself stand and go to the dead, hoping she saw no one she loved. Kel was not there, neither was her mother or Mell.

"They were putting up a fight," Pelly said, nudging a

fishing pike with her boot. "But none of their weapons are bloodied."

There were gutting knives, a few old swords and several spikes and blades more commonly at home on a fishing boat, some of them scattered on the ground, others not even drawn from the corpses' belts.

"Looks like they didn't do much damage," U'Nam said.

"At least they tried!" Namior hissed.

Mallor stepped between her and the bodies, took her hand and guided her onward. "We can do nothing here," he said. He signaled the other two Core and they passed on, and soon the scene of slaughter was behind them. To Namior, it felt even more hopeless knowing they had died fighting than if they had put up no resistance at all.

As they moved on, she saw the imposing outline of the Moon Temple slightly uphill to her right, and the harbor came into view ahead of them. The reconstructed bridge spanning the river was still piled with debris, water streaming against it and churning brown with the mud it carried.

The Moon Temple seemed silent, and sad, and . . .

And then Namior looked back to the harbor. It had not registered the first time, but she saw it now, and was amazed.

"Looks the same as the ones on the hills," Mallor said.

The rectangular surface of a tower was growing from the harbor waters. On its top, two machines worked to extrude the black stuff from their bellies, traveling back and forth across the flat surface and raising it even as Namior watched. She guessed it was twenty steps out of the water already, slightly higher than the mole.

Other shapes worked around and on the dark tower. They swam around its base in the dirty water and crawled like huge spiders up its sides. They were too far away to see properly, but Namior knew what they were.

There's something in the harbor, the woman had said. *I've only seen the ripples.*

At least they knew why the Strangers had gills.

The Core went to ground, melding with their surroundings and once again making Namior feel as though she stood out. She knelt beside Mallor.

"Was that there—?" he began.

"First time I've seen it," she said. "It must be growing very quickly."

The rain that had been promised for some time began, the sky opening and the downpour becoming torrential within beats.

"It'll give us cover," Mallor said.

Namior looked skyward, held out her hands and felt the water on her face. "It's warm."

"And?"

"The rain here is never warm."

There was one ship still at anchor against the mole, and beyond that Namior could see the hints of masts tipping slowly left and right as boats sailed away from Noreela. They were going back to the island.

"Last time I was here, there were a dozen of their ships and boats in and around the harbor."

"Maybe they've already got everyone they want over to the island," Mallor said, "and now they'll come back with their army." The idea hit Namior with a jolt. She imagined the front door of her home being kicked open by a metal-clad Stranger, her mother struggling and fighting, then being subdued and dragged out. Down the path, across the cobbles, over the bridge, past the bodies of those who had fought to the end, and then thrown onto a boat with others from the village.

Can this really be the end?

"No!" she said. "Pavmouth Breaks won't go without a fight."

Mallor smiled for the first time, and the expression hardly suited him. Namior experienced a newfound respect for the man who had sacrificed his life to a secret, silent protection of the land.

"There's something else going on at the harbor," Pelly said. She held a narrow telescope to her eye, and for a long time she said no more. "There are..." Unable to speak, she passed it back for someone else to see.

Mallor took it, looked and shook his head.

"What is it?" Namior asked.

"Something you wouldn't want to see."

Namior held out her hand, Mallor hesitated, and she snatched the telescope from him.

It was an old instrument, its lenses knocked out of alignment by some impact, and it took her a while to angle it just right. She'd looked through one before—Mygrette, the old village witch, had a collection of such objects from fishing towns and villages up and down the coast—but she had never liked the sensation. It felt unnatural to her, bringing the distance close in such a way. Magic was the only true way to do so.

There are things *in the streets*, the old woman had told them, and there were things down on the harbor. Some walked, some crawled, a couple seemed to fly, and Namior closed her eyes and remembered what she and Kel had seen over on Komadia.

"The pretense is over," she whispered.

"What *are* those things?" Pelly asked.

"They only sent those who looked like us," Namior said. "But now that they have Pavmouth Breaks, they can..." She trailed off, because she had seen something else.

The things seemed to be in a panic. They moved back and forth across the harborfront, but their general direction was toward the mole, and the remaining ship anchored there. She had never seen the Komadians moving in such a way—they had always appeared calm, and in control.

"Something's happened," she said.

Lightning arced overhead again, and the rain swept sideways for a time, as if something huge had passed quickly above the valley.

"We need to leave," Mallor said.

"My mother," Namior said. "You do what you want, but my house is up there." She pointed past the Moon Temple where she had watched Mourner Kanthia chanting so many down, what seemed like so long ago. "I'll not abandon her as well." *And Kel?* she thought. But hopeless as it felt, there was little she could do for him.

"U'Nam, Pelly…" Mallor said. He looked at Namior, silently pleading with her. She hated him for it.

At last, he turned to the Moon Temple. "Just up there?"

"Two hundred steps." Her heart fluttered with hope.

He sighed. "We'll come with you. If it means we'll leave a different way from how we came in, it helps us know the place more."

"Thank you!" Namior said, and even the stern glances she sensed from Pelly and U'Nam did nothing to dampen her relief.

Namior climbed the wall into the Moon Temple's garden first, looking at the flattened grass where so many dead had rested. There were still three bodies there, and she wondered why no one had come to claim them. The heavy rain tapped against the blankets covering their faces.

She thought she heard the door to the Temple click shut as she entered the gardens, but she did not mention it to the Core. They followed her, feet slipping on the slick ground, and the rains came down even harder, offering them cover more akin to dusk than daylight. The rain was still warm, and it tasted of something Namior could not place—stale, insipid, and painfully familiar.

U'Nam joined her, walking by her side along the paths and pausing every few steps to listen. Namior realized that the downpour would offer equally effective cover to any Strangers coming their way.

When they reached her house, the door had been smashed from its hinges, and scorch marks scarred the walls inside. The groundstone had been struck with something heavy, and a large shard of it had broken away and crumbled across the floor. Namior gasped and closed her hand around the stone hanging around her neck.

She felt Mallor's hand on her shoulder, and saw Pelly ready to pounce if she cried out again; but she bit her lip and remained silent.

U'Nam searched the house quickly, and when she came back downstairs she shook her head.

Mother isn't here, Namior thought. And those three words repeated again and again as they left, their repetition surrounding her with silence and shutting out the terrible, overbearing sense that everything was about to end.

The rain fell harder than ever. It tasted of Komadia.

Fifty steps after leaving Namior's home open to the elements, she and the Core met the first Strangers hiding in the shadows.

O'PEERIA WAS NO longer there. That was Kel Boon's first thought as he came around. His second was that his back must be broken.

He was lying on his stomach, head turned to one side so that he looked down the hillside toward the valley, and he could not move. He could see nothing other than rain striking the ground before him, and the mist it formed as it splashed back up. It was warm and intimate, trickling down his neck and sides, across his legs, and the smell was something he could not quite place—the sea and somewhere else.

Sheet lightning thrashed overhead, lighting the scene in brilliant starkness for beats at a time. Every raindrop was pinned to the air, each flash-frozen into a stilled moment in time. In those moments, through puffy eyes, Kel saw the scorched remains of one of the Strangers.

He blinked, trying to remember what had happened. He recalled Kashoomie, apparently startled and running away.

Then the fight, stabbing, punching, the Stranger's head coming toward his own, and the explosive sound of a wraith tearing its way from one of their bodies. After that, nothing.

Is one of them still alive?

He tried to bring his hands beneath his chest to heave himself up, but his arms belonged to someone else. Listening, hearing only rain and the echoes of thunder, he pushed with his legs and hands, finally rolling over onto his back. He winced in pain, squinting against the rain battering at his face.

Kel's breath stuttered, and he gasped. It felt as if someone else had been breathing with him. "O'Peeria," he whispered. She had been there, visible, taunting, then urging him to fight the Strangers. If it hadn't been for her . . .

He turned and looked up toward the dark tower, and twenty steps away he made out the second Stranger, armor melted down into a hissing slick. *Still cooling. Only just dead. I can't have been out for long.*

Kel had heard his dead love many times before, berating or scolding him in her own harsh style, and every word had been bestowed to her voice by him. He knew that, but it comforted him still. She'd been chanted down by one of the Core mourners soon after the fiasco in Noreela City, but he still liked to think that a part of her was with him always. And it was guilt that fueled that desire. If O'Peeria *was* still with him, then she did not blame him for her death, as others had. As *he* had.

But that was the first time he had ever seen her.

Groaning, Kel managed to sit up. His limbs were feeling like his own again. He touched the mess of his face, and felt a soft, sticky lump on his forehead, the swelling half the size of his fist and painful to the touch. Rainwater seemed to soothe the wound, and at least it did not bleed down his face and blind him. He took in several deep breaths, then tried to stand.

Lightning flashed and thunder cracked, and somewhere in the haze above him, an explosion shook the air. Kel looked up, biting his lip as wooziness swayed the ground. The top of the tower spat blue sparks and smoke, and a hail of shards was falling with the rain. Beats later he heard them landing at the tower's base, rattling onto the ground amongst the heavy raindrops.

"I hope it hurts," he whispered, not quite sure whom it *could* hurt, nor how.

Blue sparks. They had been similar to the lights dancing around that small box controlled by Namior's great-grandmother as she healed the injured woman.

Keera Kashoomie, surprised and running away, leaving him—her prisoner, her source of information—to the mercy of the Strangers.

The old woman, walking in the direction of the rowboat, crying, heading home.

"She did something," Kel muttered. The lightning did not sound, look or smell natural, and if the view across the valley had been clear, he was sure he'd have seen it arcing from the other towers as well. "The crazed old woman did something."

Kel knew then that he must leave. He had to find his way beyond the Komadians' influence and meet up with Namior.

He touched his forehead again, cringing at the rush of pain. The wound was soft. His skull might be fractured. Perhaps, when they reached a place where Noreela still spoke through the land, she would be able to heal him.

ONE MOMENT THERE was silence, but for the storm; the next, chaos. Mallor pushed Namior to one side, and the terrible violence began.

She huddled in a doorway, not recognizing whose house it was, trying the handle and finding the door locked, feeling ridiculously exposed, while the three Core melted away. Namior was mere witness to the carnage, not a contributor, but nothing could make her close her eyes.

She thought there were three Strangers; she could see two behind a walled herb garden thirty steps along the path, and a third was firing from the window of a house on her side. Their weapons coughed, and chunks of masonry and cobbles exploded from all around Namior and the Core. Lines of steam marked the projectile's routes through the air, quickly washed down and absorbed by the ever-increasing downpour.

Mallor lay in the gutter on his side, a few steps ahead, while Pelly and U'Nam had disappeared behind the wall across the path. As Mallor fired his crossbow, Pelly leapt up to fling throwing stars, but U'Nam remained out of sight. Namior thought she must be working her way forward, but then the Shantasi slipped over the wall and streaked up the narrow street, faster than Namior had ever seen anyone moving. Above the sound of thunder and the roar of the Strangers' weapons, Namior heard the protesting squeal of metal against metal. Someone screamed—a screech that rose higher and higher before being cut off—and then the Shantasi flitted back along the path and shouted at them to get down.

Mallor glanced back at Namior, eyes wide, but she nodded; she had seen a Stranger die before.

She curled into a ball, trying to huddle deeper into the shallow doorway. Harsh blue light flashed, reflecting from countless raindrops and splashing across the slick cobbles. Something spat and crackled, sharp sounds in the fluid cadences of the storm, and as the final explosion came, it was matched with a crash of thunder and a flash of lightning. Then the screaming of a Stranger's wraith, delving this way and that through the downpour without disturbing the falling patterns of raindrops.

Namior glanced across the path, seeing the Stranger's demise cast in rainbows through the rain. U'Nam was looking over the top of the wall and she caught Namior's eye, touching her throat and offering a small smile.

The wall beside U'Nam's face erupted in a shower of

sparks, steam and stone shards. The Shantasi fell back, hand to her face, and disappeared behind the wall.

Mallor dashed across the path, firing the crossbow on his left arm and flinging a throwing knife with his right. The Strangers' shooting subsided for a beat, then the angry coughs of their guns began again.

The cobble a hand's width from Namior's right foot shattered. She felt stone pieces impact her lower legs, then another projectile hit the stone jamb behind her, dusting her head and hands with splinters and dust. She shoved hard against the door, cursing whoever had left it locked.

A shout. Someone else screamed. Namior looked up and saw U'Nam streaking up the path again, and this time Pelly was following her, moving slower but with a snakelike grace.

Mallor sat against the wall across the path, legs stretched out before him, right hand pressed across his mouth as if to hold back a belch. He was staring across at Namior, and his throat was torn open.

Another projectile struck the side of his head, shattering his skull and knocking him onto his left side. One more hit his thigh, kicking his leg out and turning him on the wet cobbles.

"Mallor!" Namior said, appalled at what she had seen. His hand was still somehow pressed to his mouth. Blood and fluids leaked from his head. The rain washed them into the runnels between cobbles, channeling them down the path toward her home.

"Down!" Pelly yelled, and Namior responded without thinking. She pressed herself back against the door as a hail of projectiles slammed into the wall and jambs around her, peppering her with stone fragments that sliced her face and hands.

More shooting, more shouting, breaking glass, then pouring rain reflected the portentous flash of a second Stranger's imminent demise.

U'Nam dashed back down the path for the second time, slower than before, Pelly draped over one shoulder. The Shantasi threw the woman over the wall and followed, stepping in a wash of Mallor's blood without looking down.

Lightning thrashed across Pavmouth Breaks, splitting the sky in two, its roar thudding at the land. And in its brief, terrible illumination, Namior saw it touch the pinnacle of a tower just visible above the valley ridge.

From nearer came a familiar explosion, and the dead Stranger's wraith tore along the path in a death frenzy.

Namior had never felt so exposed and so terrified.

The wraith howled and screeched, dreadful and pitiful. Its voice seemed to be drawing closer. The storm cried out again, and even through eyes squeezed shut and with her arms clasped across her head, the lightning impressed itself through Namior's eyelids. Thunder rumbled, thumping at her through her knees, feet and elbows where she squatted, echoing from the doorway, across the path and from one side of the valley to the other. Everyone in Pavmouth Breaks would be hearing the sound, and Namior tried to imagine how many other people were huddled in fear.

Great-grandmother, did you do this? she thought. *Mother, can you hear this also?*

As the sound faded away, so too, it seemed, had the wraith.

Namior looked up, and there was no sign of the Stranger's tortured spirit. She saw movement to her right, and Pelly and U'Nam peered over the wall. U'Nam held up a finger: *One left.*

This time, the Stranger came to them. It ran down the path, stealth impossible with its heavy metal feet, and paused a dozen steps from Namior. It glanced at Mallor's corpse, then swung the steaming barrel of its weapon toward Namior's head.

Namior elbowed the door beside her. "Let me in!" She glanced across at the wall, but neither Core member appeared above it to tackle the Stranger. *Are they using this chance to get away? Let it kill me, escape while it does...?*

Thunder rolled, the Stranger leaned forward slightly, then something whipped through the night and wrapped around its neck. A shadow rose behind it and pulled it back, and the weapon discharged into the sky.

U'Nam stood atop the wall along the street, tugging hard on the slideshock tangled around the Stranger's throat. Sharp though it was, it could not cut metal. The Stranger dropped its weapon and thrashed, waving its hands, leaning forward and pulling U'Nam from the wall.

She hit the ground face-first, then rolled sideways, rose to her knees and pulled again.

Pelly slid over the wall and crouched down, waiting for her moment.

"Bastard!" Namior shouted. The Stranger paused in its struggles and turned her way, and Pelly struck. Again, the squeal of metal against metal as she slid a blade into the soldier's throat.

Namior ran across the path and climbed the wall close to Mallor's corpse. Dropping down into the narrow garden on the other side, she looked up the slight incline and saw the two Core do the same. U'Nam even threw her a cautious smile as they listened to the Stranger's agonized death.

When the only sound was the cry of the storm once again, U'Nam crawled down to Namior and asked if she was injured.

Namior shook her head. "Mallor."

"He was a soldier," U'Nam said. "We have to get out. There could be plenty more of those things."

"My mother—"

"We have to get out!" the Shantasi said. "Come with us, or stay behind and search for your mother. Your choice. But we're leaving."

Namior nodded, but before going with them she picked up Mallor's short sword.

U'NAM TOOK THE lead, Namior next, with Pelly bringing up the rear. They moved quickly, using the storm for cover. U'Nam frequently dashed ahead of them, disappearing into the gloom faster than Namior could believe. Each time she returned, she looked more worn. *Nothing ahead*, she would say, before leading them off again. Namior could see that the Shantasi's exertions were draining her energy, but they were also ensuring them a safe route out of Pavmouth Breaks.

The storm was the worst Namior had ever seen. Water poured along the streets and paths, gushing down between buildings from the valley slopes, falling from roofs in great sheets, surging around their ankles as they walked ever upward. The wind urged them on, roaring in from the sea and funneling between those buildings still standing. Behind the downpour, Namior could hear whistles, roars and groans as the wind twisted around and through the ruins farther down the valley. Lightning thrashed overhead, jagged lines of power scarring the sky in the same place, again and again.

Tower to tower, Namior thought, and she wondered just what that meant.

They met a small group of residents trying to make their way along the valley, less than a dozen in total, and at their head Namior found her mother. They hugged and wept, and the two Core told them they had to hurry. Namior wanted to wait, to talk, ask how her mother had escaped.

"Who are they?" her mother asked, nodding at U'Nam and Pelly.

"Friends," Namior said. "There are more coming. They're going to help."

"Have you *seen* those things at the harbor? And that thing *growing* out of the water there?"

Namior nodded. She expected more questions, and perhaps some resistance, but her mother hugged her again, hard. There would be plenty of time for talking later.

They moved along the valley path, then up the slopes

away from the village. Namior feared that every step they took would be their last.

Her hair stood on end. The air was charged, filled with potential, and sparks played around their feet where they splashed through the water. Lightning flashed almost continuously, and with every flash came the sound of impact. The ground shook, sending mad ripples and waves through the flowing rainwater. *Going back to the sea*, Namior thought. She stuck out her tongue and tasted the rain once more, and Komadia sat many miles behind her like a warm, rotten thing.

When they reached the higher slopes they saw the forbidding tower to the north, lightning dancing around its head, and as if called up by the sight, three Strangers appeared on the plain. They seemed confused and disoriented, but when they saw the Noreelans, they charged.

Namior went forward to be with U'Nam and Pelly, but the Shantasi grabbed her arm, reaching inside her own jacket and producing one of the dead Stranger's projectile weapons.

"No!" U'Nam said. "We'll hold them here, you go on. You know where to meet the others."

Pelly fired the weapon she had picked up, and fifty steps away one of the Strangers grunted in surprise and fell. "Down!" Pelly shouted, waving at the confused people.

U'Nam and Namior dropped to the ground, and the others followed. "I want to help!" Namior said.

"And this is the best way," U'Nam said. "We didn't find out quite what we'd hoped...numbers, strength. But if we don't make it back, you can tell them enough. And you have to lead these people out."

The dead Stranger erupted into flames, its demise imitated by a sheet of lightning far overhead. Namior heard her mother and the others whisper and moan when the sound of the wraith came, and she nodded and squeezed U'Nam's shoulder.

"I'm sorry about Mallor."

U'Nam grinned, and it was the first time Namior had seen such an expression on the Shantasi's face. "This is the Core's meaning!" she said. Then she turned and crawled for cover.

Namior went to her mother, hunched down, listening to the coughs of the Strangers' weapons firing both ways. "We have to go!" she said, but her mother did not need telling. The two of them stood together, and the few survivors of Pavmouth Breaks followed.

The clouds were so thick above them that it was almost as dark as night, but the lightning lit their way.

Namior's skin crawled.

Something was going to happen.

Chapter Fourteen

the weight of words

THERE WERE NO more Strangers.

They had traveled beyond the Komadians' influence, but not the storm's. Namior led the way, aiming for where they had left the other two Core men behind before heading into Pavmouth Breaks not so long ago. Her mother walked by her side. Neither of them spoke. Namior felt the weight of words between them, strung like a line ready to break, but it was not the time. At last, she was starting to believe that there would be a later.

The wind was not so terrible up there, sweeping across the high plains with no valley to funnel or concentrate its force. The rain still drove against their backs, but they could not be wetter than they already were, and the tough fisherfolk were used to discomfort. Lightning flashed, but the thunder came later than before. Pavmouth Breaks was the center of the storm. They had left that place behind.

When shapes emerged from the gloom of rain, Namior feared the worst, and she ran forward brandishing Mallor's sword. She was met with a harsh curse from Mygrette, then the two witches laughed and hugged. There were at least thirty others with the old witch, and she said she had been gathering escapees to her, hoping that with enough people they could go back into the village to rescue more.

The two groups of survivors became one, and Mygrette joined Namior and her mother in the lead.

"What's happening back down there?" Mygrette asked, having to shout against the storm.

"They're taking everyone!" Namior called.

"This storm isn't right. It's not *natural*." Mygrette grabbed her arm, eyes blazing. "I've listened to the land, and it's good to do so again. But it's *terrified*."

"Magic is afraid?" Namior asked, and the idea chilled her. She wanted to stop there and then, plunge her ground rod into the soil and join herself with the land.

"No, no..." Mygrette shook her head. "Wrong word. It's like Pavmouth Breaks isn't part of Noreela anymore. It's a blank, somewhere magic won't touch or acknowledge. As if not seeing it will make it go away."

Namior frowned, looking down as she walked. They splashed through mud. Lightning flashed again, reflecting itself around her feet. Then the thunder rolled in, a long, rumbling roar that went on and on.

"Namior!" her mother called. "Something...!"

Namior turned around. They *all* turned, because the storm had increased in ferocity even more. A sheet of lightning hung in the gloomy sky behind them, held aloft by the two towers they could see and those they could not, smothering Pavmouth Breaks, cracking and thrashing like the multiple legs of a deep-ocean scortopus. A series of explosions shook the ground, sending massive shock waves that splashed puddles and shook showers of drops from tall plants.

"The sky is breaking," Mygrette said.

Namior shook her head, because that was impossible.

And then the sky broke.

NAMIOR FELL WITH her mother close beside her, and they both took comfort from the contact.

The sky lit up, too bright to look at, too hot to touch. A wave of heat blasted at them through the heavy rains, a visible ripple originating above the village and sweeping outward, turning rain to steam and banishing the dusky darkness before it. Namior brought her arms up to cover her face, squinting her eyes shut against the brightness and holding her breath in anticipation.

The wave hit. It was a maelstrom of light and heat, a shock wave that sucked the breath from Namior's chest, and an explosion that thumped at her ears. Unable to breathe, skin stretching and burning where it was exposed, she rolled over onto her front and pressed her face into the mud.

Breathe, breathe . . . !

The noise was tremendous, far too loud to make any sense out of, and Namior was not sure where hearing ended and feeling began. The ground rolled beneath her, thudding against her body as though shaking from a series of massive impacts. The air around her grew hot, and when she finally managed to draw a breath, it scorched her mouth and throat dry.

Someone cried out, and Namior wondered where anyone had found the strength.

She heard and felt something coming then, a thing far more powerful than had struck them already. It was preceded by a few beats of relative calm and silence, like a tidal wave drawing water from a harbor before smashing itself against the land.

Namior looked sideways at her mother. The two women smiled and held each other's hands.

Namior's last sense was of being lifted from the ground and rolled, pummeled from all sides by pain. And then, for a time, her world ended.

SHE ROSE SLOWLY out of the mists of unconsciousness. Her hearing faded in first, the gentlest sigh of a breeze interrupted by something harsh and demanding, which soon resolved itself into a voice.

"Wake...wake...take your time..."

She sensed the extremes of her body, limbs splayed, stomach pressed against the wet ground. Flexing her arms and legs, there was little real pain. But when she turned her head to look up, fires erupted across her neck and face.

"Slowly," the voice said.

"Mother?"

The voice did not reply.

"Mother!" Namior rolled onto her side and opened her eyes. A man knelt next to her, his bald head gleaming with sweat, clothing and belts spiked with weapons. He looked intimidating, but his eyes were full of concern.

"You've been burned," the man said. "Lie back. I have some soothing paste."

Namior ignored him, sitting up through waves of pain and looking around. The scene that greeted her was nowhere she had ever been.

The rain had ceased, but a heavy mist drifted across the plains, blown inland by a gentle breeze from the coast. It carried with it damp hints of an extinguished fire, and even some of the mist itself appeared smeared with soot. The sun was a smudge of yellow high in the sky. *Noon*, she thought, though it felt like twilight.

People lay all around, most of them tended by others she had never seen.

"Core?" Namior asked.

"Who are you?"

"Namior Feeron, from Pavmouth Breaks."

"What happened here?"

She shook her head, dizziness turning the flat ground around her. The bald man grabbed her arm gently and leaned her against him, stroking her face and throat with paste-smeared fingers. He muttered beneath his breath as he did so, and Namior recognized the touch of a fellow healer.

"My mother," Namior said, and already she was filled with dread. Tears threatened, but then she heard her mother's voice.

"Namior." She stumbled through a patch of scorched gorse and fell to her knees by Namior's feet, holding her daughter's shins and laughing softly. "Namior, I saw you blown away, and I thought..."

Namior dried the tears with a smile, looking at her mother's injuries with concern. "Please," she said to the bald Core healer. "My mother first." The man smiled and nodded.

"Everyone else?" Namior asked.

"Those who were with us are fine, apart from Mygrette. No sign of her."

"She's hard to kill." Namior injected the comment with more hope than she felt. She turned and looked behind her, and gasped at what she saw. Shadowed against the mist, exposed here and there when a breeze parted around them, stood a line of machines. Their metalwork shone damp, and their sharp edges were out of place against the rolling clouds. There must have been thirty that she could see, and probably more she could not, hidden beyond her sight.

"How many of you are there?" she asked.

"Almost a hundred, so far. We arrived an hour ago, found you all here, and found the landscape..." He shook his head.

"Trees are uprooted. There are animals everywhere, most dead, some still alive; birds, reptiles, some sheebok and some things I believe are from the sea. Many taller plants have had their higher parts scorched black. The leaves are dead. And the air..."

"It stinks of the sea," Namior said.

"Not the sea smell I'm used to," the bald man said, passing his hands across the bridge of Namior's mother's nose.

"It's the smell of *beneath* the sea," Namior said. "Rotting plants. Dead things."

"We sent a scouting party toward the shore," he said. "They should be back soon."

"I wonder what they'll find?" her mother said.

Namior already had an idea of what they'd find: ruins. The skeleton of a village, the shattered shell of a community, inhabited only by wraiths and dead things.

"I wonder if anyone else survived," her mother continued, her voice soft and almost dreamy.

"I have to see," Namior said, standing and holding her hand.

"No, you don't." But her mother did not try to hold her back, and for that Namior was grateful.

She walked west, through the groups of stunned survivors, seeing faces she recognized and the members of the Core, whom she did not. She thought briefly of U'Nam and the scarred Pelly, and U'Nam saying, *This is the Core's meaning!* as if the Shantasi had lived all her life waiting to die. She walked into the drifting mist, and it settled damp and sickly on her face. She rubbed one hand across her throat, wincing, and realizing that she had not let the bald healer finish his work.

It did not matter. There would be time, and the burns were not too severe. At least she *could* be healed, whereas the rest of Pavmouth Breaks...

She tried not to think on it too much, not yet. Perhaps magic would still avoid the place, but she had a sense of things having moved on. She needed to know where. She had to see, not imagine.

And Kel ... her love, her wood-carver, her runaway soldier Kel Boon. It was he she was looking for really, not some old village of stone and timber, vanished people and fading memories. Kel was solid, and she still felt his touch deep inside, his love nestled alongside her soul, an eternal partner.

"Kel!" she called once, and when there was no answer she walked on.

Something large ran past her, casting a jerky shadow through the mist. She heard the wild horse's hooves thumping the mud as it galloped away in panic. Above her she could hear birds flapping and squealing, and the undergrowth to her left rustled as something emerged. It was a streaked lizard, the scarlet dashes across its flanks blazing bright in fear. It expanded its collar at her, hissed and disappeared to the east.

The creatures of the land were running or flying away, and she walked against the flow.

She met the two Core who had arrived with Mallor and the others. They guarded the crystal on the ground between them, and the ginger man's face bore a memory of deep shock. She told them of their flight up out of the village, Mallor's death, and U'Nam and Pelly staying behind to cover their retreat.

"Then there's hope for them," the ginger man said.

Instead of answering, Namior nodded down at the crystal, still covered with Kel's jacket, and asked, "What happened?"

The two men exchanged glances, shuffling nervously from foot to foot. "It screamed," the ginger man whispered at last. "When the storm came it started, and it only stopped when ..."

"When the sky fell apart," the other man finished for him.

"And now?" Namior asked.

Neither man replied. They glanced away, blinking.

"You haven't looked," she said. The ginger man shook his head. And Namior went quickly from angry, to sad, to understanding, because she would not have looked either. "Then for now, it's someone else's problem. Make sure it gets into the right hands." She smiled at the men and walked on.

Past the last of the stunned survivors, she met a line of Core soldiers strung along a low ridge in the land. They stopped her, some of them asked her questions, and she cast aside the wonder she felt at their different accents, looks and clothes, telling them that this was her home and she needed to see what had become of it. She mentioned Mallor, and told them that he was dead. They let her go.

She found herself alone, walking through the flowing mist in the direction of the sea. Pausing to insert her ground rod into the wet soil, she closed her eyes and sought the language of the land. But it was only a whisper. And when she delved westward, she shuddered with such a sense of revulsion that she let go of the rod and vomited. She leaned over and held her stomach, heaving the meager contents of her guts and trying to concentrate on the painful burns on her face. Slowly, she started to feel better.

The ground rod would not wipe clean. It was stained.

As she approached the valley, the mist began to clear. Creatures still flitted past, but fewer now, as if they had all left. The cool sea breeze kissed her face, and if she closed her eyes it felt almost normal. She had walked slightly to the south, hoping to be able to see straight down the valley past Helio Bridge and into the top of the village, and perhaps even to the harbor and the island beyond. If the air was still loaded with mist, she would not see that far, but she would go as far as was necessary to . . .

Namior topped a small rise in the land and stopped. The first thing that registered was the group of eight Core standing twenty paces down the small slope from her. U'Nam was there, and so was Pelly, leaning on U'Nam's shoulder because her left leg had been shattered at the knee and hung limp, shifting like a decorative chime from a tree's branch. *I can fix that*, Namior thought, *get her out of here, back beyond where magic is still sick, and I'll have to find some ceyrat root, and mix a paste of sheebok-liver blood and rantan seeds, but then...*

Namior closed her eyes, tried to calm her racing thoughts, breathed deeply, then looked again. All eight Core soldiers were looking down into the valley. None of them moved.

Still misty, that's why I can't see, that's why...

But she was wrong. There was no mist.

And there was no Pavmouth Breaks.

Chapter Fifteen

somewhere else

KEL HAD SPENT many dark moments imagining what it was like to be dead. O'Peeria had once told him a Shantasi saying: *The richest time of your existence is when you don't realize you're alive. Start thinking about living, and you have to think about death.* Since her terrible demise, he had tried to put himself in her place many times.

Perhaps at last he knew.

So much of him hurt that it was easier to concentrate on the parts that did not. Each of his senses felt abused, and none seemed to be working as it should. He tasted sounds, heard textures beneath his prone form and saw the smells of devastation washing over him. He kept his eyes closed for a while, afraid of what he would see of himself were he to open them. Afraid that the ground would be red, and wet with insides.

Something had picked him from his feet and carried him away. It had been the wind and rain, he'd thought, and the lightning spiking down all around him, and the power he'd felt in the ground, so much more than he had ever sensed before. If this was anything like the magic Namior knew...but he had known that was not the case. This was nothing like magic. This was something else entirely.

He moved his fingers, took in a breath, opened his eyes. His senses settled, and he risked turning his head and looking up at the sky. He felt as though he'd fall from the world if he let go, so he dug his fingers into the damp soil.

Mist drifted by him, dancing in swirls and wafts.

The violence of the moment had changed something forever. As yet he did not know what, but he was suddenly desperate to find out. Pain could try to keep him down, but he would forget it eventually, and he could cringe through it to discover the truth.

So he stood and looked around. He was still on the hillside above Pavmouth Breaks. He turned, and behind him through the mist he could just make out the looming shadow of the Komadian construction. *No*, he thought, *that's all wrong. That shouldn't still be there. If Namior's great-grandmother* did *do something to help...*

But if she *had* initiated what he suspected—if she really had caused Komadia to move on before the Elders had intended—he had no idea of what might be left behind.

Breathing heavily through the pain, ignoring his bloodied clothing and the hollow throb behind his wounded forehead, he started walking away from the structure, and down toward Pavmouth Breaks. It was time to see what was left.

The mist soaked his clothes. He looked at his feet, concentrating on heading downhill. And then the ground disappeared.

AFTER SEEING WHAT had happened, it took Namior a long time to move.

There was little left of Pavmouth Breaks. It had been scooped out of the land, lifted away with the valley and slopes, the riverbed and bridges, the harbor and houses and temples, the paths and streets and everything else that had made it what it was. A hundred steps from where she stood, the plains ended in a sheer drop, and beyond that drop was the exposed flesh of the land itself. Dirt and rock glimmered beneath the cloudy sky, wet and shocked and never meant to be seen. Scurrying things sought shelter across the new landscape; large and small, pale, eyeless and many-legged.

There were a few buildings left clinging to the untouched higher slopes, but they were ruined, shaken to their roots by what had happened to their village. They were never meant to be seen standing alone, and now they stood naked and open to view.

All but two of the tall towers built by the Komadians were gone. A stump of one remained down where the harbor had been, its unfinished top emerging and disappearing again in the raging, boiling sea. And the one they'd seen up on the northern cliffs was just visible where it protruded above the mist, crazed and pocked like some old ruin, not something new.

The sheer immensity of the scar in the land took Namior's breath away and weakened her knees. She touched her face, drawing a nail across one of the burns and gasping at the pain.

Walking forward, she stood beside U'Nam in the line of Core soldiers. None of them acknowledged her arrival. They were all somewhere else, a very personal, secret place in their minds where something like this could be observed, processed and hidden away, ready to be examined later around campfires or in private rooms, a bottle of rotwine in one hand and eyes staring into the darkness. This was something never meant to be seen.

The sea had rushed in to fill the new void on the coast. The valley was so much wider than it had been, and deeper, and the River Pav flowed into a violent inlet, the waters swirling, waves crashing in seemingly random directions as larger surges rode in from the ocean. They smashed against the new shores, the water heavy with muck and filth. Landslides grumbled down the edges of the new depression, taking trees and boulders with them. *We should move back*, Namior thought, but even her internal voice was weak with shock.

U'Nam was the first of them to speak. "The island's gone."

Namior was confused for a few beats. *That was no island, that was Pavmouth Breaks, my village, the place where my family and friends lived and—*

But then she looked up and out to sea, past the dispersing gloom to where the sun struck its surface through a break in the clouds. And all she could see was water.

"The island's gone," she echoed.

"What island?" one of the new Core soldiers said. Namior glanced to the right at U'Nam and Pelly, and they returned her look. Their faces were so blank that she could not help smiling. They smiled back. She snorted. They laughed.

"Madness," Namior said, but that one word was all she could utter. She held onto U'Nam as the laughter changed to tears and back again, and the others looked at them as if their minds had also been stolen away.

THEY SAW A Stranger to the south of them. U'Nam shouted some instructions and the Core slipped into a battle formation, but the Stranger was rushing away, metal-clad arms pinwheeling as it ran headlong down the slope. As it approached the new, jagged cliff where there had been none before, it sped up rather than slowing down. They saw its limbs still thrashing as it tipped over the edge, but it was too far away for them to hear the impact.

"What in the Black was that?" one of the new Core arrivals said.

"A Stranger in armor," Pelly said, and for some reason she found that funny as well.

The flash of the Stranger's demise was a weak reflection across the tumultuous valley.

"There might be more," U'Nam said. "Go back, tell the others to keep watch. They're hard bastards, but they have a weak spot." She reached out and touched Namior's throat. "Here."

"Look!" Pelly said. She lifted a bloodied arm and pointed back out to sea.

In the raging ocean, where waves were starting to find their directions and levels again, the remains of several ships wallowed. One was mostly sunk, its three masts snapped away and decks awash. A couple more were breaking up, and one pointed its bow and stern at the sky as it went down, broken-backed.

"Good," U'Nam said.

Namior closed her eyes, because people she knew might have been on those ships. Or people she did not know, but whose faces she would have recognized. *Oh, Kel,* she thought, and suddenly she wanted to get closer to things, drift over that sudden point where Noreela had been cut into and pulled away, immerse herself in the mud and furious waters of the new junction of land and sea. She knew that was impossible and foolish, but the urge was powerful.

She could not simply turn her back and walk away.

"Kel," she said, her voice soft. She could not cry. She was in too much shock, so much pain. But just as the taking of the village had left a hole in the world, so the loss of her love had carved a hollow in her heart.

The newly arrived Core turned around and headed back to where the survivors were being cared for, on the lookout for more Strangers. They disappeared into the gloomy mist that still hung inland, and Namior wanted to call them back, shout at them about what they had seen and why had it happened and how could they just walk away, how could they not *feel*? But they had never even seen Pavmouth Breaks. For them that was just a place of raw slopes, landslides, and a roaring, violent sea.

She wanted to go closer, but U'Nam would not let her. So she asked if they would wait with her for a while, and they agreed, even Pelly with her terrible injuries. "I can heal that," Namior said, but as she spoke she was looking down at the wound in the land.

The clouds slowly cleared and sunlight broke through. The sea settled quickly, disturbed here and there by continuing rockfalls and landslides, but always resolving its own chaos. It calmed into the eternal ebb and flow that Namior had always thought of as the beat of the land.

She sat down several steps in front of the two women, wanting to feel alone.

They took our village, she thought, over and over, never quite believing but already beginning to understand. Some of the rugged geography of Komadia, what little she and Kel had seen of it, was starting to make sense. *Perhaps it was a much smaller island when all this began...*

They waited there for some time, watching the clouds change and feeling the air grow warmer, seeing seabirds drifting across the altered part of their world as though it had been like that forever. From inland they heard the distant sound of a Stranger's demise, and out to sea Namior could see the shattered remains of Komadian ships. Soon, there would be no trace of them having even been there at all.

Apart from us, she thought. *Witnesses*. And for the first time since the cataclysm, she wondered what her great-grandmother had done.

It was Pelly who finally broke the silence.

"By all the Black, that's Kel Boon."

Kel? Namior stood, legs still weak, and she saw him immediately, walking up the slope to their right. He came slowly, pausing every few steps to look around in shock and wonder. It seemed that he had not yet seen them.

"Kel!" she shouted. Kel paused, startled.

Namior stood and ran down the slope, leaping over a fallen tree, feet rustling through burnt heathers. "Oh, Kel, I thought I'd lost you!" He looked beaten and confused, covered with wounds and blood, and as she wrapped her arms about him, his legs gave out.

"Namior, I thought…" Dry, wracking sobs finished the sentence for him.

"I've got you, I'll hold you." She appraised his wounds even as she kissed his swollen lips.

"We're still alive," he whispered, managing a dry chuckle.

"The Core is here," Namior said. "Come with me. Away from here, we have each other, and we can go away, now."

He struggled to his feet again with Namior helping him, and she wondered just how badly he had been hurt. As they walked up the slope and approached the two Core, she felt him dragging some more, finally holding back.

The two women and the man stared at each other, Core past and present, and as yet they were too far away to hear each other speak.

I WAS GOING to ask you to be my wife," Kel said softly. He heard Namior's sharp intake of breath. "When I gave you the sculpture, the cliff hawk, but it's gone now, it's…"

"It's somewhere else," Namior said. "It could be anywhere." There was wonder in her voice, and an undercurrent of fear. That was good. They all needed to be afraid.

Pelly and U'Nam stared at them, and Kel could tell nothing from their stances. He could make out the terrible scars on Pelly's face, and he remembered the sound her slingshot had made as its weight impacted her cheek. He heard the confused excitement in the children's voices, and the stench of blood as Rok took a knife in his throat. When he blinked he saw the brightness of the Stranger's demise, not the darkness behind his eyelids, and O'Peeria was screaming at him to kill her, because she knew what was to come.

" . . . away from here," Namior was saying.

"What?"

"That's when we can talk, when we're away. It's just too . . . strange, right now, Kel."

I asked her to marry me, he thought. And something inside him smiled. His head throbbed, his wounds were blazing, and he felt Pelly's stare cutting into him to add one more. But with the island gone, he had a future. *They* had a future.

"Help me walk," he said. "I need to talk with them."

Namior helped him walk up the slight incline. As they approached the two Core, Pelly's pained voice emerged from the background grumble of the wounded land. "Five years I've nursed this scar and blamed you, Kel Boon. I think back now, and I can't remember *why*."

"Hello, Pelly," Kel said. He nodded down at her smashed leg. "Namior can heal that."

"I'm chewing fledge and aker root. Can't feel a thing."

"You're the deserter," U'Nam said, and Kel looked at her sharply. Any Shantasi reminded him of O'Peeria. "But everything's changed. I believe we have much to thank you for, Kel Boon."

He sighed as Namior lowered him to the damp grass. Turning, he looked downhill at the great coastal scar once more, still barely able to comprehend the enormity of what had happened. She sat close beside him, and that felt good.

"Not me," he said. "Lots of us put up a fight."

"Some are still alive!" Namior said. "Mother made it out, and Mygrette. Hundreds more."

"Only hundreds?"

She nodded sadly. "There might be others, perhaps. Up

on the plains, too scared to show themselves." But they both heard the desperation in that idea.

"Your great-grandmother," Kel whispered, and he turned so that Pelly and the Shantasi could hear as well. "The island shifted before they were ready. Namior's great-grandmother, she left Komadia years ago and—"

"Namior's told us," U'Nam said.

"Well, she went back. That pit we saw, Namior? On the island? There must have been a mechanism, something to work with their magic and aid in the island's shifting. I think she returned and initiated it before they were ready. That old woman, fighting through her crazes, rowing out there on her own . . . she wouldn't let me go."

"You were going to?" Namior asked, and Kel looked at her without answering.

"How can you be so sure they didn't move on purpose?" Pelly asked. She nodded at the hole in Noreela. "Looks to me like they got what they came for."

"I'm sure because I was with one of them when the lightning began," he said. "Their emissary, Keera Kashoomie, who came to Pavmouth Breaks and fooled so many. She panicked, fled. Left me with two Strangers who almost killed me, and every moment from when I awoke, to when Namior saw me, I was hoping to find her corpse. But even without that, I know that *we're* the proof. Me, Namior, the others. I'll bet they've never before left a survivor behind. Noreela knows about Komadia now. The *Core* knows." He lay back on the grass, leaving that to sink in for all of them.

"She didn't only save us," Namior said softly.

"No," U'Nam said. "She moved things on. Gave us an advantage."

"It's not a Blind War anymore," Kel said. "Next time, we can be ready."

"But we can't let *everyone* know," Pelly said. "Noreela won't stomach the truth."

They sat silently for a while, warriors and witch nursing

their own thoughts as nature settled around the land's new shape.

"She was right about something else," Kel said at last.

"What?" Namior asked.

And as he looked at her, his vision began to swim. *After this, you might be the most important person in Noreela.* He was not sure he could ever leave Namior behind again.

THEY WALKED UPHILL together, toward the plains where the survivors from Pavmouth were gathered mourning their town and its dead, letting Core healers tend their physical wounds and knowing that the mental ones would last forever. They maintained a steady silence for a while, but there was something heavy hanging among all four of them.

"That crystal," U'Nam said at last. "We have to get it to the Core witches."

"What will they do with it?" Namior asked.

"It'll be examined," Pelly said. "Aggressively. See how much more we can find out about those bastards."

Kel breathed heavily against the pain, but his head was clearing. He saw what he had to do, and knew that there was no other way. But he was terrified to say it. Terrified, because Namior was beside him, and he did not want to drive her away ever again.

But she said it for him.

"You have to go with them, Kel. You've been to the island, seen all those *things* out there." He felt her shiver. "There's so much you can tell them."

"But you've been, too," U'Nam said.

"Yes, but . . ."

"Come with me," Kel said.

"But I'm not Core."

U'Nam laughed, and her throaty, strong voice reminded Kel so much of O'Peeria. "After all this, the Core will be looking for recruits. Pelly's right, Noreela can't know, and the survivors . . . they'll have to be talked to. Maybe even recruited themselves."

"Me, in the Core?" Namior asked, as if she had never even considered it. "I'm no fighter."

"But I'll bet you're a good witch," U'Nam said.

She turned and looked at Kel, and he thought, *Say yes.*

"Yes," she said.

"And the other thing?" he asked.

Namior shrugged, then smiled. "Show me Noreela, Kel Boon."

The mist was clearing, the sun was burning through. Kel heard voices ahead of them. And from far beyond those voices, across the plains and rivers and mountain ranges, he heard the wild, amazing places he'd believed he would never see again calling him back.

About the Author

Tim Lebbon lives in South Wales with his wife and two children. His books include *Fallen,* the British Fantasy Award–winning *Dusk* and its sequel, *Dawn, Mind the Gap* (cowritten with Christopher Golden), *Berserk, The Everlasting, Hellboy: Unnatural Selection,* the *30 Days of Night* movie novelization, and *Desolation.* Future books include two new fantasy novels, more Novels of the Hidden Cities (with Christopher Golden), a collection from Cemetery Dance Publications, and further books with Night Shade Books and Necessary Evil Press, among others. He has won three British Fantasy Awards, a Bram Stoker Award, a Shocker, a Scribe Award, and a Tombstone Award, and has been a finalist for International Horror Guild and World Fantasy awards. His novella *White* is soon to be a major Hollywood movie, and several of his other novels and novellas are currently in development in the United States and the UK. Find out more about Tim at his websites: www.timlebbon.net and www.noreela.com.